ELEMENTALISTS

INDICTMENT

SI FOOTE

LEAVES FROM THE VINE PUBLISHING

ELEMENTŌRUM

BASE ELEVATION: 25,000 FEET (7,620

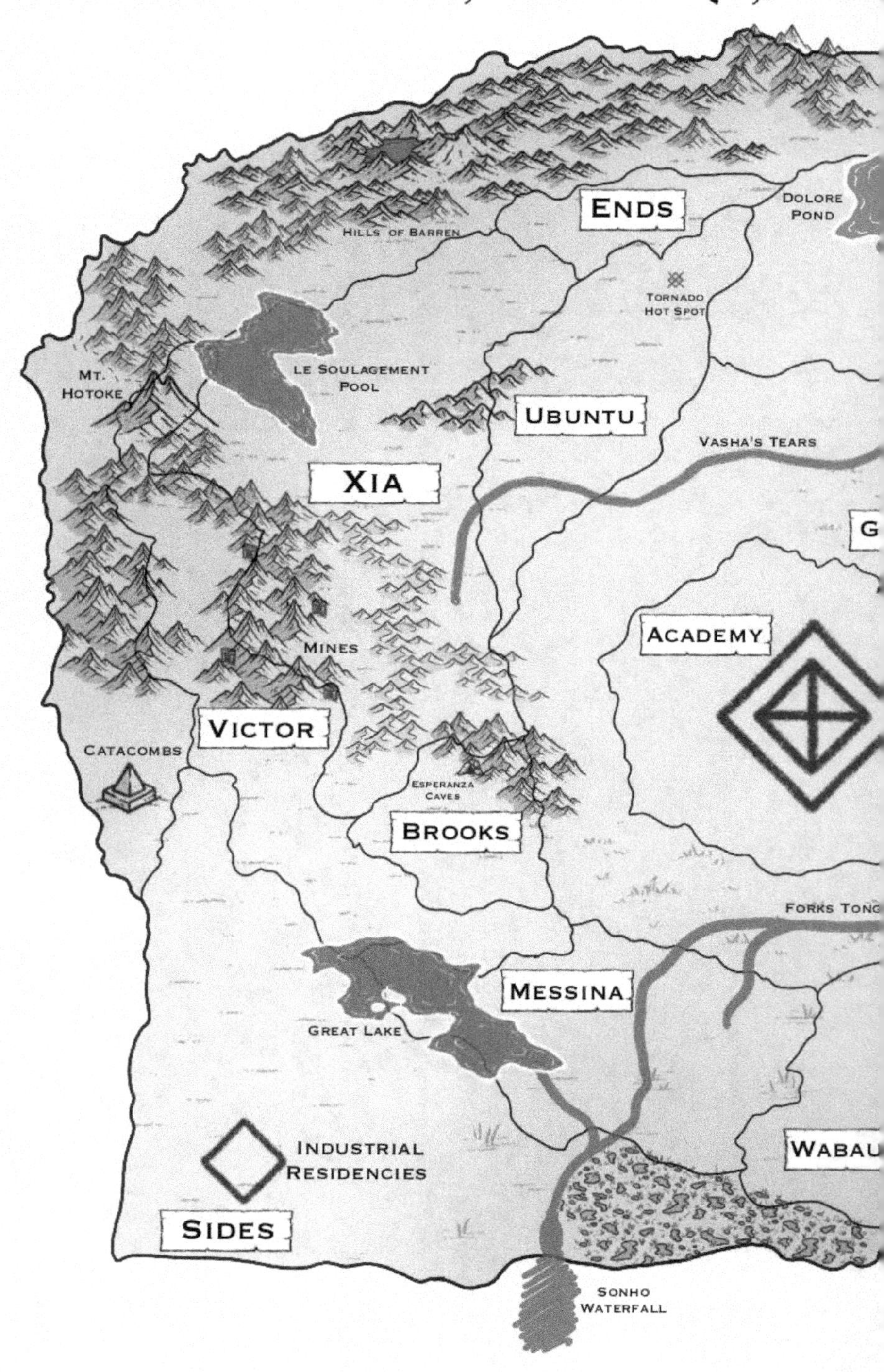

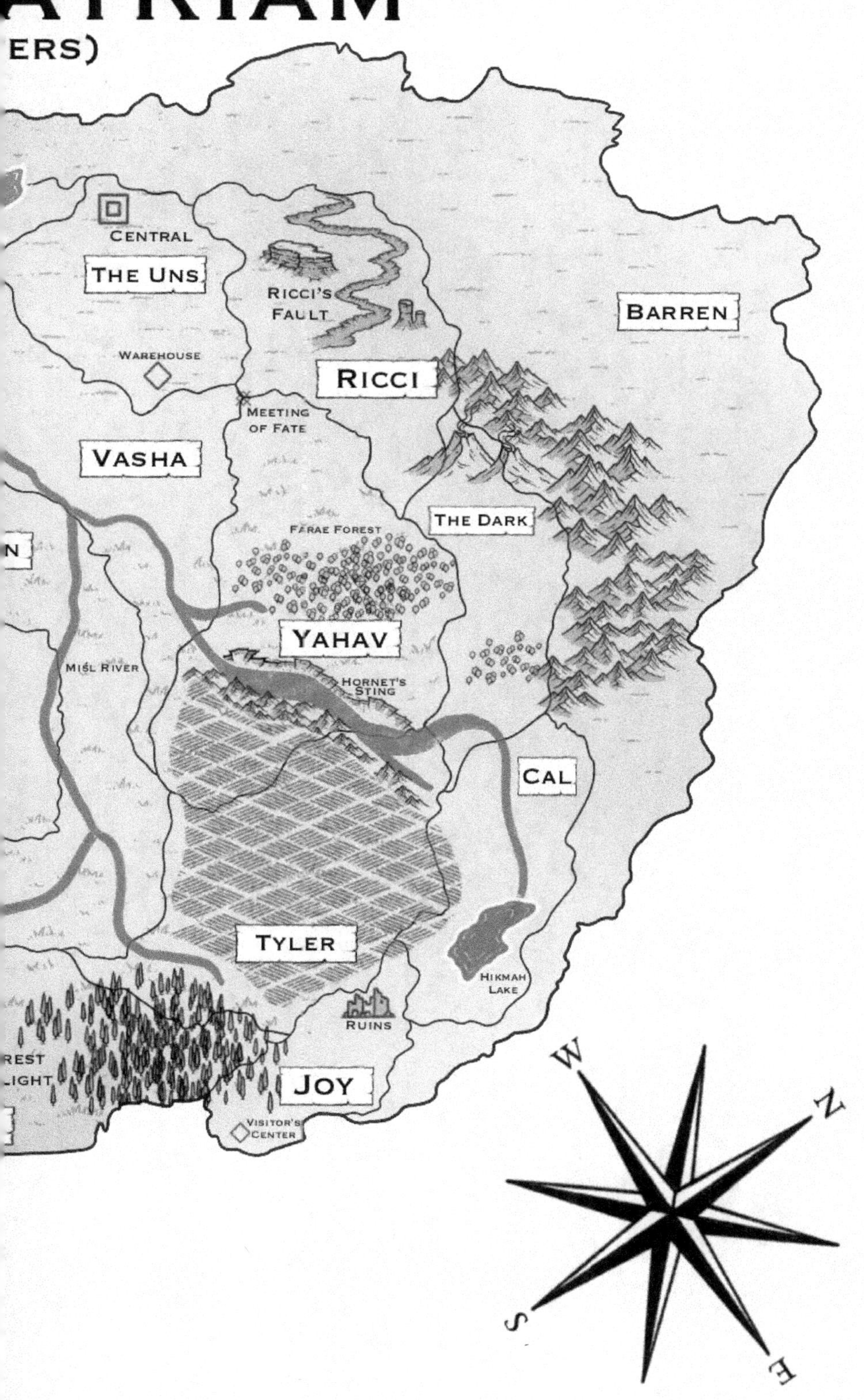
ATRIAM
ERS)
CENTRAL
THE UNS
RICCI'S FAULT
BARREN
WAREHOUSE
RICCI
MEETING OF FATE
VASHA
THE DARK
FÆRAE FOREST
YAHAV
MIŚL RIVER
HORNET'S STING
CAL
TYLER
HIKMAH LAKE
RUINS
REST
IGHT
JOY
VISITOR'S CENTER
W
N
S
E

Content includes strong language and implied sexual content.
Content includes mentions of suicide.
Content includes descriptions of human experimentation, eugenics,
genocide, violence, beheading, war, and kidnapping.

For Trevor Billings, C.L. Carner, G.T. Gretz, Sage Santiago, Izzy Krause, M.K. Dockery, Julie DeFisher, and R.M. Palumbo for all the help they gave me in my self-publishing journey. They are certainly the nicest group of writers I happened upon.

TABLE OF CONTENTS

CHAPTER ONE

Constellation

December 18, 2317

City of Wabaunsee, Elementōrum Patriam

Kristen's feet pounded against the pavement. Every step set off a ricochet of needles across her nerves. The dregs of time slipped from her grasp, and the world around her returned to a frenzy of harried people walking to their next destination. People chattered incessantly to each other and into their phone. Words blurred together where they couldn't be understood. A low hum pressed to max volume in less than a second gave her vertigo. Her smell returned next, blasting her with cuisine from street vendors—dishes and cultures that shouldn't be fused. Stench from the nearby alley overwhelmed her stomach, and Kristen fought off the urge to vomit. She staggered and tripped over her own feet.

Above the din of the busy city center, she heard the officers following her shout for her to stop. Kristen ducked behind a food stall and tried to blend into the crowd.

Her eyes darted over the skinny alleyways of the high rises and the openness of the street, hoping for an escape route. A larger alleyway, around one hundred feet from her, loomed over the square. She wound her way through the crowds knotting the sidewalk and moved swiftly away from the police. Kristen turned her head for only a moment to see them standing in the middle of the intersection scanning the masses for her. A man stood in front of the alley, checking his phone, unaware of her approach. Kristen didn't take the time to register more than his thin frame, red hair, and pale skin before she bee-lined for him. The police shouted. They spotted her.

With a small push, she felt the strands of time slide through her fingers again. She yanked as hard as possible to slow time's passage. Her hands closed around the man's bicep. Before he had a chance to register her presence, she had him pressed against the wall with her hand over his mouth. Time slipped through her grasp, again. Kristen stood on her tiptoes to press her lips against the back of her hand.

The phone in his hand clattered to the ground. The man made a muffled and startled cry against her force. He reached up and pushed her away. The police ran past. Kristen ignored the stranger and leaned out far enough from the alley to get a glimpse of where her followers went. Her hands shook against the brick building. One of the officers pulled out a handset and barked orders she couldn't quite hear into the receiver.

Kristen pulled away from the edge and wiped her sweaty palms across her jeans.

The man behind her sighed; he crouched on the ground, inspecting the phone. It had a crack along the lower edge. Kristen cringed.

"I can fix that," she offered hesitantly.

His warm, brown eyes lifted to meet hers. "Does what you did count as assault?"

Kristen dropped her eyes to the ground. "Sorry, I had to get them off my tail."

"You literally appeared out of nowhere," he said.

"That's kind of my thing." A hesitant laugh escaped her lips. The shaking traveled from her hands into her arms.

"You're an elementalist?" The corners of his mouth twitched into a smile, and his eyebrows rose with his inquiry. Something flashed too quickly across his eyes for Kristen to recognize. He rocked onto the balls of his feet, prepared to move.

"I am," she admitted.

"Why are the police chasing you?" He gestured to the main square where the officers gathered and pointed while shouting over one another.

Kristen hesitated.

Her answer defined the moment between life and death. If she could grasp time one more time, she could escape, and he would be none the wiser. He didn't know her. He had no information on her. *Although*, she thought, *he could get information from the police or report me*. He did have an accurate description of her physicality. She bit her lip before steeling her nerve and fixing him with a hard gaze.

"I'm not supposed to exist," she said.

Silence filled the few feet between them. She spun on her heel, nearly slipping against the thin layer of dirt on the concrete and leaned out of the alleyway for a second time. With a semi-clear path, she took her first step away from the police. A hand wrapped around her wrist and pulled her back.

He held the phone in her view and waved it. "I think you said you could fix this." He blocked the exit with his frame. "Also, what do you mean you're 'not supposed to exist'?"

Kristen took the phone gingerly between her fingers. "It means I don't belong anywhere. I don't have a home." She focused on the crack in the screen and dug into the recesses of her mind. Something tickled the edge of her thought, and she pulled at the string end until it unraveled. A moment later, the crack sealed itself as if it never existed. Kristen handed the phone back, pushed past him, and made a few paces down the street.

She tucked her hair in the hood of her jacket. The Storm elementalists made the day light and breezy like fall on the surface instead of the dead of winter like the northern hemisphere should be in. She tucked her hands in her pockets and slouched to match the height of the crowd. Kristen weaved to the edge of the sidewalk nearest the trees and shrubbery. She hoped it would hide her more effectively.

The man fell into perfect sync with her steps.

"People don't normally kiss me out of the blue," he said. Kristen peered far enough past the edge of her hood to see the grin adorning his lips. He continued a moment later, "Of course, I'm not sure anyone would be brave enough to kiss me—let alone get within a few feet of me."

"I didn't kiss you." She had noticed the strange berth the people on the streets gave him. A group crossed to avoid them altogether. She pointed to the behavior. "Am I supposed to be scared of you like everyone else is?"

He shrugged. "I suppose you didn't kiss me, not really, and that depends."

"On?"

"If we are mutually aware of who each other is."

Kristen narrowed her eyes. "You're asking for my name."

He played with the bun he had his hair pulled into. A few of the strands escaped and rested around his ears. "I am. Though, I have to say, I'm more surprised you don't know who I am."

Kristen examined him closer. He didn't wear anything notable. A loose and breathable shirt, a little more stylish than someone out for a casual stroll, and a pair of jeans. His tennis shoes looked new, but nothing about him stood out other than his lack of freckles. An unusual occurrence for someone with red hair. "I highly doubt you're a celebrity," she said.

The man laughed. "You wound me."

"If you're not a celebrity, why should I know you?" Kristen asked.

"Are you a resident of Elementōrum Patriam?" He hesitated and fell a step behind her. "Or, since you said you don't have a home, where do you sleep at night?"

"Trying to find your way into my bed?" She covered her growing unease with a smirk.

His relaxed posture faded, and his voice lowered an octave when he said, "Answer the question."

"I am a resident. Do I need to show you my ID?" She put a hand to her back pocket where she kept her physical card from America. She didn't have an ELE ID.

She bought a round-trip ticket to the visitor's center in the City of Joy and never got on her return transportation pod. Instead, she escaped in the hopes of finding a life in the country she belonged to. Or, at least, she believed she belonged to. No one among the known elements had her abilities. She would most likely be labeled a Rogue if she didn't run away from home in Virginia as a young teenager and already be dead. When she settled farther inland than the outer cities along the edge of Elementōrum Patriam, she caught sight of someone else's ELE ID and managed to guess a number to register under for housing and a job.

"Yes, actually," the man said. He folded his arms across his chest.

Kristen contemplated running. The stranger had maybe a half a foot on her in height, and he wasn't bulky. He would move easier than some of the officers chasing her. Even with her ability active, they kept a steady pace with hers. If she ran, she would have only a moment. She normally had more control over time and would have no issues, but the chase through three cities depleted her powers to their limit. Without further hesitation, Kristen opened her mouth as a feint before turning to run in the opposite direction. She reached out to the strands of time, but she couldn't feel it prickling at the edge of her senses.

Kristen collided with something solid. Her head snapped back from the force, and she hit the pavement. Her butt ached from the impact, and she recognized the telltale sting of an injury along her elbows.

"What do we have here?" The newcomer leaned over her with a grin. The warm afternoon sun lightened his dark skin tone to a soft, raw umber and highlighted the smile lines etched there.

"Not sure," the first stranger said. "She says she isn't supposed to exist."

"Interesting." The second ran a tongue across his lips. "In which way are you not supposed to exist? Undocumented immigrant? Human out-of-bounds? Rogue? Un who made it out of the gate?" He glanced over her scraped hands. "I don't see the scars for that one to be plausible."

Kristen debated running again, but her powers fizzled on her fingertips in a smattering of purple sparks.

"If you're thinking about running, I wouldn't do it," the second man warned. "You don't know which elements we have on our side here."

Kristen let out a heavy breath and pushed herself to her feet. "My powers," she held out her hands, "the things I can do—they aren't supposed to exist. I don't exist here or in the human world."

The two men exchanged a meaningful look. The first man gestured to her hands in reference to the purple sparks.

"We'll help you figure that out," he said after breaking eye contact with his companion. "That's part of our job, I think."

"Officer," the second man raised his hand to signal the police still scattered across the intersection, "bring me your handcuffs."

The officer in question startled, found confirmation from his coworkers, and quickly jogged over. He handed over the metal rings with a simple, "Yes, sir." He didn't dare look either man in the eye.

Kristen recognized the handcuffs from rumors. The design would lock away any ability she had during the transport of a prisoner.

"What's your name and unit number?" The second addressed the officer.

"Jonas Vogel from the ninety-ninth precinct, sir."

"We'll send over the money to requisition you a new set of handcuffs." The smile remained in-tact.

"Thank you, sir—Tautona Tebogo, President Silverspoon."

Kristen's breath quickened. She didn't know their faces, but she knew their names. "Tautona? President?" she whispered.

"Recognized us, now, have you?" Ethan Silverspoon quirked his left eyebrow. The words *Death elementalist* rang in her head. If she made any unsavory attempts to escape, he would kill her before she had time to blink. The only one of his kind known in Elementōrum Patriam. Of course, the elementalists knew there would be more. They announced a few months prior the information regarding the two lost elements. They never had high population numbers, unlike the other seven, and would occasionally fade. The Council also admitted they killed a few without knowing it because of the lost history.

"You're the Council members," Kristen said.

"Yes, newly unveiled and at your service." Dwayne Tebogo playfully bowed.

"I fake kissed a Council member." She let out a half-whistle in the same high-pitched tone of her voice. The Council ruled over the country as the strongest of their respective elements. She stood in the presence of Life and Death, literally. "I am so dead."

"Kissed?" Dwayne took his turn to raise his eyebrow, but at Ethan instead.

"I'll tell you later." Ethan waved him off.

"We have the ride back to the Academy," Dwayne suggested. "So, the one who isn't supposed to exist, what's your name?"

"Kristen Delavida Reyes." She hung her head. One of her toes poked out of a hole in the side of her worn tennis shoes.

"Miss Delavida Reyes, sorry to say, you'll be going before the Council to plead your case for what happened here today."

"I understand."

"Namune, get the pod, will you?" Dwayne asked.

"On it," Ethan said.

Kristen's brows pinched together. She didn't remember the name "Namune" from the press conferences with the Council members. He responded without hesitation or confusion. *It must be a nickname*, she thought.

"I'm not normally the person who fake kisses people I don't know," she clarified for Dwayne.

"Why'd you do it?" His voice carried a hint of amusement.

"To get away from the police. Public displays of affection make people uncomfortable."

Dwayne chuckled. "Quite the situation you put yourself in." He crossed his arms and kept an eye on her from the corner of his vision.

A transportation pod moved low and slow inches above the ground. Most traveled in the sky unless landing. It navigated carefully through the throngs. When the circular door swung open, Ethan already reclined against the plush blue Ultrasuede with his feet on the center console.

Dwayne gestured for Kristen to step into the pod, and she took a seat inside the capsule on the left. Dwayne moved to the empty right. The door closed when he pressed a button on the console, and the pod lifted straight into the air before moving horizontally once above the buildings.

"Dwayne, are you sure Luana won't be mad at us for not completing our task?" Ethan asked.

"I may be relying on Solo to help cover for us." Dwayne stretched out his legs to the sides instead of fighting Ethan for real estate on the console.

The barrier effectively blocked Kristen from accessing the door first. She frowned. "Are you going to ask me more about my ability?" she asked.

"Later—the whole Council will need to hear your story." Dwayne yawned and pulled out his phone. "Wouldn't want you to tell it twice. Be awfully redundant. Namune, I'm going to reschedule a few things. We'll need to return to Wabaunsee tomorrow."

"Anything you want me to prepare?" Ethan collected his newly repaired phone from his pocket.

"Nothing more than you've already done. Molelo might give us something later—we'll reevaluate then."

"Are you sure you can discuss these kinds of things with me here?" Kristen cut in.

"Have you learned anything?" Ethan dropped his legs to the floor.

She bit her tongue and thought. Neither Council member said any specific information about their tasks. She only knew they existed, and she had a couple nicknames, but no one to tie them to. "No."

"Then, does it matter if we talk in front of you?"

She stayed quiet and let their conversation fade into a hum behind her. Despite what Dwayne told her, she expected more curious questions from them. Especially Ethan after she repaired his phone.

The Council members didn't scare her as much as she thought they would. After the rumors about the Council and their actions around the world, she thought they would be dangerous. *Perhaps they lied to her about their position on the Council?* She shook her head. The Council uncloaked themselves a few months prior—the officer they took the handcuffs from called them with honorific titles, and Dwayne and Ethan scared him. The others in the street actively avoided them.

She supposed the blood red robes created an atmosphere to sway most people to fear long after their removal. The unknown often created the most naturally terrifying ideas. Behind the robes, the Council members could be anything or anyone—disrobed, they were still the strongest elementalists in the nation. The Council acted like real people with what Kristen qualified as "normal" issues on top of the responsibilities of running a nation. She didn't anticipate the reality.

Kristen brought her thumb to her lips and bit the nail. The edge cracked under the pressure. Thinking logically, two Council members didn't scare her, but their abilities did. Ethan wouldn't be nearly as dangerous as she perceived without the label of Death elementalist. In only a matter of minutes, she would sit not just in front of two Council members, but in front of six others. Six more unknowns, other than name and element. Eight judgements would condemn her to life or death in the society she worked so hard to illegally enter.

When Kristen first traveled to Elementōrum Patriam, she wanted to fly under the radar longer to explore her abilities. She wanted to learn why she was different from everyone else. Her leg bounced, and her breathing quickened. Despite her desires, the Council caught her. Her past and secrets sought to break free of the fetters she imposed.

If she never saw Ethan standing at the entrance to the alley, she might've chosen another path to run. Kristen knew she had little opportunity to escape the police. Her inexperienced powers failed her at the most crucial moment.

Their voices filtered over her thoughts. She recognized the word *war* and knew they discussed the plans to proceed against Tyr Slattery who declared war against the elementalists. His declaration, and the subsequent pulling out of nations to support Tyr's movement of genocide, led the Council to reveal themselves. Kristen's eyes wandered over the informal dress of her unwitting captors. They had similar tastes, a loose shirt with jeans. Ethan chose a cotton t-shirt while Dwayne opted for a muscle shirt, but neither left an impression on her as "all powerful" like their titles suggested. *What business are they conducting in non-professional clothing?* she wondered. *Maybe they rely more on their presence?*

Ethan interrupted her thoughts. "We are curious about why you say you shouldn't exist."

Kristen jumped and blinked unsteadily at him for several seconds. "What?"

"Earlier, you said you shouldn't exist. We are both curious, but anything you say to us will need to be repeated later in front of the rest. There's no point in asking the same question twice."

"Oh," Kristen hummed. He answered her question from earlier at the very least.

"As for how we're dressed," Dwayne said, "doesn't really matter when you're part of the Council. Intimidation factor."

Kristen's eyes widened, and her hand fell from her lips to her lap. "Can you read minds?" she asked.

Dwayne pursed his lips. "I'm accomplished at reading people."

A text notification sounded through the pod, and Ethan's breathing deepened when he checked his phone. He showed the message to Dwayne who nodded and straightened his posture. Kristen angled herself to see the screen, but she only caught the letter S. Frustrated and anxious over the lack of information, she reclined in the seat and let out a small huff.

Ethan rolled his eyes, or she thought he did, but neither said anything about her attitude.

Kristen wracked her memory for anything she heard in passing about the Council members. They had a few conferences to explore their past and their abilities on the Council. They gave speeches to inspire their people about progress and plans. She could recall Ethan mentioning a sticky past with a lot of death following him, a tidbit she found entertaining. Dwayne, however, she couldn't remember anything about his personal life. He always focused on his life on the Council and never mentioned anything about his past.

"Which of us do you think is more threatening?" Ethan asked.

"Huh?"

Ethan repeated his question. "What do you think?"

Kristen pressed her tongue into her cheek. Her initial reaction would be to label Ethan as more dangerous because of his element, but something about Dwayne, despite his jovial personality, made her leery of him. Sure, Ethan could cut her down in less than a second, but Dwayne could hold her in the balance between life and death as long as he desired.

"I doubt she finds you the most threatening," Dwayne said. "She 'fake' kissed you." He used air quotes to emphasize the word fake.

Kristen didn't settle on a response and chose to watch the landscape pass under the pod instead. The Academy rose above the City of Garden not unlike Mount Olympus. The building had a collection of Mediterranean features, including outdated aqueducts used as walking paths, floating medieval castle turrets, deep pools of water with buried cities, and mazelike gardens filled with flowers and fountains. The main building resembled the architecture of a Greek temple with Doric columns, but the large set of stairs led into architecture imitating Israel. Waterfalls spilled around the Academy and under the aqueducts leading into the deep pools. The myriad architecture of City of Garden climbed the elevated landscape. Italy. Greece. Spain. Palestine. Lebanon. Libya. Cyprus. She couldn't name them all. Farther out from the city, she spotted mountain ranges high enough to imitate Switzerland and its low valleys. A smorgasbord of cultures—if only she could explore it.

Tears gathered in the corners of her eyes as the pod descended to the rear of the Academy. She knew the Academy was one of the most magnificent buildings on Earth, even if it floated twenty-five thousand feet above the surface, or rather, the Gulf of Mexico.

The pod pulled into a large garage structure with mechanics and engineers working side by side on all the vehicles. A group of mechanics took over their pod immediately after they climbed out in front of a set of double doors. Dwayne courteously opened one of the doors, and Kristen walked into a stunning hall lined with windows filtering in natural light. She gasped. The light echoed off the opposite wall, and small rainbows glittered across the floor inside the marble's calcite crystals.

They moved down the hall to an open atrium with a set of stairs leading into the inner Academy. Students and staff moved out of the way of the Council members, but they continued their paths along the halls. Curious whispers from a few students relaxing in small study nooks or walking to class followed them. The further they walked, the colored stripes along the wall vanished one by one. On a particularly bare stretch of wall, painters stood on ladders, adding a purple and black stripe in sections. They passed with nary a word, and Kristen didn't take her eyes off the process for a stretch.

"They're adding the Death and Supernatural elements," Ethan said. "We opened some of the unused classrooms and boarding areas to the new elements, but we don't have people to fill them in yet. I'm still the only one."

"I see," Kristen said.

One blood red line followed them until they reached a single door in the middle of an empty hall.

The door held no exorbitant decoration on its brown wood, only a gold sign with two words: **THE COUNCIL**.

"Welcome, Kristen, to our home." Dwayne opened the door for her a second time and waved her into the small atrium.

A single light embedded in the ceiling lit the front room and a part of the attached corridor. Inside the door, nine hooks hung empty on the wall; each had an element name on the wall above it. It took her a moment to realize their blood red cloaks used to hang there. She lamented the emptiness and wondered if the hooks would be removed during the course of the new order.

Dwayne and Ethan led Kristen through a confusing maze of near dark hallways until she knew she wouldn't find her way out again.

In the middle of one of the halls stood a messy haired brunette with her arms folded. Her pale skin took on the sickly green hue of her camouflage shirt. She had a distinct military style attire, from the combat boots to the dog tags hanging around her neck. Kristen knew they had to be a decommissioned set since green plastic gems covered one side entirely. Names nudged the edge of Kristen's memory, and she struggled to remember who the short woman might be. She easily had half a foot on her in height.

Dwayne and Ethan's postures straightened in her presence, and the name hit her immediately. Luana Ford. The leader of the Council. The member who joined at eight years old. Raised in the system, she knew it the best. She rattled off laws with speed Kristen couldn't hope to manage. Luana had firm control over the press meetings and made it known when her fellows said something she didn't approve of. Kristen wouldn't dare face the small woman even with her powers intact. She sensed the ferocity of a wild animal lurking under her glare.

Luana shuffled to the side and allowed Kristen to enter. Long steps formed an aisleway leading into a brightly lit Amphitheatre style room. A single chair waited in the lower arena. Bright spots of color burst across her vision, and she nearly stumbled. She carefully descended with the lithe grace of a cat instead of a prisoner to her death; she tried not to look at anyone.

A man around Dwayne's height with a similar bulk and tawny skin stood guard by the door with his arms crossed. His light brown hair grew out since she last saw him on television and fell into his eyes, but she recognized him as Hans Aliyev, the Earth elementalist. He shared a tragic backstory during one of the interviews about his older sister being labeled as a Rogue and killed and his father committing suicide after Hans joined the Council. His mother and older brother were still alive, but the brother didn't have any elementalist powers and lived in the gated community of the Uns. Kristen didn't fully understand the Uns' presence in Elementōrum Patriam, and she didn't dare ask.

In the seats nearest the front, looking into the pit on stage left, she recognized Eilene Vos, Water elementalist, reclining in one of the seats with her feet on the railing. Her blonde and blue balayage cascaded across the seat. Eilene absently adjusted the strap of her bright pink tank top. She smiled when Dwayne took the empty seat on her right.

The eyes of the man on Eilene's left flickered to Dwayne for a moment before returning to his phone. He had his fingers poised over the screen playing a game. His black hair fell into his eyes and reminded Kristen of the emo kids in some of her middle school classes before she ran away. He dressed in black to complete the look, and it took her longer to place him as Scott Everton, Wind elementalist. He rarely talked in press conferences and generally bled into the background. Kristen thought she didn't know much about Dwayne, but she knew even less about Scott. Luana cleared her throat as she moved down the steps to a seat on stage right, and Scott put the device away. In the corner at the end of Luana's row, a woman dozed against the wall. Her round features and lack of lines across her sepia toned skin labeled her as the youngest, Series Pahona, the Fortune elementalist. Her long brown hair extended far past what she could see, and Kristen remembered it hanging past her butt in length during interviews. Series came from the Hopi, an indigenous subgroup of the Anasazi in Arizona.

Ethan clambered over the seats to sit between Series and the last Council member, Lí Scarlet, Storm elementalist. Scarlet twirled a lock of her own black and blonde balayage between her fingers and snapped a piece of gum with her tongue. Luana glared at her sharply for a moment, but she acted completely unfazed. Scarlet caught Dwayne's attention and said a word in Mandarin which made him smirk. When she shifted to lean against the railing, the light caught the gold undertones of her honeyed tan skin.

Hans moved from the door to the end of the stairwell where he could block Kristen into the arena.

"Would you state your name for the official record?" Luana demanded.

"Kristen Elizabeth Delavida Reyes." She took a seat on the chair.

"And what is your intent for illegally entering Elementōrum Patriam?"

"I wanted to discover more about myself and the abilities I have." Kristen folded her hands across her lap and picked at her nail beds. "An elementalist already told me when I was little that I shouldn't exist, and I should hide my powers. I only wanted answers."

"What are your abilities?"

"There are a few of them." She tried to calm her racing heart. "The one I use the most is to slow down time. If I drop something, I can catch it before it breaks or spills. I can also slow down time if I'm running late and still move at a normal pace to make up for those lost moments. I can separate the elements around me and control unstable ones. If I want to, I can see the stars in space as if I'm right next to them, but I stay safely bound on earth. There are many planets which are beautiful up close."

Scarlet grabbed a book from the seat next to her and flipped through the pages. She handed it to Luana. Luana read the page before nodding and holding it up for the others.

"Is this the general consensus from everyone else as well?"

A few Council members shared looks or shrugged before agreeing with whatever the book claimed.

"Kristen," Luana said. "We'd like to see a few of your powers in person. I wouldn't recommend trying to run."

"I understand," Kristen nodded obediently, "but, I'm struggling with my powers a bit."

Dwayne lifted his eyebrow. "Overexertion?"

"Yes," Kristen said.

"We'll have to wait until tomorrow, Molelo," Dwayne said. "Overexertion just needs time. She'll be good by breakfast."

"You'll stay here?" Luana glared at her.

Unease settled over Kristen, and she considered refusing; except she had no powers and eight people were ready to fight her with force. She licked her lips and said, "Yes."

"Great," Scarlet stood before Luana could turn her near refusal into a fight. "I'll show you to your temporary room. I can remove the handcuffs as well. I can't imagine it'd be comfortable sleeping in those."

"You don't think I'll try to run?" Kristen asked.

"Oh, I don't think you want to take that risk." Eilene's eyes lit up at the prospect. "We're all itching for a good fight."

Ethan cracked his neck. "With Slattery on the down low right now, we could do with a little action."

"Hush, the both of you." Scarlet gestured for Kristen to follow her through the halls.

December 19, 2317

The Academy, Elementōrum Patriam

Kristen sat on the couch across from Robert Hatchbrooke, her best friend. Robert's mother moved from Elementōrum Patriam after meeting his other mother in an online college class. They adopted Robert as a toddler, and moved into Kristen's neighborhood where they met and grew up together. They had the same elementary school classes and organized their middle school classes together where possible.

"I want to see space," Robert said. "Fly around in it like you said you did the other day."

"Okay!" Kristen leaped from the couch. "It was really cool. I stood on the rings of Saturn."

"Can we see Pluto?" Robert joined her in front of the television.

"I think so." Kristen grabbed his hands. "Hold on tight. I always feel like I'm going to fall."

Robert's hands tightened against hers. She sensed his breathing quicken, and she tried to comfort him with a soft squeeze. Her feet lifted off the ground, and they floated toward the ceiling. The ceiling vanished, and the whole room filled with the emptiness of space.

"It's cold," Robert said uncomfortably.

"I haven't noticed," Kristen said. His fingers felt like ice. Her eyes traveled from the majesty of the Milky Way to his face.

Robert shuddered and his lips turned blue. "It's. Hard. To. Breathe," Robert choked. His chest heaved raspy rattles.

"Robert?" Kristen gripped his hands tighter. Panic seeped into her nerves. The planets spun around them. Purple sparks arced from her fingertips and slapped Robert across his face. The skin cracked like ice, and the blood froze inside the wound. "Robert?"

The door burst open below her. Robert's mother stared at them, mouth open and eyes wide. A wave of flames rushed toward her. Kristen let go of Robert's hands to protect herself.

With a loud gasp, Kristen rocketed out of her bed, ready to fight. Her limbs shook with adrenaline as the dregs of the memory faded. Cold air blasted into the room from the air conditioning system, and she quickly reached for the blanket to wrap around her shoulders. She tapped the corner of the nightstand and the clock inside showed two in the morning. Kristen figured she might get a snack from the Council kitchen, which Ethan showed her at dinner time, to tide over her rumbling stomach. She needed a break to let the memory of Robert fade or she'd have the same dream again.

On her way through the halls, she noticed a door partially open. She crept toward it. With the restriction of staying so the Council could see her powers in the morning, she didn't want them to think she planned to sneak off.

"Our population is one billion making our count for each infantry..." Luana's voice filtered from behind the door and drifted off. "That can't be right." She tapped a screen rather hard in quick succession. "Two-hundred and fifty million people in a single infantry? That's too many."

"Lu, children." Hans.

"Right, children and elementalists still studying at the Academy—we wouldn't draft them." A pencil scratched a few notes. "Adjusted to two-hundred million."

"Try one-hundred and fifty." Another pencil. "There are going to be a number of people who do not wish to fight. We need to allow them mercy—even if we don't want to."

"That's a total fall of seven-hundred million not fighting." Distraught flooded her tone.

"We need people to run the country. We can't have all of them fighting or we will have no production. Our people will starve on the front lines—we will have no means to fight outside of our abilities. I think it honestly may be too much to expect that many of our people to join us in war. There is so much which needs to be done to sustain our lands while we fight for our rights. Even if we do not reach these numbers, we will have a substantial army. Most strong nations only reach a few million, and we've counted far above that. We should count on much lower numbers overall."

"We'll also be facing multiple armies at once. All who are able should fight. I want this over quickly. There has been too much talking of late, and

I'm ready to fight—I'm ready to get it over with. Be done. Kill Tyr Slattery and, with him, his ideals." A soft pounding on the table as something impacted it.

"That won't be easy to do. Slattery is preying on the weaknesses of humans. Their lack of compassion for the differences between even their own race will help to bring about their downfall, but those ideals will always persist in the ideals of men who search only for perfection."

Kristen ducked quickly past the doorway and continued to the kitchen. She grabbed an apple from the fruit basket on the counter. She took a bite and turned. An open doorway led to a dark hallway. Curiosity got the better of her, and she followed the hall to the front atrium. She stared at the nine hooks. The last in line said *Supernatural.*

Kristen glanced the way she came before pushing the Council door open. A familiar tingling warmed the tips of her fingers, and the threads of time called for her control. She let the sensation wash over her body, and time slowed around her. She moved at her own leisurely pace without a care for the Earth's rotation across the night sky. The blood red line kept her on the right path to the main entrance hall of the Academy.

At the doors to the Academy, she let go of her control and slipped through with the smallest crack.

The marble steps glittered under the moonlight and the view of the City of Garden greeted her like the night's smile. Peace swept over her as she stepped away from the canopy of the roof and found the face of the universe watching her in its glory of rich purples, pinks, and blues. Her feet clicked against the steps as she descended and watched the night's freckles wink and dance above her. Halfway down, the stairs came to a long landing with a rudimentary path to the right side. Curious, she departed the well-worn path for the dirt one.

Kristen walked a few yards away and came to a pond which reflected the majesty of the night-sky with such complexity she believed it to be a mirror. She sat on the edge for several minutes before she ran her fingers across the surface and watched the ripples interrupt the stars' parade. She smiled and scooped the water into her hands before it trickled like a fountain into its home. In the beginning of February, cold on Earth's surface, she didn't expect it to feel warm and welcoming. She liked the comfort of controlled weather courtesy of the Storm elementalists. They could have any weather they desired at any moment. It left her in awe of the greatness they boasted as a race. They had all parts of the world folded under a single banner.

"I've always found water to be a strangely beautiful element."

Kristen jumped and splashed a large amount of water onto her lap. She turned and found Hans standing behind her. He chuckled at the wet stain and ran a hand into the brunet pompadour of his undercut.

"Water has so much power over our world, over me, yet it's all the more fascinating to explore." He joined her on the ground. "You should be glad I told Luana I would search for you outside. She isn't as forgiving of rule-breakers. I'm sure she'll be waiting to give you a piece of her mind when we return."

"How did you know?" Kristen asked.

"The front door has a silent alarm. It triggers in case of intruders—or in this case, escapees."

"I had a nightmare. I feel more at ease when I am closer to the stars." Kristen pointed up.

"It is easy to feel cooped up in the Council chambers. Even when you feel like you adjust, there are days when you want to escape and be free from the pressures again," Hans said.

"Did you often want to escape when you first joined the Council?"

"Of course. I think we all did at one point. After joining, we would see the consequences of our sudden end in the world out here." He waved to the trees. "Our names no longer existed outside of the Council. We had fake graves made in our name. The Council told lies about our disappearance and every bit of it, we agreed to willingly. There were many times when I considered running away. I wished to void the pact I made because I thought running would provide me some peace of mind—reunite me with the family I lost."

"And now?"

"Now, I am free to be known by my name again, but it doesn't change the losses I suffered in the years I vanished," Hans said. They sat quietly for several minutes. Hans waved a hand in the direction of the sky. "It is a beautiful night. A perfect one to settle thoughts."

"Are you going to drag me back to the Council chambers?" Kristen pulled at her wet jeans.

"I think if I tried, you would use your abilities to your advantage. If you didn't, I would feel guilty. Instead, I think it's best to wait until you wish to go back. It's quite easy to get lost." He smiled and lay in the grass with one foot balanced on the other and his hands under his head.

Kristen joined him but in the opposite direction. She lifted her hand to the sky and traced constellation patterns across the stars. Each star twinkled a little brighter as her fingers trailed between them.

"Have you ever wanted to see a star up close?"

"I haven't thought about it before," he admitted.

"The dying ones are the most spectacular. When you watch them implode and leave behind trails of color as they turn into nebulas from the supernova. Although, the star nursery nebulas are stunning. They birth new stars as if mothers of the universe itself. How miraculous space is. It expands and acts completely on its own will, separate from our own. We have no control over it. I have no control over it. I can merely watch it unfold. In the grand scheme of things, our lives on this planet mean nothing to the universe. Our struggles are irrelevant."

"I wonder if you can control it, and you don't know it. If you've hidden your powers for so long, it's possible you do not know their extent," Hans sighed. "I would also suggest you stay away from motivational speaking. I feel saddened after your speech."

Kristen laughed bright and bold. "My apologies, Hans."

They watched the sky for a while longer before Kristen stood and dusted grass off her pants. Hans followed her and walked at her side. He had his phone out for part of the journey to the Council chambers, but he didn't mention anything urgent from the device. When they arrived, no one waited for them behind the door.

"Is Luana not upset?"

"I talked to her." He waved his phone. "It'll all be alright, provided you don't go sneaking off again."

"I won't. I am going straight to bed."

"I'll see you in the morning, Kristen." He nodded and headed down the hall.

She followed at a slower pace. In her mind's eye, she could still see the swirling sky above her and the haze of approaching dawn.

CHAPTER TWO

First Light

"Fun adventure last night?" Scarlet asked with a warm smile as she slid into a chair at the table.

"Uh, yeah, I suppose so. I just needed some air," Kristen said.

"Here." Dwayne set a vial of black liquid in front of her at the table as he joined.

"What's this?" She lifted it but quickly set it down again when she saw the caution label warning her of radioactive material.

"Carbon-14," Dwayne said. "If you're what we think you are, you should be able to drink that and have no adverse effects unlike the rest of us." He opened the dumb waiter with a momentary frown. "Well, except maybe Namune. Haven't thought about feeding him that yet."

"What am I eating?" Ethan asked. He joined Dwayne in front of food delivery.

"Carbon-14, maybe. We're debating whether it might kill you."

"Huh," Ethan considered for a moment. "I could try?"

"Rather you not." Luana slipped into the chair at the head of the table while Hans collected their food.

"It brings up a great point, though." Dwayne watched Eilene enter and drift lazily to the counter to wait for her morning cup of hot cocoa. "Could Ethan survive it as the Death elementalist?"

"That's why I want to try," Ethan said. "Know my limits."

"It makes me think about other elements, too." Dwayne nodded to Scarlet. "Think about it. Mulan could logically survive a lightning strike or a volcanic explosion because she can control those."

"Yeah," Scarlet said. "We already know that."

"Exactly, but what about Namune? Sure, he can't control the element, but he sure as hell can't die any of the normal ways. What is his upper limit on damage?"

"Take a crack at me, later. When we're training," he offered. "Dwayne can supervise to make sure I don't actually die."

Once Scott and Series arrived with their own breakfasts, the Council took to interrogating Kristen about her abilities and testing them. They had Hans drop an object from across the room and watched her catch it before it ever neared the ground.

She showed them, cautiously after her nightmare, space through a window. They toured other galaxies, nebulas, and planets up close. Eventually, Dwayne gestured to the Carbon-14 still sitting on the table.

"What will happen to me if I'm not what you think I am?" The vial shook in her hand.

"You'll die. Radioactive material isn't made to be ingested." Dwayne shrugged. "You're in no danger, really. We know you're safe already. This is just to make absolutely sure."

Kristen's eyes widened. She knew her death would be a big possibility once captured by the Council; she didn't expect it to come without care for the end result. She thought they would deliberate like a court trial, but one of the tests for her survival had a high chance of killing her on the spot. Panicked, her breathing quickened, the vial slipped from between her fingers, and her hands flew into her hair. She never heard it crash to the floor.

Sound lost all meaning. Kristen tugged at the strands and tried to remember how to breathe. She felt a steady hand on her back, and her mind cleared.

A concerned Dwayne watched her carefully. He held the unbroken vial in one hand, and a faint green glow seeped over her shoulder where his hand rested to keep her steady.

"Panic attack, nothing else wrong," he concluded. "Don't worry, everything will be fine. I'm here in case anything goes wrong."

"I'm sorry. I'm sorry."

"Kristen, deep breaths. Stop thinking. Take one thing at a time. It's not a big deal," Dwayne reassured.

Kristen uncapped the vial. The Council waited with bated breath. Dwayne raised his hands in front of him ready to read and document any of the results. She quickly pressed the tube to her lips and knocked it back at full force. Whiplash ran down her spine. The chemical burned for only a moment before it settled in her stomach. She let out a small burp, and the exhale of air lit concern in Dwayne's face.

"What is it?" Luana took a step forward.

"After ingesting Carbon-14, the breath expelled should be radioactive, and it is, but it only remains so for a few milliseconds. It stabilizes immediately after—almost as if her body is stabilizing the chemical."

"I'm not the only one who can drink weird things!" Ethan cheered. "Anyone want to crack open a bottle of poison?"

Dwayne rolled his eyes. "What do you want to do, Molelo?"

"We'll keep her for a couple days. Confirm a few more things and make sure there's no adverse reactions to Carbon-14. I trust your medical diagnosis, but it would be best to know our ideas are on the right page." Luana folded her arms. "We won't do what we did to Ethan, of course. She'll be our guest."

"Kristen?" Series leaned into her field of view, and Kristen jumped back. Series grinned. "Do you have clothes we can collect and bring here? If not, you and Eilene are similar heights, you might wear the same sizes."

Kristen looked the other blonde woman up and down. Her clothes hugged her figure. "I think I wear larger clothes. I had a suitcase in my—

uh—illegally obtained apartment."

"We'll get it back," she said.

"Tell us more about your ability," Luana said.

Kristen slid into her seat and lifted a spoonful of oatmeal from her bowl. "It's dangerous. It can kill people when I'm not careful with it—sometimes even when I am careful." She swallowed her oatmeal. When she put her spoon back to take another bite, a queasiness settled in her stomach, and she pushed the bowl away.

"You have experience with that," Hans said. He knew.

"My best friend as a kid into young teenager—he recognized my abilities as something special at school because his mom is an elementalist. She told me to hide my ability, but over time it became too much to handle. I had an outburst one day and killed him without meaning to. I've been running ever since. Always a new home. A new job. A new state. I never stayed in one place too long."

"Where are you from originally?" Ethan perked up curiously. "I ended up all over, too—passed between one family member to another."

"Virginia," Kristen said.

"I was born in Montana." Ethan grinned. "We're almost on opposite coasts."

"I'm from South Carolina," Scott said quietly.

"Oh, another Southern state." Kristen perked up. "What was it like growing up a little more south?"

He shifted uncomfortably. "Lots of hurricanes."

"I remember quite a few tornadoes in Tennessee, but I didn't live there long enough to really know. It's kind of more... relying on news knowledge." Luana frowned. "There really are too many of us from America."

Eilene laughed. "It helps to make those of us not from America all the more special and diverse."

"Where are you from?" Kristen hesitantly pulled her bowl toward her. She leaned away when the queasiness didn't back down.

"City of Barren, the Netherlands sector. I grew up speaking Dutch," she paused, "Praten over koetjes en kalfjes." The group stared at her for a few seconds too long, and her brows furrowed. "I forgot, I'm the only one who speaks Dutch. I need to use it more."

"I'm learning a new language today, apparently." Dwayne clapped his hands together. "Off to the library."

"If you're going to the library, take a team with you and research strategy and weaknesses we can exploit instead," Luana growled.

"I'll take Scott, Eilene, and Scarlet," he agreed. The three chosen turned to him in surprise.

Luana frowned. Dwayne knew she liked working with Scott and Scarlet in particular. "Alright, I'll allow it for today. You four better bring me some promising information. Hans and I will work on the public call for recruits to the army. Series and Ethan, I'd like you to work with Kristen and see what you can figure out about her abilities."

"Agreed," Series quickly cut in, "We'll do our best with her."

"Everyone split." Luana stood and took her plate back to the dumbwaiter for its return trip to the kitchen.

Kristen considered her oatmeal for several more seconds before she decided against it entirely. She placed the half-finished bowl into the dumbwaiter and waited for Ethan and Series to lead the way.

"What room can we use for this kind of thing?" Ethan shoved his hands into his pockets and fell into step next to Series.

"There's a gymnasium we never really use—it's set up for a few different sports. I'm sure we could figure out a few things to do there," she said. "Kristen could show us more space."

Unease settled in the pit of Kristen's stomach. Her fingers went numb, and she could see the crystalline blood in Robert's veins. *Never again*, she thought.

Kristen learned more about the Council members from Ethan and Series during their morning training. Hans Aliyev was a second-generation elementalist in Elementōrum Patriam. His parents immigrated from Russia, and he grew up in the Russian sector of the City of Vasha. When Kristen questioned the origin of his name, Series explained how it came from his German grandmother who never had a son. According to Series, Luana and Hans had an undefined relationship and secrets the two newest Council members didn't know.

The question of Hans' older brother, Maxim, also emerged because of brief mentions during press conferences. Ethan and Series spoke uncomfortably about the Uns and their treatment. For years, the Uns lived behind a gated community in the country "for their protection" as the law quoted. However, the fence the Uns lived behind would burn them if they tried to escape. The Uns, Series said, were humans born to elementalists, a regression of the mutation that allowed them to use the nine elements. The regression remained a main part of why they kept the two societies separate. Ethan explained how he helped quell an issue with the Uns along with Hans and Scott. Series argued they only delayed it. She thought they would revolt again.

Kristen asked about Dwayne to move away from the heavy and complex topic of the Uns. Dwayne immigrated from Botswana as a child, but he never talked about his family. Apparently, he only confided in Eilene and Scarlet, but everyone knew about his resentment toward being the Council doctor. They told her how Dwayne had a nickname for everyone among the Council, and he never referred to anyone by their given name. Molelo for Luana, Solo for Hans, Mosupologo for Scott, Mulan for Scarlet, Dickens for Eilene, Muuyaw for Series, and Namune for Ethan. Ethan and Series believed Dwayne would have a nickname for Kristen in no time. She didn't know how to feel about it. She did have open concerns about Scarlet's name, but Ethan reassured her since he'd thought the same thing.

Scarlet immigrated from China as a child, and her name in Mandarin, Zhū Hóng, translated close enough into her English name. They didn't know too much about Scarlet's life beforehand either, but they knew she admired Mulan. The reason she chose her nickname.

As for Eilene, who Kristen thought of as friendly and bubbly, they knew just about as much about her as they did Dwayne. They looked puzzled for a long while as they tried to figure out why they thought they knew Eilene so well. Kristen requested they give up trying to tell her about the other Council members.

Ethan's story had a lot of similarities to her own. He lost his parents at five in what the town still considered a mystery in his survival. He lived with his grandparents until the Black Riders invaded the town to ethnically cleanse it of elementalists. His grandparents, and the town, perished. His other grandmother appeared to take care of him then drowned in the Mississippi River. The first orphanage burned down around him. The last orphanage he lived in was he met Lulu before it tumbled into the ocean. The Council collected him for education in Elementōrum Patriam.

"How'd you come to join the Council?" Kristen nudged Ethan with her foot as they reclined on the couch of the game room. She had a bowl of chips in her lap, and she watched Ethan play a video game imitating life in the medieval ages. Series left them alone a couple hours previous to take care of a task Luana wanted completed.

He didn't respond right away as he fought off a wolf attack with a knife. "They tried to kill me."

She raised an eyebrow waiting for more information.

"You already know they retrieved me from Washington when I was fourteen to train me here at the Academy. Problem is, no matter what element I was in, I couldn't do much more than accidentally almost kill everyone. If anyone talks about the infamous incident where they had to evacuate the entire Academy Infirmary—that was me."

"You didn't!" Kristen kicked her feet in the air as she laughed.

"Little methane, ammonia, and hydrogen sulfide. Works wonders." Ethan gave her the classic OK gesture.

Kristen's laughter slowed, and she leaned her head against the couch. "It's lonely not having anyone else like you. You don't know how to control anything."

"Yeah." Ethan swallowed hard. "I think I felt the loneliest when the Council locked me in a cell before they knew about you and me. I was alone, and I became weak. Anything could hurt me when it normally can't." He ran a hand through his hair. The long strands clung to the between spaces of his fingers before falling to his neck. "Nobody can adequately explain my powers to me either because there's only one book about us."

"So," Kristen flung her legs onto the back couch cushion, "we are the ones currently setting the limits and understanding of what our powers can do."

"Pretty much." He tossed the gaming glove onto the coffee table. "It feels like I'm always watched like a lab rat. I just want to discover things about myself and my powers without everyone staring at me waiting for something awe inspiring to happen."

"Can we practice together?"

"There's cameras all over this place." Ethan pointed around the room. "No matter what, they'll be watching something."

"It's like we aren't really members of the Council. I'm sure they don't watch each other."

"They know each other too well for that." Ethan stretched his arms above his head. "They're all awesome people in their own way, but it's still lonely being the new recruit."

"I imagine it would be," Kristen said.

"Tyr Slattery, the one who declared war on us last year, he made it a point to call me and others like me out," Ethan said.

"I remember seeing the video. I didn't find it convincing, but so many countries pulled out following it. It scared me a little."

"Why?"

"Well, I'm already a Rogue. If I came here, I knew I had a high chance of being killed. I know Rogues are considered unsafe for the world because they can't control the elements, but I didn't want to die. I also didn't know what Tyr had planned." She played with the hem of her shirt. "I actually recognized him in the video. He and two other men followed me for a while when I lived in Mississippi. Some coworkers helped me escape him, and it was narrow."

Ethan didn't say anything, but he watched her carefully.

"There's some interesting irony in Tyr's plans," Kristen said.

"Why do you say that?"

"In the video, he showed that he planned to kill and injure children. He had a kidnapped child in the video who he clearly tortured and so many countries immediately backed him. They are so scared of us that they're willing to kill any version of us."

Ethan let out an amused breath. "Yeah, I get where you're coming from. He's doing it all to get his daughter back, and his daughter is one of us. It's messed up."

When lunch arrived, the Council gathered as a group to eat and discuss the things they did during their team time. Eilene sat at the lunch table with three tosti sandwiches on her plate along with some slices of cold meat and an ice-based dish Kristen didn't recognize. She sat immediately next to Scott who had a large plate of fries and three fried chicken sandwiches. Eilene scooted her dessert toward Scott. Both worked their way through the fries and dessert together—it felt as if Kristen intruded on something she shouldn't see.

Scarlet had her own version of the same ice-dish and several dishes she couldn't name but identified as Chinese. All the Council members had large plates of food. Hans worked his way through several servings of a tomato-based stroganoff, while Luana had three double cheeseburgers in front of her; she polished them off quicker than Kristen could blink. Ethan had two large enchilada style burritos, stuffed to the brim with beans and rice. Series had a plate full of beans, corn, and venison hash. Dwayne had two separate dishes: one consisted of a deep-fried bread covered in honey and ground beef; the other, a bowl full of an unfamiliar bean.

"Do you all normally eat this much food?" She felt embarrassed to only have a single American style taco in front of her with a side of seasoned tater-tots.

"We started training recently for the upcoming war," Scarlet said. "We are eating a lot more carbs to help sustain our diet as a result since we burn through them."

"We didn't eat nearly this much a few weeks ago," Eilene said with a grin.

"Training can make you hungrier?" Kristen popped a tot in her mouth.

"Oh yeah," Dwayne said. "We must keep our status as the strongest elementalists in the country. If we don't have a wide range of control on our powers, and if we aren't able to fight properly, it'd look bad on Elementōrum Patriam. Part of proper understanding and control is all in the training elements. We'll be fighting right alongside our people—we have no intentions of sitting and commanding from the sidelines."

"I think it'd be more terrifying to know you're up against the strongest elementalist in the world as well. We're hoping some fear might drive a few away." Series chewed her meat thoughtfully. "Though, in some countries, dying in war is a badge of honor."

Eilene finished off her food and twirled her hair between her fingers as she waited for the others to finish. "Will we be doing the same tasks in the afternoon?"

"I would like us to continue—though Kristen, you can have free-time as I need Ethan's and Series' help." Luana nodded to her companions.

"Of course. I think I'll check out one of the entertainment rooms," Kristen agreed politely.

"Ugh, I need to dye my hair again," Eilene muttered under her breath as she dropped her hair back into place with a little more curl. "I'm heading off to the library."

"I'm right behind you." Scott quickly stood from his chair, and the two headed off together.

Kristen's brows furrowed together. "Are they dating?"

The others shrugged, but Dwayne shook his head; they stood and headed off to their own tasks. Left behind, Kristen polished off the last of her food before she went to find something to entertain her for a few hours.

December 20, 2317

Eilene shuffled into the room in a daze and made hot chocolate in a mug which read DON'T TALK TO ME UNTIL MY THIRD CUP on the side. Scott appeared to be in a similar state next to her, sans drink. They passed yawns back and forth several times.

Kristen pulled the yellow strap of her tank top into place on her shoulder and collected her breakfast from the dumbwaiter in the corner.

"What do we have on the itinerary for our workout today?" Ethan took a seat at the table next to Kristen with a plate of pancakes and syrup.

"Strength training and hand to hand combat. In the afternoon, Luana wants us to focus on increasing the capacity of our abilities," Series reported as she polished off her own breakfast.

"Where is Luana?" Ethan looked around the sparse table.

"Already in the workout room. She's been up all night, I think. Hans and Dwayne are with her," Scarlet said. She took her and Series' dishes to the dumbwaiter. "She's pushing ring work, I hear."

"Lovely." Eilene let out another unwilling yawn. She used the hair tie on her wrist to pull her hair into a messy ponytail. She stood and placed her own dishes with the others before heading out of the room with Scott hot on her heels.

"Do you have a water bottle?" Ethan asked as he retrieved his own from under the table.

Kristen shook her head. "Lost it. I think I dropped it in the Forest of Light when the police caught up to me. I had to drop it to get rid of the weight."

"No problem, we have a cupboard full of them." He opened one of the cabinets and produced a purple bottle for her to have. He headed toward the door. "I'm sure the rest expect you to join us for the day."

"Do you have workout clothes?" Series asked.

"I don't."

"I can order them, and they'll arrive shortly." Series sat in the empty seat on her right. "This is the styling app. Choose as much as you like."

Kristen browsed the catalogue and chose a few different outfits she thought looked comfortable and a sports bra she hoped would fit based on the online measurements.

"Do you need any other clothes as well? It's no problem to add them."

"I can look through it later," Kristen reassured. "I have enough clothes for a few days right now. These are just the essentials."

"I'll put in the order and have it delivered to the locker room directly." Series took over control and tapped the screen to place the order.

"You can do that?"

"There's a lot of old delivery systems set up throughout the Council quarters since renovations here are rare. It's not hard to have them use the older ones."

"Terribly efficient." Kristen smiled. "Thank you for ordering me clothes."

"Of course." Series stood. "It'll only be a few more minutes before they arrive. I'll show you the way."

"You go ahead. I still need to fill my water." She shook the empty bottle. "I can find my way on the map."

"If you're sure." Series hesitated but left at the affirmative nod.

Kristen walked over to the sink and ran the water until it turned cold. She filled the bottle and took a few sips before she refilled the gap and screwed the lid on tight. She followed the map on the phone to the locker room and found the clothes Series ordered waiting for her on one of the benches. She smiled and changed quickly before she joined the others in the large gymnasium area. Her outfit consisted of a nice pair of tennis shoes, a bright galaxy themed tank top, and a simple pair of small, black, exercise shorts.

On the far side of the room, a covered pool waited stagnate. A boxing ring raised above the rest of the room showed off Dwayne and Hans practicing against each other. Luana worked out on the gym equipment lined against the walls all the way around the room. Ethan and Scott took over the mats next to the ring—they practiced melee with wooden weapons in place of the real plasma ones. Scarlet sat on an elliptical on the other side of the room and sweat beaded across her skin. Series laid out on one of the yoga mats. She moved fluidly between each position.

"Welcome!" Scarlet called when she spotted Kristen. "Choose anything to start working on."

"Thank you." She nodded and headed to the unoccupied sets of treadmills. She placed her water bottle in the cup where she could access it before she started her workout.

After several minutes running a few laps around the projected track, she noticed the Council members gathered around her to watch. She slowed her pace to a walk and considered turning the machine off.

"Did you know you activated your ability while running?" Hans said.

She froze and the conveyor belt pushed her dangerously close to the end of the machine. Ethan grabbed her arm and pulled her off before she fell. It took all her thought capacity to convey: "I didn't mean to."

"It was like watching a cartoon where the legs move, but the body doesn't," Eilene laughed. "It's amazing. You shouldn't try to hide it."

"If you stop hiding it, you'll be able to recognize when you use it more and control your powers better," Dwayne said.

Kristen tried to walk, but her legs felt shaky under her after running for so long.

"Come stretch with me." Eilene took her hand and led her to the yoga mats. "You should rest after exerting yourself like that."

She followed obediently. Before she stepped over to choose her mat, she placed her water bottle in line with the others. A rumbling under their feet set them off balance and the room swayed around them.

"An earthquake?" Hans stared at the ground. "I don't remember having fault lines this close to the Academy. Most of them are in Ricci and Barren."

"Someone's abilities?" Scarlet suggested. "It would be Earth or Storms."

"They'd have to be pretty strong to hit that kind of impact." Scott pointed to the cracked support beam nearest them.

Hans took a deep breath and held out his hand. A few of the others grabbed onto each other or stable objects as Hans reversed the damage.

"We'll investigate behind the scenes." Luana grabbed her phone and typed.

The Council spent a long while deliberating during their meeting over the topic of Kristen becoming a Council member and a more permanent fixture in the Council chambers. The decision would be made in less than twenty-four hours, and they had a lot more time to make the decision about inviting

Ethan. Logically, they didn't want to just invite the first person they encountered, but they also had no other elementalist to give them a run for title of "strongest" as the Council dictated.

"I think we should," Eilene said at the end of another thirty-minute debate. They took a break from the topic to discuss other issues about the war, but they needed time to get a Council trial run set-up for Kristen.

They also had a meeting in a couple days to split the regions, and it would be easier to split it into nine first than wrangle it into nine later, on the off chance there would be another Council member. Granted, that only applied if Kristen accepted the position.

Many arguments against Kristen's placement included her unfamiliarity with Elementōrum Patriam and its laws. She only had a few months experience living there and all of it had the illegal undertones shading her view. Ethan argued that he didn't have the most experience with leading a country either, but he learned. They reminded him he spent six years at the Academy studying the seven elements before joining the Council as the eighth representative. No one dared point out Luana's short education prior to her induction.

Only two Council members could claim any heritage from the country in the first place. Eilene and Hans, and Eilene's family had more history than Hans'. Eilene's family didn't remember when they came to Elementōrum Patriam. Many guessed they existed since the foundation of the country at the time of the splitting of Pangea.

"Should we rule by majority vote?" Dwayne suggested as the argument halted again.

"I would prefer a unanimous decision," Luana said.

"Do you honestly see us getting there within the next year?" Hans asked. "Either we need Kristen to complete the nine, or we don't. We'll find a place for her to stay in the Academy and move on with our lives. Those are the two options. Whether we say yes or not, we are going to war."

"Nine would be better than eight in a war," Scarlet said. "I think we should do it."

Everyone except for Luana agreed. They stared at her waiting for the final call. They sat in silence for a couple minutes while Luana doodled on the screen in front of her before she finally said, "Let's be nine again."

The others breathed a sigh of relief.

"We have another important question to get the answer to before we choose her run," Eilene said. She gestured to Dwayne. "What's her nickname going to be?"

"Naledi," Dwayne said immediately. "It means 'stars.'"

"She's officially one of us." Ethan grinned.

The few hours between their morning exercise and lunch, the Council left Kristen to wander as she pleased. She couldn't find anything interesting to calm her mind and settled on walking the halls in never-ending circles. On one run, she decided to turn in a different direction to create a new circle— for variety. Her pacing took her past a large meeting room. She noticed the Council members gathered around a table. Scribbles covered the walls and more appeared as she watched. She tried to read the words backward and recognized the name: Tyr Slattery. Others graphed war expectations—battle formations, plans, rations. On a single panel by itself across the room, she recognized her name with several remarks under it. She quickly ducked out of the way of the walls and leaned against the door as quietly as she could.

She couldn't hear anything than a low hum of muffled discussion. She peeked around the corner and hoped they wouldn't see her through the wall. She couldn't make out any of the notes under her name at her angle, and she frowned. Eventually, she gave up and crawled back the way she came and retreated to her room.

Kristen busied herself with reading an eBook on her phone, but her mind kept wandering to her name on the wall. She knew the Council needed to discuss her and her abilities, but she also wanted to know what they thought. She wanted to know their plans. If they wanted to kill her, she wanted to be ready for it. To write a final goodbye—though, she didn't know to whom.

Her bedroom door slid open to a dark hallway. Startled, Kristen didn't dare go near it, but she also didn't know where to hide in an open white room. She stood out compared to everything else. After several long moments of nothing, she crept toward the door and peered into the dark hallway. She didn't recall it being incredibly dark when she returned to her room a couple of hours before.

A light triggered at the end of the hall, and she curiously followed it. She thought it might be a strange ritual for the Council to kill their victims—but either way, she wanted to know. The light vanished as she approached and another further down the hall attracted her. Eventually, they led her to an ajar door at the end of a long hall. When she pushed it open, she thought she accidentally stepped outside of the Academy. Several hundred feet up on a platform, floating rocks created an uneven path and guided her across the open sky. She tried to turn back, but the door behind her vanished, and she didn't know how she found herself outside.

With no other option, she geared herself up and jumped between each platform. On the last one, her foot slipped, and she started to fall. Her abilities activated without her thinking; she managed to grab onto the rock and pull herself into a position where she could make the last jump. When she landed, the sky faded, and Kristen stood in the middle of a large octagon piece of rock. On each side stood a stone arch with a single gem embedded at the top. Each of them glowed with a different color: orange, blue, green, white, red, yellow, gold, and black. The floor under her shifted and raised her on a pedestal far above the ground and as high as the gems in the doors.

"Kristen Delavida Reyes." Luana's voice boomed around her. "We bring you before us today with a proposition—as the return of the Supernatural elementalists, we offer you a position by our side on the Council."

Kristen collapsed to her knees in shock. She didn't expect the invitations. She also didn't have an answer immediately available. The day before she thought the Council would label her as a Rogue and kill her—as they did all Rogues. She didn't know about the Supernatural element, but they knew and wanted her. Her powers were of value to them; she was worth something. *I don't know about this country either,* she thought. She would be hopeless leading a people she knew next to nothing about.

A moment later, she remembered that most of the Council didn't know much about Elementōrum Patriam before they joined. Luana learned by growing up with the laws—she killed Rogues as a child. Ethan thought of himself as a Rogue for nearly six years. The people rejected him from the Academy and revered him as a Council member. She could have the same opportunity. She could bring a new opinion and change to the Council, maybe. If she saw places for improvement.

Ethan's jovial voice came across the line. "I get the opportunity to ask you for your commitment to our ideals. We want to ask you if you are willing to serve for the rest of your life as a member of the Council which protects the elementalist people? Do you swear fealty to the people of Elementōrum Patriam over your own gains? Are you willing to negotiate with those who oppose us? To keep peace between humans and ours? Currently, are you ready to fight and lead in the war for our continued existence alongside humans? Are you prepared to set clear lines between our laws and those which govern the Uns? Are you willing to be the ninth member of the Council?"

"Yes, yes, of course. If you'll have me." She nodded eagerly. "I will do it all for a place to belong."

The room shifted with a low groan of gears, and the octagon transformed into an enneagon. The pillar Kristen stood on lowered slowly to meet the floor under it. The large archways opened and revealed eight Council members behind each appropriate door. The last one opened into an empty hall. The stone above it flickered before glowing bright purple.

"Welcome to the Council, Kristen Delavida Reyes," Eilene said. A surge of power erupted around them all at once. The wave rocked them on their feet, and they threw out their hands to keep from falling.

"Whoa," Series gasped. "I guess that's what it's like when we actually have a full Council."

"No kidding," Luana said.

"Now you get to join us for meetings. You won't have to be alone anymore." Ethan held out his hand for her to take.

Kristen gripped his tightly, and he hauled her to her feet. She said, "I definitely like the sound of that."

December 22, 2317

The winter solstice morning dragged on, and Kristen thought it would never end. They had the morning news on in the background so low the voices of the hosts hummed. The subtitles flashed across the screen in the corner of her vision. Currently, they had to go through all the responses from the elementalist people after their voluntary draft went out to all fourteen and older. They didn't need to sort the yeses from the noes or sort by elements—the system automated those answers. No, they needed to review qualifications to give them their titles and ranks in each region.

Since the machine couldn't do all their tasks, the Council worked with all-hands-on-deck until further notice. They barely had enough time for four hours of sleep the previous night. Kristen flipped to a new page on her tablet with the name INAYA AHUJA across the top. Ethan paused noticeably next to her. She nudged him with her elbow.

"What?" Kristen asked.

"I know this name." He pointed at the tablet where the name LULU MORRIS stood out on the information sheet.

"From your time studying at the Academy?"

He shook his head. "We were in an orphanage together. The night the Council took me, the orphanage fell into the ocean. I thought everyone there died. I never thought I might see her again."

"Are you sure it's the same one?" Something in Kristen's stomach tightened painfully. She understood Ethan the most as the other lost element.

He scrolled to the picture. Lulu had her brunette hair tied in pigtails, but she looked much younger than Kristen first estimated. He smiled. "That has to be her, a little grown up."

"She must be very special to you." Bile rose in the back of her throat.

"Yeah, she is." He scrolled through the pages of information lost in thought before he *finally* said, "Look, she's fourteen now. Just barely past the age limit to fight."

Kristen choked on the sip of water she took. "Fourteen?"

"Yeah—a Water elementalist, too. That must be how she survived falling in the ocean."

"And you're interested in her?" Kristen's high-pitched squeak caught the attention of a couple of other Council members.

"Interested?" His brows pinched together. "I suppose—I mean she's in my region, so I do want to know if it's her. If it is, I'll have my little sister back."

Kristen's mouth fell open, and she expelled a burst of air imitating a laugh. "Right, little sister."

Dwayne snorted from across the table. "You weren't the only one worried about the implications of that."

"What were you..." Ethan drifted off.

Kristen watched as it clicked in the way his jaw went slack just before he pulled a face and gagged a little.

"I am not a—I have absolutely no desire to date her." The words came out of him in a rush trying to clarify. It was panic.

She knew the reaction well. "Yeah, we picked up on that," she laughed. She turned back to her tablet and clicked one of the rank options listed to the side. She had several greyed-out options she could no longer select. "You'll have to tell me more about Lulu later."

"Sure."

December 26, 2317

Ice Stadium, Belarus Sector, City of Vasha, Elementōrum Patriam

Kristen adjusted the uniform again against her skin. Dressing in military attire would take getting used to. They had a while before they would go on stage. The recruits had already been there for quite a while exchanging their regular phones for the new military grade issued ones and receiving their official uniforms to change into.

She peeked through the curtains of the temporary stage into the stadium. It filled quickly with recruits. The ice rink was covered by temporary flooring, and those of higher rank sat quietly in the main stage area.

"You, okay?" Ethan appeared behind her in black camouflage.

She nodded and tugged at her own purple fatigues again. "Nervous."

He laughed. "We don't have much to do."

"Still. It's the first-time people are really seeing me as a Council member, isn't it? People are going to be taking pictures." Kristen turned to face him. His new haircut still threw her off. Most of the Council went for semi-new haircuts for service in the war. She kept her basic ponytail, but Ethan chose an undercut with a ponytail of his own.

"President Delavida Reyes, we need to finish your styling." A woman called her over to the row of mirrors and make-up kits.

Kristen bit her lip and walked over to let the woman pamper her. She didn't like the idea of looking runway ready for a press conference regarding war, but she had to for professionalism's sake. The make-up artist finished in only a couple minutes as they flattened some of the wispy hairs against her scalp and added a bit of color to even her skin tone.

Ethan grinned at her from his own chair, long done with the styling experience. Behind Ethan, Hans, wearing red, stood near the wings with his hands on Luana's shoulders as he spoke quietly. Luana nodded along, and her mouth formed the word "okay" over and over. Hans looked quite nice with his new undercut, but he had a shorter pompadour on top compared to Ethan's ponytail. She had never seen Luana with nicely styled hair before. She had the same ponytail, but Kristen was used to the strands messily spilling out of the hair tie. Instead, it pressed ramrod straight against her scalp and swung below her shoulder blades against her orange uniform. The color washed out her skin tone.

Scarlet joined them a couple of moments later in yellow. She had her hair pulled into a half-bun. Hans let go of Luana to include Scarlet in the conversation. In the corner, waiting for Eilene to finish at her own table, Dwayne made animated conversation while Scott and Series listened politely.

Kristen liked the change she saw in Scott. When they first met, he came off as a traditional "emo", but he exchanged the shaggy fringe for a textured French Crop; it highlighted his bone structure, sharp enough to kill. The offset of his white uniform made him look a little tanned for once. Eilene reached out and grabbed his wrist as her hair stylist finished tying the Dutch Braid into her own half-up, half-down style. Scott smiled briefly, and his lips barely moved as he replied to Eilene, dressed in blue. The uniform was several shades darker than the dyed portion of her hair and almost clashed.

Series laughed and flipped her fishtail braid over her shoulder before moving away to stand in line at the wings. Her gold uniform resembled the one Scarlet wore.

"It's time," Luana called through the backstage area.

Kristen climbed stiffly from her chair and followed Ethan to line up in the order in which they joined the Council. Scott slid between Hans and Scarlet immediately followed by Dwayne, in a traditional deep green, and Eilene. Ethan stopped just behind Series, and Kristen nearly crashed into him. He laughed softly, and it eased some of her nerves just before they shot sky high as Luana made her way on stage with her shoulders rigid.

Cameras flashed from the area directly in front of the stage, and Kristen felt blinded by the lights. She could see the news cameras rolling for a broadcast across the nation. She leaned toward Ethan and whispered, "This is way worse than what I predicted."

He laughed again but did his best to hide it as they took on the personas of the strongest and most respected in the nation.

"Thank you all for the warm welcome." Luana stepped up to the microphone and held up her hands to bring silence among the crowd. "We wanted to take this opportunity to introduce ourselves to you. If we are going into this war together, trust is the first foundation in building a strong army. It is hard to defend your fellows on the battlefield if you don't trust them with your own life."

The Council members took their turns sharing details from their lives. By the end, Kristen saw quite a few of the recruits completely zoned out. It had to be boring hearing your governmental leaders talk about their own lives.

Luana smiled stiffly as she took control of the microphone again. "We hope to be able to continue to build our mutual trust as we move into fighting side by side on the battlefield. You all are going to start with ten days of basic training before we move into field work, which means we are only a few weeks out from meeting Slattery's forces face to face." The Council leader read off statistics about expectations. She told them about the division of supplies and planned arrangements to have regions work together. Kristen did her best to imitate listening to the important information.

Once the main meeting finished, Luana dismissed the crowds of new military personnel. Those on the rink stayed; the Secretaries of the Army and Field Marshals had further meetings with the Council members to discuss the upcoming war. The Secretaries of the Army would function as their right-hands and have extensive responsibilities. Some of which included cleaning up after the Council and making decisions that contradicted them if it bettered the war. The Field Marshals would serve as the next rank down, and they had a lot of military members to manage.

Ethan turned to leave the stage to collect his water bottle, but he paused when they all heard a faint shout of his name.

He turned back to the crowd with crinkled brows searching for something familiar.

"Are you okay?" Kristen put a hand to his bicep.

"I thought I heard someone." Ethan pursed his lips.

"Hearing weird snippets are my thing. Why are you encroaching on my territory?" Series jokingly jabbed him in the stomach. He laughed and opened his mouth with a rebuttal, but the panicked voice interrupted again—clear above the vacating crowd.

"Ethan, it's me, Lulu! Turn around."

The Council turned and saw a brunette jab one of the guards trying to restrain her with her elbow. He dropped her on instinct as pain burst through his nose just before it started bleeding.

Ethan watched her with wide eyes and stumbled back. "Lulu?"

"Hi," Lulu said.

The officer put a hand on her arm and pulled her back.

"Hold on, I know her." Ethan held out a hand. "I doubt she'll hurt me."

The man nodded and stepped away.

Ethan pulled her into a long hug. "How are you?"

"I'm great, really. I'm a Water elementalist."

"And you're in my region." He pulled away and gestured to the black fatigues.

"I was excited. I know I broke a ton of protocols to see you—but I had to. I never knew what happened after the orphanage. I'll take any punishment as deemed necessary." She bowed respectfully.

He looked back to Luana for confirmation. The woman had her lips pursed as she watched them.

"She's in your Region. Punish her or not." Luana turned away with an annoyed eye roll.

"I never would've guessed you'd be an elementalist, too. What happened to everyone?" Ethan crouched to look her straight on.

"After we landed in Cape Meares, the strongest swimmers started diving to rescue people. Since I could manipulate water, I stayed under longer, and I helped pull a lot of people out. The Council intervened and helped rescue more: dead and alive. They brought several of us here to the Academy as it turned out many of us are elementalists."

Hans cleared his throat. "I remember that night. It was with several people from the Council before the current members. You were very brave."

"Thank you." She nodded at Hans. "I'm sorry to have taken up your time."

"You're fourteen now, aren't you?" Ethan's eyes narrowed.

"I am."

He sighed. "Look, I can't let you go without punishment because I know you. It wouldn't be fair."

"I understand," Lulu said.

"Your squad will be in basic training for a week longer than the rest—which means you'll join the war later than everyone else. You'll spend seventeen days in basic training. You'll also need to write a sincere apology letter to the officer you injured." Ethan looked at the officer at her side.

"I'll report it as such to the squad leader." The man nodded and took

Lulu's arm. "We'll let you get back to your important duties, President Silverspoon."

"Thank you. I enjoyed seeing you again, Lulu. You'll always be my little sister. We might see each other again on the field." Ethan turned away, and Lulu watched him go.

Kristen fell into step next to him. "I think you went a little easy on your little sister."

Ethan smiled and knocked her hip with his. "Definitely, but sometimes mercy is better."

They didn't watch Lulu leave with the officer as they had duties to attend. However, something settled in the bottom of Kristen's stomach she didn't have a name for.

January 29, 2318
Lesotho Sector, City of Ubuntu, Elementōrum Patriam

The Council sat in a glass box above the military compound watching the training process. Several experienced groups already waited on the surface to hear of planned attacks, but there was nothing over the last month and a half from Slattery or any of the countries sworn to eradicate them. It made them anxious. Every day, the protests outside the Academy grew, but they rarely spent time in their well-known home. The Council waited on edge for the threats to come true.

Kristen watched a news broadcast on the wall with subtitles as most of the others watched the recruits practice drills. A line from the broadcast caught her attention.

"While military units have been in basic training for a month now, we've heard little on the war front and the progress in defeating the humans."

Kristen rolled her eyes. From the expression on the broadcaster's face, she knew his tone wouldn't be much better.

"In other news," his female partner cut across him, "protestors of the war are currently demonstrating outside the Academy building."

Curious, she reached for the controls. The increased volume caught everyone's attention.

"Thank you, Molly." The field reporter appeared on screen. "I'm here amid the elementalists protesting the war against the humans. They are currently outside the Academy building where the Council resides. I have here with me Theo Iraklidis. What are your concerns about the Council declaring war?"

"The humans are obviously disadvantaged. It'll be a massacre of human life. They can't compare to us. There's no reason to take their threats seriously," Theo said.

"Turn that o—" A low and warbly beeping cut Luana off; the emergency warning sound broadcasted through the Council system. Everyone grabbed their devices where it showed the words: S.O.S. Novo Mesto under attack. It appeared on the broadcast a moment later.

"I'm sorry, Viggo," Molly reappeared on the screen. "We interrupt this broadcast to bring you news of an attack against the Elementalist Harbor city, Novo Mesto, Slovenia. A live broadcast feed from the human armies is currently showing on television worldwide, and we are picking up coverage from their feeds which we will show now."

The camera flipped to show a helicopter style vehicle view of the entire city burnt to the ground. Smoldering remains wafted thick, black smoke across the winter sky. The snow drifted to rest among the ruins and vanished a moment later.

"It's time." Luana scowled.

CHAPTER THREE

Sunrise

Novo Mesto, City Municipality of Novo Mesto, Slovenia

Once a haven of the elementalists, Novo Mesto became the humans' first successful stand against their oppressive power. Mason Ford crouched in the middle of the road leading into the heart of the city and watched the ash and snow drift to the ground around him. The pavement was warm to his touch despite the darkening weather. He didn't want to be there, among the rubble, but he couldn't walk away—no—Tyr would notice. He kept Mason and Ryan close for reasons Mason couldn't fathom anymore. Tyr went mad for his quest—and the world followed him.

"We're to head out in the morning." Ryan Everton stepped up behind him with nary a sound, and Mason jumped.

"That's *his* orders?" Mason's stomach dropped.

"Yes."

"And our task?"

Ryan took a shaky breath of frigid air; it rattled in his chest. "Testing center."

The faces of one of the families trapped in their house as Mason lifted the flamethrower under orders flashed through his mind. They didn't look scared but sad and resigned. He would stare at those faces forever and only add more to the number while trapped at Tyr's side. "What's he doing with the testing center?"

"Countries under his banner are investing in genetic testing."

Mason bit his tongue and tasted blood.

"Some have started ghettos," Ryan continued. "Tyr is sending us to work with the top brass on the testing center."

"Away from the fighting?" Mason lifted a hand to shade his eyes from the fading light on the horizon. He could see a mass of black dots growing bigger.

"For now." Ryan spotted the same shapes. "The elementalists are arriving."

"We should go." Mason turned his back on the smoldering ruins and followed the wet pavement.

Ryan fell into step next to him. "What's your rush?"

"If Luana is in that convoy, I don't want her to know I'm mixed up in all of this."

"Do you believe the same things as Tyr?"

"I don't know anymore."

January 30, 2318

Mason packed his last bag. They would ship out in a few hours. If he wasn't on the airfield in time, he would be left behind. Tyr would castigate him further. The elementalists didn't bother to do much with their camp over the last sixteen hours; they focused on the town—or the piles of ashes. Mason and Ryan would help with the testing facility, but he also knew Tyr wouldn't keep them out of the line of fire permanently. No.

Tyr wanted them to meet their children on the field. He wanted the reality of the situation to drive a further wedge between the elementalists and the humans. Mason slung the strap of the bag over his right shoulder and stepped out of the nearly empty tent. The lower ranks would arrive later to pack away the beds and disassemble the tent.

He raised a hand to shield his vision from the bright sun overhead and saw the swarm of activity in the lower town. Green uniforms moved among the remains. Mason breathed a little easier. No orange uniforms meant Luana wasn't there. The same went for white; Ryan wouldn't have to face his son—yet.

"The Life branch." Ryan joined him with his bag over his left shoulder. "I doubt they're all life elementalists, though. That'd be a stupid strategy."

"It'd leave the element without a military presence, and the others without medical aide."

"Exactly." Ryan scratched his eyebrow. "Either way, it's a smart idea to send the Life Council member. Have you seen what he can do?"

"Not personally. You?" Mason led them through the crowds of people to the airfield a little closer to the town.

"In video—and I heard from Tyr what he saw the day they took his daughter. It's intimidating to think someone has so much power to keep people from dying. How many of our people would kill for a blessing like that?"

Mason grinned. "I suppose that's why they're here." He stopped walking and watched a unit pull people out of one of the houses from a distance. They looked alive. Mason's brow furrowed. "Do you know where Tyr is planning to attack next?"

"You mean HISS?" Ryan asked.

Mason laughed. "I'm sorry, what?" He started to cough from laughing and couldn't focus on Ryan's identical grin.

"The Human Inquisition for Systematic Suppression. It's the new name they've fashioned for the movement—Tyr is at the head, but it makes the backers feel more involved."

"And they went with HISS?" Mason rubbed his hands across his face. "I'm glad I wasn't in that meeting."

"Same here." Ryan's eyes dropped to the city again. "I heard they want to go after all the safe cities first—HISS is planning on the Philippines."

"Want to make it more difficult for HISS?"

Ryan imitated a fish for a few moments. "How?"

Mason tilted his head toward the town. "There's a whole military down there looking for information. I think we ought to have a little conversation."

January 30, 2318

Kostanjevica na Krki, Municipality of Kostanjevica na Krki, Slovenia

"Reconnaissance units stationed in Novo Mesto reported the humans have plans to launch their next attack against Quezon City in the Philippines." Salama Ahmed, the Secretary of the Army in the Fifth Region, reported. She stood with her arms clasped behind her back and spoke steadily.

"And we are certain this will be their next strategic attack?" Dwayne set his phone down on the desk in front of him. She didn't flinch under the full weight of his gaze like the Field Marshals did. She made a perfect Secretary of the Army.

"Yes, sir. It seems they plan to attack our harbor communities first—the cities which host the largest number of elementalist populations. Intel believes they are also going to attack the original nine cities."

"The ones founded by the first Council?"

"Yes, sir."

"I'd like to reinforce those cities with a military presence, provided the host country agrees. Of course, we can leave out Pompeii—I doubt they would attack an archaeological site." Dwayne laughed, and the woman nodded.

"Who should I relay your message to?" Salama didn't retrieve a writing utensil.

"Send the 873rd rank to reinforce Jerusalem, Israel. 842nd will go to Moscow—but they will operate as a retrieval team since we are at war with them. I hope Russia will not see our presence as an invasion. 787th will need to go to Ekurhuleni, South Africa. 948th will go to Venice, Italy. 774th and

924th will also be retrieval teams for those in Hong Kong, People's Republic of China and Chicago, USA, respectively. 947th will reinforce London, England while the 782nd will be over Cochabamba, Bolivia. I will confer with the Council on how we will defend the harbor communities. Tell the others to wait for further communication."

"Understood, Tautona Tebogo. We will await your call." Salama saluted before she left the room.

Dwayne pressed a button on his desk and initiated a video call with the other Council members. He moved the register pad to his desk because he preferred sitting for meetings. The black plating on the floor had an engraved image of his elemental symbol. The other eight plates were organized in a circle from his, following the traditional power structure of the elements. Anything on the projection pad would be visible to the other Council members. The others, also at their desks, appeared around the room as they joined.

"Reconnaissance in Novo Mesto turned up information on where Slattery plans to have his forces attack next—but there is a wide range of possibilities post a planned attack on Quezon City in the Philippines." He opened a projection of the world and highlighted nine areas as it rotated slowly in front of them. "They have plans to attack our harbor cities first and later, the cities founded by the first Council. I sent eight ranks to defend or rescue those cities. As for the nine harbor cities, we have a choice to make."

"Can we double up on reinforcements to the eight original cities?" Eilene jumped in first. "If it looks like we plan to occupy or fortify the cities, it may drive back the armies."

"It would be better to leave Moscow, Chicago, and Hong Kong as rescue operatives under the curtain. We aren't trying to invade those countries at this time—though I'm sure many of them will come sooner than later." Dwayne shook his head. "I would also like to keep the numbers low in London, as we don't yet know what allegiance they plan to swear. Should we need to evacuate any of these cities in an emergency, a large body would put more strain on them."

"I think we can get away with two ranks in Cochabamba, Ekurhuleni, and Venice—but Jerusalem is under too much pressure from human wars. It will put us in a bad light if we try to occupy too much," Scarlet said. "Eilene, if you want to send three ranks to those cities it will be fine for backup. Make sure your ranks know to be prepped for evacuation protocol should we make the call."

"As for the nine harbor cities, we could send one of each of us to them," Hans offered.

"Would one region be enough to defend against them?" Series worried her hair. "You saw the mess they made of Novo Mesto. Two regions responded as soon as we received word of the attack, but there was a lot we couldn't do."

"Then, we need to decide which cities we think will be the most likely for their next attack and reinforce the harbors with three regions. We'll have three cities covered and another six waiting in the wings." Ethan shifted in his seat and narrowed his eyes.

"Some of these cities are relatively close to each other." Kristen pointed to the globe. "If we assign three cities to three regions based on their distance from each other, we may be able to cover more territory. If something happens, we can respond quicker to the attack."

"We can also calculate the probability of the human army attacking a city based on the current climate in that country." Scarlet nodded along and typed into her computer. "Traditionally, humans are more likely to attack countries with a weaker economy or less people than the larger ones as it runs less risk of civilian casualties."

"Some of the cities have a lower population compared to the rest of the country as well—look at Inuvik, Canada for context," Scott said. "It's up in the colder weather and farther away from the majority of where Canadians live."

"How likely do you think it'll be for them to go up into the cold weather?" Dwayne quirked an eyebrow.

"Likely, the humans do it often. Napoleon. Hitler. Teivel. Drozdov. They tried to take on the north and met fierce winters which killed a lot of their armies." Luana set a hand on the edge of her desk and tapped a finger against the corner.

"Okay, well," Hans paused for a moment, "I'm still inclined to cut them out from our initial protection wave. If they do travel north, depending on when they do it, they could find fierce cold and incur a lot of deaths. It would put them at a disadvantage. At the very least, we could warn Inuvik to be on guard. If we give them the info ahead of time, they could prepare for whoever manages to break through the weather."

Eilene cleared her throat. "Are we assuming they will choose to attack Inuvik this winter?"

A few of the Council members shrugged.

"Alright, this is a bit far for one group, but, if need be, the other could serve as a backup." Dwayne used his pen to circle cities on the globe. "We can assign three to cover Philippines, China, and Uzbekistan. Another group will cover Togo, Georgia, and Canada—Canada being the only far reach. Meanwhile the group covering Panama, Belize, and Paraguay will serve as backup for Canada. If one of the cities in Central and South America aren't attacked, they can get to Canada the quickest, and we'll hit it hard with six regions."

"It is an awkward set-up, but I think it does give us the most coverage. If we station the three regions assigned to the southeast here," Scarlet used an X to mark Kaifeng, People's Republic of China and Quezon City, Philippines, "then they can also respond to Canada as an aid if their cities are not under attack. It may not be wholly ideal, but it's better than nothing."

"Canada should feel lucky, they're getting the attention of all nine Council members for defense," Ethan laughed.

"We still need to decide who will cover which cities." Eilene ignored him.

"While my Mandarin isn't as strong as Mulan's, I can cover the east." Dwayne offered. "Mosupologo also knows Uzbek, I think."

"I do," he agreed reluctantly.

"Take Kristen with you." Luana nodded.

"Are you sure you don't want me for South America? Paraguay and Panama are both Spanish speaking countries. The dialect would be a bit different, but it shouldn't be a problem." Kristen's lips thinned.

"That would be a good idea," Scarlet joined in. "We should be able to communicate with the people we are talking to."

"By that logic, I should send Dwayne to Africa." Luana pursed her lips.

"Woah, when did we get racist on the Council?" Dwayne sat up straighter in his chair. "Africa is not a country—nor do I speak every language in Africa even if I am from Botswana. Togo speaks French, which I do not know. Georgians speak Kartvelian, which I also do not speak. To top it off, Georgia is in the Middle East, almost European sector. If we're gonna pull the race card out, we should send you to the European cities."

"We're already aware we don't speak all sixty-five hundred languages in the world, we merely wanted to try and ease some tension in the cities we do visit if we happen to know the language," Series argued.

"I didn't mean it the way it came out." Luana frowned.

"For some reason, I don't really believe you." Dwayne stood fully from his chair. "It's not the first time you've pulled something like this. As an F.Y.I., you are the only Council member who never learned a foreign language. You are the most disadvantaged of anyone serving our country. If you want Naledi to join my group, I will gladly have her by my side, but know we all recommended her for the American sectors because she volunteered, and because she's the best bet we have at communicating effectively with them. Race aside."

"Kristen is going with you," she told him hoarsely.

"Alright." Disappointment washed over Dwayne. "Solo, where do you think we should send everyone else?"

Hans cleared his throat before speaking. "I'll take the hardest to defend sector with Luana and Ethan. We'll send Scarlet, Eilene, and Series to the Americas."

"Good, we have everywhere covered. It'll be a good idea to have the girls backing you up for Canada. I'm going to get my things together and head out. Naledi, Mosupologo, I'll see you and your regions soon. We have a war to win," Dwayne said.

"Before you go," Luana said with a small voice. "Our code breakers have been unable to crack through the code on that page you found in the book."

The book. *Elementalists Across the Ages*. The text, a lost history for Elementōrum Patriam, broke down the nine elements and saved Ethan's life. Eilene found it almost one and a half years previous in the British Library. On one of the pages, it had a drawing with four different codes imbedded into different parts of the image. Eilene and Scarlet requested a team a few weeks after finding the book. Scarlet had a niggling suspicion the coded image would reveal further information about the elementalists, and the Council.

Eilene pulled up the page on her phone. "Did you get a team of linguists or foreign language speakers together to look at the codes alongside them?"

"I got an Italian translator to work with them."

Eilene rolled her eyes. "I highly doubt every piece of the code is in Italian—that would be a poor code. Did the code breakers at least get anything back from the binary?"

"They said they ran it through every type of encoding, but they never got anything except gibberish back." Luana pulled up a document on her tablet. "These are all the results of each type of code. They made sure to record the translations."

Eilene pulled up the same document and scrolled through the list of results. About half-way down the page, she stopped. Her brows pinched together before she turned the tablet around to show everyone. "On the ASCII/UTF-8 binary code output, this is clearly a character-based language which requires translation."

Dwayne leaned closer. "I don't recognize it, but I'm sure we can find someone to translate it."

Luana turned a faint shade of pink.

"This is why we requested a translation team alongside the code breakers. How is a code breaker supposed to run an entire language they don't know through the system and expect to get a message on the other side?" Scarlet pulled at the skin under her eyes to relieve her itch and avoid her eyeliner.

"We need to get a proper team on this." Eilene examined their other futile attempts to break the codes. "Other than the translation of the Italian, all their work is worthless for us."

Series read the Italian translation aloud, "Granted to the guardians of our race, the power to raze and protect—the nine send their hoarded knowledge to establish the world order."

"What does that even mean?" Ethan turned his tablet in vain hope of the upside-down English revealing some new message. "How are the nine sending forth their knowledge? What is the world order? Who are the guardians of our race?"

Everyone shrugged.

"The other codes might give us a clue." Hans scratched the end of his nose. "I'll reach out for a team of translators to come in and start working on this right away. They'll work with the code breakers to see what they can run through. Hopefully someone will recognize the binary."

"Right, if we have nothing else to discuss—we will be leaving this time." Dwayne nodded to each Council member.

"Of course, you are dismissed," Luana said.

"See you soon." Kristen logged out of the call and vanished from her place.

Scott gave him a nod and followed suit before Dwayne also disconnected. He slumped into the chair, shaking. He never thought he would have the guts to stand up to Luana like he did. Something in him went off during the call and punched it from zero to one hundred on adrenaline. Of course, she deserved to be told everything he said, but it still felt weird going against her seniority on the Council. He took several steady breaths to try and calm the shaking of his nerves, but they didn't slow. Instead, he stood hesitantly on unstable legs and stumbled out of his office toward his temporary lodgings to collect his things. He could sleep in the transportation pod, hopefully, and be fully relaxed about the incident by the time he met up with the others.

"Prepare the remaining ranks for war," Dwayne told the first Field Marshal he saw on his way to his room. "We're going to Quezon City. We will run rescue and protection operations for the surrounding areas and fight Slattery's armies head on."

"Yes, sir." The marshal saluted and rushed off toward the barracks.

Dwayne took a deep breath and prayed to anyone who would listen that he would make the right decisions as they landed and went to war.

February 7, 2318

Quezon City, Metro Manila, Philippines

Dwayne supervised the men as they erected tents matching the green color of their uniforms. In the distance, he saw the white and purple of Scott and Kristen's tents. He made sure everyone pulled their own weight and helped organize supplies equally throughout the encampment. The tent nearest his own hosted the weapons. The Field Marshals distributed them according to rank, position in the military, and fighting style. Each group called in smaller numbers to decrease the flow of people congregated in one area. Dwayne already had his preferred weapons waiting at his side. Like most of the other Council members, he preferred close-range fighting which meant they equipped themselves with Lūcis Armōrum. Every Council member opted to carry one type of Lūminis Tēlōrum with them in case of a long-range fight. They needed to be versatile on the battlefield.

"Tautona Tebogo, it appears we are short on ranged weapons." One of the messengers approached him with hands clasped.

"Did you already check with the other distribution units?"

"Yes, sir. We do not have enough for each person." He bounced from foot to foot as if itching to run away.

"Tell the men to hold out for a couple hours—I will check with the other regions and see if our supplies mixed with theirs."

"Understood, sir." He saluted and ran back to the Field Marshal.

Dwayne headed over to the canteen to check on their dinner's progress. They would need a hearty meal before bed. They didn't know when the fighting would start, but they could see the rise of military tents on the horizon. The enemy waited.

"Do you have enough supplies to cover dinner for everyone?" he asked the head chef.

"Yes, sir, but I'm worried about breakfast in the morning." The chef frowned and recounted something before making a mark on their clipboard.

"And why is that?" Dwayne pulled out his phone to make a note.

"It seems several crates of eggs and other ingredients went missing during setup. I am personally recounting and relocating all our stock to make sure it isn't an oversight."

"Keep me updated."

"Of course."

Dwayne progressed through the camp and kept stock of more and more items which went missing. His frown deepened. The strain on his muscles made his jaw ache. They had a problem—most likely a mole in their camp feeding the enemy lines with their supplies. Only a slim chance they didn't ship the right number of supplies. He would need to check with the others and Luana.

"Dwayne!" Kristen called above the crowd as he discussed lacking medical supplies with one of the fellow Life elementalists assigned to his region. He turned and saw her and Scott pushing their way through the swell, dressed in their civvies.

"If you'll excuse me." Dwayne nodded to the elementalist. "Compile a list of what we're missing and send it to me. I'll get it corrected personally."

"Of course, Tautona Tebogo."

"You must've found something concerning?" Dwayne approached the other Council members.

"Missing supplies," Kristen said.

"You both as well?" Dwayne narrowed his eyes and gestured for them to walk in the direction of his residence.

"Do you have an idea of what's causing it?" Scott adjusted his black leather jacket across his shoulders.

Two sentries stood at the entrance to Dwayne's tent.

"I'm ruling it as a mole currently—I think it may be best to reach out to Luana and the other Council members. If it's only something on our end, it means a human blended in with our people, and I have to wonder how." Dwayne pushed the tent flap aside and held it up for the other two to enter.

As the leaders of the country, they had the most technology in their tents for communication and battle plans. They had the ability to create maps on a large table in the middle and send them immediately to the Field Marshals for distribution.

Kristen and Scott stood in their respective spots for a Council meeting. Their forms would be projected to the others if they deigned to join. Dwayne took the helm of the tech, already set in his spot, and triggered the call. Luana joined shortly after along with Hans. Ethan and Series joined them as well. Dwayne wondered if they planned to be there as mediators in case something turned sour in their meeting like the last one.

"Are you missing any supplies in your regions?" he asked immediately; looks of surprise crossed their faces.

"Did the shipment not go out?" Luana shuffled through documents of their orders and stock.

"Either that or there is a mole running around our camp pretending to be one of us." Kristen shifted her weight to her other foot.

"It's near impossible to tell the difference between ourselves and the enemy." Ethan folded his arms.

"Especially if they've got ahold of one of our uniforms." Dwayne glanced at Scott. "Should we have the ranks check for the impostor among us? I'm not sure they would've stuck around."

"If they did, we could figure out what they did with the supplies," Hans offered. "There's only a couple of ways to assess it. Elemental control strength and temperature."

"We'll test their abilities. I have a feeling the temperature check would be more obvious. We can play off the power check." Dwayne reached for his tablet to make a note. "What if we aren't able to recover the lost supplies?"

"I had an idea as a resolution," Scott spoke up. "As we are already checking strength of elementalist ability, it would be a good idea to have them send their strongest elementalists to us. If we take the ones with the most power, we can give their weapons to other fighters. We'll swing out at the humans full force with our abilities. It might scare a few of them off if they realize we're serious about not playing on an even battlefield."

"Eilene said that could also backfire and make them hate us even more—since we aren't playing fair," Series said.

Scott turned a faint pink, chastised.

"Is she not joining the meeting?" Luana looked up.

"Scarlet and Eilene are both here with me. They're working on some projects and didn't want to step into the projection. They are listening and participating," Series defended them quickly. "We are drafting emergency evacuation plans. It may be best to get the people out of these cities should it come to war. Eilene recommends it for Quezon City. We don't want bystanders to sustain injuries or die."

"And where are we to house them, exactly?" Luana leveled Series with the glare she typically reserved for Eilene since she stood as proxy.

"The Academy has more rooms than we can fill with students. I'm sure they'd appreciate a place to stay and not worry about food for a while." Dwayne cut in. "I'll talk with Mosupologo and Naledi on this end and negotiate with the people of Quezon City to see what they would like to do. I'd hate to force them out of their homes if they'd rather stay."

"That is a great solution." Hans nodded as well.

"Naledi, will you go tell the sentry outside to have all three regions host a performance check on all persons?" Dwayne asked. "Anyone who is unable to use their element in good capacity is to see the doctors in the medical tent. The strongest of each element will need to come see us three personally to receive a briefing on fighting without weapons."

"Of course." Kristen stepped away from the projection.

Dwayne scratched his nose. "We'll get everything running on our side. I've heard Dickens' concerns, but I think Mosupologo's plan may be the way to go. The army didn't face any true elementalist power in Novo Mesto. I think it's time they had a taste of what we can do. If they did take our supplies, it's only fair we hit them back a little harder."

"Let us know what you find out about the supplies," Hans said before stepping away from the projection.

"We'll keep you updated on war efforts." Dwayne ended the session.

Scott sat down in one of the lounging chairs and looked through files on his tablet. Kristen joined him as she returned from talking to the sentry.

"They'll have the strongest rounded up within the hour to speak with us."

"Good. Shall we look at formations?"

February 10, 2318

Dwayne honestly couldn't remember most of their first battle against the humans. Everything around him passed in a blur. He remembered swinging his Lūcis Bipenne, a type of double-edged axe with a two-handed grip, and he could still feel the reverb from the impacts against other bodies, but he had no recollection of their faces. He didn't know who he killed—much less if he killed them in the first place. He remembered seeing his own people with grievous injuries. He recalled the blood and how he touched them and watched as they healed on the battlefield right in front of the enemy.

It took two hours for both sides to call a ceasefire. The wounded evacuated first for the medical tents while those still intact, despite their exhaustion, searched the bodies on the field for the living among their ranks. Dwayne walked past one of the members of the human recovery team and kneeled to check the pulse of an elementalist wearing Scott's region colors.

"What do you hope to gain from fighting this war?" the human asked with dropped shoulders.

"I can ask you the same thing." Dwayne stood after finding no pulse. "My people are threatened with genocide. Are you merely fighting because you serve your country as I do mine?"

"As you said, I serve my country."

"I suppose, in the end, we are all the same." Dwayne walked away to the next body. When he found a pulse, he looked for their cause of injury before healing them to a stable condition.

"I think we are different after all," the human said as he passed with an unconscious body draped across his back.

"Oh?"

"You can help your people immediately, while I have to wait until the fighting stops. I saw the arm you reattached through touch earlier."

"I am the most powerful healer in my country. I'm the only one who could help my people in that way. I don't think it's any less noble than waiting until the dead are catalogued. After all, you put in more effort to carry them home." Dwayne gave him a warm smile. The blood dried on his cheek cracked and itched.

"You are an incredibly optimistic person."

"I'm told that often." Dwayne hoisted his own companion into the air and waved for Scott to carry the body to the transport vehicle with a stretch of wind. "I hope you can reunite with your friends."

"The same to you."

Dwayne found the next body all the while listening to the labored breathing of the human moving their way across the rough ground. Maybe when the war ended, they could meet again—they could discuss how it felt to fight in a war perpetuating genocide and if they regret their involvement. Perhaps Dwayne would even come to regret the war protecting his own people. They could suffer innumerable losses which would affect the Council as much as the rest of their society. In a two-hour span, they lost many great elementalists.

"How many more do you think are alive?" Scott appeared at his shoulder.

They watched other elementalists lift dead bodies into a transport vehicle. They would be prepared for burial in the morgue before returning home in a funeral procession.

"Of us as a total or of the bodies still around here?" Dwayne bent and pressed a hand against the pulse point in another person's neck—one in his own region.

"Out here on the field."

"I think the majority is dead bodies." He flagged down one of the elementalists to come join him. "They just need medical treatment, they're alive but stabilized already. My guess would be a blow to the head and knocked unconscious."

"Yes, sir. I'll get them there right away."

"Have you seen Naledi?" Dwayne walked to the next body.

Scott shook his head.

"Worrisome." He pushed himself up from a dead body and signaled for the corpse collectors. When he took another step forward his legs gave out, and he collapsed.

CHAPTER FOUR

Order

"Dwayne?" Scott rushed to his side.

"I think the adrenaline wore off," he choked out.

"I'll get you to the medical tent." Scott lifted them both into the air on a current.

"Don't. I can self-diagnose in my tent. I'll be fine."

"Not allowed. Eilene would kill me if I didn't have someone take proper care of you," Scott said sharply.

"At the very least, put me at the end of the line. I don't want to cut ahead when I know my treatment won't be as grievous as some of the others who fought today."

"Alright, fine."

Scott brought them down at the end of the line. Startled whispers moved away, a poor game of telephone that they knew would give Dwayne a more grievous injury with each iteration. He'd be half dead by the time he saw another Life elementalist. Scott supported Dwayne over his shoulder until they reached the edge of the medical tents where crates were set-up as temporary seating.

Kristen blew past them in a blur carrying her own rescue to the emergency medical bays. She stopped on her way back to the field. "You okay?"

"I'm pretty sure it's just an adrenaline crash, but I'm not allowed to self-diagnose." Dwayne glared at Scott.

"You can do that as a Life element?" Kristen clasped her hands behind her back and looked at the long line to the medical tent.

"Yes, it's as simple as doing this." Dwayne placed his free left hand over his heart. He frowned a moment later.

"Something wrong?" she prompted.

"I can't use my element."

"What?" Scott's voice broke on the vowel.

"I can't currently access my ability. I wouldn't be able to heal anyone if I tried."

"Is that kind of thing serious?" Kristen examined the line again and debated moving them forward.

"It's usually caused by extreme exhaustion or stress. When I talk with one of the healers, I'm sure they'll tell me I need rest."

"It's better to be safe than sorry," Scott said. "Not being able to use your element is serious as a Council member. We're stronger than the average elementalist—stronger than the strongest elementalist. If our power fails, it's only a matter of time before theirs fail too."

"I'm sure it's caused by overwork. I did a lot of healing between fighting out there." He grinned. "I picked up a person's arm and reattached it while fighting off two other attackers. I bet my body is tired and needs sustenance to recover."

"I'll grab you a banana while we wait." Kristen headed toward the kitchen.

"Tautona Tebogo, are you sure you don't want to cut ahead?" The person in front of them looked uncertainly back. She had a large gash across her arm, but the blood caked over and looked easily curable.

"I'm quite sure. I know how to read health well. If I could help you right now, I would." Dwayne flashed her his near permanent smile. "Just because we're Council members doesn't mean we should put our safety or health above yours. You are our people, and you deserve the same care we do."

"I really don't mind waiting, sir." She tried again.

"You might not, but I do. You should be cared for first. You've lost blood. I have no such wounds, no matter how stained my clothes are. Most of this is blood of the enemy." He gestured to the browning splotches on the green fatigues. "I'm more concerned about you getting your gash repaired."

"Thank you for your kindness, Tautona."

"Here." Kristen handed him the banana as she arrived back at their side.

"Thank you." He quickly broke it open and ate the inside. "If this recovers enough of my strength, I can get out of the way for the rest of these injured people."

"Your metabolism isn't that fast." Scott rolled his eyes.

"Don't doubt my awe-inspiring powers, Mosupologo." Dwayne laughed long and hard. It infected those nearby into their own peals of laughter.

The line shuffled forward several feet.

"We should probably send someone to check on the collections and lookout. We need to keep an eye on what the humans are doing." Dwayne folded the banana peel, held it in his hand, and turned it into manure; he sprinkled it on the ground. "See, my powers are back, too."

"Alright you freak, do your job then." Kristen pointed to the other people in line.

"And you two, go do your job." He bit back with a laugh. He reached out to the woman in front of them. "May I?"

"Only if you are able, sir."

He touched her arm gently over the wound. In his mind's eye, he could see the severed nerves, veins, and skin. He had to line each up carefully with their original placement. It took longer than what he normally needed, like when he was first at the Academy studying the element, but he managed to heal the deep cut. "You'll still want to check in with them on blood in case you lost too much. At least now it can be washed off. I'm going to grab some food and head back to help more people. You have a good day."

"Thank you, Tautona Tebogo."

February 11, 2318

The second battle lasted an hour longer. Dwayne ate a larger breakfast in preparation for the battle when he heard the human army approach. He didn't want the same thing to happen as the day previous. He faced the next person in his way and swung his Lūcis Bipenne down in front of him. The blade caught the human across the chest. The human dropped his weapon and stumbled back till he fell to the ground. His body convulsed as he bled out. He coughed as Dwayne passed him by and spit blood over Dwayne's shoes.

Dwayne moved forward with the weapon ready. Across the field, some fifty feet, he saw Scott raise himself into the air with his Lūminis Sclopētum ready. He tore his eyes away from the sight when he felt a tug at his shoulder from the bullet of a close-range weapon. He turned to the aggressor and saw the man from the day previous. Dwayne lifted the Bipenne, the edges of the axe arced with green light, and the man dropped his gun.

"I'm sorry—I'm sorry," he stammered and ran in the opposite direction.

Dwayne put a hand to his shoulder and tried to find the bullet as he avoided hits from other humans. It rested in his muscle tissue, close to the bone. He wouldn't feel any major impact on his overall health if he treated it right away, but the bullet would not be easy to retrieve. If he planned to use his arm in battle, he needed to address the wound as soon as possible. From the corner of his eye, he saw a sword descending on his arm. He slapped the bracelet around his left wrist and the Lūcis Scūta expanded to protect him from the impact.

Pain surged through his shoulder, and he cried out. Someone from above him hit the attacker hard, and they fell. Dwayne used the Scūta to push himself off the ground and watched the human's sudden retreat. He turned to thank the person and saw the woman from the day previous.

"Merely returning the favor." She smiled before parting to join her region.

Scott lowered himself from the sky, along with several other Air and Earth elementalists. He landed at Dwayne's side.

"You, okay?"

"Think you can dig a bullet out of my shoulder?" He pointed to the wound and deactivated his shield.

Scott took a closer look at the wound before he nodded. He used wind to create a pair of tweezers. Dwayne hissed as Scott dug around for the bullet, but it took only a moment before he pulled it free. Dwayne held his hand to the wound and healed the torn muscle and skin.

"Thanks." He patted Scott on the shoulder and moved to the bodies to repeat the same process as the day before.

Three hours they spent in battle. Three hours and more losses to their army. He guessed their fighting would end only when one side had no one left to fight for it.

"The humans made a signal they plan to retreat." Scott pushed open the flap to Dwayne's tent.

Dwayne had his shirt off as he inspected the scar left behind by the bullet. "Do we think they are backing off Quezon City?"

"Lookout says they took down half their tents and started packing supplies."

"I suppose that is a good sign." Dwayne pulled his shirt over his head. A message notification pinged on his phone, and his face followed the known crinkle patterns of a smile when he saw the message. He typed a quick reply before tossing the phone back to his bed.

Scott didn't say anything, but he also didn't leave. Dwayne watched him ball his fists several times over; Dwayne knew it was a tic of Scott's when he tried to calm himself down.

"Is there something else you wanted me to know about, or am I supposed to find out on my own?"

"Is that Eilene?" He gestured to the phone.

"Yeah."

"Are you both okay—after—everything?" Scott fixed his gaze on the ground and moved his hands jerkily around an invisible topic.

"I came out as asexual ages ago, and you're concerned now?"

Scott didn't respond. Dwayne leaned back on his hands and watched the other for a long while before he sighed.

"Dickens and I are not romantically involved. We never were. I know she had feelings for me at one point, but those are long resolved." Dwayne swung one of his hands to his phone and unlocked it. He opened it to the messages. "Dickens and I are close friends, like siblings, I would say. She's definitely closer to me than my real sister."

"You have a sister?" Scott looked up in surprise.

"An older one. It's been many years since I last saw her—the year I was identified as an elementalist." Dwayne held out his phone. "I can tell you're in love with her. She deserves someone like you, provided you don't hurt her."

Scott stared at him with round eyes and parted lips.

"Go on, take it. You can see our messages for yourself. They're innocent bickering." He waved the phone in the air until Scott approached and took it from him.

The image in the message included a picture of someone standing in front of a map of papers and red lines trying to find a mysterious person. The caption above the image read:

> ***Me waiting for the fighting to start.***
>
> > **We're at two battles and counting. What do you think of my battle scar?**

Dwayne included a picture of the miniscule leftover scab from the bullet wound.

> **Are you okay? Is everyone okay?**
>
> > **Don't worry. I'm the only one injured. Everyone else got off Scott free.**

Hardee-har-har.

**Also, your meme template is
really old.**

**Certain things never go out of
style.**

As Scott held the phone, another text came in.

**I'm glad everyone is okay. Scott
wouldn't tell me himself, and I
don't know Kristen well.**

He held the phone out to Dwayne who took it.

"Mosupologo, you mean well. You really like her, and she needs to know about it. Confronting me on my end isn't going to change anything from her side. You're going after a threat you've perceived, but it doesn't exist. The only thing I want is for my sister to be happy—to be loved. After all she went through, she deserves it."

Scott swallowed but didn't reply.

Dwayne stood and placed a hand on Scott's shoulder. "If I expect you to take care of her, then I also expect you to not pick fights with her family."

"I understand." Scott nodded. He *knew*, but that part of him that wanted to see Eilene happy above everything else reared its head and always placed Dwayne before him. Dwayne was always first, and Scott second—but Eilene had been concerned for him. A small spark of hope flickered under the pressure to give in and hide away. It was just enough to send something warm and new sparking across his nerves until he could hardly stand the feeling. He almost missed what Dwayne said following his warning.

"Unless it's her birth parents. You can pick a fight with them. I'd participate myself." Dwayne's well-worn grin appeared on his face again. "Try talking to her."

"Okay."

"Now, I don't want to see you back in here unless the humans changed their mind about leaving. Or if someone needs desperate medical attention."

April 5, 2318

Kolkheti National Park, Guria, Georgia

"Don't follow blindly."

Hans' eyes flew open to the sound of an explosion from a nearby tent. Several shouts and a cry of pain followed the sound. He jumped out of bed, in only a pair of sleeping shorts, and pushed open the door of his tent.

"Someone set off an explosive on themselves while moving equipment," one of the Field Marshal's informed him. "They'll be fine. It was an unfortunate accident, not an attack. Nothing else went off."

"Good." He dropped his posture. "Keep me updated if it does turn into something else."

"We will."

Hans returned to his makeshift bed and decided it would be the perfect opportunity to dress for the day. He donned his red camouflage fatigues and adjusted the cap to fit over the height of his pompadour without letting the strands escape. He stepped into the field and wandered through the camp until he reached the sea of orange where Luana had her group set up. As if knowing he would come to her, she stood waiting on the edge of their groups.

He raised an eyebrow upon his approach. "You are allowed to come over to my tent, too."

She didn't smile. Instead, she turned on her heel and led him through the maze of tents to her own. He followed obediently and saw Ethan standing outside the tent waiting for them.

"What happened this morning with the explosion?" she asked as they stepped inside.

"Accident during moving. Taken care of."

Luana nodded.

"Dwayne sent the reports this morning of deaths and injuries in their first couple battles." Ethan held his tablet a little higher. "I think it would be good to review the numbers and statistics to see if we can avoid similar results in the future."

"I agree, this would be a productive part of our day," Hans paused before hesitantly broaching a contentious side project, "Lu, have you heard an update on how the new weapons are progressing? If the results of the war are bad, we will need them sooner than later."

"We can't unleash the full brunt of our power against the humans." Luana frowned sharply with a small and pointed glare.

"Dwayne's unit already did, and it didn't deter them."

"He released only a few elementalists because weapons crates went missing. He did not order the full army to attack with their powers. Those few should be enough. He chose the strongest. Not to mention we are fighting on the front lines among them with our own abilities." Luana pushed her tongue into her cheek.

Hans bit his own to keep from replying with something snarky. If the humans declared war against them, he knew their abilities wouldn't be enough to deter them from further battles. They felt confident in the weapon Tyr boasted. They thought they could successfully destroy the elementalist people.

"They weren't enough, though. Are you not hearing what we're saying?" Ethan narrowed his eyes.

Hans' head snapped around to look at Ethan. Still new, he was a braver man than all of them to challenge Luana and her thought process. Hans knew her so well he could feel her eyes narrowing and her tongue sharpening.

"What did you say?"

Ethan didn't back down. "Ah, so you are experiencing trouble hearing. The humans aren't afraid of our powers. They aren't backing down. Those 'few' you claim to be working is not. The strategy needs to be revised."

"Do you know who you're talking to?"

"I thought I was speaking to Luana Ford, am I not?"

"You are speaking to the leader of the Council."

"In what capacity? The government of the elementalists is ruled by nine people, not one. You may have seniority for serving our country the longest, but you are not some all-powerful leader. There are nine of us to decide. Currently in this room, you are outnumbered."

"Outnumbered?" she hissed.

"Two to one."

"Hans?" Luana glared fiercely at her usually most loyal companion.

Hans shifted uncomfortably between his feet and swallowed. He turned his attention to her and tried to possess the bravery he never had around her before. *Let Vasha give me strength*, he thought then said, "You heard my reservations at the beginning of this discussion and waved them off. I think you can add one plus one."

She looked as if he slapped her. Hans felt no remorse—instead, it felt good. He felt like he had a voice. For the first time, he felt like Earth truly had the upper hand against Fire.

"I think," Luana started, clearly rattled, "we should continue this meeting later today."

Her hands shook, and Hans fought back the urge to reach out and calm her down. He said, "That would be for the best—with the nine if possible. I will contact them with optional meeting times and get back to you."

"Thank you, Hans." Ethan gave him an appreciative nod.

They both walked out of the tent to leave Luana to her thoughts. Once outside, some of the adrenaline left Hans' body, and he stumbled. Ethan caught him deftly as if he expected it.

"Thank you."

"No problem, I was honestly surprised you backed me up." He grinned and tossed his head back to get rid of the strands dangling in his eyes. He didn't have it pulled into the half-pony like normal.

"I need to start standing up to her more. We all do. Your courage is going to give us all strength."

"Just as Dwayne's did almost a month ago." Ethan clapped him on the shoulder. "Anything you want me to prepare for the meeting this afternoon?"

"Bring some ideas of new strategies. Talk with those under you, they'll have good ideas as well." Hans pulled the tablet from his cargo pants pocket. "I'll look at what time will be best for a meeting then do the same."

"Sounds good." Ethan walked through the orange tents to the black.

Back in his own tent, Hans sat at the computer space. He spent several minutes figuring out how to calculate the difference in time zones to find an optimal meeting time. Something not too early for those in the earlier zones, and something not too late for the later. Strategically, Eilene's team decided to set-up in Panama since it put them closer to Inuvik. Meanwhile, Dwayne's team was still fighting rigorously in the Philippines. They originally thought the humans planned to retreat, but they quickly traded out the troops with new and refreshed fighters. Almost a month later, the battle for control of the harbor city raged on just as viciously. The best time would be four in the afternoon for Hans' zone in Georgia. It would still be only seven in the morning for Eilene, but eight in the evening for Dwayne. He had to hope the humans wouldn't attack at nightfall.

He sent the official message through the correct channels to every person and gave instructions to come up with strategic solutions to gaining the upper hand. They needed something more immediate than the hope of their own new weapons. Hans would suggest the unleashing of the elementalists at full power against the humans, no more weapons. Tear up the entire field. *They had to prove themselves as the superior race*—Hans' thoughts halted abruptly. *What would that say about us? Is the whole war being fought on supremacy ideals?*

He pushed back from his desk. Hans folded his hands and leaned forward where his elbows rested on his knees and his head bowed. *Had anyone from either side paused to look at what the outcome of the war would be, no matter which side won?* He understood Tyr Slattery wanted to wipe their race off the Earth, a genocide, *but what would become of his daughter? Would he be so hardened to kill her as well? What about all the carriers of the genetic mutation?* He highly doubted if any human would be entirely free of the possibility of passing on the elementalist gene coding. *What would happen to the next generation? Would they be prenatally tested? How did Slattery plan to ensure a population without genetic defects? Did Slattery take any of these questions into consideration during his cry for war?*

Hans spiraled around the thought process, but he couldn't come to any conclusions. He had no idea how the enemy would act at the end—*but how would we act? If the elementalists win, how will I respond? What will it mean for the fate of the world? Will we be taking over the rest of the world? Will they fear us? Are we seeking to be feared, or are we seeking equality with the humans? Survival and preservation of our genetic code is only one goal—one which is complicated and tied to many other complex ideas.*

Hans leaned back in the chair and spun in slow circles. Providing a solution would be much more convoluted than he originally thought. *Did Luana consider these same ideas when forming her speeches and plans? Does she know more than me?* Grabbing the tablet and attached pen, he scribbled down the thoughts and questions affecting their decision on what to do moving forward. It wasn't up to just one of them to give an answer, it would be a group decision.

Just as every previous decision should've been. Hans bowed his head a second time. They certainly had a lot of room for improvement on the Council, especially to better help their people. He needed to decide what would help the most—but it wouldn't be based on his own opinions. Determined, Hans stood and walked to the tent entrance. Two people stood guard just outside, and he sent one of them to get the Secretary of the Army, Mateo Paewai, who served as his right hand. Each of the Council members had a secretary to rely on.

In the time waiting, Hans wrote out a list of questions he wanted answers to. It took several minutes before Mateo entered his tent. He stood at attention with his hands behind his back.

"You wanted to see me, sir?"

"Yes, I have an important task for you that must be fulfilled as quickly as possible." Hans held out the sheet of paper. "We're going to be making some changes, potentially, and I would like answers from as many of our soldiers as possible before twelve hundred hours today. If you have time, delegate someone to send a survey to Elementōrum Patriam and randomly select citizens to ask. Those answers can be back to me at fourteen hundred hours."

Mateo looked over the sheet of questions and nodded. "I will have the responses to you by twelve hundred hours."

"Thank you." Hans watched him leave with a bit of contentment settling in his chest. If he wanted to help his people, he needed to know what they thought would help them the most. He wanted to know what they thought of the outcome of the war.

Hans jumped when his phone rang a few minutes later. Surprised, he saw Scarlet's name on the caller ID.

"It's late there. Isn't it?" he asked immediately upon answering.

"Not too late—not recently, anyway. We are getting less and less sleep by the day here. There are so many things to prepare and many people to take care of. I'll be up for a while longer." Scarlet sounded half-asleep already.

"Do you need me to push the meeting back later than planned?"

"No, no, that's not why I called. Besides, nine in the evening is already pushing it for Dwayne's group. I can take a nap tomorrow if I really need it. I think Series is taking the brunt of the work—the entire camp is currently enchanted with luck. It may be staving off attack a while longer. We have yet to see the enemy armies, however."

"Is she getting enough sleep?" Hans leaned back, and the chair creaked under him.

"Less than myself and Eilene. She's adamant she is fine, but we are both worried. We refuse to give her any more tasks to do. I told her to relax while I look at the message you sent us. She's confident Eilene and I will have appropriate answers."

"Then the reason for your call?" he prompted.

Scarlet sighed on the other end of the line. "We wondered what influenced this kind of a discussion to occur. What is out-of-bounds to suggest?"

"Nothing, at this point. Luana will be reluctant to change anything. It'll go to majority vote."

"How in Elementōrum did you get her to agree to those odds?"

"We forced her to agree."

She made a puzzled noise.

"Ethan and I—not long ago. I'm sure she's refusing to talk to either one of us now. I've never seen her so quiet."

"You actually stood up to her?" Scarlet shifted in her chair, Hans assumed, as the sound of crinkling leather infiltrated his ear.

"With some help." He laughed lowly. "I am not yet brave enough to speak up on my own. Ethan started it and gave me the strength to agree."

"So, we have our newest member to thank." She returned the laugh. "It seems finding the eighth and ninth for our number were to our benefit."

"As I'm sure the original Council would know."

"They would," she agreed softly. "How did Ethan bring about this change?"

"I pointed out the obvious. Luana's reluctance to consider other options and recognize what we are doing as a Council. It's clear she didn't process what I said, and Ethan pointed it out. He told her we rule as an office of nine and not one. She took offense, and I backed him," Hans said.

"I think Luana's world is crashing down around her in tandem with the war."

"It started before the war," Hans countered. "The moment Eilene found Ethan's abilities. It should've broken years ago. She grew up with the Council and expected to be seen as important. It messes with your head being considered the most powerful from a young age."

"What answers are you hoping we bring to this meeting?" Scarlet asked.

"Something I was deeply considering myself." Hans pushed himself out of the chair and paced. "I talked a big game with Luana and Ethan, but I realized how complex our answers are going to be. There is no simple solution to the problem proposed. There is no strategy I can think of where we do not become the villain."

"So, our answer may come down to whether or not we want to be the villain."

"The question I can come to is how many human lives are we willing to sacrifice to preserve our own survival? Does that make us any better than the other side?" Hans sat on the bed.

"You've been spiraling," Scarlet said.

"That's one way to put it." He clutched the phone a little tighter. "I sent out a survey to those under my command to know their thoughts. I think we can only govern our people if we know their thoughts and feelings on the matter."

"It's a brilliant idea. If it wasn't late at night, I would do the same." Her smile bled into her voice. "I would send a message to the others, maybe not Luana since she won't do it, but it's a good idea. Although, Dwayne, Ethan, and Kristen will be fighting, I'm sure of it."

"They would. I'm already adding much to their plate by asking them to propose strategies to move forward. They'll be exhausted during our meeting."

"Then this is something we should handle and propose to them. We'll move forward, assuming Luana will veto anything we put forward," Scarlet said.

"So, whatever solution we provide, we are aiming for the will of only eight," Hans said.

"Exactly. I would say we all know each other a fair more than we know Luana with how often she shut us down and out. You'd be the only one who has a hope of convincing her of anything, Hans."

"You keep saying that, but I've never seen it."

"Because you are blind to your own influence."

"I have no influence, Zhū Hóng." Hans listened to her laugh as if using her given name would change her mind. He knew it wouldn't, but it did show their understanding of each other. "If I had influence, things would be very different from the world we currently live in."

"Oh? You would change that much about our society?"

"It wouldn't be a lot of little changes, it would all come back to one big change."

"You can color me intrigued," Scarlet said.

"It's something I've dreamed about since being offered the Council position."

"I think your dream has gone on long enough. You should manifest it as reality." The *pop* of Scarlet's chair almost startled him as she stood in her corner of the world.

"I don't think it would help us in the war, otherwise I might listen to your sage advice," Hans said.

Scarlet yawned. "Well, now I know your intent for our early morning meeting, it's best if I let Eilene know and also start on my own solutions."

"Make sure you both get plenty of rest as well. I think Series can rest for the night."

"I agree." Scarlet shuffled to the door of the tent. "Thank you for the enlightening conversation."

"Good night," Hans said.

"And good morning to you."

The call ended, and Hans put the phone on the bed next to him. He wouldn't use the word *'enlightening'* from his perspective, but the conversation certainly helped calm his mind. He had a good idea. He had a starting point. He just needed to wait for more information before he could make a more informed decision.

Hans gratefully took the survey answers shortly before noon from Mateo. Just before two, Mateo surprised Hans by entering his tent with responses from the civilians in Elementōrum. Hans would have to see if their budget would provide a bonus for Mateo. He certainly did his job well. During the unoccupied hours, Hans compounded all the questions without clear answer—questions he felt the Council would need to address as one. Hans didn't see or speak with the other members during the empty period until their meeting. He had no idea what they would bring, let alone how Luana felt in her isolated camp.

His plan gave him hope. He didn't think it would be the best plan, but he built it based around the people. His own desires had to come last.

Five minutes before the start of the meeting, Hans wheeled his desk chair over to the register pad. Anything in the vicinity of the circle would broadcast with him, and he certainly would like a place to sit if the meeting ran long (as he assumed it would). He organized his piles of paper notes onto a table in front of him, just out of view of the pad. Around the same time, Ethan joined from his tent and Eilene from hers.

"We can see who the early planners are." Ethan grinned widely, and Eilene laughed.

"I simply want to be prepared." Her hair looked more haggard than usual. Hans guessed she hadn't brushed through it properly after waking up.

A moment later, the projection blurred from a long-distance signal before connecting Scott to their group. He sat in a chair with his eyes closed; he breathed unevenly, and a pained moan slipped past his lips.

"Scott?" Eilene put out a hand; she knew she couldn't touch him.

"I'm fine." His blue eyes peered up at her through a slit. "Battle worn."

She shook her head. "This is more than battle worn."

"I didn't realize you were the Council appointed physician." Scott closed his eyes again and took a rattling breath.

"I've learned enough from Dwayne that I can give a basic diagnosis," Eilene snapped.

He didn't provide a response.

"How did the battle go?" Hans asked.

"We won, in a sense. At a heavy cost, however. They don't plan to retreat."

"How many of them do you think you'll have to kill?" Ethan dug at some dirt under one of his nails.

"No one in our group would have an exact number. I don't think even you could find one." Scott shifted in the chair, and a short *wheeze* issued from his chest.

"If I'm being harsh, all of them." Ethan folded his hands and pressed them to his lips as he leaned forward, clearly on an unseen desk. "Then the worry of retreat would not exist."

"Don't tell me you're going to suggest our new plan becomes killing all our enemies?" Hans laughed.

Ethan grinned. "No, that would be stupid."

"At least you still have reasoning." Eilene shook her head with her own smile taunting her lips.

"Very little of it," Ethan said.

Dwayne's line blipped, and he appeared in his own chair, head lolling off to the side of the backrest. His characteristic smile in place as he looked around the group. "Are we placing bets on who will be the last to join, or who will be late?"

"We started neither, but a wonderful suggestion." Eilene gave a nod toward Scott, and Dwayne's eyes obediently followed the motion.

"Mosupologo?" Dwayne said.

"What?" There was a sharp rattle in Scott's speech.

"So, you did lie to me about your injury." The smile vanished.

"I'm perfectly fine," Scott said.

Dwayne scowled. "You are using your own ability to keep your lung from collapsing. I can hear it in your breathing."

Hans sat up a little straighter and saw the other two stiffen from his peripheral vision.

"I'm alive," Scott murmured.

"Not for much longer if I don't fix your damn lung." Dwayne stood. He used air quotes as he spoke again. "If I'm 'late', it's because I'm tending to this idiot in his tent."

The feed disconnected just as Scarlet and Series joined.

"Who left?" Scarlet asked. They generally directed their questions and comments to the senior Council member present. Without Luana there, Hans filled the *leader* role.

"Dwayne has to go heal Scott—collapsed lung," Hans said.

"How did you sustain that injury?" Eilene only had eyes for Scott.

"I got shot. I removed the bullet. It's fine."

"Scott!" she admonished.

"I'm sorry. Am I expected to not get hurt during this war? I don't remember covering that rule." His face settled into a sharp glare.

"It's strange hearing him talk this much." Series lowered herself to the floor to sit. "He's opening up more to us."

Scarlet hummed; her eyes fixed on the exchange.

Kristen sank into her chair a moment later with her arm in a sling and her hand bandaged as one lump. She noticed their concerned looks immediately. "I'm on the mend. I've already seen the healing tents. There were more severe things they needed to treat immediately. I'll be fine by morning."

"Today was rougher than expected?" Hans asked.

"Yes. Dwayne certainly has an advantage to getting out unscathed." She looked around. "I'm sorry for being late, but is Dwayne not here either?"

"Actually, we're waiting on Luana." Hans looked at the empty space. "Dwayne will be with Scott shortly."

"I'm here." He stepped onto Scott's register pad. They weren't built to support the projection of more than one Council member, so he spoke quickly to step away again. "This idiot will be back to normal in no time."

Hans looked to the empty spot again before turning his gaze to Ethan, who nodded. Hans stood from his chair and cleared his throat. "Something has held up the Fire elementalist representative, but we can go ahead and continue with the majority—a Council of eight."

Everyone stilled, a little surprised by the boldness of excluding Luana from their discussion.

"I called this meeting because it's clear our on-the-field strategies are not working. I think our strategy to spread out and cover as much ground as possible since we have little reconnaissance is still a good idea, but those in the Philippines are faltering. We are taking heavy losses by the day and the humans are not deterred. We need to think of ideas we and, most importantly, they can use as soon as tomorrow. We need to turn the tide."

"I'm assuming the answer is so much more complicated than just unleashing everyone's full abilities against the humans." Series looked to Hans for further direction.

He shook his head with a small smile, the motion contrary to his positive response. "You assume correctly."

"Which means none of us are asses today." Dwayne leaned on the pad just enough for it to register him, so his comment would come through. Laughter rippled through the members, though it turned into a worrying *wheeze* for Scott. "Sorry, I'll hold off on jokes until I have you healed."

"I think it may be the only answer we have," Eilene whispered. "I'm afraid to say it aloud."

"I agree with you." Hans covered his face with a hand and rubbed.

"Have we all come to the same conclusion?" Scarlet folded her arms.

"We saw firsthand in our battles that they won't back down in the face of our weapons." Kristen nodded. "If we are to preserve the elementalist race, we need to show them what our true ferocity is like."

"I think, and my soldiers agree, that the humans got away with thinking we were only separate and not more powerful, not stronger, not better off for too many millennia." Ethan massaged his fingers as he spoke. "I took Hans' lead and asked those who I'm commanding for their responses. They are itching to prove they are worth something. I can see our people falling under active command. If we can spare their lives in favor of the enemy, I cannot fault our decision."

"The humans are already thinking along those lines. They are not going to give up." Dwayne appeared in his proper place. "We have an advantage, but we will all be substantially more drained. I overexerted myself after the first battle. It's harsh conditions."

"But the reality of war," Series said. She watched them all with glazed eyes. "We cannot ask our people to die to conditions they can stop."

"Like my bullet wound." Scott turned his gaze to the floor. "They would've never got that close to me."

"All our people are thinking along the same lines, including those still on our homelands." Hans returned to his seat. "My Secretary of the Army is adept, and he retrieved responses from those not in the field. The over-whelming majority consensus is that we should face them with everything we have."

Series inhaled sharply, and she slid to the edge of her chair. They waited patiently for her vision to focus, although they were worried about her injuring herself.

She returned to the present a moment later and gripped the arms of her chair to pull herself back up. She squeezed her eyes shut. "We have to use our elements," Series said. "I can see it. It lines up with what I saw with Scott wielding the nine—the strange glow that surrounded him and me in our element colors. We will unleash our powers against the humans before the end of this war. I don't think timing matters."

"Then, I believe we are in majority agreement," Eilene called their attention. "We can put it to a formal vote."

"For the democratic process, I put forth a motion to allow our military to use their powers to the full capability," Scarlet said.

"I second the motion." Hans nodded at her.

"All those in favor, vote 'aye'." Eilene listened as everyone spoke at once. "Then, as a majority, the motion will move forward as approved. We will need to inform our armies."

"And the consequences of this decision?" Hans asked.

"We will shoulder all of them when the end of the war arrives," Ethan said. "There is no point in accounting for it now. Things will change. For now, I do not believe there is an answer."

"Agreed," Dwayne yawned. "If this is all we needed to discuss, I think it's time we closed the meeting. We will be fighting again at dawn's first light."

"Of course, you are all excused."

They exchanged courteous farewells matching their various times of day before the projections vanished and left Hans in silence. A moment later, a notification pinged on Hans' phone.

> *By order of a majority vote among Council members, all elementalists serving in the military are authorized to use all abilities to protect and serve Elementōrum Patriam. From this moment forward, use of any of the nine elements against the enemies of the elementalist people is permitted.*
>
> *Prime Minister Eilene Vos*

CHAPTER FIVE

Ablutions

May 12, 2318

Hans stared into the mirror in his tent, awoken from a nightmare involving Maxim. He felt glad Series could see the future instead of him. He wouldn't want *that* future to exist. For a moment, he thought he saw a flicker of Maxim's reflection watching him. He pressed his tongue against the back of his teeth as he tried to steady his breathing. In through the nose. Out through the nose. Five long breaths and hold.

Maxim didn't exist in the mirror. He didn't stand behind Hans. Brothers separated by the laws he had to uphold. *Or do I?* he thought. He turned slowly and stared at the Council circle. *Asking for forgiveness is sometimes easier than asking for permission.* He pulled his phone from his pocket. He could get a majority agreement—at least, he thought most Council members would agree with him. If he succeeded...

It might destroy everything he built with Luana. *Does that matter?* Hans froze. Of course, it did. He spent years building a relationship of trust with

Luana, and in the last several days he destroyed large portions willingly and without contemplation of what it would mean. Ever since Eilene sent out the official declaration, Luana didn't speak to him or Ethan. She refused to leave her tent, and no one could enter.

He loved her. He did. He couldn't keep denying it. Love, however, couldn't continue to negatively impact his people. Centuries of harm at the hands of the Council took time to correct, but blatant policies in opposition to their needs and freedoms only caused more pain. If Luana refused to change, they would move forward on majority votes.

Except for one thing.

Hans needed to do it. He needed to apologize in person. He would go alone, but he would tell someone in case anyone went looking for him. Ethan would be the best choice. He would support Hans' decision.

He had no idea where the humans would attack next. Once the southeast units unleashed the full capabilities of their powers, the humans retreated with heavy losses. The enemy's retreat gave their military time to clean-up properly before determining where they would move to protect next. Several factions worked tirelessly in the city to restore damaged buildings and wildlife.

Several media outlets spun their fighting as proof of their need to dominate the world, but they had to push it off.

They had limited options; Hans made his decision without the approval of anyone else. He would go to the Uns and request their help in the war. They could prove useful as spies and infiltrators. In return, he could only promise eventual reform of their lives in Elementōrum Patriam. He hoped they would prove willing.

Banana, Kiritimati, Republic of Kiribati

"Sir?" Mason asked.

Tyr stared at him, unwilling to repeat himself. He knew Mason heard the order loud and clear. "You'll ship out in the morning."

"I thought I was to remain here, to help with the testing facility."

"Orders have changed. Ryan can handle what needs to be done for now."

"But sir—" Mason said.

Tyr banged a closed fist against the table. "Your loyalty lies with HISS, does it not?"

He grit his teeth. "Yes."

"In the morning, Ford. War front in Georgia. Lead the cavalry against those monsters."

May 13, 2318

City of Uns, Elementōrum Patriam

Maxim supervised the construction of several new houses down the lane. With funds reallocated, and additional temporarily granted, they spent time designing and building appropriate houses for each family in the Uns. Someone called for help with a large support beam, and Maxim helped lift it into place. He picked up his tablet on the way out and heard the workers pass whispers as they carried the supplies to different construction sites.

Council member.

Walking among them.

Looking for the leaders.

Dressed in war fatigues.

Maxim looked toward the city center where he caught a glimpse of red moving amongst the people. Red—the color of Earth. His feet carried him away immediately. His mind didn't condone the idea of it being a figment of his imagination or a desire to see his brother again. When he reached the square, he did see Hans standing among them, almost overwhelmed.

"Hans!" he called above the crowd.

He turned immediately and smiled. His whole figure relaxed, and the crowd parted to let them through.

"Maxim," he whispered as he pulled his brother in for a hug.

"What are you doing here?" Maxim whispered in Russian.

"Either something brilliant or stupid. The jury is still out," Hans said.

"Alright, keep your secrets." The corner of Maxim's mouth quirked up as he held back a laugh.

"I'll tell you, but in the official meeting. I need to call for one, but I don't know your customs." Hans had the decency to look sheepish at the blatant ignorance.

Maxim laughed. "We're still developing customs. Your people never allowed us to have them."

Hans opened his mouth briefly to respond before closing it again and nodding.

"I'll send a text to the others. It may be a while." Maxim frowned, completely uncertain of his brother's schedule.

"I have time. My unit has yet to see war. There's no sighting of the enemy."

Maxim nodded. Several minutes passed before he received responses. "They can free up time around three."

"Perfect. Is there anything I can help with in the meantime?"

"Are you any good at construction?"

"I don't know." Hans stared at the ground.

The frown on his face felt almost permanent. "The Council stunted your ability to learn practical skills." It wasn't a question.

Hans ignored him and gestured for Maxim to lead the way. Maxim walked into the outskirts of Central where the new constructions started. As it turned out, Hans made quick work of digging out the areas for the new foundation. He needed only a short look at the plans before he could lift the earth away with very little thought.

Maxim bit his tongue. His brother wasn't one of *those* people, but he did enforce the laws which kept them separate. Even while oppressing them, he could do more for them than Maxim could. All because he was born cursed into a family who produced only one Elementalist. Only one of the three siblings was an all-powerful being. He didn't want to resent his brother, but it felt like he could see the fence between them again. Maxim stared down at his palms where the diamond scars crossed each other—permanently seared there. Almost every Un had a pattern of diamonds burned into their skin. It was of their own volition that they threw themselves against the fence, hoping that the next searing hit would be the one to break the wall and take them home. It never came. The diamonds were Maxim's reminder of what he was and where he was. He clutched his hands into fists and watched the white outlines strain and shine on his forearms before vanishing into the sleeve of his shirt. His nails left crescent patterns on his palms.

"It's almost three." Hans' voice directly next to his shoulder startled him.

"Right, we should go." Maxim swallowed past the lump in his throat. He looked to the foreman on the job. "I'll be back later to help."

He nodded and had the men return to their digging pattern. They didn't look much happier than Maxim about the new foundation spaces; the help removed several days of work from their schedule, but something about it felt patronizing.

"I'm sorry my help couldn't be more welcome." Hans kept up the drivel of Russian between them.

"A double-edged sword." Maxim tried to smile, but he knew he failed. "We haven't heard anything about the war here."

"We split into three groups to cover the most ground. Only one has seen fighting thus far."

"Are you winning?"

"What do you consider victory?" Hans' face was uncharacteristically open. His sincerity bled into the curve of his brows, the biting of his tongue, and the darkness hiding behind his eyes.

Maxim placed a warm hand on his little brother's back. "I'm not sure I am philosophical enough to answer that question."

Hans sighed. "Nor am I. I used to think war was black and white. Fighting for this or against another thing, but it's so many shades of gray I can never find the right answer. I feel like I'm running in circles."

"Are you coming to us for answers?" Maxim stopped walking. "You are coming to the people your kind oppressed for answers to your war in which we will receive nothing from it?"

He shook his head. "I don't want you to not receive anything from it. I want things to change. Here and now. That's why I'm here."

Maxim thought he could hear the gears spinning in Hans' head as his thoughts tried to grasp the conclusion he so desperately wanted. "What are you planning?" he asked.

"I only have about five percent of it worked out."

Maxim bit his lip. "Hans, are you telling me you came here with no plan and only an idea? You had the last two hours to figure this out. Were you thinking of nothing while you worked?" He let out a sharp laugh. "When we were little, I prided myself on always knowing what you were thinking. You went into every action with a plan fully worked out and at least thirty contingencies considered. If you got in trouble with mama or otets, I could explain everything to keep you out of trouble. Your strong mind led you well, serving on the Council, but now—I'm not sure I know who you are."

Hans worked his jaw for a moment before admitting, "I think Hans did die the day I joined the Council—just as it was reported."

"What do you mean?" Maxim folded his arms.

"It feels like there is the past me who had a family with siblings and parents, but he doesn't exist anymore. Instead, there's just this man born late in life who became a Council member and hid so much of himself it was buried. It was lost and mourned over. It feels like I don't know who I am without the red robes—without the safety of the chambers which closed out everyone. I was the arm of the law. I followed it without question. I didn't stand up to oppressive policies—I perpetuated them. Now, I walk around without the safety of people not knowing who was responsible for their suffering. It feels like yet another death and birth," Hans said.

"And that means you are back to the infantile stage where you have to learn who you are and what you stand for."

He nodded. "I have two families now mashed into one, and I'm being forced to choose loyalty to only one."

Maxim ran his tongue over the front of his lower teeth. "Do you know who you are swearing loyalty to?"

Hans' expression closed off again, and he stared at Maxim with his muddied green eyes. "I am standing here, aren't I?"

Maxim shook his head. "You want to play a dangerous game with our lives. You want us to join this war in exchange for our freedom. That's your half-assed—no, not even half. That's your five percent plan. A trade. We stay locked up here, or we help you fight the war. Uns who can't even fight without weapons, who can't hold a candle to what you can do."

"We have weapons. We're releasing the elementalists on the humans without restraint."

Maxim laughed again. "And how many of us will be caught in the crossfire as well? Hans, we are humans, too. Your people don't see us as humans because we came from your kind, but we are. We can't stand on a battlefield and fight or shield ourselves against what you can do. If someone in your unit set the entire field on fire, we'd be dead where we stood. You can shield yourself with Earth. Others can combat the Fire with Water or fly away. We have nothing. Asking us to fight in the war is asking us to throw down our lives for a cause that doesn't affect us. We have nothing to fear from the humans defeating you. They would be the first to welcome us back. We'd be seen as unwitting captives to a corrupt system because that's what we are."

Hans swallowed but made no reply.

"This is why you can't just walk in here with a five percent plan. I would love to have my freedom, but not at the cost of my life. Mama can't lose another member of her family. She already lost me once."

"I can protect you."

"You think you can protect me," Maxim sighed. "You better start thinking fast with that mind of yours. We're already late to the meeting."

"What is one of *them* doing here?" Esebelle Berlusconi demanded in English as soon as they walked into the main governmental building conference room. She swung her black hair over her shoulder with an annoyed flip.

Esebelle lead a riotous group, along with Maxim, against the corrupt Un politicians the year before. While the Council removed those politicians in power and sent liaisons to watch over returning the Uns to a more prosperous place, they did little else to help the Uns. The Uns lived behind an electrified fence designed to keep them in their corner of Elementōrum Patriam. Away from the elementalists. The Council traditionally swore it kept the Uns safe. Their scars told a different story.

"I came with an offer," Hans spoke quietly, unsure of his plan. He produced a tablet from inside his uniform. Using the attached pen, he scribbled onto the surface. Maxim recognized the spikey movement of his handwriting. "I've just had a slight change to the offer. It is open to discussion as well."

They watched him scribble frantically across the page, and Maxim grinned. A rebirth into both worlds would take time to adjust to. Hans' brain working at full capacity certainly left something to be feared. He had a mind for strategy. If Maxim had to guess, he knew Hans would already be working out the contingencies of every piece of his offer.

"And this offer? We do have other things to get to," another one of the new officials said.

Hans' stare pierced through him. The official shifted in his chair and redirected his gaze to the table. A moment later, Hans recognized his position at the head of the table; the new Governor of the Uns, Mikhail Tyche. He did his best to soften his gaze and wrote a few more notes on his tablet. When ready, Hans cleared his throat. "Your freedom with no strings attached."

Maxim leaned back in his chair. He really didn't know his brother. Hans had traces of the boy Maxim knew before their separation, but Hans matured and grew into a man who he couldn't fathom.

Esebelle broke into laughter which held no hint of humor or genuineness. It sounded as cold as her words. "You would never."

"I can have the fences taken down today." He shrugged. "I can do it myself."

"And what are you expecting in return?" Another official spoke from their chair. They had cold, sharp eyes.

"Nothing," Hans wrote another quick note on his tablet. "However, I will take anyone who volunteers to help us in the war. There are several different places we can put you to work with increased wages. We'll send in crews to help build out the rest of the city as well."

"Do you honestly think anyone would be willing to help you in your war against the humans? After you locked us behind this fence?" Esebelle's eyebrows shot upward.

"Which is why I am not making it a demand. Should you have a desire, you are welcome to join us. We will provide weapons training and anything else that's needed. I'm already aware you would be at a disadvantage on the battlefield with us wielding our powers to full capacity. I thought we might be able to recruit some of the Uns as spies. It's much easier for an Un to approach the humans as you are already human."

"The Council never recognized us as humans before." A short woman piped up from down the table.

"That is our mistake. I take full responsibility. I wanted to make changes regarding how we handle Uns ever since I joined the Council, but in the face of more experienced members, I backed down from my convictions. I cannot make that up to any of you, but I hope to be able to make some reparations. It's time we do recognize you as equal to our other citizens." Hans stared at the center of the table as he spoke.

"We are not citizens of your country. We are captives," Esebelle hissed. A murmur of agreement swept around the table.

"I believe Hans when he says he will work to make changes for us and with us." Maxim watched her carefully. They were confidants for many years, but it could fall apart in the blink of an eye. Esebelle never truly trusted anyone other than herself. "They could have houses for all our people within a few days—we probably wouldn't live in a desert anymore, either. The Council is already proving themselves as willing to overturn archaic laws."

"You're betraying us." Esebelle fixed her fierce gaze on him instead.

"I'm not betraying anybody. I'm looking at the ideal. We would have better paying jobs, full-citizenship, a city without borders—"

"You are forgetting everything you went through as a child because your brother came back for you."

"I am not forgetting it." He scowled. "The current Council members had nothing to do with my removal."

"How can you be sure?"

"It's an assumption." Maxim admitted. He looked at Hans.

"Luana joined the Council in twenty-two-ninety-five. She has seniority over everyone. I was the second member of the current Council in twenty-three-oh-six. We have separated many other children from their families. I would love to figure out how to make reparations and reunite families."

"Yet, you are here alone." Mikhail still refused to look Hans in the eye.

"Yes, I came alone."

Esebelle laughed forcefully. It sounded as if she would choke and start to cry. "And you promise our freedom when it is not a decision offered by all of your government?"

"I don't need to ask them for permission. There is only one person on the Council who will oppose what I am offering. I am done being afraid of them, and I will not stand down when I know this is the right decision." Hans placed a hand on the table. "I am offering your freedom, guaranteed work, and a reunion with your families all in exchange for nothing because it's what you all deserve. We have no reason to fear you—"

"But we have every reason to fear *you*." Esebelle thinned her lips into a line.

"I suppose."

"Isn't your original reason for separating the humans and Uns from the elementalists because you are too dangerous to be around?" The woman from down the table spoke with such surety that Maxim felt the ripple of fear cut through his fellows again.

"Only when we aren't trained. You won't be in the Academy with those still learning. You'll be in the city with graduates who are in full control of their abilities. You can be back with your families who I don't believe would harm you. If they would, we can find alternative arrangements to keep you safe."

"How many of your people consider us the dangerous ones?" She shook her head. "This is all just too much to be believed. We hoped for this for years, but the damage is already irreparable to all the people you locked away. Is it not common practice to separate us because we are a regeneration of your supposed great blessing to carry the elementalist gene mutation? Are you not afraid of your civilization losing its power?"

"Of course, the discourse will be dealt with, but the damage of it is already done on many generations inside our country. There is no doubt that you will experience forms of oppression as we move the country into a new age. It's why it's even more important for us to work together to resolve these issues and find solutions which will help all parties involved."

"And all of this is offered in hope that a few of our people will be willing to volunteer themselves to serve in your army—to act as your spies among your enemies and feed you information you need to win the war." Esebelle sucked on her teeth. "A war in which you will only yet again prove your superiority and breed the fear you claim to hate."

"Yes, the war is complex, and we cannot determine all the outcomes. Our intent is to let the war conclude where we can rebuild together. We discussed these ideas already as a Council and decided to tackle the harder ideals once the war is over. There is no point in harassing ourselves over them when we do not yet know how the ending is written."

Esebelle scoffed but didn't say anything more.

"Will you allow your country to make reparations?"

"We don't have a country." A tremble of fear infiltrated Mikhail's words. "Any semblance of nationalism left us when we received our title."

The others nodded.

Hans sighed. "Am I to understand you don't want me to take down the wall?"

Maxim watched as each of the leaders voted to stay within the electric fences. "Why?" he asked.

"They are fighting a war. There is no one left here who will protect us from the elementalists if those walls come down. We are safer here for now. After the war's conclusion, if you still feel the same about us, we expect the fence to disappear."

Hans stood. "I understand. Thank you for at least hearing me out."

They took the meeting as dismissed and filtered out of the room. Hans sunk slowly into the chair, defeated.

"You, okay?" Maxim moved to sit on the table over his brother's hunched form.

"I knew it was a long shot, anyway."

"But you still had hope they would be willing." Maxim pulled his right leg onto the table and bent it, so his foot rested against his other thigh. "I hoped as well. You impressed me with how quickly you revised your plan. It felt much more than five percent. It wasn't a complete plan and had a lot of holes to fill, but it was better at the very least. Next time, you definitely need a full plan."

Hans laughed. "I should be getting back to the war front. I need to know if we have any other information about their movements."

"Do you still need spies?"

Hans' brows crinkled against the bridge of his nose. "They did not accept my offer."

"You said the volunteers were not contingent on our agreement to fight in the war."

"It's not, but why would anyone want to join us when we are not bringing down the walls?"

Maxim laughed. "I know a few people who would probably be willing to get outside of the fences."

"I couldn't ask you to ask them. I have nothing to give in return," Hans said.

"The ability to see the world outside these fences sounds like a wonderful deal." Maxim jumped off the table. "Come on, we have to get people quickly and get a move on. We have a war to get to."

"We?"

"You weren't expecting me to let you do this on your own?" The corner of Maxim's mouth quirked up. "Please, you're my brother. I trust and support you. I'm going to be one of your spies. Now, get me out of here."

Maxim did have a small group of volunteers who were compelled to join based on the premise of their immediate freedom and freedom for their people later. Hans assured them they would receive great pay for being spies, in addition to receiving combat training. The ease with which they left the city surprised Maxim, but he knew their absence would be treated as treason later. He would accept the consequences only after the war. He had no intention of returning to the city.

Their small team fit comfortably inside the transportation pod. Maxim remembered riding in them only a few times, always on trips to see their family in Russia as a child before his expatriation. He could tell only a couple of the Uns had the experience he did. Carmen panicked when they lifted away from the edge of Elementōrum Patriam and flew high above the ocean.

"It's okay," Hans told her warmly. "The pods have never failed."

She nodded, still incredibly uncertain.

"Perhaps we should get to know each other a bit. We'll be working together after all." Hans licked his lips. "I'm Hans Aliyev, Maxim's younger brother. We both lived in Vasha in the Russian sector."

"Carmen Castillo Fuentes, my family has lived in the Dominican Republic sector of Victor for several generations—we were a heritage family until I came along."

"I'm sorry you had to be separated from them." Hans' knee bounced.

"I'm Zawadi Wanjiku. My family had a rare abnormality—everyone was always a Life elementalist. We hailed from Yahav—very fitting, I suppose."

Everyone chuckled.

"Mpendulo Tembe. My family is from Eswatini, I was second generation. We lived in Wabaunsee."

"Ulrick Forestal, I grew up in the neighborhood next to Carmen. We knew each other before being pulled."

"Is your family Dominican as well?" Hans asked.

Ulrick shook his head. "Haitian."

"It's good to at least know all of you on the most basic level. I hope we can know each other better as we work together." His leg stopped bouncing. "Do any of you have combat experience or weapon experience?"

Everyone except for Maxim shook their heads. Since Maxim helped Esebelle lead what they meant to be an uprising the year before, he handled the Sclopētum a couple times but never used it against another person. He felt ill prepared. He told his brother he would spy, but he had no experience.

"Right, well," Hans placed his tablet in front of them, "I'll get some of these commissioned for you all as well. I can show you the weapons you'll be working with."

May 14, 2318

Kolkheti National Park, Guria, Georgia

A man with a large build walked toward them as soon as they departed the pod. Maxim registered the moko kauwae adorning his skin; it enhanced the softness of his movements.

"Mateo, I need you to get an additional tent next to mine immediately for our guests. I also need to see Luana and Ethan in my tent." Hans told him.

"Yes, sir."

Hans led them through the temporary streets of the encampment. A few people looked over with curiosity when they saw people out of uniform, but they didn't pry as they walked with a Council member. At the center of the camp, the largest tent bore the elemental symbol for Earth. Hans pulled the door aside and gestured for them to enter. Maxim performed a quick inventory of the room. A bed for Hans separated by a false wall, a work desk, projection pads for each Council member, a three-dimensional projected map of the surrounding area and small tokens to indicate armies and numbers. A yellow light cast hazy and deep shadows across the floor.

"I want you close to my tent, so you are better protected." Hans explained as he pulled up chairs from their storage spot against one of the walls. "The four of you will sleep in the tent they're setting up now, Maxim, you'll stay here with me. Once you're trained with the basics, we'll look at dispersing you around to the others as well."

"What's going on?" Ethan pushed the tent flap to the side and stared with wide eyes at the five new people. When he spotted Maxim, his expression turned to confusion.

"Hi, I'm Maxim, Hans' older brother." He put out a hand to the Council member.

Ethan took it warmly. "Ethan Silverspoon, Death elementalist. Aren't you an Un?"

"Yeah." Maxim didn't expand.

"I thought we could use some spies," Hans covered.

"They would pass the temperature checks." Ethan grinned. "Did you convince Luana to let you do this?"

Hans paused as he unfolded the last chair. "I'm choosing to ask for forgiveness than permission."

Ethan patted his fellow on the back. "I'll help you stand up to her."

"Thanks." Hans rolled his eyes and took a seat in his office chair.

Maxim wandered over to one of the chairs and took further inventory of the tent. It had the appearance of a studio apartment more than a tent, and there was no obvious entertainment. The nine dark projection pads on the floor hummed softly, only audible because of their proximity and quantity. He traced the symbols of the elements.

"What are those for?" Zawadi asked.

Ethan looked to where she pointed before responding. "When we have meetings as a Council, they project our appearance to everyone else. We can all be in our own tent, or together in a group."

"And it crosses any distance?"

"Yep. Super nice since we're currently in three factions. Much easier than texting or trying a phone call."

"Are the others in different time zones?" Carmen pulled her feet onto the chair.

"Yeah. We have the clocks set on our phone as well as on the wall." He pointed to the four digital clocks. "One of them is tied to home."

"What did you do?" A woman with messy brunette hair demanded with her hands on her hips. Her orange fatigues, the top of her battle dress uniform gathered around her waist, shimmered under the light and imitated the fire burning under her skin. Maxim recognized her from the news broadcasts. She and Hans were practically inseparable. Luana Ford.

CHAPTER SIX

Noon

Luana didn't know she was capable of being furious with Hans. She couldn't recall ever pointing anger toward him. He was her rock, her foundation. He betrayed her.

He stood, stony faced, waiting for her inevitable explosion; almost like he expected it. Hans knew her so well, he predicted her reaction and acted on his own anyway.

Of course, she recognized the man sitting in one of the chairs. He looked like a slightly older version of her most trustworthy ally. She recognized him from the photos of Hans' young family despite the age lines, scars, and stubble lining his jaw. He had the same face as their father, Yerik. The strong Russian genes overrode their mother's German. The problem: he was an Un. He should be behind the electrified fence in Elementōrum Patriam. Yet, he sat in front of her. A flicker of fear passed over the Uns—she made an educated guess based on their civvies—and Luana checked herself in case she had any flames leaping off her body.

"I got spies from the Uns." Hans positioned himself between her and the others as if she were a threat.

Rage set her leg bouncing as she tried to keep it from rising into something more. She didn't plan on attacking the Uns. She needed to send them back to where they belonged.

Ethan rose from his chair and came to stand next to Hans. He was a little taller than Hans, he had an unexpected growth spurt since joining the Council, and in the face of her barely over five-foot stature, they made an intimidating pair. Both had over a foot on her.

"Did you consult anyone on your plan?" she asked.

Hans' Adam's apple bobbed as he prepared his next words. "As Maxim told me, I had a five percent plan going into it. I got us five spies who are willing to be trained and infiltrate the human military where possible to bring us information."

"No. They're going back."

"They're not."

Luana buried her hands into her hair and let out a frustrated cry which sounded like an eagle screaming—high pitched and squeaky. "What is it with you and your attachment to fixing things for the Uns? Things were fine the way they were."

The Uns looked as if she slapped them, mouths open and brows furrowed with justified anger, but under the power radiating from the Council members, they quickly directed their gazes to the ground instead of watching the growing fight.

"Have you ever thought to look at anyone besides yourself and the Council's old rules?" Hans remained eerily calm in the wave of her anger, and it threw her off. He usually apologized and agreed with her. He would drop everything to follow what she said. He didn't fight.

"You've changed," she whispered.

"You haven't."

Luana froze. He had to be wrong. She changed a lot. She allowed the Council to remove their robes. She declared war on the humans. She allowed the other eight Council members to decide; she refused to debate. *Are those changes or concessions?* Luana opened her mouth to say something in response, although she didn't know what, when an explosion rocked the ground underneath them.

The chairs tipped the Uns to the floor, Ethan fell against the desk, and Luana collapsed to the ground. Hans remained steady and rushed toward the tent flap.

"Sir, it's a surprise attack by the humans. They're besieging us."

"Mobilize everyone immediately, remember they are allowed to use their elements in full capacity to drive them back," Hans ordered.

Luana stood on shaky legs. "Here? At night?"

"They wanted the edge of surprise, and they got it." Ethan checked his belt for his weapons which never left his side.

"Maxim, stay here with the other Uns. Do not leave this tent for any reason. You are not trained yet to deal with this," Hans said.

"Got it." Maxim nodded firmly and helped the others back to their seats.

Hans hesitated for a moment before removing the Lūminis Sclopētum from his belt. He activated the weapon before handing it over. "Keep your finger on the trigger aimed at the door. Anyone who is not wearing an elementalist uniform, shoot first and ask questions later. If you disable it, it'll be useless since it's registered to me."

"Understood. I'll aim it when you're all clear." He kept it pointed upward for the time being.

Hans nodded before his fingers wrapped around Luana's upper arm and hauled her out of the tent. Ethan followed on their heels.

"We need recon on how many people are attacking," Ethan said.

"I'm the only one who can get into the air." Hans placed a foot on the ground and the earth rose underneath it. "Go protect our people."

Luana shook with every step she took in Ethan's wake. As they reached the edge of the camp, a ferocious scream came from behind them as a human raised a crude weapon, something like a sickle, into the air and swung at them. Luana closed her eyes and ducked behind a tent. When she opened her eyes again, she saw Ethan with a hand on the man's face. A moment later, the attacker crumpled, and Ethan tossed him aside, dead.

"You're supposed to be our leader, and you're cowering from the fight?" Ethan shook his head. "If you don't plan on helping, get out of here."

"I'm sorry," the words felt heavy in Luana's mouth, and she struggled to form the correct sounds.

"Don't apologize. Fight." He vanished into the crowd of fighting elementalists.

She watched as human after human collapsed, dead in front of their quarry. Rolling black smoke swept across the ground with Ethan at the epicenter. Even the elementalists moved out of the path of the force until they saw him retreating.

"Keep going! Secure the border of the camp!" Luana shouted. She ran through the gaps of the tents. She pulled her Lūminis Sclopētum from her belt and aimed the small hand weapon in front of her. The elementalist military personnel heeded her and ran off to create a border in the cleared area.

Luana moved quickly between the tents. She kept her eyes peeled for more human invaders. As one rounded the tent, she fired. The sagittae ripped through the man's shoulder with a bigger hole than she expected. He grunted and raised his gun toward her. Luana lowered her Sclopētum just far enough to shoot him in the leg. He buckled. The weapon from his hand fell and fired a shot at random, luckily away from Luana. She knew he wouldn't die from his injuries. He scrambled for his gun, but she kicked it away. She placed her foot on the wound. He locked his jaw, but the pain escaped his teeth in a soft hiss. His eyes squeezed shut, and he flexed his fingers to keep feeling in them.

"Who ordered this attack?" she hissed.

"I don't know."

"You don't know?"

"Please, we were just told to attack via our commander. I don't have contact with the top military personnel."

Luana spat onto the ground next to their face. "What do you know?"

"Nothing, I swear."

"President Ford!" A voice from behind her interrupted the impromptu interrogation. She looked up to find one of her Field Marshals watching her.

"Take this one as prisoner. Get them healed. We might be able to use them as ransom."

"Yes, ma'am." They moved forward and helped the human off the ground before moving toward the medical tents.

Luana continued with her weapon raised. Instead of more enemies, she found the camp fully defended by her own. The borders remained secure. She pushed her way through the main defense line and into the fray of panic. Weapons fired around her without a care for who they hit. Scared of being trampled under the onslaught, she tapped the band around her wrist; the Lūcis Scūta erupted in a blaze of blue and parted the crowd in front of her. With the shield's assistance, she pushed away the heavier bodies as she tried to grasp the situation.

Black tendrils of smoke snaked their way along the ground in front of her. She gasped and tried to back away. It looked like gas with a form. Screams ripped through several throats before the mass of bodies collapsed. Ethan stood in the middle of the wreckage, and his eyes landed on her, completely black. He nodded before stepping over the dead body nearest him and moving toward the crowd of humans who caught onto what he could do.

The commanders' shouts drifted across the battlefield, too distant to make out the words. It floated like the seeds of a dandelion blown into the wind, scattered wide and only a few seeds followed the command. Some tumbled out of order rushing their path to the devil. Luana's mind worked double-time to keep up, but everything around her moved with a pace she only associated with Kristen's ability. The commanders fired their weapons in Ethan's direction, but the bullets passed through him without harm.

The black smoke swept toward them in a wave; those closest were obscured inside the fog. The ensuing stampede trampled those who couldn't keep up under their feet. Lives that Ethan didn't have to take to instill fear in their presence. Luana shook in the presence of sacrosanct death. Luana's grip on her Sclopētum slipped. Her breathing turned cold and tight in her chest. Only Scarlet would have a chance at stopping Ethan if he turned on any of them. The breadth of his power brought Luana's world crashing around her. She tightened her hold on the grip and pressed her way into the fog.

"How long have you been able to do that?" she gasped when she managed to stumble her way over the bodies to his side.

"Not long. Takes a lot of focus and energy to make sure I don't just kill everyone. It's not exactly discriminate on its own." Ethan let the smoke retreat into his skin.

"Can you wipe out their entire camp with it?"

"Not in a million years. I can get it to go maybe fifteen feet when I'm really focusing. It's incredibly draining."

"Do you think they'll be back?" Hans landed on the ground next to them.

"Unwillingly." Ethan nodded.

Luana turned to the elementalists. "Look for survivors! Rest if you can. We don't know when they'll attack next."

The message passed swiftly through the crowd, and they dispersed.

"What did you see when looking at the army?" Ethan asked.

"It's bigger than their attack size, which is already formidable. I cornered one of the commanders, and he confessed they are bringing in even more people by the day. He's in interrogation now. It's like they plan to make a big stand here. They knew we were here." Hans shook his head. "Somehow they keep getting our information, and we have nothing on them."

"Which is where a spy would be useful." Luana chewed her lip and didn't dare look at either man. "Summon the Council members, here, physically. Just the Council. We'll make a stand with the nine of us at full power. None of this shit." She gestured to the gun-like weapon in her hand. "Ethan proved tonight that they run at the sight of our powers. If we plan to win this war, we must use every part of us."

"Glad to know we're finally on the same page," Ethan said.

She didn't need to see Ethan's grin to know it sat wide above her in winning triumph.

The second tent Hans organized for the Uns was ready, so only Maxim remained. Hans refused to let him leave. She could tell he wanted to give them privacy by the uneasy shaking of his leg, and the way his eyes darted between her and Hans like a tennis match. Luana didn't want their talk to turn into a fight, but she already had a feeling it would. It didn't feel avoidable on her end.

After the dead were counted and the survivors ushered to the medical tents, the three Council members agreed to meet in Hans' tent. They needed to discuss the attack as well as the Uns in their midst.

Luana sat on a folding chair near the projection pads. "We still need to talk about you acting without informing anyone on the Council about your actions."

The tent flap opened behind them. Ethan peered inside with a sheepish expression. "Sorry to interrupt, but did your meeting with the Uns not end well, Hans?"

"What? No. We came to a half-conclusion with a promise to make reparations after the war." Hans' brows furrowed together.

Luana looked at Maxim.

"That is how it ended." He shrugged. "Hans offered them their freedom with no expectations in return other than to take volunteers as spies, but they refused because they thought they would be persecuted without you there to ease society into the change."

"Yeah, that's not how they're spinning it." Ethan held out his phone.

UNS CLAIM KIDNAPPING OF THEIR PEOPLE TO FURTHER
WAR EFFORTS ON ELEMENTALIST FRONT

City of the Uns (ET) — Esebelle Berlusconi of the
Uns reported the kidnapping of five Uns from their
city earlier today after a visit from Council member,
Hans Aliyev. She told reporters he came with the
offer to remove the walls from around the Uns city
in exchange for the use of fodder in the war against
the humans. According to Berlusconi and the other
Un governmental leaders, excluding the newly
appointed Governor Mikhail Tyche, President Aliyev
wanted to train the Uns to use weapons and send
them into the front lines of the war.

When they refused his request, he left the city with five Uns, one of whom is his brother, Maxim Aliyev. The other four kidnappees are Carmen Castillo Fuentes, Zawadi Wanjiku, Mpendulo Tembe, and Ulrick Forestal.

The Uns are requesting the return of the victims, or they will start an assault on home front against the elementalists who they believe think of them as expendable. We reached out to the Council for comment, but we haven't received a response.

This is a developing story.

"Ty che blyad?" Hans immediately caught Maxim's attention.

"What is it?"

Hans held the phone out to him.

Maxim's eyes skimmed the article. When he reached the bottom, he whispered, "Suka blyad."

Luana covered her face with her hands; she paced furiously around the space until she came to a stop near the back. "Why'd you do it, Hans?" Her voice bounced off the other tents and echoed around them several times over. The low murmur of conversation outside the tent died away.

"Because we are out here pretending as if we are so much better, so much loftier, more informed, more accepting, more everything than our human counterparts, yet we have the Uns locked up like animals in a cage. We act as if we are the emblem other countries should strive for while we hold our own people captive. The Uns are a regression of our DNA, that's all it is. They are humans born into our society just as we are elementalists born into human society. You yourself came from the surface—only Eilene and I are true blooded Elementalists, Eilene more so than my own family line. We are tearing our country apart from the inside. We needed help, so I went to our people.

"Yes, it backfired, but I tried to do something. If anything, this brings to light how destructive and messed up we are. Tearing children away from their parents based on their DNA—in what world is this a perfect system?

So, we are now at war with the Uns. I get it, war on two fronts is not ideal, but honestly the Uns should've raised their flag against us years ago—before we ever got to the positions we are in now. My brother is an Un, Luana. I can't deny his existence or pretend his life doesn't matter. The scars on his hands from the electric fence keeping them inside—" he choked. He brought up a hand to pull at his lips and wipe away the spittle. "Even if we fix this now, I can't ever take that away from him. I can never pretend like I didn't continue to perpetuate the system which hurt him. The Uns are traumatized by our decisions—but at the end of the day, they're our people. The elementalists and the Uns shouldn't be separate. I became the instigator for change once in my life, and I stand by that decision."

"And what do you plan to do to fix this problem?" she asked coolly. She could hear the crowd building outside the tent.

"I plan to fight alongside my brother. If it is against you, I'm afraid I already committed to supporting the Uns."

"Hans, you can't do that." Maxim touched his brother on the shoulder. "You can't fight a war against your own people—your friends."

Luana's eyes fixed on the lattice of scars across his hands and up his arms. She never saw Maxim outside of photographs taken before his time in the City of the Uns. She never considered him more important than her. She never saw the Uns as equals, following the laws of the old Council without question. She didn't even register what the Council did or what they asked of their society.

She crossed her legs and sat smoothly on the floor. Everyone in the room watched her.

"Hans, really, I can go back to the Uns. If I go back with the others, you can avoid a war with us, too." Maxim clenched his hands into fists. "You can get me after the war when you can actually make a proper agreement with my people. We all came because we wanted to get out of that city, so see even a small part of the world, and we've done that. I understand the position you're in. I can convince the others."

"No," Luana said.

"What?" Ethan tucked his phone into his pocket.

"I knew when you guys told me I should've sent Kristen to the Spanish speaking countries. I know I lashed out against you incorrectly for speaking with the Uns. I just didn't want to admit I was wrong."

"Why?" Hans joined her on the ground.

"The previous Council would've never stood for this. I can't go against them."

"Luana, the previous Council is dead. We are the current Council. There is nothing wrong with change."

"We can't change. We are a perfect governmental body."

"Luana, we are people. People are expected to do some things wrong. You can't keep holding yourself to these idealistic standards. If we don't change as a government to fit the needs of our people, then the people will overthrow us."

"I don't know how to change."

"No one does," Hans laughed. "What matters is you put your best foot forward. If you mess up, you admit it and work with the rest of us to make things right again. The Council is not made up of only you. There are nine of us. We are all going to make mistakes, and we can't let that hold us back."

"Everything we do just makes sense in my head. I can always see why things are the way they are—but then there were nine instead of seven. There was Ethan who could do something I've never seen. There's Tyr who was torn apart by the standardized and lawful removal of his daughter, waging war against us. Next thing I knew, everything was spiraling out of what I knew. We removed our robes, and our people address us by name. Nothing is as it was before, and I don't know what I can control anymore."

"Lu," Hans said with such tenderness she couldn't help but lift her head.

She still couldn't meet his gaze, so she focused on Maxim instead, who had confusion written on his features.

Hans continued, "You joined the Council when you were eight. Of course, change would be the most difficult for you. During your first few weeks serving the Council you had to kill a Rogue." He paused uncomfortably, and Luana knew he couldn't face the reality of admitting she killed Odessa, their sister, to his older brother. "You may have been the strongest elementalist, but it was too young to subject you to the realities of a governmental body which makes decisions for other people daily. Raised in that environment, it's only natural that you struggle the most out of all of us to tackle change."

Ethan cleared his throat. "Hans is right. We expect that you are attached to this sense of the 'old ways' but considering everything happening—you need to understand that you are not one person leading a country. You have eight people standing next to you. We won't agree all the time, but that's why we work together to find solutions and compromises."

"I don't think I know how to do that, yet," Luana said.

"That's because we let all your seniority power go to your head." Hans took her hand in his. "The eight of us aren't going to let that happen anymore."

"Balance between the nine elements. Not one, not seven, nine." Ethan's familiar grin slid back onto his lips.

"So, am I staying or going?" Maxim bit his tongue.

"Staying. We'll train you and the other four Uns properly and use you as spies. With the others arriving in the next few hours, we can even split spies between the Council." Luana pushed herself off the floor and pulled at her pants which rode up. "We need to decide where they'll be sleeping. I doubt they're thinking of bringing their whole tent with them." She gestured to their set-up. "It'd be ridiculous to expect that."

"Now, you're thinking clearly," Ethan laughed. "We can put Dwayne, Eilene, and Scott in my tent."

"Scarlet and Series are welcome to stay with me." Hans stood and put a hand against the small of Luana's back. "You'll be okay sharing with Kristen?"

"Just put all three in my tent. You need to have time to spend with your brother." She patted him on the arm. "I'm going to see if they got anything from interrogation—then I'll try to sleep."

May 16, 2318

"It's as if the people fighting know nothing at all about what they're doing and why. None of them can even say who is making the orders to attack," Luana announced the next morning as she slipped into her seat at the main table next to the other Council members. Whispers followed the Council around the camps as more and more people heard about the supposed "kidnapping" of several Uns. They only increased when the Uns joined them at the table as well.

"You aren't actually planning on using your brother as fodder, are you?" Dwayne pointed his spoon accusingly at Hans.

Hans gave him a sharp glare in return. "No way in the nine hells."

"Just had to clarify." He glanced around the table and returned his spoon to his bowl. "It feels like forever since we last saw each other."

"It feels like a dysfunctional family reunion," Kristen muttered from down the table.

Laughter rippled through them. It felt comfortable sitting around a meal. If not for the groups of people in the canteen, they'd assume they sat in their chambers getting ready to divvy out the tasks for the day.

"Do they know when the next attack will be?" Scarlet reached for the pot of coffee to refill her mug.

"None whatsoever." Luana shook her head. "Series?"

"I haven't been able to get anything specific. I keep seeing fighting and it looks light out, but there's nothing to pin anything down. I'll keep trying, of course."

"Scott, can you get an aerial view of how much their numbers are increasing by?"

"Immediately." He stood and took off into the air.

"I'll go out and see if they are amassing a Navy," Eilene said." The Supsa Terminal port is on the river they will cross to get here. They have an advantage if they can get supplies to their camp via boat. Our only chance to fight them is myself and Scarlet." She took her leave with a reusable mug of hot chocolate.

"I need to put together a detail to train the spies." Hans hurriedly finished the last several bites of his breakfast. "Afterward, I'll categorize what supplies we have versus what we need."

"We need to review the reports from our actual assignments as well. I have faith the Field Marshals can tide it over, but I hate not being where my units are." Dwayne produced his tablet from his uniform.

"Agreed." Scarlet opened hers as well.

"I'll review military formations, I suppose." Luana left the table alone. She never felt so useless before. She usually told everyone their assignments, but they had no need for a one-woman dictatorship. They all had their duties worked out. Three units already knew the reality of the war.

Luana sat at the table in the middle of her tent where she had the movements and size of their force mapped out. She hoped Scott would also look to see if the humans had any air-force bunkers somewhat nearby. The elementalists never had a formal air force because they didn't have a need for one. They already had a high elevation and people who could manipulate the air. It seemed silly to attack the humans with such outlandish attacks as bombs—especially when not in a war time.

She stared at the little chips representing the different numbers in their military. She moved several to create a front guard against the direction they knew the human camp stood. Recounting the numbers, she changed a few of the chips to show their losses from the night raid. Once reevaluated, she moved to the enemy. They had only preliminary data, and the force looked small but targeted; except, the Council knew the humans planned to increase their numbers.

Series burst into her tent. "Dusk, tonight."

"What?"

"The next attack. It seems as if they are aiming to hit us during times when we least expect it. It's still light at dusk. Everything lines up."

"Right," Luana breathed in deeply, "inform the Field Marshals. They should make sure our people are resting where possible to prepare for tonight. We need everyone at full strength and using their powers from the first hit. Send a few extra Air scouts to get an idea of where they could attack from."

"Do you want to call a meeting?" She hesitated in the doorway.

"Only after everyone completes their tasks. It's important to have all information prior to meeting."

Series' eyes narrowed suspiciously. "Right."

Grigoleti Beach, Grigoleti, Guria, Georgia

Luana stood on the beach with the rest of the Council in a line on either side of her, the same as their traditional seating arrangements. As the sun made its descent into the western sky, it highlighted the southeast ridgeline where the humans set-up their camp. The elementalists had their camp against the shoreline of Paliastomi Lake where several branching rivers provided protection if they guarded the right bridges. However, they waited much farther south a little north of Grigoleti Lake.

Eilene found several naval ships near enough to launch smaller boats to shore during their reconnaissance. Scott confirmed their path across the Supsa River if they planned on attacking the elementalists. They took immediate action on the war front and evacuated the citizens of Maltakva and Grigoletti to Senaki, a nearby larger city. The Council carefully planned their approach; they aimed for as few casualties as possible. They would use their abilities to their advantage. They planned to launch a full-scale operation against every piece of their military. Eilene would focus on the naval units, with a little help from Hans and Scarlet, while the others would deal with the land units. If they dared use any air units, Scott would be ready with a coalition of Air elementalists.

"We all understand what we're doing as soon as we spot any of their military?" Luana asked.

"Yes, we can do it. It won't be a problem." Hans put a hand on her shoulder. The spies and a small, strong contingency remained in their camp for protection.

"We'll have them running again like they did a couple of nights ago," Ethan said.

"We should get into position, so we don't run into each other." Scarlet took several steps behind the front line.

Eilene and Hans followed her. Dwayne and Series stepped to the side and drew their weapons.

The sun sank lower in the sky; on the horizon, the naval ships carrying military personnel approached the shore from the Black Sea.

"Tell me when we move," Scarlet called.

Scott flew into the air to get a better view of the Supsa and the E70 bridge. His eyes scanned the line of trees before sweeping out to sea. The naval ships stopped their approach in favor of launching littoral combat ships. The ships sped toward the shore and trailed the v-shaped wakes behind them Scott opened his mouth to call-out the observation, but the army emerged from the trees on the south side of the Supsa and made their rush, in coordinated lines aiming their weapons, over the bridge.

He let go of the air resistance and dropped like a stone. He reengaged inches above the ground and said, "They're coming."

"Now!" Luana shouted.

Eilene stepped into the surf. Scarlet closed her eyes and held her hands, palms toward the ground. She researched the fault lines in the Black Sea, but finding and pulling at them required her utmost control. She felt the pull of the earth's tectonic plates. She closed her hands into fists and pulled like grabbing a rope. The earth rocked with the move as the plates along the Shatsky Ridge, The Ordu Fault, The Trabzon Fault, and the Rize Fault pulled in a strike slip. Eilene, Hans, and Scarlet spent hours debating the different fault movements to choose the right one for their needs. Hans advocated for the Reverse fault, but Eilene came out on top against him because she didn't want to deal with most catastrophic tsunami. They only needed it big enough to wipe out the navy and remove one threat. The tidal wave rose, and the ships launched their emergency bells.

Hans slid his boot through the sand, and a wall of earth rose into the air. Eilene planted herself unsteadily in the sand, clinging to the rising wall and praying she wouldn't fall. She would control the oncoming wave and crash it safely back in the Black Sea with as little damage to the surrounding areas as possible.

The rest of the Council ran unsteadily across the sand with their military to meet the humans head on.

Luana's feet stumbled through the sand under her as she struggled to run amongst the crowd. Amid the rush of military to meet military, Luana lost track of her friends. She couldn't tell where their armies met, but she saw the humans in front of her firing on the elementalists. She only had one purpose, to drive the humans back and scare them with her powers. Any human who got too close found themselves alight, but Luana didn't recall touching them. Dilatorily, she realized some of the human army took the E692 route, and they hadn't been spotted. They couldn't have penetrated so far into Grigoletti without sneaking through the secondary route on the elementalists' side of the river. The Council didn't plan on them using the road because of the humans' encampment in Tskaltsminda. The only other bridge over the Supsa was too far east for them to think it plausible.

On an unnamed street to her left, a house exploded. In the dimming light, a smaller lake glittered in the distance.

Something ripped through Luana's shoulder. She dropped to her knees in the sand. A line of fire erupted in front of her, and the humans took several steps back. Kristen fought her way to Luana's side. As she touched the woman's shoulder, time reversed in a small bubble and the bullet pulled its way out of her shoulder. Kristen grabbed the ammunition and threw it to the ground.

"Thank you," Luana gasped. She held her hand to her shoulder and cauterized it. "Your power gets stronger every day."

"Yours is driving the humans back." Kristen nodded to the protective line. The humans on the other side hesitated; none of them wanted to broach the flames.

"Then I'm done with playing fair." She stood on unsteady feet and swung out her arm. The flare doubled in height and intensity. A few of the humans cried out and retreated immediately.

Luana closed her eyes and took a deep breath. She imagined her body lighting on fire, a blazing inferno. She pictured her eyes glowing like coals and her hair flying into the air like the ever-changing blaze. She heard Kristen gasp. She opened her eyes and stepped across her imposed line. The humans screamed and ran. They stumbled over each other in their eagerness to get away. She followed, an undimmable ember. The heat propelled her movement forward, and she halted their retreat. With every step, she left behind a trail of conflagration burning the sand into a glass-like surface which their feet couldn't grip.

There, at the rear guard nearer the bridge crossing, the fight coalesced as the other Council members engaged the highest ranks in battle. Luana charged forward to help Hans but stumbled when she saw the familiar face shooting at him. The flames doused around her.

"What are you doing? Attack!" Hans yelled.

It caught the attention of his attacker, and he faltered.

"Dad?" Luana whispered desperately hoping it wasn't true.

His mouth formed the shape of her name.

"Luana!" Hans tackled her to the ground as one of the other commanders fired at them in Mason's stead. "Get your head out of the clouds, they are our enemy."

"He's my dad!" Luana's shrill voice rose above the spray of bullets. "I can't hurt him."

Hans lifted a shield of earth to surround them as the fighting raged on without them. "Then scare the hell out of him. Kill his companions. Make an impression and force him to retreat, but for the Nine's sake don't falter on the battlefield."

She nodded and pushed him away from her. She closed her eyes again and imagined her impersonation of a living fireball. She threw herself over the barricade and charged toward the commanders. Mason jumped out of the way in terror as Luana plowed through the group. Several fell screaming trying to extinguish the flames. She turned and raised her arms so two pillars of fire split the field in a V from her focal point. Mason scrambled toward the ocean on his outside edge, Hans let him. On the opposite outside edge, she heard the call for retreat. For those trapped in the middle, she would take them as hostage.

"Hans! Restrain the captives."

The earth immediately rose to bind them to the ground. Luana dropped the walls of flame and staggered into Dwayne's waiting arms.

"You overextended yourself there, Molelo." He grinned.

"I'll be fine with some food later."

He placed a hand on her head and nodded. "And almost an ocean full of water."

She laughed. "Don't tell Eilene. She'll drown me."

"Luana," her father's voice cut through the sounds of the retreating forces.

"If you don't go, you will be taken hostage." She didn't turn to face him; instead, she pushed off Dwayne and straightened her back. "I won't give you another opportunity like this."

"Luana, please, Slattery, he's powerful—he's blackmailing—"

"I have no interest in what you have to say to me, dad. You're the one trying to kill my people." Luana walked away on unsteady legs. She didn't hear what Dwayne or Hans said, but they joined her a moment later.

"Lu—" Hans started.

"Not right now. We need to find survivors." She turned around and felt a brief stab of disappointment cut through her stomach when she saw her father gone. "Dwayne, go find who you can, we'll grab any elementalist we can to secure the hostages and interrogate them for information."

Before Dwayne could leave, Scott landed with Eilene in his arms. She had her arms around his neck, and her fingers were white from clutching her wrists our of fear of falling. He eased her down from the princess carry to the sand.

"Hans, I never want to do that again," Eilene said.

He laughed. "It was your idea."

"Admittedly it worked, the entire navy is flattened, surrounding towns are safe from the wave, but I do not like heights."

"New fear, Dickens?" Dwayne smiled at Eilene and reached out a hand to pull her into a hug.

"A horrible one." She staggered across the sand to reach him, still wobbly from her flight. "Plus, I had to sit out for the rest once I dealt with the navy. Very boring."

"We'll make sure you have someone to drown next time." He patted her shoulder before heading back to the main field to look for survivors.

"Dwayne!" Ethan appeared out of nowhere and ran after him. "I can help figure out who's dead."

"Get a move on, then, Namune!"

"What can we help with?" Scott gestured to himself and Eilene.

"Can you do a fly over to see what the enemy is doing?" Luana looked back to the captives. "Otherwise, we need help getting the enemy survivors back to camp for questioning."

"I'll go look for survivors from the enemy side," Kristen volunteered.

"I'll go with Scott. Two pairs of eyes are better than one." Eilene staggered back to his side.

"You don't like flying." Luana frowned.

"Scott can take me again, right? I trust him."

"Promise not to vomit on me," he said.

"Got it."

Scott lifted from the ground and grabbed Eilene under her arms and pulled her up into the sky with him.

"I did not agree to be carried like this!" she shouted and kicked her legs.

Hans watched them vanish before turning to the captives. With a flick of his wrist, he made the earth roll over itself and forced them to follow.

"Just until we find the right unit," Hans whispered into Luana's ear. "Everyone keeps abandoning us in favor of more interesting jobs."

"I don't blame them." She watched them pass by reluctantly one after the other. "Who's your main commander, the one who told you to attack?"

"Mason Ford," one said immediately. "He's Slattery's right-hand."

"Lu." Hans' hand wrapped warmly around her upper arm.

"I should've killed him where he stood," she whispered.

"You made the right decision. You would be torn apart if you killed your own father." He shook his head and pulled her along with him. They reached a line of elementalists and waved them forward to take care of the commanders. Hans pulled Luana away from the crowds but continued along the beach. A wind picked up as the sun met the horizon. Hans reached down and pulled off his sweat sticky shoes and socks. Luana watched him curiously for a moment before she joined him.

They walked for a long while down the beach without saying anything. Their skin mirrored the changing sky of pinks and oranges.

"I never expected to see him, out here, fighting against us." Her voice cracked with tears she desperately needed to rid herself of.

Hans stopped walking. "I think he was surprised, too—to face you." He pulled her into a soft embrace. His hands rubbed up and down her back and offered her warmth despite the weather's best efforts. She felt comfortable.

"How are we going to win this war?" His chest muffled her voice where she pressed against him.

"By remaining strong when we see adversity." He rested his chin against the top of her head. "We'll work through this new problem together. You won't be able to spend the rest of the war without meeting your father again. We'll need a plan for the next time—the time when you won't provide him any mercy."

"Next time." The wind whipped away Luana's promise.

"Air reconnaissance shows they are packing hurriedly." Eilene announced at their meeting the next morning. "They also came back with two locations— overheard on the wind—Russia and Japan."

"They're going after Moscow? But why Japan?" Dwayne placed his elbows on the table and leaned forward into his clasped hands.

"Moscow is our best guess. We have no idea why they are targeting Japan. There are no elementalist settlements there." She nodded. "I think we need to consider reevaluating the way we have our units dispersed around the world. If we work on training our spies, we can get more reliable information to place the best people in the best locations."

"A delegation probably needs to return back home to deal with the Uns as well—although, I'm not sure how we are going to handle that particular branch of issues." Hans rubbed his forehead with his fingers.

"As much as I hate to admit it, the Uns are locked inside their city. Unless they find a way to get past the fence, they are not a threat to us. We can increase guard presence around the city by sending back a few of the lower ranks." Eilene pushed her hair out of her face and tucked it behind her ear.

"I don't like the Japan lead." Scarlet frowned.

"We don't have time to train and get an infiltrator amongst their midst before they leave," Series said.

"I think we need to focus on other areas." Luana walked over to the projected map of the world and spun the globe in thought.

"The Japan lead may be a bust, but I can get semi-close and try to get information." Scarlet's fingers fluttered, and Luana recognized it as a nervous tick. She didn't know if she'd get shot down immediately. The pain of what she did to her fellows cut through Luana's heart again. She nodded for her to continue and hoped the other woman saw it as encouragement. "Kaifeng is one of our Harbor cities, so I figure I could set up a camp there with at least one other region. Then, I could move throughout other parts of China as a spy and try to pick up on information. If there is something going on in Japan, we wouldn't be a far shot off, but I would guess it's a bum line."

"Let's redivide where we are going to gather information—this time we'll put the best people in each area. Which means, Dwayne, I want you with Scarlet since you both speak Mandarin." She nodded to him, and he smiled. "Hans will go to Russia, but since our other Russian speakers are occupied in China, I'll go with him and start working on learning the language."

Ethan narrowed his eyes. "I can't decide if this change in you is good or not."

She smiled hesitantly. "There's only one way to find out." She moved the globe around and highlighted a few areas with her finger. They glowed where she touched. "The humans have yet to launch an attack on the Americas, and it's worrying me. I'm not sure how best to split the remaining five of you."

The five exchanged looks with each other as if debating on their own.

"Why don't Scott and I go to Paraguay?" Eilene suggested. "I've been working on my Spanish since we were positioned in Ancón. I still don't have the firmest grasp of the language, but Ethan, Kristen, and Series can be in Inuvik. We'll be on opposite ends of the hemisphere with equal opportunity to protect all the cities across two continents."

"Is that alright with you?" Luana waited for confirmation.

"Yeah, that's fine. If you're sure you are fine without my Spanish skills." Kristen smiled. "It'll be perfect because Belize and Panama are practically perfectly center between us. I wouldn't mind learning more from Ethan and Series."

"And there's no better way to learn a language than forcing yourself into a place where you have to use it to communicate." Eilene straightened her posture. "I'm sure I'll be speaking fluent Spanish with Kristen in no time."

"Entonces podemos hablar a espaldas de estos perdedores."

She nodded along as if she understood before saying, "I'm in more trouble than I thought. I knew two words."

CHAPTER SEVEN

Intermission

Date Unknown

Bakhuis, Sipaliwini, Suriname

Vander shifted the dipper forward to swing the long-armed claw of the machine to the excavation point. He brought it down into the dirt and lifted the heavy material into the air. He dropped it into one of the large bins which would be carried away to remove the bauxite. Once cleaned, the dirt would be returned to the area, and Vander's team would shift to reestablishing a forest over the mine. As he turned the equipment to grab another scoop, he heard a familiar *pop* from the machine. The steering wheel vanished, a strong downside to his abilities. It would need a break before he used it again.

He shut off the machine and climbed out of the rig. He dodged between the others working until he reached the break room area. He collected a cup for water and joined a few of his coworkers at one of the tables.

"How long do you think we can continue hanging out here?" One of the new recruits whispered in crude Sranan Tongo. He didn't grow up in the area, and he didn't know much English or Dutch.

"Donkaw," Vander said as he sat down. "There's no reason for them to find us."

"But there is a whole group of us here. We're all dead men walking if the elementalists find where we are."

"We already know they won't. The number of years we worked quietly without issue, there's no reason for us to be found now. This is our society." Vander took a deep drink of his water. "Sure, our powers go off from time to time, but with the heavy machinery and our work here, it's easy enough to pass off. Bounty hunters cross through once in a blue moon. The Council has more important things than hunting wanted Rogues. Most escape for their entire lives. You're worried about nothing."

"But—"

"Donkaw," Vander repeated. "Rest your mind and enjoy the time you spend here. It is easy work with great pay. We have lives. That is enough."

The newbie didn't say anything more at the table, and their conversation turned to upcoming projects.

"Did your machine *pop* again, Vander?" His boss asked as she passed through the building.

"Yes, it did, ma'am. Most horrific sound with the metal. I'm sure it's almost cooled down now."

Their polite conversation would keep most outsiders unaware of their true discussion. While the machine would *pop* for Vander, it might do something else for one of his coworkers. Around Vander, certain things liked to "pop" in and out of existence without explanation. Part of the brokenness of his abilities as a Rogue. No one could ever tell what element a Rogue should be able to control, and no Rogue ever lived long enough typically for any certified doctors to perform medical research on them. Since they couldn't let anyone know about their Rogue colony, no one knew a whole group of people waited for answers which would never come.

"Well, I'll expect you back to work soon. Remember, the economy of Suriname relies on us."

"Yes, ma'am. I'm very dedicated to the work we do here." Vander gave her a wide grin.

"Good to hear it. And the rest of you?" She raised an eyebrow at them, particularly the newbie.

"We are getting back to work as well, ma'am—just waiting for our machines to cool as well. Mine had a little fight with a fire extinguisher," one tittered softly.

"Sounds like you might want to take your problem to the mechanic rather than take a coffee break." She swayed her hips as she left the room. "I'll be back in five minutes for another cup myself."

The room scrambled into action when the door swung closed.

"Is she not mad?" The newbie whispered to Vander as they stepped out of the room.

"She's a Rogue herself. We all know our abilities have a bit of trouble from time to time. If we do our work properly, she won't be mad. "I've got to go see if the steering wheel reappeared on my machine or not. Excuse me."

Vander weaved his way through the large vehicles again, he spotted another on fire in the distance, and he returned to his own charge. He found the steering wheel back in place and returned to work. He moved dirt for several hours before another *pop* issued through the vehicle and his seat vanished. Vander barely caught himself from being impaled on the seat pole. He considered stopping work again for another break but decided he could work without a chair.

He stood with an arched back in the cabin until a second *pop* caused the scoop to vanish. He couldn't work without one of the most important parts of the machine. Vander climbed down from the equipment and saw the sun approaching the mountain range on the west. Almost quitting time—a perfect opportunity to start a new day with a completely functional machine. He knocked on the outside of the other equipment he passed by to let the others know they could quit work.

The group of workers marched through the grounds to the outside where lines of housing waited for them. Those with families smiled when they saw their children playing in the street or their spouses greeting them at the door. Vander passed them all by to his smaller house for a singular individual. He never sought a spouse—he worried about passing on his terrible abilities to others. He wouldn't want them to be affected by the same fate, a hard life hiding from an entire government body.

Once inside, he fixed himself a microwave dinner and planned a long night of rest.

Screaming filled the room. Vander groaned and rolled over on his bed to try and go back to sleep. Some poor sap with nightmares again. Just as he drifted, he felt a growing heat outside the wall. A pounding on the door startled him, and he stumbled out of bed.

"They've set the place on fire!" a shout echoed down the street. The pounding on his door came again. "I guess they already left."

"I'm here," Vander called. "Still here. What fire?"

"The one consuming the entire area!" The mysterious person threw open the door. "Your house is about to catch next. Get out, quick!"

"Why is everything on fire?" Vander stumbled into his boots and out into the street in his pajamas.

"The humans found out we have a colony here—somebody slipped the information to one of the other cities. They came to kill us and get rid of the threat." They turned to the other houses. "Help get everyone out before all the houses catch."

Vander turned to the next house on the street and repeated the pattern. The whole work camp assembled in the main square and watched the flames grow higher. Shots rang out across the clearing. More screaming. The Rogues scattered like ants. Vander broke into a zigzag pattern, but a spray of bullets passed right by him, he realized it wouldn't help him with a large group of shooters. He grabbed the first person he saw as the next round blew past him and pushed them both to the ground. The stranger tried to fight against him for several moments.

"Pretend to be dead. Pretend like they got you. We'll have a higher chance of getting out alive," Vander whispered furiously.

His unwitting companion stilled almost immediately. They lay on the ground for what felt like an eternity while people ran around their bodies and more bullets sprayed across the burning houses. He watched the boots of one of the attackers stomp by as they continued their way down the long street looking for survivors.

Near morning, Vander pushed himself off the ground and dragged his companion with him. The newbie, he realized belatedly. They slid between the half-standing structures and behind the humans with guns. When they reached the edge of the mine, they ran for it—directly toward the Amazon.

"So much for it being a safe place," the newbie mumbled as they stumbled across the roots of the lungs of the earth.

Vander realized if they went on the run together, they would have a higher chance of surviving. First, he would need to stop calling the other "the newbie".

He held out a hand. "Vander da Silva."

"Abdiel Vicente Santamaria Quiroz." Abdiel shook his hand. "I want to work together to get out of this mess."

Vander climbed carefully over another root and became entangled in several vines on the other side.

"If you thought I would abandon you after you saved my life back there, that's where you went wrong. We're in this together—but not like in a weird way. It's just easier to survive when there's more than one person, right?"

"Do you babble often?" Vander reeled away from a large insect passing by. It looked completely unperturbed by the people traipsing through its territory.

"Mostly when I'm nervous," Abdiel laughed.

"Collect anything edible. I'll try to come up with a way for us to carry it."

"What if it turns out to not be edible?"

"You haven't foraged much in the area?" Vander checked under a log for mushrooms.

"The encampment had everything we needed." Abdiel turned a faint shade of pink and shrugged before staring at the ground. "I honestly didn't travel too far after I went on the run. I survived on the food I took with me then the boss brought me to work there."

Vander pulled free a rather large chunk of edible mushrooms before he turned back to his unwitting companion and sized him up. "You at least know fish are edible, right?"

Abdiel rolled his eyes. "Obviously."

"Good." He picked up a stick from off the ground which had a rather jagged edge from where it broke off a tree. "You can work on your fishing skills with this."

"There's not exactly a water source nearby?" He took the stick in hand.

"There are a couple smaller unnamed rivers on the way to the Coppename. We're not too far from one now as long as we keep heading east. It'll take us a few days to reach our destination, but we should make the journey relatively easy—if we can find something to store water in."

"Where will we go after Coppename?"

"If we keep heading east, it'll take us to Brokopondo which has denser civilizations around it. It really depends on where we want to go—where we think is safe for someone of our caliber." Vander slid a thumb under the waistband of his underwear to scratch an itch on his hip. "I don't know of any other colonies like ours."

"Do you think we're the only one?"

"Doubt it." Vander recognized one of the palms and immediately headed for it. Sure enough, when he peeled back the bark of the Chonta palm, he found a plentiful stock of chontacuro. "How good are you at climbing trees?"

"Why?" Abdiel eyed the larvae with disgust in his frown.

"This is a Chonta palm. There may be some chontaduros near the top of the tree which we can collect. It'd also be a good idea to collect some of the fronds. We can use it for a variety of purposes."

"And what are you going to do with those bugs?"

Vander's brow pinched together. "Cook them and eat them. They're chontacuro. They'll be good when cooked along with those chontaduros. It'll be like bacon with peaches. Delicious."

Abdiel shuddered and considered the length of the tree again.

"How are we going to cook these exactly?"

"I know how to start a fire. How to cook them—I'll figure something out." Vander collected leaves from a nearby plant and wove them into a sort of basket to store the larvae. He left no room for argument, and he heard the tell-tale sound of Abdiel's feet connecting with the trunk as he started the arduous and dangerous climb.

Finding another stick on the ground, Vander speared the chontacuro down the middle to create a kabob. He interspaced them with pieces of the mushroom. He moved away from the tree and into some of the thicker parts of the Amazon where the plants grew thicker. He found taro and yucca plants.

Vander collected as much as he could in his arms before returning to the foot of the Chonta palm where he spotted Abdiel high above picking fruit and placing it in a temporary shirt pouch to deliver it back to the ground as safely as possible. He took the time to collect some of the fallen palm fronds to create another basket for his new finds. When Abdiel returned to the ground, he placed the fruits in the basket with the other plants and steered clear of the larvae and mushrooms.

"I think we could make it to the stream before we get too hungry." He stared up at the patches of sky through the trees. The early morning light still filtered in different colors. Vander picked up the basket with the larvae. "It'll be better if we're near a water source before we cook as we'll need something to drink more than we need food."

Abdiel acquiesced without a fight, and they continued deeper into the rainforest. Along the way, Vander pointed out several plants they could use for various purposes. They picked several orchids which would add a nice taste of greens to whatever they decided to cook. They at least had variety in their food choices.

As they approached the small stream, Vander breathed a little easier at the growth of bamboo. He had no problem turning everything into a kabob but getting clean water would be a hassle without a proper container.

He set down his basket and waved his companion over to help him break down several stalks. He wanted containers for water as well as cookware—

but traversing with them would be a different story. Especially when they had no real tools.

"How do you know so much about survival?" Abdiel asked when Vander juggled the bamboo into place under his arms. He struggled to pick up the basket with the chontacuro, so Abdiel sacrificed his qualms and picked it up instead.

"Thanks. I survived for a quite a while on my own before finding the Rogue colony." He shrugged. "I'm also from here, well, not here, here, but Suriname. I grew up in Para, and I learned a lot about the basics of living off the land since we didn't live in the capital. When I had to make a run for it as a Rogue, I decided to return to my home country and just disappear into the Amazon. It worked really well, and I happened upon the colony during my trek. It was nice having a stable place to live instead of dealing with all the wildlife out here."

Abdiel considered what he said before inspecting the stream. "It's really muddy."

"Because the water is swift it churns up the bottom. If we move farther downstream, we can find a calmer place where the sediment rests and get cleaner water. We'll still need to boil it. No need to get sick just because we're living where few people dare go." Vander pointed him in the direction of downhill, and they followed the shallow water.

They eventually found a flat bit of land which had clearer water and a small place to set up a camp with some fallen logs. Vander set Abdiel to collect firewood while he found a rock to help break down the bamboo into usable containers. He had to keep them sealed properly for their use. Two were turned into cooking dishes with a hole in the middle between two of the natural seals, while another two had only a seal on the bottom. He wanted to keep the latter upright for the most part and use them to transport water. They would encounter another a stream a few hours after the current one, but they'd have no other water source until reaching the Coppename—which was a significant river with deep beds and swift water.

Vander lashed some of the longer sticks together to create a resting point for the bamboo well above the fire.

"This is really good," Abdiel said over dinner.

Vander grinned. "You had no faith when I started collecting the larvae."

"Absolutely none." He placed aside the large piece of bark they chose to use for a dish. "So, you said you grew up in Suriname?"

"Yeah, a bit more northeast from here. Where did you come from?"

"Panama," Abdiel said.

"That's a far cry from here working in the mines," Vander said.

Abdiel laughed. "I managed to catch a fishing charter along the coast, and it took me down here before they caught onto my Rogue status. Once they knew, I jumped ship and ran for it. I caught word of good work in the mines with the little English I know and headed out to the meeting point they described without an invite. Boss took pity on me."

"What's your special ability that causes trouble?"

While on the move, they didn't notice their "abnormality" as often as they did during work. Vander's reappeared with a vengeance during their sit down for dinner by "popping" the bamboo out from under the water they wanted to boil twice.

"It's not as obvious as yours." He shuffled his feet and stared at the ground. "I mean, I have some semblance of control over what I can do."

Abdiel reached down and lifted the chunk of bark again. He tossed it into the air, put out his hand, and it froze. As he twisted his hand right and left, the bark lifted higher or dropped lower following the natural pattern of gravity's pull but stuck in time controlled by Abdiel. After a few up and down rides, he released whatever hold he had on the object, and it fell.

"That's impressive," Vander grinned. "It might be less obvious, but it's really cool."

"I feel like I can teleport sometimes, too." Abdiel bounced in his seat encouraged by the compliment of his strange ability. "I mean, I can remember walking or running to wherever I needed to go, but the people around me are always in the same spot. They give me a weird look. I don't know if I imagine myself completing the action, or if I am just moving really fast."

"Like superspeed?" Vander stretched his legs out in front of him. "Can you show me?"

"I can try." Abdiel looked around the patch of trees. "If I need to get across the river, it could look like this."

He moved through the river, but Vander couldn't make out much of his movement. On the other side, he turned to face Vander whose mouth hung open.

Abdiel shrugged and returned in the same manner. "Like I said, I don't really get how I do it. I remember walking through the river."

"I believe you." He pointed to the wet bottoms of Abdiel's jeans. "There's no way you'd be soaked in water if you didn't walk through the river. It was like watching a blur of light move. You were faintly there, but I couldn't make you out until you stopped on the other side."

"I don't quite understand how I do it," Abdiel admitted as he sat down.

"No matter. We can use it to our advantage. I'm sure of it." He stared into the flames of the dying fire and grimaced when one of the logs popped out of existence. "I'll stay up for first watch tonight. I have to wait for the log to come back, so we can put out the fire properly."

Date Unknown
Raleigh Vallen Nature Preserve, Coppename, Sipaliwini, Suriname

The hike to Coppename took them nearly a week. It was made easier by Abdiel's strange control over his Rogue abilities. As they sat on the bank of the wider and less calm river eating their dinner, Abdiel finally broached the topic Vander thought about every night before he fell asleep.

"Do you think anyone else made it out alive?"

Vander set his makeshift dish to the side and focused on the river crashing over a large rock in the middle. "Alive? Yes. Still alive? Impossible to say."

"Were there others from here?"

"Oh yes, the majority of the camp, I'd say." Vander folded his arms and rubbed the skin, overtaken by a sudden chill. "I don't think most of them grew up near the Amazon, however. The more populous districts live where the forest is thinner. It's still a forest, but it's different from where we are now." He pointed to the thickness of the vegetation. "Survival is a lot easier to do when you have a companion as well."

"Where will we go now that we made it to the river?"

"That's the choice, isn't it?" Vander stood and walked over to the banks. His feet still bare from their fishing expedition, he stopped at the bank and watched the waves lap over his feet. "There are a lot of options for us."

He didn't quite know when their language changed to them as a team, a pair, but he liked how it sounded. Being with Abdiel made the sun a bit brighter underneath the forest canopy.

"Do you want to try and find another Rogue colony?" The rocks on the bank *clacked* under his feet as he joined Vander.

"Do you?"

He didn't receive a response. In his peripheral vision, he saw Abdiel staring across the river to the other side. With the width of the river, they had a great view of the sky which they usually only caught glimpses of. It felt nice to be in the sun's rays again.

"What if—" Abdiel's Adam's apple dipped down his throat, "we just started a life out here?"

"In the forest?" Vander raised his left eyebrow.

"Yeah," he said. "If this last week has proved anything, we can survive on our own. We could find a place near a water source and just live here where no one can find us."

"Surviving for a few days is different than making a life out here." Vander turned his attention to the ground. "There are certain parts of society we need."

"I'm not sure about that."

He looked up to find Abdiel watching him. "What do you mean?"

"We could hide out here. The elementalists would never find us."

"And when one of us gets really sick?" Vander shook his head. "If we were in a Rogue colony, we could at least get help. Out here, we're at the mercy of mother nature."

"Ah," Abdiel looked back to the river.

"We could move closer to other people but stay out on our own," Vander said.

Abdiel nodded. "That makes sense."

"So, do you want to go to Brokopondo? It's one of the more populated areas because of the lake. Otherwise, we can head north to smaller communities along the Coppename's edge."

"Brokopondo. It makes more sense to be near a large body of water," Abdiel said.

Vander turned and started walking up the embankment. "We'll head out at first light."

Date Unknown

Baikoetoe, Brokopondo District, Suriname

Their arrival in the city near the border of the two districts brought with it the news of the world at war with the elementalists. A few of the other Rogues from their encampment made their way to the same city, and they approached the newly arrived pair.

"There's a colony of Rogues living closer to the lake," one of the Rogues told them in Dutch.

Vander glanced uneasily at his companion. Abdiel blinked curiously, not understanding what they said. Vander asked, "Are they creating another work camp?"

The woman shook her head. "They're preparing for war. They intend to attack the elementalists, too."

Vander relayed the information in Sranan Tongo.

"Why? They want us dead. We should be hiding." Abdiel's brow creased in the middle.

She waved them closer to avoid being overhead and switched to the creole. "Rumor has it the Uns are staging a revolt or coup of some sort from inside the country. We're fighting for our liberty. No more unjust killing of our kind just because of our broken abilities. You want in?"

Vander stared into Abdiel's eyes. They communicated silently. Eventually, Vander said, "We don't know."

CHAPTER EIGHT

Libations

November 23, 2318

Inuvik, Northwest Territories, Canada

Months with no news plagued the elementalists. They grew restless staying in one area with no direction, but the humans made no moves to attack. They had nothing to defend against—nothing to offensively go after. Series hated every minute of it—especially considering she found herself stuck in the middle of a very awkward romantic situation which only worsened by the day. She begged for Slattery to move his armies against Inuvik despite the deep snow, so she'd have something to distract her from the two newest members of the Council.

"We're going sledding," Ethan announced over breakfast. "Do you want to join us?"

Series shook her head. "I have a few things I'm trying to accomplish on my own."

Kristen pulled her hand free from Ethan's under the table. "Are you trying to see more of the future?"

She nodded. "I haven't seen anything in months. It's like the cold is affecting my abilities, or something. I want to know what HISS is up to. It's strange we haven't heard anything after such fierce battles."

"Scarlet hasn't heard anything in China either. Last night, when I texted her, she said there's a lot of panic and blaming going around but nothing substantial to the war," Ethan said.

"All the more reason for me to try and see something. Our people are out here stagnant because of us."

"We'll leave you to it, then." Kristen stood. "If we can help you with anything, let us know."

"Of course, I will." Series tugged at the parka sleeves where they rode up and bore her skin to the cold air. She followed Kristen and Ethan, their hands brushed, before she split off toward her portion of the camp where she could find privacy in her tent.

The guard nodded briefly at her. She heard them whisper in the communicator about her location before the tent flap swung closed. She pulled off her gloves and a single layer of coat before moving farther into the tent. It wasn't so much a tent as it was a version of their Council rooms at home. Made from the same materials as the Lūcis Scūta, it kept the area well-protected and insulated. They merely covered it with fabric to give privacy. Series greatly appreciated it. She pulled the blankets from her bed and arranged them on the floor next to the heater in the middle.

She curled into the blankets and did her best to clear her mind. She needed to see something. She needed to help the Council. They needed to stop camping in the cold region of Inuvik.

She burrowed there for an hour slowly lulling to sleep. Frustrated, Series pushed the blankets away and stood up. She didn't want to sleep to see the visions, although she didn't have any of those either. She wanted to have control over them—to see as she wanted. She wanted to manipulate it to get the best information for their purposes. The blanket caught around her ankle as she stepped out from the cocoon, and she fell to the floor. Gasping in pain, Series rolled over only for her vision to blur before sharpening in on something which was not her ceiling.

She recognized the interconnecting supports of the underside of a wooden table. Series managed to enter another vision—but it always came at the cost of her own pain. She braced her feet against the table leg and pushed herself free of the small space when the voice above stopped her.

"We're building a facility to house the elementalists. Any we capture will need to be sent there when its fully operational."

"And how can we promise this facility will contain them?"

A clink of something set on the table. The occupants of the room laughed—but it wasn't friendly. Series sucked in a breath. She pushed off the leg and grasped the outer rim of the table. Just as she pulled herself up, the image changed, and she stood above a spiraling city. Sick from the sudden height, she stumbled back from the ledge. Except, nobody was at the top of the skyscraper with her.

Series pounded her fist against the concrete finish. She had her opportunity to hear something—to operate within the vision, but she couldn't hold onto it. She couldn't control it. She recognized the spire as the one on top of the Academy building. *Home.* Something would be happening there—if only she wasn't on the roof. Focusing, she stood and walked forward. Nothing changed. She had control to an extent, but something else held her there. Series stepped onto the ledge and felt the wind pull at her clothes. A shot echoed in the distance. She focused on the horizon. A cloud of smoke rose into the air. *Where is it?*

Series spun carefully on the ledge until she located the sun falling to the western horizon. Using it as a guide, she knew the smoke came from the south.

She only knew of one location which produced black smoke. "The industrial sector," she whispered. Still unsure of her control over the ability, she took a deep breath. "Take me there." Series closed her eyes. She stepped off the edge. She expected to fall. Her foot met something solid. She found herself in the middle of a burning building. *Not that close,* she thought. Series walked through the flames and into the street where elementalist people ran screaming. She weaved between them.

Lines of humans marched forward with their weapons pointed into the crowds. They fired again. Series watched the line at the back fall. Scott landed in front of the encroaching army. He swung his arms through the air, and a blast of wind lifted them off their feet and sent them flying.

"When is this?" Series whispered against the wind—and as if requested, she spotted a digital calendar through one of the open windows of the burning building, but she could only make out the year. 2319. "Too far. I need something sooner. What is Tyr doing now? Where do we need to fight?"

She pushed forward again. Water sprayed across her skin. The ground under her moved with the fierce wind and she recognized the railing and equipment of standing on a boat, a sealift, at sea. High waves and dark clouds obscured the horizon. She couldn't make out any nearby land.

"Supplies won't be coming till later this morning if they can make it in the weather." The wind whipped past her with the faint words of a crew member. Wrapped in wind breakers, they stood on the deck and squinted into the rain.

"Doubt they'll make it from Kiritimati in this weather! We'll have a day off today. Tomorrow, we'll work."

"But we still have to stand in this blasted rain until we get official word over the radio."

"But the radio is inside?"

The men paused for a long moment before heading toward the door to the main office. Series didn't blame them—there was no reason for them to stand in the rain. She kept her mind focused on the ship as she followed. There had to be something inside with a clue as to what Slattery planned. Spread across one of the tables inside were several sheets of paper, each one had different logistics to show a complex building. It looked like a cruise ship and a building at the same time. There were several long spar buoy's, labeled as approximately three hundred feet, attached to the underside of the ship on the drawings which indicated how they would keep the location mostly stable and resistant to wave motion. Series briefly wished she understood floor plans, so she could give her companions accurate information on her findings. Although, the plans gave no evidence the new building related to Slattery in the first place.

"Show me something useful," Series hissed. The ship heaved with the curl of a wave, and she slipped and rolled across the floor—except she kept rolling right down a hill into the mud.

She knew the location. The place with the mysterious man fighting Tyr—Scott wielding the nine elements. *Yes*, a grin spread across Series' face to match the thought. She could see more. She had no date—no timeline—but she knew the path. She would manipulate it. She could see something she wanted.

Series ran through the crowds of fighters and dodged weapons which passed through her if she tried to interfere. She spotted herself fighting with the ring of fortune spread wide around her. Someone went flying backward from the strength of the swing of her weapon, and she spotted a necklace around her neck glowing gold. It was tied unprofessionally with a simple leather cord to a mess of metal; one good blow would send it flying. She didn't own any jewelry like it.

Pushing forward, she recognized Scott again, but this time she noticed the same kind of necklace on him as well. It glowed white. Her brows pulled together further as she continued to the focus of the battle. The person battling Tyr. Series saw the back of the man and realized why she didn't recognize him before. Ethan changed substantially in the months since she first met him. He grew several inches, the tallest of all the men on the Council, and grew out his hair for his bun. Ethan would face Tyr.

A strong wind propelled her freewheeling into the sky, and she opened her eyes in the familiar tent. She pounded her fists and feet against the ground like a petulant toddler to exhaust some of the adrenaline from her system. When spent, her hands came up to cover her face. Series couldn't deny she learned a lot from her exploration, but most of the information felt completely useless. She would only bring the Council more questions she couldn't answer—which would provide no comfort.

Series sent the others a text with the main details. She would try for more the next day.

"So, I'm the one who has to face Tyr?" Ethan sat in one of the chairs in Kristen's tent. He leaned forward against his elbows on his knees, supported by his clasped hands.

Series nodded. "I'm sorry."

"There's no way to change what you see in the future?" Kristen sat next to him, tucked against his side in a way Series could only figure would make anyone uncomfortable. Holding hands would seem too *casual* for the situation. She disliked public displays of affection only when the people involved acted as if they would die of not touching. It made it hard to look in their direction.

"Even with warning, I've never heard of an alternative—there are no records of avoiding what is seen by anyone with my ability." Series leaned against the desk, although it acted like a vanity.

"¡Por el Amor de Dios!" Kristen's hands, trapped between her thighs, formed fists. "What will become of Ethan or Tyr at the end of this battle?"

"I wish I had an answer." Series crossed her arms.

"Then, go back into whatever state you have to be in and see what happens!"

"It's not as simple as that."

"¡Los cojones! You just don't want to because of what you might see." Kristen pushed herself away from Ethan.

Series was rather surprised to not find them glued together. She scowled. "I'd appreciate it if you didn't tell me how my own abilities work. I don't pretend to know how you look at the stars up close. I'm the most powerful Fortune elementalist in the country for a reason." She turned on her heel and marched out of the tent. She rather regretted leaving her coat behind, but she didn't want to turn around to go back for it either.

Instead, she jumped her way between tents, briefly startling the occupants by using their tent to warm up before making another short bid down the line.

Ethan met her at the line between Kristen's and his encampments. He held out her coat, and she put it on begrudgingly. "Sorry about Kristen."

"It's not you who should apologize," Series said.

"No, it's not." Ethan gestured for her to walk next to him. "I'm not afraid of facing Tyr—not if it's what you saw."

"But what I saw was incomplete. I don't know the outcome."

"We don't need to know the outcome." Ethan bumped her elbow with his. "I'm the Death elementalist—I'm practically immune."

Series frowned. "We already know Slattery is developing a weapon with the potential to work on you. If you're facing him, there's no way he's taking any chances. You have just as many chances as the rest of us to die in this war."

"What weapons do I face Slattery with?"

The banner bearing her elemental symbol rose in gold above the snow topped tents. She tried to recall the snippet. "I think you were dual wielding something, but I don't remember the specific weapon."

"I figure I should be fully decked out with whatever I can carry and comfortably use."

"Ethan—"

"You already said what you see is unavoidable. We have warning. I have time to train and prepare to meet him. There's nothing to worry about." He placed a hand on her shoulder which she could barely feel beneath all the padding of her coat.

"Are you sure?"

"Absolutely." He pulled away as they reached the line between her camp and his. "In fact, I'm going to thank you for the warning. We need all the help we can get in this war, and your power is undeniably the most useful." He winked. "Thank you, Series."

"Ethan—" she tried again.

"I know." The smile faded from his lips. "Go find something to entertain yourself with. I'll take care of Kristen."

"Entertain myself? Like I'm a child?" Series shook her head. "You don't need to tell me what to do with my time, Ethan."

"Sorry—force of habit with Lulu." He pulled at the bun he tied his hair in until it released into a ponytail.

"I've seen her hanging around you any chance she gets." Series kicked at the snow. She didn't want to say anything horrible about the teenager, but she wasn't on their level as Council members. Despite numerous reprimands, and the punishment for her display at the recruitment assembly, she still followed Ethan around like a puppy.

"She plays the part of an annoying little sister very well." Ethan looked around as if expecting her to be nearby. "I haven't seen her in years—I always thought about her, but it was more out of regret than anything else. I realize that now."

"But you can't tell her that."

"Certainly not," he said. "So, keep that quiet."

"I have no one to tell." Series rolled her eyes. "You need to be firm with Lulu," she paused, "and Kristen."

"Are you telling me to 'man up'?" Ethan narrowed his eyes at her.

"Never. I'm not that blasé." She grinned. "I'm just recommending you have more confidence and more force behind your meaning. Make what you want undeniably clear. She'll catch on."

"Right. Get used to the confrontation thing."

"You haven't had nearly as much practice as we have." She patted his arm. "You'll get used to it after a while. Granted, none of us ever really used our voice against Luana 'til Dwayne finally stepped up the pace."

Ethan didn't say anything, but he shook his hands. Series noticed he didn't have his gloves on.

"You'll freeze." She put a hand on his back and pushed him toward the heart of his encampment. "I'll go find something to *entertain* myself with."

He nodded. "I'll spend the next five minutes psyching myself up to speak with Kristen."

"At least do it inside your tent. I'd hate for you to lose your fingers in this cold."

"Sound advice," he tucked them into his pockets and winced as the cold ligaments tried to bend. "Good luck."

"You need it more than I do." She watched the small line of gold rush across the snow to Ethan. He looked considerably warmer when it touched him. "I always have luck on my side."

Series sat on the floor in her tent, again, with her head tipped back to stare at the ceiling. She chose to use the cloaking mechanism this time and watched the Arizona sky move at its own pace. The clouds drifted lazily over light blue, not a single care for the people below. She knew it would be warm. With the heater blaring next to her blanket cocoon, she could almost imagine herself there.

She wished she were there.

She saw the houses lining the paved road. They had no grass yards to take care of, and cars parked outside on any empty land they wanted. She could see the people sitting on their porches, some were crafting—it wasn't a daydream. She stood on the familiar street leading home. She knew the trees pressed close to houses as native to the land as her own people. The Joshua, Chinaberry, Desert Ironwood, and Emory Oak. She remembered sitting in their shade and playing in the dirt.

Series walked forward several steps toward the house she grew up in. The table where her mother made jewelry to sell at the Four Corners monument still stood on the porch. She could see the beads in a bowl. An unfinished project, attached to a needle and thread, waited for her return. A moment later, the front door opened, and a hand pushed at the screen.

Her father.

Still as handsome as she remembered, although, he had more gray strands in his braid. He said something to someone in the house which she didn't catch. She ran forward, eagerly climbing the steps to stand next to him. He was still taller than her, but she came up to his shoulder. In several ways, it felt like looking in a mirror. His nose had the same shape, and his eyes the same sadness—loneliness.

"Are you finishing this project?" he asked.

"Yes, I'll be out in a moment." Her mother.

Tears poured down Series' cheeks just to hear their voices. Her father continued down the porch steps and onto the main road. "I'll be down the road at Dextra's. She's hosting a board game night."

"Alright." Her mother stepped onto the porch, and Series' breath caught in her throat.

They were the same height, and if Series thought she could see herself in her father, it was almost tenfold in her mother. From the way she held herself to the way she walked across the porch, every bit felt like watching a doppelganger.

"I might join you a little later. It shouldn't take too long to finish this piece."

"Everyone will be excited if you come."

Her mother smiled a little sadly. "Yes, I'll bring something to snack on at the very least."

She sat at the folding table and picked up the project. Series stepped behind her mother to inspect it closer, and her hands flew to cover her mouth. It wasn't jewelry as she first assumed, instead it was an intricately carved and beaded headdress. It splayed out like the wings of a butterfly and had yet to be painted—she would recognize it anywhere.

"I don't think Series will return home to wear it," her father said standing just below the railing.

"I think she will." She smiled. "I know my daughter will participate in the butterfly dance."

Series breathed a momentary sigh of relief. She was not forgotten by her family—they didn't let her existence fade.

"Well, after all this work you put into it, I expect her to be the most beautiful," her father said.

"As if she could be anything less."

"Thank you," Series whispered.

The image faded, and Series found herself in her tent in Inuvik. She wiped the remaining tears from her cheeks on her comforter. It seemed as if thinking about where she wanted to be, really longing for it, gave her the most control over potentially seeing the future. She could use her longing. The thought struck her, *Maybe—because didn't I long to see Slattery before, and nothing happened?* There had to be something else triggering what she could see.

"I want to see where I am now. What will occur here?" She closed her eyes and repeated the mantra. When she opened them again, it didn't work. She bit her lip and stood.

A walk in the cold air would release tension at the very least. She felt stalled staying in Inuvik. She pulled on her winter items before pushing out of the tent, but she wasn't met with the tranquil quiet of fresh snow—the people around her ran in a panic. It was still dark, but the light meant little in the far north.

"What happened?" she called desperately, but no one would stop to answer her. She reached out for the arm of one of the elementalists who normally stood guard at her tent, but her hand passed through the woman.

"The Council members are already on the hill. Get everything distributed as quickly as possible. They're waiting to give orders on the situation."

"Yes, ma'am." The soldier saluted before turning away to relay the message. Bundled in her coat when she didn't need to be, she waddled her way through the snow following the crowd of people who had their weapons ready.

Series, Ethan, and Kristen stood on the crest of the snowy ridge and faced northwest toward the Happy Valley Territorial Park. They wore their thick winter uniforms, and, when she crossed in front to see their faces, she recognized the annoyed scowls of someone who didn't want the truth to be their reality.

"I can't believe he dared to send his armies this far north." Kristen folded her arms.

"The infallibility of the human race." Ethan crouched in the snow. "How many do you think I can take out before they realize what's happened?"

"From here?" Series' eyebrow quirked.

"Nah. When we get down there."

Somebody check the date. Somebody tell me when this is. Series begged silently. She knew how important it was to know information—her future self would, too. Sure enough, she pulled out her phone and pressed the button to check for notifications. *December 3* displayed under the clock. She jumped up and down with increasingly higher hopes of having something useful in one of her visions. She forgot their brutal nature. They liked to play tricks with her because in the next second, she missed what Kristen told Ethan, and her feet slipped in the snow. Series closed her eyes as she slid down the mountain.

She felt a cold floor under her fingertips and opened them to find herself sitting in a pristine facility. It resembled a cross between a prison and a hospital, a bit like the asylums they only had photo evidence of. The walls were made of heavy steel and painted a clean white. The floor vibrated under her feet, and she couldn't figure out why until she looked through the porthole windows and saw a roiling ocean outside. She could be almost anywhere in the world at sea.

She recognized Tyr standing in the main atrium. The doors had scanners for authorized personnel to pass through. Several guards held ten people in cuffs. She recognized the build design as their power suppressing ones. Each "arrested" person kneeled on the floor and stared down—except one.

She had dark brown hair and big brown eyes like Scarlet. She kept them trained on the people in the room, but she tilted her head every so often as if trying to see the person speaking.

"You let the others slip through your fingers?" Slattery vociferated at one of the military personnel.

"It was not intentional—we were binding the captives, and they broke free."

"And every single one escaped?"

"No, sir," he pointed to the girl watching them. "She stayed behind when the others ran."

Tyr settled his gaze on the small teenager. She stared back without flinching, her gaze curious. "Why didn't she run?"

"I don't know, sir."

"What's your name?" Tyr asked.

She shook her head but made no verbal reply.

"She might not speak English, sir. We captured her in Singapore."

"Never mind. Take them into the facility for testing. The Ls won't know what's coming to them." Tyr grinned.

Series' brow furrowed. His words could mean almost anything, but she had a bad feeling about the "capture." One of the guards opened the side door. She expected to see a hallway or more of the facility. Instead, a bright flash of light nearly blinded her. Series screwed her eyes shut. When she opened them again, the sun sunk low over the mountains. A guard stood to her right and left. The same tent entrance she walked out before but no panic. Inuvik. The snow sparkled orange and pink in the early afternoon sunset.

"Are you alright, Kikmongwi Pahona?" Her secretary of the army, Gloria, held out a hand to steady her swaying.

"Yes, thank you." She tried to give Gloria a reassuring smile, but Gloria still looked concerned. Series continued, "I'm heading into the other regions to discuss matters with the Council. Please send a messenger to me if there's an emergency."

"Of course." Gloria nodded.

She walked carefully across the snow and only slid a couple times before she found herself outside Ethan's tent. The guards shuffled their feet at her approach. She raised an enquiring eyebrow, but they frowned and looked away from her. Feeling uncomfortable with the treatment, she stopped. They didn't say anything, so she pushed through the tent entrance.

She wished they would've warned her.

Ethan and Kristen stood in the middle of the tent, almost glued together. Series watched one of Ethan's hands slide along Kristen's back and into her hair. Series couldn't quite see their faces, but she knew.

Series cleared her throat, tried not to retch, and averted her eyes. "My apologies for the intrusion, I wasn't informed you were otherwise occupied."

They broke apart, but Kristen didn't move away from Ethan. She stayed attached to his side despite the uncomfortable expression on his face.

Ethan said, "I'll better inform the Field Marshals in the future."

"I'd appreciate that." She focused on a spot between them on the wall. "I have some information to share with the Council. I thought it would be better to have us all meet in the same room."

"Right," Ethan stepped away from Kristen, and a flicker of annoyance crossed her features. "I'll put in the call for everyone to meet."

"What exactly is so important to report? Something else about Ethan fighting Slattery?" Kristen spat.

Series' brow pinched together in annoyance. "I'd prefer to tell the Council all at once."

"Kristen, I already discussed this with you. Please don't antagonize the person who has the best access to what HISS is doing." Ethan sighed. "Series, half the Council is probably still sleeping at this time."

"Push the notification, it's important."

He nodded and sent the call.

They each took their places on the projection pads—Kristen still scowling. Scott and Eilene joined almost immediately holding plates of food.

"Caught us during dinner," Eilene said.

"It's okay, we're calling at like three in the morning for Hans," Ethan laughed.

Eilene crinkled her nose. "Ew. Scott, pass the ketchup."

Dwayne flickered into his space. He looked completely alert for the four o'clock wake-up call. "Mulan will be on soon. She's still waking up."

"Why are you so chipper?"

"Well, Dickens, I never went to sleep last night. This is pure adrenaline."

"Pure adrenaline is right." Scarlet appeared in her pajamas with a yawn. "You need to sleep."

"I'm fine."

"Thirty-six hours without sleep is not 'fine'," Scarlet mocked.

"You haven't slept for three days?" Eilene nearly dropped her plate.

"Only two nights—been a bit busy with some underground stuff. We don't have enough information to report on it yet." He shrugged.

"Dwayne, you need to sleep." Eilene's brows pinched together. Her face flooded with concern.

"I promise I will sleep after this meeting, and if another one is called, then Mulan can fill me in. I'll sleep through the whole thing." He held up a hand imitating an oath.

She frowned.

"It is *three* in the morning," Luana hissed as she joined the call.

"I'm sorry, it couldn't wait." Series chewed her tongue.

"Hans is putting on clothes, he'll be with us in a moment." Luana immediately sobered from her sleep—on full alert.

"Oh?" Dwayne quirked an eyebrow in the air. "Solo was naked? With you?"

Luana rolled her eyes and opened her mouth to respond when Hans joined the call himself. A scowl set deep in his features.

"I sleep without a shirt. The old Council rules don't really apply anymore."

"Hey, I'm not asking for the details." Dwayne put up his hands in surrender.

"Ignore him, he's not had any sleep in a while and is going loopy." Scarlet shot a glare at her companion.

Scott looked as if he had an epiphany, and when Series raised an eyebrow in his direction, he shook his head.

"Right, so, I called you all because I have important information." Series clasped her hands behind her back. "I started having visions again after being blocked. There's going to be battle here in Inuvik on December third. I only saw the three of us, so I'm assuming nobody else planned to fight—but being prepared in case we are overwhelmed is a good idea."

Luana nodded and made a note on her phone.

"Of course, that isn't the only thing—otherwise I would've texted. I think HISS is building an elementalist testing center."

"What?" Eilene dropped her plate. Luckily, it was empty.

"Last time, when I texted you, I omitted that I was on a ship somewhere near Kiritimati because I couldn't connect it back to HISS. It made no sense until just a little while ago. In the first vision, I saw a construction project planned that was like a cruise ship crossed with a regular building. It had those spar buoy's that allow the ship to remain stationary, for the most part. This time, I was on the finished construction project." She took a deep breath, but no one interrupted. "Tyr was in this main entryway with a bunch of guards. They had people there in handcuffs resembling the power-suppressing ones we use. I think they were elementalists. They said one of them was found in Singapore—"

"Singapore?" Dwayne's eyes darted to Scarlet.

Series nodded. "Yes, but there wasn't much else to go on. Tyr told the guards to take them into the testing center, and we would have no idea what's coming."

"They've been clearing districts here in China and putting known elementalists into ghettos." Scarlet confirmed. "If they're rounding people up, it could be for this testing center. Having elementalists already in groups would make it easier to transport them."

"We haven't heard or seen anything like that here," Scott said.

"Nothing," Hans said. Ethan shook his head as well.

"Well, I think we need to move against these ghettos as they pop up." Luana massaged her fingers in her other hand. "Anytime we hear about them, we send our military out to intercept it. The more people we can get safely back home the less HISS will be able to *test* on." She spit the last few words. "We obviously won't be able to intercept him fully, but we know there's something near Kiritimati. Hans and I may be able to relocate."

"Kiritimati is too small. It won't be able to sustain your branches." Dwayne had the statistics on the country pulled up on his phone.

"If it is something like a ship, then they're most likely going to travel." Scarlet pressed a hand to her lips. "They are probably using Kiritimati as a shipment port—a place to bring the materials. Once they're at sea, they'll be near impossible to find."

"So, our focus should be on land. We know he's going to get a few of our people, but we can't possibly protect everyone. We know countries are starting to form ghettos. It might be a good idea to split our forces further, get units in every country to keep an eye out and run rescue operations where we can." Hans grabbed a tablet and a stylus and wrote notes on it.

Series received a notification on her phone saying a new file was added to their shared drive.

"I think this meeting is about to go a few hours." Dwayne pulled a chair into his area.

"We should get breakfast." Scarlet agreed. "Give me like fifteen minutes? We're still on our solo stuff, and I have no one to order around."

"Yes, yes, let's all take a break to get things in order. Grab whatever you might need." Luana vanished.

"Dwayne, take a power nap," Eilene said.

"Nope, that'll kill me at this point. I promise to sleep for like twelve hours after this meeting is over." He turned his head as Scarlet said something behind him. "Mulan promised to drug me if necessary."

Eilene laughed.

Scott touched her arm. "I'm going to send for some snacks."

"Thanks."

"We should do the same." Series headed for the tent door. Except, it opened long before she got there.

"Ethan?" A brunette head appeared in the doorway—Lulu.

Ethan shuffled his feet. When he swallowed, they watched the bob of his Adam's apple. "Ah—Lulu. I'll be right back."

Series grabbed his wrist just as he waved for Lulu to go back outside. "Be gentle. She is only fourteen."

"I know," he squeezed her fingers before disappearing.

She shifted to Kristen. "I'll be back with snacks."

Kristen nodded tersely in reply.

"You know, I don't mind joking about relationship drama, but watching it in person is so much worse." Dwayne's voice faded as Series left the tent.

"I can't agree more," she mumbled. Gloria glanced at her before realizing Series hadn't addressed her.

"Okay, final plans one more time," Eilene said four hours later.

"Each of us are going to go through and find at least twenty-five units we can send to other places in the world to get recon on where more of the 'ghettos' are cropping up. Then they'll need to plan extraction missions to get our people back home where we'll deploy at least one other unit per region back home where they will focus on helping them adjust to life in

Elementōrum Patriam." Luana rattled off the first part of the plan.

"However, our units are temporarily suspended from the order until the battle with the humans starting on December third is over." Ethan rubbed his right eye before massaging his temple. "Dinner is coming to us, right?"

Kristen gave a soft verbal confirmation.

Scott took over the next part. "Until further notice, the rest of our units are to remain where they are. Dwayne and Scarlet will continue working undercover in Kaifeng searching for ghettos and digging for other information—Singapore is just a bit far away to hear anything on the one known person from Series' vision."

"Singapore will be a priority for getting spies," Scarlet paused, "I want to suggest again that we speak with our people and ask if anyone would be willing to be captured."

"And how will they get us a message from out at sea?" Luana pulled her hair from her ponytail and the messy strands fell into her eyes. She attempted to blow them away with puffs of air before pushing them back with her chapped fingers. "It would be useful to know what Slattery is doing in the facility, but we don't know what experiments they'll run. I don't want to risk their lives."

"But the lives of our people are already at stake—many of them are going to be captured whether we like it or not." Ethan's voice cracked with emotion. "If we had someone on the inside, someone who could control Water or Air, it might just give us the advantage we need. They could find a way to escape and give us a report in person."

Eilene raised her hand. "I could—"

"No," Scott said at the same time as Dwayne's emphatic:

"Absolutely not."

"It would be a better solution than sending in one of our own people." Eilene frowned.

"And it would put you at risk of being severely damaged, Dickens. We're not sending in anyone on purpose—no matter the advantage it would give." Dwayne glared at the other Council members, and they nodded in acceptance of the ruling.

"Right, so, back to the last thing." Series cleared her throat. She hadn't shared the vision of her parents with the Council. "Ethan will be the one to face Slattery, but I know it won't be the upcoming battle."

"Why not?" Ethan asked. "I was getting prepared."

"Still a good idea to be prepared," she placated, "but the version of you I saw was fighting Slattery in the pouring rain on a muddy hill." Series gestured outside. "That is the exact opposite of what's outside right now. I'd be surprised if we manage to dig up any mud under this depth of snow."

"I'd take that as a challenge." Dwayne tried to lighten the mood. "See how much mud you can dig up when you fight."

"We'll prepare for battle. Everyone close by will be on call—and then we'll go from there." Kristen stood from her seat to stretch. "That was everything, wasn't it?"

Luana nodded stiffly and reached up to massage her own neck. "I think we should all get some rest."

"I already drugged Dwayne about twenty minutes ago." Scarlet winked at Eilene.

"I thought my water tasted funny," Dwayne yawned. "Alright, I'm going to collapse in bed. If there's an emergency, wake me."

Both logged off.

"Series, if you see anything else—"

She cut Luana off, "I'll inform everyone immediately."

She nodded before logging off with Hans.

"Promise you'll all be safe during the battle?" Eilene's hand hovered over the disconnect button.

"It's a war, Eilene. None of us can promise that. We will fight our hardest." Ethan smiled weakly.

"Have a good night," Series said.

December 3, 2318

Over the dark hills, Series watched the headlamps of their military forces dance across the snow like their own personal sky. The Aurora Borealis faded out of view in the early hours of the morning. The sun would appear for maybe an hour and a half. The elementalists paced with anticipation as they waited for the call. Training amped up since they had warning, and it set everyone on edge.

She bundled into her warmest clothing and left the tent. She would wait on the crest of the hill until the time came to notify her troops. Series told one of the Field Marshals to send someone with supplies to light a fire where she would wait, and they hurried off to do her bidding. She walked through the camp with all eyes on her. She kept her posture straight and tried not to shrink away. In a way, she hated not wearing the Council robe. It provided a lot of privacy.

Series sat in the snow when she reached the northwest point. A few minutes later someone showed up and helped build a fire.

"Thank you," Series told them.

They nodded before walking back up the hill. She sat alone watching the town lights twinkle. A few vehicles passed by on the road winking their lights through the fog settling into the valley.

"How long do you think we'll have to wait?" Ethan appeared next to her.

"I honestly don't remember the time on the display."

He laughed. "I think we all have to check our phones about seven times before we really process the time when we look for it."

He joined her on the ground, and they sat in the quiet air watching new flakes of snow drift lazily from the sky.

"Kristen doesn't believe we're really going to be at war today."

Series pushed her gloved fingers into the snow. "She doesn't trust me."

"No, I'm sorry." He sucked on his teeth. "I tried talking to her. I told her what you saw before, and it was true. She won't listen."

"Thanks for trying."

"I think she just doesn't want to accept I have to face Tyr—but it makes the most sense. I'm the only one who stands a chance."

She nodded stiffly.

He nudged her with his elbow. "If you had to take a guess, when do you think they would attack?"

"It would make the most sense to attack in the dark, because it would be harder to see them coming." She pointed to the base of the ridge. "I mean, most of that is probably trees, but even now I can't be certain."

"Okay, so logic would dictate almost any time during the day."

She laughed. "However, they're humans, and their eyesight, frankly, isn't as good as ours. My guess is for the limited daylight we have—just so they know where we are. After that, I'll bet they're more strategic."

"Dare to put money on it?" Ethan pulled his legs up against his chest.

"Not when our people's lives are on the line."

"Fair enough."

While they waited for anything to happen, they ended up in a snowball fight, played several rounds of eye spy and twenty questions, and debated over how many variations of rock, paper, scissors could be considered acceptable. Kristen joined them just after noon carrying plates of food.

"Nothing yet?" She smirked at Series.

"Not yet—but they'll come."

"How can you be so sure?" Kristen asked.

Series narrowed her eyes. "That's kind of the entire point of my element. I'm not there just as a luck boost."

Kristen didn't reply and crossed her arms. She stared out across the horizon blurred by snow. They couldn't even make out the rivers and lakes pockmarking the landscape.

Ethan and Series stood to stretch and walk around just as the sun crested over the horizon and brought their moment of daylight. There, in the late dawn, as they faced the Happy Valley Territorial Park from the ridge, she spotted the army gathering in the lower town.

"There they are," Series breathed.

"I'm sending the call." Ethan grabbed his phone and triggered the alert.

They watched the enemy army march through the deep snow.

"I can't believe he dared to send his armies this far north," Kristen said.

"The infallibility of the human race." Ethan crouched in the snow. "How many do you think I can take out before they realize what happened?"

"From here?" Series' eyebrow quirked.

"Nah. When we get down there."

A smile crept onto her face, and just to be sure, she reached into her pocket for her phone. She pushed the button to trigger the home screen and saw the familiar clock staring up at her just as her vision promised. Word for word. Moment for moment.

"How do you want to get down the ridge?" Ethan looked for a safe place to climb down.

"Wouldn't it be better to wait and see if they come to us?" Kristen suggested.

"We could invade from the south through the solid waste site. Won't smell pretty, but we'll have the ridge as protection." Series pointed toward the snowy road.

"I like that idea. Safest way down." Ethan turned to find several units already behind them and waiting for orders. He nodded to them. "Let's head out."

They slipped their way down the ridgeline until they met the road into the main town. As they neared the buried golf course, they saw the human forces sliding their own way down the Marine Bypass Road. HISS saw them coming.

Series reached out and touched Ethan and Kristen on the shoulder. Good fortune swept across them like a warm flame, and they proudly raised their weapons before initiating a run through the snow. It wasn't ideal, and many of their own fell face first into frozen piles. Life elementalists stopped to help the more damaged members while the others struggled onward and slid across ice.

Series couldn't keep up, but she could see the black tendrils of smoke extending from Ethan as their front line met the human's. The line fell, but everyone pushed on. A bullet passed through Ethan's head and *pinged* off the Lūcis Scūta of one of the ranged fighters.

Series checked to make sure the bracelets of her own shields rested on her wrists before reaching for the weapons on her belt. She was a close-range fighter typically but had no chance to get close to the army, not with Ethan tearing up the field. She kept running with the handle of her Lūcis Jacula clutched tightly in her left hand.

As she neared the edge of the front lines, where several humans ganged up on elementalists to bring them down, she activated the weapon and swung it through the air. Unlike a real javelin, its shaft was fully made of deadly plasma light which meant any part of it could pass through the victim at any angle—the name was more of a description of the look than its purpose.

Series swung the weapon around one-handed, a bit like a baton, and the shaft passed through one of the humans. She watched as shock overtook his features just before he slid to the ground in two pieces. Blood spilled across the snow and melted patches under the stains. The companion flanking one of her own turned to Series, but she repeated the same slashing movement before they had an opportunity.

Nose nipped by the cold run, she sniffled and looked for her next victims. Series watched a group try to flee in a pack only to be chased by the dark tendrils of smoke billowing from Ethan. They fell as they ran with panic etched in their death masks.

"Use your abilities! Drive them off!" Series' voice was hoarse over the wind, but the shout repeated across the armies. She pushed forward alongside her people and fought her way to Ethan's side.

His cheeks were stained red from the cold, and his coat was torn open. On her approach, he said, "Something's wrong."

"What do you mean?" Series swung her weapon forward as a human tried to rush Ethan. It caught his free hand on the back swing, and he hissed in pain.

The back was open and bleeding. "That's what's wrong."

Series stared at the wound with wide eyes and missed the soldier running up behind her with his own plasma weapon. Ethan grabbed her arm and pulled her out of the way. She fell into the snow, and Ethan parried just in time by raising his Lūcis Scūta. Series dropped her Lūcis Jacula on the impact, and she lost the handle base in the snow. Instead, she reached to her belt and pulled free the Lūcis Fucsinae. She speared the soldier across the triple point like a fish.

"You alright?" Ethan's element withdrew from the battlefield.

"I should be asking you." She searched the snow for the shaft of her preferred weapon.

"I think it's the cold." Ethan sniffled as his nose ran. "You know, extreme scenarios, and all of that. I could use my ability up until a certain point, but now the cold is taking over."

"Like when we had you in the prison cell."

He nodded stiffly. "Extreme points are the only way to take me down."

She watched as a water elementalist stepped forward and pushed water from the snow into the air where it froze several humans in their tracks. Other water elementalists joined in, and soon soldiers were frozen in place all over the open area like grotesque statues. The handful remaining dropped their weapons and held their arms in surrender.

Ethan frowned. "That was more anticlimactic than I expected."

"Yeah," Series said still staring at Ethan's injured hand. "We should get you to the medical tent."

"It's not a deep cut," he said. "We need to focus on the more important things right now. Those who surrendered and the wounded."

Series nodded, and the pair headed toward the bulk of activity to organize operations.

"This feels inhumane." Kristen joined them as they walked around the field. She stared at one of the frozen humans, their mouth frozen open in pain, and their eyes stared unblinking at the sky.

"It's only a small part of the difference between us and them." Series shrugged. "We were told to use our abilities in this war. It may be the only way to get the point across that they can't get rid of us."

"Still—" Kristen turned away from the encapsulated body. "What else needs to be done?"

December 5, 2318

Their victory in Inuvik plastered across the headlines of almost every single news site, each with varying takes on the outcome of the battle.

ELEMENTALISTS SLAUGHTER FORCES IN FROZEN TUNDRA

ARMIES FROZEN AND IRRECOVERABLE IN INUVIK

ELEMENTALIST FORCES RAGE AGAINST TRUTH AND FREEZE BRAVE WARRIORS

HUMAN FORCES FALL IN UNPRECEDENTED ATTACKS FROM ELEMENTALISTS

Only a few variations of the same headlines dominated the human papers, but in Elementōrum Patriam, the win was quite celebrated. Praise came in from almost every corner for their handling of the battle. The elementalist people were proud to show off the extent of their power and laud it over the humans seeking to destroy them. It spread hope even among their own army who grew weary of the cold.

Series' phone rang as she reclined against the bed. It startled her amid her doom scrolling, and she dropped it onto her chest with a hollow *thud*. She quickly picked the screen up and answered the call flashing Luana's name and blaring her ring tone.

"What's up?"

"We're relocating your regions."

Series smiled, and her laugh bled into her next words, "Is this because we froze all those humans? Because, you know we still don't have cryogenic technology."

A small huff of breath from the other side of the phone indicated Luana found it funny, but her tone was still businesslike when she said, "No. You've had a victory there. I don't think HISS will be keen to send more of his armies to Inuvik this time of year. I need you to prepare the Uns for deployment."

"Oh?" She sat a little straighter. "They finally completed their training?"

"Just about. I want you to help refine them for at least another month. If you're willing."

"Yeah, I can do that. Where are we going to be?"

"That's the thing," Luana paused, and she could hear the shuffling of the phone as she put it on speaker. "I've got Hans with me, and we were thinking of splitting up your region. We can put you and a bunch of your units back in Elementōrum Patriam to help in case the Un situation worsens while taking the smaller units and creating more of a global spread to get more info on where those ghettos are cropping up."

"Sounds great."

A smile eased into Luana's voice. "Great, because I want the spies ready to go for the next attack. They weren't ready for this one, though admittedly, it wouldn't be the best time to get them to infiltrate another army."

Series nodded although Luana couldn't see her. "There were too few survivors, it would be more noticeable."

"And we need to get them appropriate documentation." A tapping audible from the other line.

"Where will Ethan and Kristen be sent?"

"Somewhere warmer," her voice hesitated over the syllables like she didn't want to admit it.

"Anywhere is warmer than here. I'm not going be jealous—I was just curious."

"They'll be moving frequently with smaller groups through the different harbor cities and the first cities founded by the Nine." Hans' voice filtered over the call from a distance. "We'll split up their regions as well."

"I'll be glad to be back home, personally." Series stretched one arm over her head. "Send me the details, and I'll start sending my units on their way."

"Thanks, Series. We appreciate what you do for us." Luana turned off speaker.

"You'd be lost without me." Series grinned and pressed the "end call" button. She would be going home.

CHAPTER NINE

Prayer

December 6, 2318

Xiaoqiao Residential District, Chuanhui District, Zhoukou, Henan, People's Republic of China

"Have they taken all the elementalists?" a voice whispered to one of the street venders.

"There are more in the neighborhood over. I heard they're moving them into the ghettos tomorrow once enough rooms are available. They had to expand—more humans are evacuating their homes every day to give to the Republic, but they need time to pack," the vender said just as softly if not more so.

Scarlet adjusted the strap of her backpack as she inspected the vegetables on display at one of the stands. She needed to visit the wet market to get more supplies (and information) for her and Dwayne, or Nuò as he went by in Mandarin. It worked well for their cover in China. They hadn't seen anyone from their regions in months as they moved underground. They were in contact, but they had to be careful about it. Their military presence in Kaifeng painted a large target against them, but the country did little about it since the city had laws in place to protect the elementalist people. Everywhere else, not just in China, the military noticed similar behaviors as elementalist people either fled to Elementōrum Patriam or found themselves rounded up in various "ghettos".

Scarlet tapped her phone against the automated pillar at the shop and confirmed the money transfer. The owner smiled at her before Scarlet stepped to the side to put the vegetables safely into the backpack. It afforded her a few precious moments closer to the *gossip*.

"Where are they sending the monsters?"

Scarlet pulled a face at the question but covered it by clipping her bag closed again and pretending as if it pinched her finger.

"The Renhe Residential District—by the river. I saw them putting up fences a couple days ago."

"Where are the people who used to live there being moved to?"

"The capital, last I heard."

Scarlet swung her hair over her shoulder and spotted a popular vender near one of the building supports where it would be more protected from the weather. Inside the artificial warmer hung several cooked ducks. *Nuò would like one of those*, Scarlet thought. Since returning to China, she felt less isolated. Her thoughts and speaking reflected her mother language.

She joined the line of people waiting for their request, and she noticed a secondary vender selling various pickled items and some sweet pink rice pudding. When her turn at the counter came, she requested some pickled items and the duck; she couldn't buy the pudding due to the rice wine in the recipe. The alcohol wasn't cooked out, and she didn't fancy dying.

"Má fan nǐ le," she said as she took the bag of items from the owner. Scarlet felt bad for causing trouble with the inquiries about the rice pudding. It did look delicious. She worried her refusal of the item might tip them off to her status as an elementalist, but they were already onto the next customer and didn't appear worried.

She spotted Dwayne above the heads of the crowd waiting on a street corner for her to finish the shopping. She did a much better job getting everything they needed. Weaving her way with the sack still in her hand, Scarlet tapped him on the shoulder to get his attention.

"For you." She handed him the bag.

"Xièxiè nǐ," Dwayne said.

"I have something important to tell you back home."

His gaze wandered over the crowd, never settling on anyone long enough to remember their faces. He scanned the people closest to them and imitated their shopping behavior. The hairs on his arms rose, and Dwayne surreptitiously looked over his shoulder.

"We're being watched," he whispered into Scarlet's ear.

A stone sunk in her stomach, and she curled her toes. They would have to move on sooner than later—choose another location to dig for information. Maybe move closer to her old home.

Dwayne took her hand protectively on their short walk to the apartment they rented short-term. When the door closed behind them, Dwayne switched to English without a single thought. "The duck looks delicious."

"I thought you might like it—I know it's not the same as they make in Botswana."

"That doesn't matter. I like duck just about any way it's prepared." Dwayne grinned. "So, what did you need to tell me?"

Scarlet watched him place the pickled items in the fridge. "There's ghettos nearby."

He shut the door quietly as his familiar smile faded into a frown. An all-too-common expression since the start of the war. "Our people?"

She nodded.

Dwayne pulled his phone from his pocket as he set the container of duck on the low table. He typed out a message before asking for the location. "They'll be mobilized within a couple days."

"We'll need to move before then." Scarlet moved into the kitchen to unload the other items from her backpack. "We're already suspected."

"Yes," he took a bite of the still warm lunch, "I did hear something today in passing. It was down a highly populated alley. I'm pretty sure they assumed I couldn't understand them, but they still spoke in whispers."

"About?" She grabbed a knife from the block and chopped the white radish.

"There's ties to the underground here."

Scarlet hesitated as she pulled a box of broth from the cupboard. She didn't often make her own out of convenience; it was never as good as her childhood memories. "Here?"

"There are people hiding elementalists and helping them escape the country before they can be put into the ghettos. I heard a whisper about Slattery planning to do something with the captured elementalists, but I don't think anyone really knows."

"But they're risking their lives to run this underground."

Dwayne nodded. "There's always good people willing to help out during times like this."

"Can we trace it?"

"Possibly." He pushed the container away to bring out a computer system. "I think we may be able to get ourselves into it."

"Which would be better." Scarlet dropped the radish into the boiling broth. "What do we need to get into it?"

"That may require more work." Dwayne pulled up the web browser. "Especially if we're moving, we'll need to find the network running through that area."

"I want to move closer to Jingzhou." She leaned against the counter and stared at the floor, but she sensed his halted movements.

Scarlet counted every breath—time stopped moving—her heart raced; she knew only about a minute passed by the clock on the stove.

"You know why we can't," he said.

Her eyes traced the pattern of linoleum under her feet. "I know they're probably being watched, but we don't have to meet them."

"Scarlet—"

"Never mind—I know." She bit her lip and returned to her soup boiling softly on the stove. "Rather than moving, I think we should get into the underground. Let them move us around, so we can see what's going on."

"I agree, but not here. The ghettos are too close of a threat." Dwayne shook his leg under the table. "I'm thinking we should be a little more blasé with our powers when we move. Get their attention. Make it seem like we're messing up."

"We might draw the enemy to us as well."

Dwayne cleared his throat and leaned against his palms on the floor. "I think that's a hazard of any plan we come up with. There wouldn't be an underground if humans weren't trying to hide people like us from the ghettos in the first place."

"So." Scarlet's feet padded against the floor. She tucked herself under the table across from him. She opened her tablet and the maps app. "Where are we moving to?"

"Somewhere without ghetto activity. While they may be working in tandem, it'll be safer for us to dig around."

They sat in relative silence, searching the web. Dwayne scrolled through an online forum for information about the ghettos. He didn't notice Scarlet turn off the stove and collect a bowl of soup. Her feet brushed his under the table, and he playfully kicked her as he closed the tab to look at a different one.

"Hubei," Dwayne said.

"What?" Scarlet looked up from her doodles on the tablet page.

"We'll be in Hubei—not Jingzhou, but we'll be there. I'm narrowing down what neighborhood we should be in."

"You're serious." She blinked several times.

"Yeah—I mean, Hubei is literally the province south of here. It'll be a little closer to home without giving away our cover."

Scarlet scurried around the table as fast as she could on all fours. She threw her arms around Dwayne in a tight hug.

"Thank you." She pulled away quickly from the show of familial intimacy. "Seriously, thank you."

"We're not going to be near Jingzhou, Scarlet—you're not going to see your family."

She pulled away and pressed a single hand, balled into a fist, against her lips. "I know—I swear I know that. I'm just happy to be in the same province."

"Your family could've moved in the last—how many years?" Dwayne returned to leaning on his palms.

Scarlet shook her head. "They haven't." Her cheeks flooded with color when he raised an eyebrow. "I've checked every once in a while through the official channels. Never more than their registered address."

"You're scared of what you might learn." Dwayne crossed his hands.

"They're old." Scarlet sat on her heels. "I'm not stupid. I'm avoiding a broken heart."

"I get it." He rolled his shoulders to relieve the tension.

"Do you ever wonder about your parents?"

Dwayne sucked his teeth. "It would do no good. They gave all of us up—I know enough to know they're already gone. They were in their thirties when they had me. Can't say I'm particularly attached to my birth family." He nudged her knee with his elbow. "I'll be a lot more broken up when you all start passing in thirty years."

She grinned. "You're bound to go first—you're the oldest."

"Nah, I'm gonna live forever. I'm a Life elementalist. I can find the secret to immortality."

Their laughter echoed around the room.

"How does the Yong'an Residential District sound?" He pointed to the map on his screen.

"Which one?"

Dwayne paused, tongue between his teeth. "There are multiple?" At her nod, he looked back at the computer screen. "The one in Xian'An." He turned the screen to face her.

"Ganhe River." Scarlet nodded. "Right off the G351."

"Sijixin Commercial Street a couple blocks away."

She scratched her cheek. "I'll look at rentals in the area—see what we can't get on short notice. What made you choose there?"

"Forums. People talking about the hospital. Someone mentioned experimentation."

"Medical?"

"Possibly." He shrugged. "We'll be in the thick of everything, so we will need to be obvious and cautious."

"You always enjoyed a challenge."

December 7, 2318

Series twisted fitfully in her sheets. She only needed a few hours of sleep. The pods would take her and the select units home in the morning—everyone else was already vacated from Inuvik. Something about the emptiness of the area made it harder to sleep than she expected.

Untangling from the bed, she poured herself a glass of water and pushed herself onto the cleared desktop. Series swung her legs as she cleared her mind. Her heels connected softly with the drawer creating a dull and methodic beat against the wood.

Thud, thud, thud.

Something flickered in the corner of her vision—lush and green. She looked up but saw an abstract painting hanging on the tent wall. She forgot to take it down during the packing phase.

Thud, thud, thud.

For a moment she thought she heard people screaming outside, but when she paused the swinging, it was silent. No one moved to open her tent and ask for assistance.

Thud, thud, thud.

The action transformed the scene around her fully. She sat atop supply crates across from a man throwing a tennis ball, watching it bounce back to him. The rhythm changed.

Pop against the dirt ground. *Thud* against the box. *Pop* on its return to the ground. *Thwop* into the hand of the thrower.

Pop. Thud. Pop. Thwop.

"Vander?"

Series investigated the face of a newcomer. The low light of the shady area gave a sort of golden glow to his cheeks. His dark hair curled over his forehead still dripping water. He recently washed. His clothes looked worse for the wear. He had several holes near the seams and a tear up one of the pant legs.

Pop. Thud. Pop. Thwop.

"Ai?"

"Den wani unu besroiti." He stood quietly for a long while, but 'Vander' didn't respond. "Fa musu mi taigi den?"

Pop. Thud. Pop. Thwop.

He stopped throwing the tennis ball. "Taigi den wi o miti kon na wan." He rolled the tennis ball between his fingers.

"Yu no abi misi?"

"Ai." Vander gave his companion a hard look. "Mi abi noiti moro no abi misi ini mi libi."

The shady scene slipped from view. Series had no idea who they were, or what they said, but it sounded serious. She wished she knew more information. The scene reformed around her, and she recognized the landscape. *Home.* The Academy rose above them in the distance. It struck her how much the city of hovering towers and Grecian inspired buildings looked like a castle. She stood in the City of Garden in the Tunisia sector. Date palms outside the buildings climbed high toward the sun.

While some of the business buildings had a sandy stone exterior, the houses were white and blue with nearly flat roofs. Drainage holes were open on the top floors to release water from any heavy rains. The slight slope of the roofs pushed the water toward the open holes.

Curtains were drawn over the windows, and one house on the corner was blasted half-open. Belongings spilled across the road trampled underfoot. A child's doll lay on the dirty ground with a ripped dress. Half its face crushed in.

Series turned amidst the screaming of battle and saw the large fountain in the main square. The top was busted, and the statue lay in several pieces in the water. The fountain spewed water at an angle and soaked those fighting around its brim. She spotted Eileen standing on the parapet of one of the businesses. She reached out her hand and pulled the water from the fountain. It swept down the main street in a flood carrying the unprepared humans away. The current swept several under, and they didn't resurface.

A familiar blonde figure climbed the center podium of the fountain.

"What are you doing?" Hans yelled across the square as he lifted the earth. A rumble moved through the ground and nearly knocked the woman off the plinth.

"Ending the war!" she shouted.

"Then get in the fight!" Dwayne swung a Lūcis Jacula through the air, passing it fluidly between both hands and cutting down four people in one go.

"Trust me!" Kristen turned to face the bulk of the crowd with arms spread wide toward the sky. It ripped open above her, and they could see the vastness of space. Several humans and elementalists stopped fighting to stare in awe at the majesty of the universe. Kristen clenched her right hand into a fist followed by her left. Then, ever so slowly, she dragged her left hand to her right. They couldn't feel the shift, but they could see it.

The sky above grew darker, and the air chilled around them. Within minutes the buildings frosted over, and gooseflesh rose on everyone's arms. Their breaths came out in freezing crystals. Several people huddled in on themselves or with others to try and stay warm.

Series tripped as she tried to run forward, and she found herself falling off the desk in her tent. She crumpled to the floor and spilled the glass of water. Her body shivered as if still affected by the cold. One thought struck clear and cold as crystal in her mind. Kristen would destroy the entire world.

December 8, 2318

A modern pop song reverberated off the walls of their apartment in the middle of the afternoon. Scarlet jumped and accidentally closed her tab of available rentals. Dwayne exited the kitchen, wiping his hands on a towel to collect his phone from the table.

"Hey, Muuyaw." He put the phone on speaker. "Scarlet's here, too."

"Kristen's going to destroy the world."

The cacophony of people on the street below, arguing, filtered through the open window. Dwayne and Scarlet stopped. Dwayne licked his lips and chewed the corner where his teeth latched onto a bit of dead skin.

"What did you see?" he asked with a slight warble of hesitation.

"There was so much—" her voice trembled around a breath, "destruction."

Scarlet stood and closed the window. "How do you know it was Kristen?"

"That part wasn't her. She was—Kristen was trying to 'end the war'. It's what she shouted."

Dwayne exchanged an uneasy look with Scarlet. "Start at the beginning, that might help," he paused, "skip the small details. Tell us the story."

Series' hair brushed against the phone. Static filtered through the line, and they assumed she nodded. Her following swallow was more audible. She gave them a brief description of the events, including where she fell off her desk.

Dwayne pressed his thumb against his lips, ignoring the last bit of her story. "Do you think she actually pulled the Earth, or did she fake it by showing space in a way she wanted it to appear?"

Series stuttered her hesitation on the other side. "Everything was freezing over, Dwayne."

"Yes, but Eilene or I could freeze the area if we wanted to." Scarlet walked to Dwayne's side to make sure her voice came across clearly. "Something like what you described, everything freezing over, would be incredibly easy for us to recreate, especially since you mentioned how Eilene washed water from the fountain across the armies."

"It could be a ploy to scare the humans into ending the war. If they breeched that far, I don't know if the ploy would work." Dwayne pursed his lips. "Did you see anything else?"

"Yes, but it wasn't related. I think," Series said.

"You're not sure?"

"What I saw, it was in a foreign language. I couldn't understand what they said, nor could I repeat a single word of it. Well, one of the people I saw is named 'Vander'. I picked up on that much. Their tone was serious."

"We'll disregard it for now," Scarlet said.

"So, could it be a farce? Could we do something like that late in the game where our civilians are directly involved in the slaughter?" Dwayne sat on the floor with crossed legs, and Scarlet followed him, sitting on her feet.

"It didn't look like Eilene knew what was going on either," Series hesitated, "but it's possible she did. I mean, I was staring at the sky—at what it looked like."

Dwayne set the phone on the table and covered his face with both his hands. He took a deep breath through his nose, and the sound echoed under his palms. "What do you even do with this information?"

"I trust Kristen," Scarlet said. "I know we barely know each other and out of everyone, her and Ethan are the two we know the least—but I trust her. I don't know what Series saw, I don't know the reality of a moment sometime in the future, but whatever is going on, I don't think we should agonize over it like we're doing. It only builds our mistrust of each other. We are all Council members. We'll all do the right thing."

Dwayne gave Scarlet a side-eye as he pressed his palms together in a prayer position and rested the pointer fingers against his lips. He pinched the under portion of his jaw with his thumbs. *Would they?* he thought.

Scarlet swallowed before continuing. "Series, I don't know what it's like to have your power. I can't imagine the burden placed on you to know snippets of the future—of what will happen to us or yourself—but if we are always worried about this future, we'll never live in the present moment. You're going back home today. You'll be protecting our people. We don't know everything about the situation with Kristen. I think it's better to confront it when we get there."

"I agree with Mulan." Dwayne cleared his throat. "If you see something giving us information—a leg up on the enemy, we need to know that. We don't need to worry about the decisions of the Council members in ending this war. It's why we all agreed to unleash the true strength of our powers."

"I don't know how to not be terrified of what I see. I don't know how to not worry about it and wonder if there was something I should've told you all sooner," Series whispered.

"I think," Dwayne chewed his next words, "you have to trust your instincts. Not your reaction immediately after seeing something, but what do you sense in the moments after as you reflect on what you saw? Does it feel like something we need to know? By all means tell us, but if it's a slight shadow of doubt where the truth of reality is muddled—it'll do nothing for any of us to dwell on it."

"Like the information on Ethan facing Tyr," Scarlet said. "In the end, it just scared Kristen. Ethan can't do anything about it."

"So, I should keep information to myself?" Series asked.

"Not necessarily," Dwayne said. "I mean, if we're going into a battle and the location is familiar—like the beach in Georgia—then I think you should help guide us to what you saw. Like, there will be an explosion here, armies will invade from this direction, these people should be at the front lines."

"That's a fair judgement. We'd know you're helping guide us in the way things are meant to play out without feeling like our future is dictated—even if it is." Scarlet smiled at Dwayne. "Series, does that work for you?"

"I'll do my best," her voice carried her hesitancy with the idea. She would have to keep a lot of information to herself.

"If you do find it to be too overwhelming, you know my number." Dwayne ended the call.

December 20, 2318
Yong'an Residential District, Xian'An, Xianning, Hubei, People's Republic of China

Scarlet shuffled the last box out of the moving truck with a small grunt over its weight. She nodded to Samuel, her right-hand Field Marshal, and he closed the back of the truck before climbing into the cab and driving away. At the top of the stairs of their new apartment building, she saw Dwayne in the kitchen unpacking the cooking supplies.

He glanced at her as she squeezed through the doorway. The box corner tried to catch on the frame, and she let out an annoyed *huff.*

"Need help?" Dwayne held the spatula in his hand a bit like a sword.

"I've got it." She nodded to the five open boxes. "I see where your priorities are."

He waved the spatula like a wand. "I'm fixing us lunch." Their eyes flicked to the empty stove. "Once I get the boxes unpacked."

"Now that's a skill we need." Scarlet set the box on the dining table. They had a little more room in the new apartment and opted for the more traditional large party round table with chairs. "An unpacking elementalist."

Dwayne laughed. "Their ability is to unpack boxes?"

"Exactly. The most important of all elementalists."

He lifted the teapot from the box in front of him, and his eyes glanced off the plants lined against one of the windows. He noticed a person passing behind the pane. Dwayne clicked his tongue to capture Scarlet's attention before nodding to the plants. She glanced at the front door, still open.

"Think you could water the plants?" he asked clearly in Mandarin.

She licked her lips, recognizing their first opportunity. "Of course." Scarlet wiggled her fingers and small storm clouds gathered over the stalks before drizzling a slow pattern.

The pedestrian stopped in surprise just outside their door. Scarlet gave a soft smile before closing the door in their wide-eyed face.

She leaned against the door facing the room. "A little more warning would be helpful in the future."

"We'll plan better," he said. "I just saw them outside and figured 'why not'."

December 22, 2318

They had a plan.

Sort of.

It involved a lot more danger than actual planning and really put them flying by the seat of their pants with the hope they would reach the right parties before falling prey to HISS. Being reckless with their powers would certainly lead to more people noticing them than they wanted.

They quickly encountered their first problem: they were too used to their powers in a combat capacity. Scarlet couldn't think of anything she could do with her powers other than water some plants with rain which only went so far.

Dwayne sat cross-legged on the floor, staring at their list of ideas for what they could do. *Pitiful.* They made a great match for the area, but not in terms of ability. He watched Scarlet grab a snack from the fridge. "You could create a small earthquake."

She chewed the pineapple bun. "A small earthquake could still cause quite a bit of damage. I'd also worry about triggering another fault line with mine and hurting much more than a small area."

"What are we going to do?" Dwayne pushed his fingers against his temples.

"You could get a job at the hospital?"

He lowered his hands. "How do I do that without a doctorate?"

She laughed.

"At any rate, you know how much I hate being the 'doctor'." He used air quotes. "I never really seemed suited for my ability." Dwayne saw her skeptical look. He was a Council member for a reason. "Personality wise."

Scarlet nodded sagely. She struggled with her own abilities when she first arrived at the Academy, considering she could control the very thing that stuck her grandmother dead in front of her. "So, when are we going to the wet market?"

"Tomorrow? We have enough food for today. As we wander around, we'll just look for opportunities." Dwayne deleted the list from his tablet. "I think we work better without a plan."

"We do make a great team." She nudged him with her foot as she walked past him to the bedrooms. "Early tomorrow morning."

December 23, 2318

Dwayne awoke to Scarlet shaking him frantically. He couldn't process her harried whispers. He garnered enough consciousness to find the alarm clock showing two in the morning.

"If I knew this is what you meant by early morning, I wouldn't have agreed to it," he groaned.

"There's someone trying to get into the apartment," she hissed.

"What?" He shot out of bed.

"I think they are, anyway. Tried opening my window. Heard them at the front not that long ago."

"And you came to me? What am I going to do? You have the power to kill them."

"Great, then we have a body on hand. We're not trying to get arrested!" Scarlet's nails dug into his arm. "What do we do?"

Dwayne bit his lip before sliding out of bed. He peered out of the door and into the hall where he could hear a scratching at the front door. "If it was HISS operatives or the government rounding up elementalists for a ghetto, wouldn't they just bust down the door?"

"I don't know!"

Dwayne padded across the hall with Scarlet on his heels. Shadows played across the curtains, but they didn't look quite human. He slipped to the window and pushed the curtain back far enough to catch a glimpse of the outdoor light brightening the exterior walkway. He couldn't see a figure in front of the door, but the shadow didn't lie. Dwayne waved Scarlet back, and she darted to the kitchen area.

It only took a moment before she returned to his side, holding a kitchen knife. He raised his left brow at her.

"At least if I stab them, they have a better chance of living than if I electrocute them," Scarlet hissed.

Dwayne buried a laugh, but she didn't miss the jerk of his shoulders. "Alright, open the door and stab on my signal."

Scarlet held the knife in her left hand. Despite it being her non-dominant, it would be easier to stab since she had to open the door with her right hand. She quickly unclicked the locks, and the shadow moved.

Dwayne held up a hand as a warning. The shadow shifted again.

A lithe figure jumped onto the railing, and the shadow followed. A rather large cat flicked its tail through the air.

"Who is it?" Scarlet's hand shook on the doorknob.

"A cat."

She started laughing and locked the door. Dwayne watched the cat follow the railing until it jumped onto the balcony again.

A moment later, a head peaked over the lower part of the balcony where the stairs were. He quickly signaled for her to be quiet. Scarlet went on full alert again.

Dwayne let go of the curtain and slid to the side of the window. They listened with bated breath as the footsteps stopped outside their front door. Scarlet grabbed Dwayne's sleeve and pulled him toward the dark kitchen. Just as they hid, the person moved to peer through their window. The living room would be slightly visible from the light on the wall plug-in, and their figures would've been in plain sight for the unwanted visitor.

Dwayne crouched and tried to get a good read on the person through the window, but he couldn't see more than the outline of their figure.

"They're watching us," Scarlet whispered in his ear.

Dwayne jumped violently as he hadn't noticed her close approach. His foot kicked the cabinet as he fell over. The figure ran.

"Sorry!" She reached out to help pull him off the floor.

He pushed her away. "I think it's safe to say they noticed us."

"Should we play it a bit more cautiously?"

He nodded before he remembered they couldn't see each other. "I think so. We'll do just enough to try and draw out those with information. Nothing reckless."

January 7, 2319

The incident at their apartment frightened them enough that they stepped back from reckless behavior for several weeks. While they still used their powers around the house, public spaces took on a case-by-case use; they could count on one hand the times someone noticed their interference. Occasionally, they could feel eyes watching and following them through their various tasks in the city, but not once did anyone approach them.

"Are we sure they're in the city?" Dwayne whispered one day as she paid for some vegetables.

"I'm sure of it." Scarlet returned her phone to her pocket and thanked the merchant. "We've all but had online confirmation. I've also heard whispers. You have to get in close while shopping."

She had an advantage over Dwayne because she blended in. Dwayne's height did him no favors in getting into small spaces or dense crowds.

Someone shouting in Mandarin interrupted Dwayne's response, and the small fight caught the attention of most of the crowd. The stall had a long line of waiting people, but the workers running the stand came to a standstill to fight. A larger crowd gathered.

"How could you be so stupid?" The woman running the stand yelled at the teenage boy. She barely refrained from hitting him. "Go find some ice, idiot child."

He turned away from her, cradling his hands to his chest. Seizing the opportunity, Dwayne slid around the crowd and met the boy as he navigated the back roads away from the wet market.

"What happened?" he asked.

The boy turned in surprise. He hesitated before showing Dwayne his blistered hands.

"I touched the inside of the oven by accident putting in the meat to cook."

"Here." Dwayne held out an expectant hand toward him. The boy cautiously placed his hands on Dwayne's. The familiar green light appeared between them almost immediately, and the blisters healed over with nothing but smooth, new skin. "Is there any other pain?"

The boy shook his head and flexed the ligaments. "It's better than before."

"Good." Dwayne smiled. "Go back to work. Be a little more careful with those ovens."

"Yes! Thank you, xiānshēng."

"You're welcome."

Dwayne followed him to the main market where Scarlet stood with crossed arms, staring into the distance. He watched the boy excitedly return to work and explain the situation to the older woman. His explanation drew more than her gaze—he even saw an officer catch word of the event and turn hesitantly to watch him.

He shuffled to Scarlet's side and followed her line of sight to the wood post of the building. Carved in vertical letters, archaic Chinese scripts combined to create a message.

"Hey, people are starting to notice us," Dwayne whispered in her ear. "I may have drawn a bit too much attention."

She raised her phone and snapped a picture of the characters before grabbing his hand. Dwayne pulled her down the street to their temporary apartment.

He pushed the door closed behind them. "What did you see?"

She pulled out her phone and displayed the picture in the air between them. "This is archaic Chinese, two different forms. The first is known as zhuànshū, while the second is jiǎgǔwén. I think if we translate it, it will tell us directions to go for smuggling elementalists to safety."

"What makes you say that?" Dwayne inspected the script, but he couldn't read it.

"The zhuànshū characters are the word 'yuánsù', and if I'm not wrong, the jiǎgǔwén are the locations. To anyone not from here, it might look like scratches or graffiti."

"I'm not familiar with the scripts."

Scarlet smiled and one of her eyebrows quirked upward playfully. "Well, you weren't raised in China." She pointed to the symbol directly under the seal script. "This is běi followed by tián. Lastly, is shān." She used her finger to circle the characters. "If I took my best educated guess, I would say the translation is Elementalists go north to the field by the mountain."

"The fact you figured that out by only looking at it for a short while." Dwayne walked over to the table and set down their shopping. "I'm amazed."

"I think we should follow it."

"You don't think it's a trap?"

She shook her head. "I don't think Slattery would have enough foreplanning for that. He has the ghettos. Why would he write secret messages?"

"Fair point." Dwayne looked at their shopping. "Think we can turn this into food that travels without spoiling?"

Scarlet grinned. "Definitely. I'll message our regions, and the Council, and let them know of our plans."

"We'll pack out in the next few days." He walked to the window and pulled the curtain aside. His brow furrowed as he watched the street below. "We may be able to get a delivery of equipment during the night. Have someone bring us a couple backpacks and water canteens."

"I'll start planning food." She wandered into the kitchen.

January 10, 2319

Dwayne checked each item off the long list on his tablet as he safely packed it away for the journey. He would carry a lot of weight, but he needed to be prepared for the worst-case scenario. They would be hiking, and they needed most of their food packed with carbohydrates. If Dwayne had to do any significant healing, he would need something particularly potent.

He had the forethought to order large amounts of whole grains prior to their planned exit date to make a dense trail mix style snack with sixteen of the main grains. He didn't fancy eating rice uncooked. Most of them would be hard to swallow dry—but it was better than nothing. Scarlet did her best to cook food that wouldn't spoil, and they didn't dare cook in the open in case it drew unwanteds to their area.

On top of the grains, Dwayne took care to pack the water tight. Among the bottles, he had a fair amount of coconut water for electrolytes and other important minerals; he used it frequently to combat blood loss. Lastly, he piled the fruits and vegetables that would keep the longest without consistent refrigeration. The temperature wouldn't get anywhere near what they needed.

He didn't want to ask Scarlet to create a bomb cyclone, either. They wouldn't be able to travel, and it would mess with the ecosystem.

Dwayne's phone vibrated with an incoming text tone, and he picked up the device.

Council meeting in ten.

Luana

He spotted the transmission pads glowing faintly under the light from the window drained of their distinguishing colors. Dwayne stood and closed the curtains from prying eyes, and the walls reflected yellow and green behind him. Scarlet walked into the room a moment later with her phone in hand.

"I'm almost packed with my stuff."

Dwayne glanced at his nearly full backpack with the bulk of the food. "I'll be a while yet." He'd need another pack at the very least—but one hanging off the bottom somehow. Their sleeping gear would be tied at the top.

She examined his packing. "Do you need me to carry some of your clothes?"

"I'll figure it out," he said. "I probably need to repack."

Scarlet stepped onto her pad and activated the call on her app. The projections of Ethan, Kristen, Eilene, and Scott populated in their living room. "Dwayne's here, he's just packing," she said.

Dwayne stepped onto his own pad. "I was trying to pack. Rethinking how to do it."

"You'll both be safe going underground, won't you?" Eilene's brows pulled together in the middle and gave her a pouty look.

"As safe as we can be." He gave her his familiar, warm smile. "Mulan won't be in any danger with me around."

"I thought I would be the one protecting you like the damsel in distress." Scarlet crossed her arms with a slight scowl.

"Oh, you will be." Dwayne nodded. "You have to protect your healer, after all. That's how it always works in these games."

They laughed.

"At any rate, we'll be off grid for a while—as much as we can. We've got plenty of charging devices packed; if we absolutely need it, Mulan can zap us a little electricity." He wiggled his fingers through the air. "We'll try to make contact again once we're in the system."

"What will you do once you're inside it?" Scott leaned back, and his desk entered their view.

"Follow it to the other side," Scarlet said. "We have no idea where it comes out—how many people are hiding in plain sight. Of course, we'll arrange for transportation to get everyone to safety."

"We're hoping to get some clues about what HISS is doing, but it may be hard in the underground." Dwayne crossed his arms.

"And you're sure you'll be going into somewhere safe, not straight into HISS?" Ethan tapped the toe of his shoe against the ground.

Scarlet shook her head. "No way to tell. Of course, if it is HISS, then you'll see a report about a large group of people being electrocuted. Maybe frozen in a freak storm. Swallowed by an earthquake." She pursed her lips. "I have options."

"Killed in a freak volcanic eruption," Dwayne pitched in. "We could even name it after you. Mount Li."

She rolled her eyes. "You do that."

Luana, Hans, and Series joined in the middle of their laughter. Once calm, Luana started the meeting with, "Before the both of you go AWOL—"

Dwayne interrupted. "Hold on, this leave is definitely official."

Luana threw her hands in the air. "And, interestingly enough, official AWOL would still use the same acronym."

"Clearly, it's not about spelling. It's about connotation."

"Whatever it might be," Luana rolled her eyes, "before the both of you are out of contact, we have an update on the implementation of our spies."

The group sobered immediately.

"Carmen and Ulrick work great together. They've successfully infiltrated HISS and were assigned on work duty for a project near Kiritimati. Last I heard, they were on the island. Apparently, they don't come to shore often to make calls, and reception on the ocean is non-existent. No one with information has told them what they're doing—but it's some sort of construction project."

"I texted about the project a couple months ago," Series said. "It was in the set where I was learning to control my powers. I just kept getting snippets of what felt like useless information."

"Do you remember where it was?" Hans asked.

"Somewhere near Kiritimati. They were getting supplies shipped there by boat—but I've never seen it again."

"Think you could?" Hope glimmered in Luana's eyes.

"I'm steadily getting better control, but it's still iffy. I mean, it's never been a situation where I can just see everything." Series clenched her fists out of frustration.

"Well, if you could, that'd make life awfully boring!" Ethan grinned. "It's no fun to say how things will play out word for word all the time."

Scarlet latched onto Ethan's attempt and added her own sentiment about the importance of seeing only pieces to guide them in the right direction. "Which you've already done! Don't stress too much."

Series pulled a face but didn't say anything. The Council hoped they hadn't insulted her by refusing help from her ability.

"So, we'll wait on the spies to give us more information about whatever is happening near Kiritimati."

"Why don't we move against the construction project? It's a waste to let them build whatever it is," Ethan said.

Hans sighed. "It comes down to the laws of armed conflict. While our enemy may not plan to follow those laws, we will because humans already don't trust us. Also, the people who are working on whatever this project is—are they military or civilian personnel?"

"Most likely civilian," Scott answered for him. "It's the Principle of Distinction. If we could solidify through espionage that whatever this building is, is for is a military objective, we would have an opportunity to attack. However, we don't know that. Until we know whether it is a civilian project or a military one our hands are tied."

Eilene nodded. "Indiscriminate attacks are prohibited because it could result in easily preventable deaths. Even if it is a military objective, if we can't confirm civilians aren't harmed, we won't be attacking the facility. I think our hope should be that Carmen or Ulrick manage to find out any information which tells us its purpose. Then we can counter HISS."

"And what about Zawadi and Mpendulo?" Dwayne asked.

"They are currently working through the lengthy registration process to join HISS from a country aligned with the movement," Luana said. "We've had a hell of a time giving them an appropriate backstory and paperwork to help define their presence where they are instead of in City of the Uns."

Scarlet cleared her throat. "And Maxim?"

"He's remaining with me," Hans said. "He's fully trained, but since he is solo, we may be able to build him a good enough backstory to get him invited into the top ranks—with Lu's dad."

"I think that's everything worked out, then," Kristen yawned.

Luana crossed her arms. "Dwayne, Scarlet, you both have everything arranged to avoid suspicion?"

"Of course. Our replacements will move in during the cover of nightfall as we leave. They'll live here for about a month before moving away permanently." Scarlet ticked off each part of the plan on her fingers. "Meanwhile, Dwayne and I will be moving across the countryside in search of the farm by the mountain. We hope to successfully infiltrate the underground and figure out its movement and where elementalists are being taken."

"And if it turns out to be a clever ruse by HISS, Mulan will blow the entire operation to smithereens," Dwayne said.

"Great." Luana clapped her hands. "Keep in contact when you can." She ended her side of the call, and everyone followed.

CHAPTER TEN

Justice

January 11, 2319

Lijiajizhen, Huangpi District, Wuhan, Hubei, People's Republic of China

Even though Dwayne and Scarlet headed out on foot, they still used public transportation to travel through the Wuhan area. They disembarked in Lijiajizhen near the base of the Tongbai mountains which hosted the Shuangfeng Mountain National Forest Park. Farmland dotted the rises and falls of the topography. They had a lot of ground to cover until they found the right farm.

"Have you figured out how we're going to know which farm it is yet?" Dwayne lay on his stomach over a cliffy outcropping. He held out a hand to pull Scarlet up.

"No idea. I'm not sure whether we should ask anyone either if we see them working one of the farms."

"Right, so, any particular reason why we're not just following the main roads through the mountain?" Dwayne reached the top of the next cliff. He grunted lowly as he pulled himself along the smooth rock. Scarlet helped brace his feet under him.

"I have a feeling it's going to be more secluded and cut-off from the main roads."

Dwayne didn't lay down immediately to help her up, so she tried to climb on her own. He quickly dropped to his stomach and reached for her hand. "Sorry, but I didn't realize you had access to Series' powers."

Scarlet huffed and pretended to bat him away before taking his hand in a fierce grip. "Well, Xia did hail from Hong Kong. Maybe I'm absorbing her power being here."

Dwayne laughed but didn't pry further. He trusted her gut instinct.

They hiked for a few more hours, scaling cliffs and resting to eat and drink. As they crossed a particularly rocky patch, Scarlet pointed out a small farm in the distance. They would check there before moving on.

Unknown Date

Southern Tongbai Mountain Range

Dwayne and Scarlet lost track of time as they hiked the long-range leading into the Henan prefecture. Scarlet knew they wouldn't cross prefecture lines to find the farm, but Dwayne thought they had too few mountain farms left to search. They stopped whenever they came across one of the reservoirs in the mountain, and even once in the Mulan Tianchi Tourism Area to refill their water and bathe.

"I can see a farm another two kilometers or so from here. At the very least, we might be able to get a bit of shelter." Scarlet pointed toward a farm in the distance.

The sun rested on the western horizon in a blaze of pinks and purples. Scarlet told him earlier of the inclement weather—they didn't want to be stuck outside in a snowstorm. Even the edge of a roof would be preferrable to the tree cover. They wouldn't reach the farm until after dark, and they forgot to pack flashlights. Their path would be treacherous if they didn't hurry before the light faded.

They increased their pace. Scarlet sensed the storm rolling in faster, and she had no desire to mess with it unless necessary. She thought it might draw too much attention to them—even in the middle of nowhere.

Purples and pinks highlighted the western ridge above the small two-story farmhouse rising over the hill. Twilight shadows fell over the valley and darkened the shingled roof. The concrete-like exterior walls crumbled near the corners and offset windows. He didn't like the three ranked style (with a missing upper window on the left) or the recessed bay entry. The tabbed door surround, laid with uneven brick, drew his attention to the double front door with a quarter light. The asymmetry and deepening shadows sent an uncomfortable tingle down Dwayne's spine.

Scarlet grabbed his arm as they approached the small fence outside the farmhouse. "Something's off."

Dwayne froze, and the pair found a nearby set of trees to hide behind. He sensed it, too, but it faded quickly when he saw no lights shining from inside.

"What are you thinking?" Dwayne crouched behind the tree. Weeds grew over the small road to the farm. However, someone cleared at least a bit of the snow previously as it hung around in piles.

"I'm not sure." Scarlet reached for the first tree branch and climbed. "I'll get a view from up top."

Dwayne stood when she returned to the ground next to him.

"I'm not sure what I'm sensing," she said.

"The fact it's empty?" Dwayne gestured to the dark windows. "There's no way anyone's home. We may be able to take a closer look or stay inside."

Scarlet nodded hesitantly, and they made their way up the cleared path to the low wooden porch. She grabbed his arm again; the last dregs of light highlighted a mark on the door. "Look, yuánsù."

Dwayne also recognized the zhuànshū characters—he brushed up on their history after Scarlet told him about the languages used in communication messages. "I think this is the place to be." He tried opening the front door, but the handle wouldn't turn. "Locked."

"Maybe we missed a date somewhere, and we were supposed to be here already?"

"I'll check for another door." Dwayne made a full circuit of the large farmhouse, but he didn't find any other easily accessible doors. A window on the second floor looked slightly ajar, but he had no idea how they'd climb high enough to reach it. Especially if it wasn't open. He had a feeling it was built on a slight angle via natural error.

He told Scarlet about it when he returned to the front, and she insisted on checking it out. He held her steady on his shoulders where she could just reach the bottom lip of the window—but the window was firmly shut.

"Should we wait to see if someone comes back in the next couple days?" Scarlet asked. They returned to the covered porch.

"Can't say I'm particularly inclined to stay outside in this snowy weather if we don't have to." Dwayne inspected the door. They could kick it in, but a broken locking mechanism would reduce the safety of the house. He had one other option. "I'm going to punch out the glass."

"What?"

"If I break the glass, it'll be easy enough to patch up inside." He raised his fist, but before he could swing, Scarlet wrapped her hands around his bicep.

"You can't do that. Surely, you know what happens when people punch out windows."

"You forget who you're talking to." He wiggled his fingers through the air. "I've got this." He coiled his fist again, but realized how much his heavy coat restricted him, so he quickly removed it.

"At least use your left hand, so it's not your dominant one."

He nodded. "Stand back."

Shattering glass echoed off the mountains around them. It clattered to the floor and tinkled and rolled near their feet.

"Shit, that hurts." Dwayne held his arm out in front of him. The skin split from his wrist, down the main artery, and to his elbow. "This is why we listen to Scarlet."

"You're not going to die, are you?" Scarlet touched his left shoulder softly.

"Not if I heal it quick enough."

She spotted the green light under his skin. Slowly, the wound knit itself together. She had a feeling the spliced nerves and tendons would also return to their natural state, even if she couldn't witness it. Dwayne gasped a moment later and clutched his forearm tighter.

"Dwayne?"

"Nerves are not the nicest when healing." He tried to steady himself with several deep breaths. "Can you get the coconut water I packed?"

She reached into the bag and held out the can. He opened it clumsily with his right hand and chugged it.

"Better?" Scarlet examined the bloody window and tugged uncomfortably on the straps of her own bag.

He pulled his bag out of her hand and dug around until he found a bag of nuts and another bag with some fruits and vegetables. "Almost."

A chill swept through the valley. He tore open an orange.

"Are you sure you can't eat inside?"

Half the orange, still stuck together instead of broken into slices, hung out of his mouth. He lowered it slowly. "Sure, just stick your arm through the window and open the door."

Scarlet crinkled her nose and stepped over him to the door. Carefully, she reached past the shards of glass and blood to click the lock out of place. A moment later, she swung the door open to a dark entryway.

"It feels like we're walking into a horror movie."

Dwayne grinned. "Well, if we are—you already know I'll die first. Gives you time to run away."

"And you nearly bleeding out is not at all a foreboding sign of what's to come."

They shuffled into the house and closed the door. Dwayne reached for a jar of peanut butter near the bottom of his pack.

He stared into the jar. "Think this place has a spoon?"

"Don't use someone else's silverware." She rolled her eyes. "Just use the one we packed."

"Yes, but I did not clean the one we packed this morning—and it's at the bottom of my bag." Dwayne made to step further into the house. "Should we take off our shoes?"

Scarlet looked around the room. "We can clean any footprints later if needed."

He nodded and stepped out of the lowered entryway. The first door, next to the stairs, led into a nicely decorated sitting room. Dwayne left the door open, and the next one lead into the kitchen. He rifled through the drawers until he found a spoon for the peanut butter. He moaned softly into the taste.

"Alright, I'll leave the two of you alone." Scarlet opened the last door across the hall that led into a cute dining area with a long table. Moonlight flooded through the curtains over the front window. Shadows curled around the walls and filled the room with hulking figures. Shivering, she closed the door behind her. She found Dwayne still in the kitchen working his way through the jar methodically now with a bit of kale on the side. "Bottom floor is cleared. Want to check the second floor with me?"

He used the spoon to put peanut butter on another leafy bite. "Let's go." The snack traveled with them.

The stairs creaked under their weight—they heard a movement in one of the rooms on the second floor. Dwayne sucked some of the peanut butter from his teeth as they considered continuing.

"You should go first," he whispered.

"Why me?" Scarlet's voice squeaked at the sudden change of plans.

"You're the one with a combat ability! How many times do I need to establish this?"

She grumbled the entire way, switching places on the stairs. He made a sly joke about her proving her worth as Mulan, and she elbowed him hard. He shuffled his snack into his backpack.

"I hate not having our weapons."

"That was probably a bad decision on our part—but they felt way too conspicuous." Dwayne frowned. "It's left me very vulnerable."

"If we get into the system, we could always arrange a safe location to have someone deliver our weapons to us." Scarlet reached the top of the stairs. She put her hand on the first handle. "Be ready to heal me."

He nodded, and she opened the door. Moonlight bathed the room from the upper exterior window, and the curtains hung limply at the side. Unlike the dining room, no ominous shadows creeped along the walls. A bed sat in the middle with a wardrobe in the corner. Outside, a few snowflakes drifted lazily toward the ground. Peaceful.

Dwayne pushed past Scarlet and did his best to stealthily walk across the room to the wardrobe. He raised three fingers to give her a countdown before he pulled the doors and used one as a shield to hide. A woman tumbled to the floor in front of Scarlet.

"Don't hurt me!" She raised her hands in surrender.

"We don't have any intentions to unless you hurt us." Scarlet put out a hand for her to take. "Are you an elementalist?"

The woman nodded hesitantly and took the offered hand.

"Perfect. We are, too. We thought this might be a safehouse, but it appeared empty when we turned up today."

"My friends and I arrived a few days ago, it was empty then, too. A window was open on the second floor, and we closed it."

"We checked the window earlier." Dwayne stepped out from behind the door. "You have friends here?"

"Yes," she said.

Scarlet pressed a warm hand to her shoulder. "Mind introducing us to your friends? It'll be better if we work as a group."

They chose to sit in the living room. Scarlet found the dining room too creepy, even with the lights on. They made sure the curtains were closed, but the light would be obvious through the window.

"Lǐ Zhū Hóng," Scarlet introduced.

"Dwayne Tebogo, call me Nuò here." He nodded politely.

"Council members!" the woman from the wardrobe whispered harshly.

"How'd you end up here?" the man asked.

"We were trying to infiltrate and figure out what's going on, so we can better help and assist the war front." Dwayne scratched his nose.

"And nobody recognized you?"

"Right? You'd think out of everyone in Elementōrum, we'd be the most recognizable," Dwayne said.

"It's probably the robes," Scarlet said.

"True, we only stopped wearing them a year ago." Dwayne folded his hands behind his head and leaned back. "Still, you'd think we'd be a little more recognizable than the average elementalist."

"Tautona Tebogo—"

Dwayne cut the man off, "Nuò."

"Right, Nuò, I didn't know you spoke Mandarin."

Dawyne grinned. "All but one Council member speaks at least two languages. Mulan and I have four under our belts."

"Three," Scarlet corrected. "My fourth language is only conversational. I wouldn't trust myself with much else."

"We were chosen to come here because we can speak Mandarin. It's hard to track the movements of elementalists in a country if you can't communicate with the people." Dwayne leaned against the soft cushions of the couch. "Now that we found this place, we need to figure out its purpose. I'm assuming it is a safe house of some kind, but the question comes down to whether we're just supposed to hide here as a community or if we'll be moved."

"We haven't found any additional instructions since we arrived," the second woman of the group said.

"My apologies. We never asked for your names." Scarlet clasped her hands in her lap. "That was incredibly rude of us. Please."

The woman from the closet introduced herself first. "Cài Měi Liān."

"I'm Gāo Bó Chéng, and this is my twin sister Lè Qí." The man pointed to himself and the other woman in turn.

"It's great to meet you." Dwayne clapped his hands together. "I think at the very least we should hang around here for a while. Maybe search through some stuff. There might be more clues—or whoever owns this place might show up again."

"Could be a runner and delivery system," Scarlet said. "There are a lot of options before we start thinking about moving on."

"And you'll be welcome to travel with us if we decide to search for another location." Dwayne gave them a comforting smile.

The next morning, they broke into two teams to search the house for further clues. Scarlet refused to search the dark house at night in case the lights triggered anyone to think someone was there.

The trio swore up and down they searched the house prior to the Council member's arrival, but they still wanted to double-check with their own standards. They made sure to upturn every bit of furniture they could find. The fridge was well stocked despite having the three eating through some of the supplies.

Scarlet passed through the hall from the kitchen toward the dining room when she heard a short whistle of wind to match the roaring outside. She stopped short and turned, trying to trace where the sound originated from, but the hall was quiet. Dwayne stepped out of the living room and paused. He quirked an eyebrow and watched her confusion.

"Find something?"

"Maybe. There was a sound of wind from over here."

Dwayne joined her. They waited for the next strong gust outside to howl through the valley. When the wind picked up again, the whistle whipped through the hall, and they traced it to the underside of the stairs leading to the second floor.

Scarlet touched the wall, searching for a gap. The wall moved under her fingers, and she pushed against the wood paneling. When she pulled back, a door swung open. The space under the stairs was primarily made of concrete with another set of wood stairs leading into a dark tunnel.

"Well, we know where we need to go."

"I'll go upstairs and get the others. You should focus on packing supplies." She pushed him toward the kitchen.

"Should I bring the spoon?"

Scarlet rolled her eyes.

"I'm going to bring the spoon."

Dwayne, Scarlet, and their crew lost all sense of time walking through the tunnels. They slept when they felt tired and ate when they felt hungry.

After what they assumed was a week, Dwayne decided to briefly boot up his phone to see if they could get a signal. They wanted to get a sense of their location in case they needed to *ping* someone—and to arrange for someone to bring their weapons on the other side. Scarlet wished they'd thought to send a message before they left, but they were caught in the opportunity to continue their journey.

His phone wouldn't give them a time or date because it wouldn't connect. The tunnel cut them off from the real world. Frustration inundated them as they continued to hike. Their bodies hurt, and they had no information about where they would be on the other side.

Eventually, they heard voices and saw light flickering around the bend of the tunnel. Their pace slowed on approach. The voices didn't sound harried or hostile, so they continued around the bend to where a collection of people sat around a barrel fire.

The cavern was roughly carved and had several tunnels leading in various directions. A small puddle of water gathered near the center of the room from where it dripped down the walls.

"Newcomers!" A few of the people ushered them over.

"You've made it in time for the next transfer truck. We're supposed to be a few hours out," another said.

"Come eat some food while we wait."

The trio quickly bled into the crowd of elementalists, but Dwayne and Scarlet stayed back and watched with wide eyes. There were at least fifty people waiting for rescue.

Dwayne pulled one of the elementalists to the side. "Do you know the date?"

He shook his head. "Sorry."

"No problem—just how do you know they'll be coming to pick up another shipment?"

"I rely on the leaders of the underground, honestly." He pointed into the middle of the circle where five people passed out fresh meals to each of the elementalists arriving.

Another group of four wandered in from a different tunnel. Similar shouts called to bring them in. Scarlet and Dwayne opted to sit to the side of the cavern and wait. They didn't know how long they waited, but the roar of an engine echoed around the cavern. A moment later, someone removed a piece of the ceiling and daylight flooded the open space. A ladder dropped down, and the elementalists scurried toward it.

Dwayne and Scarlet waited until everyone, except the organizing group, evacuated before they climbed their way out of the cavern.

What first felt like daylight in the darkness of the cavern turned out to be twilight. Several vehicles waited for them, and the organizers shuffled them to a truck with space to carry them. They peered into the hole and gave further instructions to the organizers who remained behind before they pulled up the ladder and closed the hole again. Someone knocked on the back of the truck the Council members sat in, and it moved.

Dwayne powered his phone on again, and the system ran an update before connecting to service. He quickly sent a location tag in a text message to the Council along with a small message saying they made it out of the underground system.

"Date?" Scarlet asked.

Dwayne slid the control panel menu down from the top. His jaw dropped. "February sixteenth."

"We were gone for over a month?" Her face copied his. "How?"

A moment later, Dwayne's phone started vibrating with fury as text messages from the Council rang in all at once. He was glad he didn't have the text tone on.

I THOUGHT YOU WERE DEAD

EILENE

Did you find out anything important? What's going on in

the underground?
Luana

Why did it take you so long to contact us?
Series

Things haven't changed much in the time you've been gone. To assuage some of your worries.
Hans

Similar veins of texts followed those before he had a chance to think about typing a reply.

We're currently in a transport truck. Mulan and I were not aware of how long we were gone. We literally ended up in a tunnel underground.

No cell service when I tried to connect. I don't know how that much time passed by without us knowing.

They're splitting people up in this underground system. Don't know where we or the others are going. Will get transport out as soon as we can.

It's good to know there aren't any significant changes with HISS.

Glad to know you're okay. Keep us updated.
Scott

I think I read a study once that said when people don't have access to sunlight or a clock, they lose all sense of time. I bet that's

what happened to you if you were in tunnels.
Eilene

I also don't know how long we spent hiking the mountain range looking for the right place. Those days really blurred together— and we had the sun!
Scarlet

As the truck approached the next street, the driver turned off the headlights which alerted them to something fishy. The driver requested they also stifle all light from any electronics for the time being. Scarlet and Dwayne, and several others, tucked their phones away. The vehicle slowed to a crawl as it prowled the dark street. It stopped outside a house in the dead of night. The lights weren't on, but something felt eerily familiar to Scarlet.

Someone rushed toward the truck. The back clicked open, and the elementalists scrambled out upon her command and into the house. The voice struck a chord of memory in Scarlet, but she was eager to get to safety. Another dark figure inside the house ushered them down the hall and to a basement.

Downstairs, the light was on, and the people shuffled to fill in whatever space they could. A moment later, the stairs creaked as the owner of the house hurried into the room with a pile of blankets. She set them on a nearby table and told them to share. Scarlet knew why the voice had been familiar.

"Māmā?" Scarlet stood ramrod straight, and Dwayne joined her a moment later. The small woman with graying hair turned slowly.

"Zhū Hóng?" Fei Hong raised her hand to cover her mouth.

"A mā!" Scarlet ran forward and pulled her into a tight hug despite the strangers in the room.

"What are you doing here?" her mother whispered.

"My fellow Council member and I were following the underground to figure out how we could help our people get back to Elementōrum. It's impossible to bring them home if we don't know where they are entering and leaving from."

"To think you were here." She pushed some of Scarlet's hair behind her ear. "You've grown into such a beautiful young woman." She froze. "Your father!" Fei Hong ran out of the room; her bare feet padded against the stairs calling for Wang Lei.

"Huh, so we ended up at your parents' anyway," Dwayne laughed quietly behind her.

"I can't believe they're helping our people." Scarlet's eyes filled with tears. "I thought they hated me when I was taken—but they're here helping us despite the danger."

Dwayne gathered her into a side hug. "I'm glad you could see them again."

Her parents came down the stairs together with a small boy following them.

"Zhū Hóng!" Wang Lei gathered his daughter into a hug. He was still taller than her.

"A bà."

"I saw you on the news report when you took off the Council robes—we were so surprised and pleased to see you alive," he said.

"And proud!" Fei Hong gently pulled her husband away. "We have someone to introduce to you." She reached behind them and placed a hand between the shoulder blades of a teenage boy to push him forward. "He's only a human, but this is Yuxan."

"Jiāodì," Scarlet said.

"Dàjiě," Yuxan greeted politely with a bow at the shoulders.

"Mulan's a big sister." Dwayne grinned at her. Her family appeared startled by his knowledge of Mandarin.

"Mulan?" her mother repeated.

"Nuò—Dwayne—gives every one of his close family members a nickname. Mine is Mulan." Scarlet turned a faint shade of pink.

"How fitting of our warrior." Fei Hong pushed Scarlet's hair away from her face a second time. "Is this Dwayne your boyfriend?"

Dwayne quickly stepped back with his hands in the air, and his head connected with the basement light.

Scarlet laughed brightly. "No, a mā. Dwayne and I both aren't interested in relationships. We're not dating."

"After the war, will I be able to visit you in Elementōrum Patriam?" Yuxan's eyes shone brightly under the swinging basement light.

Scarlet nodded. "One day. I promise."

"Upstairs!" Fei Hong said suddenly. The elementalists looked around. "You should sleep upstairs in your old room."

"Dwayne can share with me," Yuxan volunteered excitedly.

"I couldn't impose—and you can call me Nuò while we're in China."

"No, no, of course you should stay upstairs." Wang Lei ushered them to the stairs. "Quickly. We'll get everyone settled down here."

Scarlet grabbed Dwayne's hand and pulled him up the stairs. She led him to the entryway and quickly slipped off her shoes. With the amount of foot traffic, her parents decided not to have their guests remove their shoes because it was controlled and not all over the house, but she knew they'd appreciate not having the outside tracked upstairs.

Yuxan joined them at the foot of the stairs and led Dwayne to his room next to Scarlet's old one. All her belongings, the ones she couldn't take with her, were still there. She opened the drawers of the dresser, and she was glad to see her parents discarded her old clothes. Scarlet stepped into the hall to collect some sheets for the bed, and Dwayne exited the other bathroom.

"Are you fine sharing a room with my brother?"

He laughed. "Are you fine finding out you have a brother?"

She hummed softly. "I'm glad my parents could have another chance at a proper family. In the morning, I'll contact my Secretary of the Army and have them bring us our weapons and additional gear."

"See if we can't get a few military personnel as well. We can send them back with the coordinators and get evacuation committees everywhere we need to." Dwayne checked his phone again. Scarlet saw a few notifications on the screen, but the screen was too bright to make out the colors. "Have a good night."

February 26, 2319

Hongu, Jingzhou, Hubei, People's Republic of China

Dwayne took a seat on the couch next to Scarlet where they waited to be officially picked up and relieved of their reconnaissance mission. They were fully decked in their military gear which Yuxan marveled at. He asked them about each of their weapons, and the two provided a small demonstration of their use in the backyard during the middle of the day when less neighbors were likely to be home.

Scarlet even showed off her ability in the safety of the house, so he could get an idea of the basics. When her mother cut herself fixing dinner, Dwayne showed off. Yuxan definitively told them Scarlet had the better mutation. Dwayne called the vote biased.

She was sad the only family member she could take with her when they left was Dwayne. She held onto the hope her family might join her in Elementōrum one day.

The TV played quietly in the background. The streaming service defaulted to a commercial. Neither of them were paying attention. The news report came on again, but they ignored it until Fei Hong told Yuxan to turn up the volume.

"Some countries under the influence of HISS are encouraging children to drink alcohol to root out any elementalist children. However, this process is also killing the elementalist child. Some parents who followed this advice are now being charged with homicide."

Scarlet stared open mouthed at the news report. Dwayne's grim expression from across the room did nothing to assuage her worries.

"It is apparent from discussion with Life elementalists who work as doctors in elementalist cities or in Elementōrum Patriam that the consumption of alcohol is a fatal and irrecoverable event. Elementalists are pleading with parents to not give their child alcohol."

Francisco Choc, Elementalist In Corozal, Belize flashed on the screen. "I think that willfully giving your child alcohol to see if they are an elementalist is criminal. People are so scared they want to kill not only a group of people, but their own child. That's what it is. Murder."

Orlando Cowo, Human In Corozal, Belize flashed on screen next with a new face. "It's horrible. I can't imagine killing a child you wanted. I mean, it's far better for my child to be alive even if they can't be with me."

Gloria Flowers, Human In Corozal, Belize. "I can see where parents are coming from. It's a fear with my own children. I don't want an elementalist child, I want a human one. If they're developing a way to test for that before birth, I'm all for it. These are merely ways to weed out the hurt and pain caused by the elementalists when they take our children from us."

The newscaster reappeared. "However, most parents now incarcerated and charged with homicide are saying they would go back and change their minds if they could. We'll be keeping you updated on further developments in this story."

Bile rose in Scarlet's chest. "Fuck."

Dwayne clenched his fist. "It was only a matter of time before HISS found out and used it to their advantage."

"We have to be worried about biological warfare." His phone rang in his hand and lit up blue. Eilene. "You saw it?" he asked upon answering.

"Luana wants to call it an act of bioterrorism." Her voice filtered through the speaker phone. "She needs our opinions immediately."

"That's exactly what it is," Scarlet said.

Dwayne's grip tightened around his phone. "We make no laws regarding abortion, but killing a living person with this act is terrorism."

"It's malicious," Eilene whispered. "To desire your own child to die." Fabric rustled on the other side of the line. "Thanks, Scott."

"I think," Scarlet began, "the parents who listened to HISS when they didn't know the outcome—if they can confirm what they were told, and it didn't mention death, they should get a lighter sentence. It wasn't intentional."

"But if they show no remorse—"

Dwayne cut Scott off. "Different case. They wanted it to happen. If they knew it would kill them, no mercy. It was homicide plain and simple."

"I'll inform Luana."

CHAPTER ELEVEN

Abundance

February 25, 2319

Fuerte Olimpio, Alto Paraguay Department, Paraguay

Eilene leaned further into Scott's side as he cradled her after their conversation with Dwayne. She drifted in the quiet atmosphere and the warmth of Scott's arm. When a group of people walked past their tent laughing loudly, Scott spoke.

"You, okay?"

"Yeah."

He raised an eyebrow but didn't say a word. Eilene pressed her face against his chest.

"I suppose I'm lucky," she said, "that my parents didn't kill me as a child."

"You really think your parents would've?"

She nodded roughly against the canvas of his uniform jacket. He subtly tried to shift, so she could press against the cotton of his undershirt instead.

"I mean, if they had just bought some alcohol off the black market, I would be gone."

"Why would they?" Scott ran a hand down her arm. She cricked her neck to look at him. "If they thought you were an Un, they knew alcohol wouldn't work. If you turned out to be an elementalist, they would be charged with homicide. The best they could do was ignore you until they knew the real results. Either way, the Council would deal with you."

"You mean if I turned out to be a Rogue in the other worst-case scenario."

He nodded and apologized when his chin hit the top of her head harder than he intended. "We're absolved from homicide because of the law."

"Does it ever feel—" she paused chewing her tongue, "icky?"

"'Icky'?" He raised a single eyebrow. "That's the best you could come up with?"

She nudged him with her elbow, but the angle prevented it from doing more than uncomfortably pushing against his side. "Wrong, then."

A smile bled onto his lips. "Erroneous. Unsound. Reprehensible. Unethical. Unjust. Ill-advised—"

She elbowed him again, harder. "Stop with the synonyms."

He didn't respond for a long minute. "Yes. It does." His hand drifted up her arm again, and his fingers curled around her bicep. "But it's also the law. Rogues were deemed too dangerous for the world a long time ago."

"We could change that."

Scott rubbed his thumb across her bare skin, and a frown sunk into his features. "Why?"

"We've only ever seen the Rogues when they're terrified. Even our powers misbehave when our emotions go haywire. Maybe Rogues aren't as dangerous as we were told. Maybe with help, they can live a normal life."

"What happens if they can't?"

"I think we should focus on seeing first. We keep running ourselves crazy with 'what ifs'." She used her free hand to add air quotes. "We've done it for years on the Council. It's time to stop and focus on the issue we can fix, even temporarily. Just like Hans did with the Uns."

"Or attempted to do." Scott smirked.

Series' presence back in Elementōrum helped quell some of the ill feelings of the Uns but not completely. Debates over their freedom would come after the war.

"I think we could do it."

Scott used his freehand to fish his vibrating phone from his pocket. "Luana's sending out the official message."

"I won't bother checking my phone, then." She pushed away from his side and used his leg to help her stand. Uncomfortable tingles coursed through her nerves. "We should probably review supplies and battle statistics. Make sure we're prepared."

Scott didn't like the uncomfortable chill bleeding into his left side. He quickly followed her lead and tried to adjust his jacket to replace the warmth.

February 28, 2319

5.41, -143.16, Devil's Gate

"This is the facility?" Mason stepped aboard the tower from their smaller fishing boat.

"Yes, and we already have several arrivals." Tyr adjusted the lapel of his suit. The wind wanted to dishevel his appearance. "I know everyone is eagerly waiting to get to work. You are as well?"

Mason's footsteps hardly stuttered across the deck. "Of course, sir. This is noble work we are doing." He clenched his jaw so hard he knew he'd need medication for his headache later.

While Ryan worked to recruit Rogues in a remote location, where he was isolated with knowledge of HISS' plans, Tyr made immediate plans for Mason to be relocated to the new testing facility. He would oversee running the testing center and managing the employees—nothing too difficult. Mason wouldn't have to run any of the tests himself, but he would report on weapon construction to Tyr what worked and what didn't, so he could meet with the investing nations.

"We should have around fifty test subjects waiting to be assigned rooms. When we get to the main atrium, I'll send you ahead to work with the guards in assigning their rooms." Tyr stepped into the elevator, waiting to take them to a lower deck.

"Understood, sir." Mason triggered the elevator floor button.

Tyr checked his appearance again. He used the reflective metal of the elevator to adjust the few hairs out of place. Once ready, he used a liquid breath spray and a travel tube of cologne. Mason resisted the urge to cover his nose.

The floor dinged as they arrived, and the doors slid open. The atrium was painted a bright white color to cover the heavy steel walls. Mason knew the plans; he visited it once with Ryan during its construction. The architect was instructed to build it reminiscent of asylums. The room had a couple windows on opposite walls, both the style of a porthole, and Mason saw the choppy waves outside beating against the side of the ship. However, only a slight rumble of movement sounded under his feet. Despite the ill weather, the ship was stable. The atrium had two main doors, one to his left and the other to the right. The left led to the room where test subjects would be kept while the right led to the administrative offices. Both sets of doors had the familiar TSA scanner equipment to make sure nothing unwarranted passed between the areas.

Fifteen guards and five nurses stood in the room with a group of ten children ranging from elementary to teenager. Each subject wore a set of handcuffs designed to suppress their elementalist ability. Tyr never said how he got his hands on the cuffs since they were a design only used in Elementōrum Patriam.

Tyr stepped hesitantly from the elevator, but none looked quite as terrified as the staff. His jaw set a little harder. "Who here is to take Mr. Ford on a tour of the facilities as he assigns the subjects to their cells?" he asked.

A short male nurse dressed in pale blue scrubs, and one of the guards, wearing a full Kevlar kit, stepped forward. They vibrated with nerves at the hint of retaliation from the head of HISS. However, Tyr waved them off. Mason quickly introduced himself and followed them through the scanner on the left.

"I was under the impression we would have fifty test subjects on the first shipment." Tyr slid his phone from his pocket to check a notification. "Was there an error in the paperwork?"

"No, sir. We did have fifty."

None of the guards looked at him, and he couldn't tell who spoke other than registering the deep tone.

Tyr pretended to do a careful count of the subjects. One subject caught his attention. An older teenager, if he took a guess, stared at him while the other nine stared adamantly at the floor. She had dark brown hair and eyes. Despite her fixed gaze, she didn't seem to understand the situation. Her eyes slid across the others, searching for something before settling on Tyr again. Tyr cleared his throat and spoke a little slower, "One-fifth of what was promised. That seems a bit odd to me."

The girl's eyes narrowed, but she didn't make any note of understanding what he said. Tyr decided to ignore her in favor of looking at the guards who shuffled from foot to foot uneasily.

"They made a coordinated escape attempt. We caught and rounded up those we could."

"You let the others slip through your fingers?" Tyr castigated.

"It was not intentional—we were binding the captives, and they broke free."

"And every single one escaped?"

"No, sir," the man with the gruff voice pointed to the girl still watching them curiously. "She stayed behind when the others ran."

Tyr watched her again for a moment. She stared back with a firm jaw, challenging him. He chewed his tongue thoughtfully. The guards caught fifty elementalists originally; they managed to retain ten, only one of whom remained behind when the others bid their freedom. Finally, he asked, "Why didn't she run?"

"I don't know, sir."

Tyr bent down to her level. "What's your name?"

Her nose crinkled as if trying to process what he said before she shook her head. She made no attempt at a verbal reply.

"She might not speak English, sir. We captured her in Singapore."

Tyr straightened and grinned uncomfortably. "Never mind. Take them into the facility for testing. The Ls won't know what's coming to them." He stroked the stubble along his jaw. "I'll be in my office speaking with our investors about this error."

Mason examined the paperwork from the nurse and guard. "You really didn't gather any information about those you took for experimentation?"

"We ascertained they were elementalists, then took them." The guard had the humility to look embarrassed.

Mason sighed. "How do you expect us to run appropriate tests when we don't know anything about them? Say they have an allergy. We could kill them without meaning to and think it's something related to being an elementalist. Not having their names is going to be a whole other hassle. What country do they come from? You're starting us way before square one in terms of getting information our investors can use."

"I'll talk to the other guards and see if we can't backlog any information."

"I can speak with the doctors about running some basic allergen tests in the meantime," the nurse offered.

"Those take a few days, right?" Mason rubbed the bridge of his nose and closed his eyes.

"Yes, sir. We should have the results in approximately ninety-six hours. However, some allergies do take a longer time to show up, so those results may still be preliminary."

"How many days would it take for your guards to track down the information on who you captured?" Mason asked.

"About the same timeline."

"You both should be glad I'm not Tyr." He ran his tongue over his bottom teeth. "Right, do both. It's always good to have double the information. Make sure you inform your men for all future captures that the information travels with them. I don't care if you have to break into secure places and files to retrieve their medical information. We need all of it. Communicate with governments—if you're taking people from the ghettos, then the country is already aligned with HISS, and I'm sure they'd be more than happy to hand over those files without question."

"Yes, sir." The guard saluted.

"So, let's bring in the subjects and assign them to the first ten rooms here. There's no point in feeding them back too far. It'll just delay the tests when we collect them. The room should be secure. We used the best material." Mason examined the invisi-material. Tyr learned the elementalists used something similar on their Uns. If the subjects tried to escape, the wall of the cell would burn diamond patterns into their skin.

The guard left the hall to return to the main atrium and summon the guards and captives.

"Do you want me to grab tablets to make sure we spell each of their names correctly?" The nurse asked.

Mason pointed at the cells. "Is that not what those are?" Every cell had a tablet on the front to be used mostly as a control for the door. "Have them write their names on the cell. If it's something in a foreign language, we can access the file later and find it. I just hope they understand we want them to write their name."

"I'm sure they'll pick up on it if even one person understands," he said to comfort Mason.

Mason rubbed his left eye in lieu of answering. HISS had several mistakes under their belt already, and he didn't need to deal with more than necessary. Mason could tell Tyr sensed information slipping from his grasp, and he didn't trust Ryan or Mason. Sending Ryan to Suriname to recruit Rogues isolated his options. Locking Mason away in Devil's Gate kept him out of reach of the elementalists who had previous contact with him. Tyr methodically reduced the threats to HISS.

It took a few minutes for the children to shuffle in. The guards stood one to one with the extras congregating next to Mason and the nurse. Mason stepped forward and pointed at the tablet on the cell.

"Write your name." He figured a simple sentence would come across clearest. Several of the children understood at least the word "name" and immediately moved to write. Mason gave each of them a thumbs-up to convey they did the right thing. The children who didn't pick up on his command copied the others except for one.

The girl at the very first cell, the one who hadn't looked down among all the captives. Mason curiously walked over to her. He pointed to the tablet again and repeated the one word they understood. She watched his mouth form the word a second time. She shook her head.

"Do you not have a name?" Mason asked. He wished the captors did it properly the first time.

A male teen, close in age to the girl, said something in a language Mason didn't recognize. The boy pointed to himself then the girl. "Bāngzhù."

The guards looked uncertainly to Mason, and he nodded. The boy approached the girl and said, "Xìngmíng." He pointed to the tablet. "Xìngmíng."

She nodded and quickly wrote her name on the tablet in a character-based language Mason thought might be Mandarin. The name was followed by three letters: JOY. The boy returned to the door in front of his cell.

"Thank you," Mason said.

The guards opened each of the cells and ushered the children inside.

Mason turned away before he could process the turmoil of emotions on their sad faces. He put a hand on the shoulder of the nurse. "Make sure they're always well-fed, yeah?"

"Of course, sir."

Tyr sat at his desk staring at Mason who refused to budge on the issue at hand. They argued for fifteen minutes and made no progress.

"I cannot proceed with testing if I do not know which element each child can control. If none of them are of the Death element, we have no hope of ever developing a weapon to use against the elementalists." Mason crossed his arms.

"You are asking me to allow all of them to be in a room together." It wasn't a question.

"Yes, a room where they feel safe in each other's company."

"I will think about it." Tyr clicked his pen closed. He stood a second later and collected a small binder of papers and his electronics. "For now, proceed as directed. I have some other places to be. I expect you to run this facility in top shape. I've also arranged for a new group of Ls to be transported here as soon as possible. I'll let you know about the element testing."

"Understood, sir."

Date Unknown

Tan Qíng Yí Joy sat on the floor of her single cell room where she could feel the vibrations of movement under their prison. She had her eyes focused on the unseeable wall to her cell. She touched it enough times to know going near it would only cause her pain. Small diamond patterns traced her skin from where the wall burned her. The room had a slight smell to it, and she assumed it came from the toilet. A light flickered at the end of the hall and chased the shadow of someone walking to the main hallway door outside her cell. Moments later, a guard stopped in front of her door.

She watched them unlock the cell via the tablet on the outside before they waved for her to stand and join them. Qíng Yí pushed herself up. The tiles felt cooler in the hallway under her feet. The guard grabbed her upper arm, but she shook them off. Instead, they pushed her toward the door, and she walked. The door opened on their approach, and the guard tapped her shoulder before pointing to the left. She followed the direction obediently. It wouldn't do any good to resist. It only made the procedure worse.

She spotted two people dressed in lab coats at the end of the hall. They paused their discussion to glance up, but when they saw her, they returned to what they were doing. One pointed at a clipboard, but Qíng Yí couldn't make out the words on their lips. The guard pointed her into another room. Inside, the walls were made of tinted glass that only worked one-way.

She climbed onto the table in the middle of the room and laid down. A low rumble started in the room, and it only took a short while before she welcomed the cold realm of sleep.

When she awoke next, the room looked the same except for a tablet with a pen waiting on a side table for her. Qíng Yí picked it up and wrote, in Mandarin: *What did you do to me?* She showed it to the window but didn't receive a response. Annoyed, she glanced around the room before erasing her message.

She kicked her legs against the table, and the vibrations titillated her spine. She didn't know how long she sat there before one of the windows projected: *How do you feel?* She paused to think about it before writing. *Normal. Tell me what you did to me.*

We're sending you back to your room.

TELL ME WHAT YOU DID.

The door opened, and a guard entered. They waved for her to exit.

You can take the tablet. The last message flashed as she stood.

Qíng Yí let the pen magnetically snap to the edge and carried it with her. In the hall, the next guard with the next subject passed on their left, but she didn't look up until she noticed a new vibration passing through the air. From the corner of her eye, she saw the other patient swinging their limbs in any direction they could. Her guard had an arm out to protect her, but she had enough room to turn around and see the other person screaming and fighting against their guard. Qíng Yí strained her eyes to spot the muddled words on their lips, but she couldn't make out anything. Shaking her head, she followed the guard to her cell.

She used the tablet to draw doodles for a couple of hours. It was the most stimulation she had in a while. The guards didn't let them interact with the other prisoners. The closest she came to any of them was during the rotations for experimentation. She never knew what they tested on her, but the tests gave her a sense of comfort. Whoever captured her didn't have the information they wanted yet. Therefore, Qíng Yí was still alive.

Somehow, she had something over them. Something made her special.

The door at the end of the hall opened, and a guard appeared escorting the subject from earlier. They spotted her through the door to her cell and stopped. The guard tugged on the subject's wrist, but they pulled back before pounding against the invisi-fence material of her cell. Qíng Yí blinked slowly.

She didn't know them. They didn't appear to be Singaporean like her—but she had no idea what their ethnicity might be.

The guard tugged on the subject's arm again. More apparent shouting, but Qíng Yí couldn't hear it. She gave a slight wave before returning to her doodles on the tablet. Unless the person knew Mandarin, and she highly doubted it, there would be no point in trying to write a message. She also didn't know what the guard would do if she did write a note—let alone the facility who were nice enough to let her keep the device.

Qíng Yí found a few other apps installed which had games, so she entertained herself with them until the guard came with her meal. She didn't realize they were there until several rough vibrations crossed the floor. The guard stomped his foot to grab her attention, and she quickly retrieved the meal from him. She tried for a voiced thank you but wasn't sure if the sounds came out right. The vibrations felt correct in her throat.

The guard nodded and closed the door again.

March 15, 2319
Various Locations, Council Projections

The Council heard less and less about parents giving their children alcohol to root out elementalists. However, rumors spread claiming HISS figured out a way to use alcohol as a biological weapon. It left the Council feeling incredibly uncomfortable as they had no way to combat such a weapon depending on its use.

"Is that what they're developing in the testing facility?" Eilene asked during their now weekly Council meeting since Dwayne and Scarlet's return from the Underground.

"We aren't sure—they could be." Luana flipped a few pages on her tablet. "I wrote down the information passed to us from Carmen and Ulrick recently. They have been moved from building duty to guard duty within the compound. They say it's something like a boat and a hospital tied up in one. Tyr had it designed after old asylums. They stay on the employee side watching security cameras most days. There are only ten cells being used.

Their job is to watch the cells and the coming and going of the guards. Those who are captured do not receive any stimulation. However, one occupant was recently allowed to keep a tablet. This is apparently a huge change in HISS' approach to the facility. The reason why is undefined."

"The captives, are they elementalists?" Dwayne picked up a nail file and corrected a hang nail.

"Presumably. Although, they haven't shown any abilities in the cells from what I understand." Luana flipped another page. "We're not sure if the cells are capable of suppressing powers or if they have no desire to. It's a little unclear as to what the facility is being used for. They've noticed guards will intermittently arrive at each cell in turn and take the subject to a room where there are no cameras. At least, not ones hooked up to the observation of the average facility guard."

"I think Tyr may be using the facility to test and build a weapon to use against us. That may very well be biological, but—" Series held up her phone to the original video Tyr made two years previous. "It's more likely he's working to perfect whatever this weapon is. It resembles the one I saw in my vision where Ethan faces Tyr on the battlefield."

"So, in whatever room they are taken to, they test the weapon on them to see what it can do," Scott said.

"Or they test what their bodies will react to, so they can forge the weapon and test it later." Luana pulled her feet onto the chair. "Carmen said she signed up for training to be able to help guard the main cells instead of just the security cameras. Eventually, we might get more information, but the guards aren't in the room with the captives, either."

"Too bad we can't disguise me as a doctor." Dwayne cracked his knuckles. "Think Maxim could pass as a nurse if we gave him the right documentation? I could do a crash course.

Hans shifted uncomfortably in his chair. He liked having his brother nearby. He didn't want to send him into danger even if that's what he signed up for by leaving City of the Uns with Hans. "I can ask him."

"Great." Luana turned off her tablet and set it aside. "Anything else we need to discuss in this meeting?"

When she received all noes from everyone, they ended the call.

April 2, 2319

Baikoetoe, Brokopondo District, Suriname

Vander sat next to Abdiel in the small building they used as a meeting room. A representative lectured at the front with a travel projector about all the great things HISS planned to implement once removing the elementalists from the world.

Genetic testing prior to birth.

Gene therapy to remove defects or mutations.

Someone raised their hand and asked what would happen to the Rogues—they were elementalists after all. The presenter didn't hesitate when they explained how Rogues would have their own place in society among humans, reminiscent of how they made their own communities after escaping the Council. When the time came, they would experience the revolutionary tech of HISS. Their mutation would be removed and no more of the nasty "uncontrollable errors" would occur around them.

What would happen to them during the interim?

The presenter didn't have an answer. They simply reassured the Rogues that HISS had no issues with their existence since they weren't the reason for two separate worlds. *No, the Rogues were safe,* they repeated. It wasn't an answer. Vander clasped his right hand over this left fist and pressed them against his lips, deep in thought.

Abdiel shifted uncomfortably in his chair. He crossed his legs at the ankles then back again, accidentally kicking the chair in front of him and whispering an apology in Spanish. Vander grabbed one of his knees briefly and squeezed. The presentation was in Dutch. Abdiel didn't understand a single word, but he sat watching the reactions of everyone in the room. Mostly Vander.

Vander returned to his previous position as the presenter forcefully moved them forward to show the progress HISS made on Earth's surface against the elementalist people. The slide show included pictures of the

ghettos in various countries with confused families standing behind invisi-
fences topped with barbed wire. HISS claimed to use a similar fencing
material as the elementalists did against the humans held hostage in their
country—the Uns. Nobody pointed out several elementalists could fly; if
they wanted to escape—HISS had nothing on them. The elementalists most
likely didn't know what was happening.

The presenter marched on with their mission to show the strides of HISS
which included showing off a new building. They planned to use the facility
as a testing center for experimentation on elementalists. Vander's eyes
narrowed at the revelation, and he caught Abdiel turning to look at the
screen. Abdiel didn't understand the maps and diagrams any better than he
understood the language.

He grabbed Vander's wrist and pulled the hand between them. Abdiel
threaded his fingers through Vander's and rubbed his thumb along the
irritated skin where Vander didn't realize he'd bitten. "It'll be okay," he
whispered roughly in Sranan Tongo.

Vander nodded stiffly.

The presenter concluded their pitch session with the black end screen.
"So, if you'd like to join HISS, let me know. I'll be here for a couple hours
accepting applications—if each of you would take one." They waved a stack
of papers in the air. "It's a bit old-fashioned, but I didn't know if everyone
would have electronics because of being Rogues and all," they coughed.

Vander rolled his eyes. He tugged Abdiel's hand. "Come on."

"Do we need the—" he waved his free hand through the air searching for
the right word, "papers?" He said the last word in Spanish, but Vander spent
so much time with him the change in language didn't throw him off.

"Maybe—it depends on what we decide."

Abdiel pulled his hand free. "I'll go grab them and meet you outside. Just
in case."

Vander let him go and found a secluded spot just outside the building in
the shade. HISS, in his opinion, chose the plan where they threw everything
at the wall and hoped something would stick. When Abdiel leaned against
the wall next to him with the paper applications, Vander explained all the

large ideas of the presentation and a few of the smaller interconnecting ones. Abdiel did his best to follow along, and he asked frequent questions for clarification.

"So, if we join HISS, they're going to find a place for us in society after they destroy the elementalists?" Abdiel's eyes glimmered with hope.

Vander nodded stiffly. He didn't have any of the same hope. He knew HISS had no plans regarding the Rogues. If they did, it would be like the system already in place. *However, do we have much of a choice?* he thought. They had next to no chance of finding a Rogue community again. They could live on their own in the forest, but they had just as much chance of the Council finding them there as they did in the Rogue community. They could fight with HISS, but the chance of dying amid battle was high. If they faced the Council on the field, they'd be killed without question. Even HISS could turn on them at any moment. No matter how Vander approached the situation, the outcome wasn't in their favor. They had no direct benefit. He explained so to Abdiel.

"You don't want to fight?" The muscles in Abdiel's face twitched as he processed the disappointment.

Vander sighed. "If fighting came with a sure answer of our freedom and safety—I don't want to die." He nudged Abdiel's elbow with his own. "I don't want to lose you."

Abdiel reached out to grab him, but Vander pushed him away.

"Let me think for a while."

Abdiel nodded and stayed near the main presentation building with both applications. Vander took a stroll through the small village area and wandered between houses. He kicked a stray tennis ball across the ground and watched it bounce off a building. Vander followed its path and picked it up. He rotated the soft, felt ball between his fingers. While his mind would run in circles about whether to join Abdiel and HISS—he knew if he declined, Abdiel would follow him—he tried to entertain the energy coursing through his veins, the kind causing things to *pop* around him.

Vander sunk to the ground in a small alley between two buildings where a group of crates stood stacked on one another. He listened to the ball's methodical *Pop. Thud. Pop. Thwop.* He didn't notice the fading light in his shady corner of the world. He could only think of certain death and the sound of the tennis ball on each careless throw.

"Vander?" Abdiel interrupted his pondering. He stood at the end of the alley with a fresh, golden glow. His dark hair curled over his forehead, still dripping water. *He took a shower.* Vander tossed the ball again.

"Yes?"

"They want our decision."

Vander threw the ball again as he took in the raggedy appearance of Abdiel. He deserved so much better than running around the Amazon with Vander. If the world had to go down in flames, he would much rather do it at each other's side.

"What should I tell them?" Abdiel didn't have the papers in hand anymore.

Does he think I won't agree? Vander caught the ball on its return and dropped his hand to his lap. He rolled the ball between his fingers. Debris cluttered the felt and gave it a rougher texture. "Tell them we'll join."

Abdiel's breath hitched quietly enough that Vander nearly missed it. He said, "Are you certain?"

"Yes." Vander watched as the sparks of fighting grew into embers in Abdiel's eyes. He made the right decision. They would be together at the very least. "I've never been more certain in my entire life."

CHAPTER TWELVE

Prosperity

April 5, 2319

Fuerte Olimpio, Alto Paraguay Department, Paraguay

Eilene sat in her computer chair and chewed her thumbnail. The other Council members projected in her tent.

"So, the other two spies, Mpendulo and Zawadi, found their way into HISS. There's a battle coming for Eilene and Scott."

"Really?" Eilene moved her hand away from her mouth.

Luana nodded. "They managed to infiltrate a recruitment facility in Suriname. HISS decided Fuerte Olimpio was close enough to send them without a high cost. From what I understand, this particular military force won't be as well-trained, but they are fierce in numbers and will. I wouldn't be surprised if they put up a strong fight, but I see no reason why our forces there can't handle it."

"However," Dwayne interrupted, "I think the Council should make a full presence at every battle moving forward."

The line went deadly silent as they stared at one another.

"That would be a waste of resources—" Luana started.

"I didn't say our whole regions," Dwayne said, "I meant us. Just the nine."

"We can't possibly be at every battle." Series frowned. They already hadn't. With their regions broken into smaller groups, many skirmishes broke out in random areas—none so related to any of their cities on the lower seven continents.

"He means the big battles," Scott said. "The ones where HISS is focusing their largest groups and possibly their highest-ranking officials."

Dwayne nodded.

"With the nine of us there, we would have more of an opportunity to penetrate to the farthest line and take prisoners of war who have information." Scarlet combed her hands through her hair and used a ponytail holder from her wrist to move it out of her way.

"I think the Council should stick together. We can still send our regions off to battle, but we are so much stronger when we're together. We work fluidly with each other," Hans said.

"Not to mention all the workarounds with time zones—it's ridiculous trying to arrange for meetings." Eilene stretched her arms over her head.

"Alright, moving forward, the nine of us will remain together as a group. We'll fight in every battle at each other's sides." Luana shifted in her chair and reached for an off-screen snack. "Let's plan to meet up with Eilene and Scott for their upcoming battle. It'll take a few days for us to arrange everything on our end to leave."

"We can hold them off in the meantime. No need to rush to our aid." Scott kicked his feet onto the small coffee table in his tent. "Eilene and I make quite the team."

"Oh?" The corner of Dwayne's mouth dragged into a smile until it matched his usual roguish grin. His left brow rose with the quirk of his smile, and his nose twitched as he caught the scent of Scott's unintentional admission. "It's good you work well together."

Scott leveled Dwayne with a glare Scarlet was surprised didn't kill him. It only increased the wideness of Dwayne's smile, and his shoulders shook with hidden laughter. Eilene glanced curiously between them.

"It... is... good," she said with a pause after each word.

Scarlet rolled her eyes at the antics of the trio. "Right, so once we get all our stuff taken care of, we'll come bother the both of you and mess up your *teamwork*."

"What is going on?" Luana slid narrowed eyes across the group of troublemakers.

"I have no idea." Eilene threw her hands in the air. "If we're done, I'm going to check supplies *again*. I'll also have my groups amp up their training over the next few days. Now they have warning."

"Of course." Luana disconnected the call.

April 9, 2319

"Eilene?" Scott called into her tent hesitantly. He didn't want to walk in on her changing if he could avoid it; his imagination had enough fodder.

"Come in," she said. When he entered, she sat on her bed with a book in hand. She asked, "Any news about what is happening?"

"Tyr's forces are moving closer, but there's something different about this group."

She quirked an eyebrow at him.

"They don't look like military personnel. They're equipped with some weapons, but they look like civilians."

"Did the spies have any information on who they are?"

"Rogues."

"What?" Her mouth fell open.

"When they recruited out of Suriname, they targeted Rogue colonies," Scott said.

"Colonies?"

"We sent the spies a list of Rogues who managed to escape, and there are a large number from our list among this army."

Eilene reached up to run her hands through her hair before she remembered she had it pulled into a Dutch braid. She didn't want to have it redone when battle marched on their doorstep. "We're going to be fighting Rogues?"

"And some of HISS' actual military. The spies are unclear on how trained they are—they're part of the medical crew."

"I can't help but think this is some type of opportunity," she said.

"How is this an opportunity?" Scott asked.

"The Rogues. The colonies. If they've lived together without killing each other or anyone else—it proves they aren't dangerous. This could be our chance to show we don't have to kill them anymore."

He shook his head. "This is the last moment to be thinking about that. They're coming here to kill us. It doesn't matter if we could possibly change things, it's either kill or be killed out there on the battlefield. What are you thinking?" He covered his face with his hands.

"I understand clearly, thanks." Eilene crossed her arms like a petulant child. "It's not like I'm going to hold my punches when it comes to the battle because of who we're fighting. Who do you think you're talking to?"

He ignored her question. "Good." Scott wiped his mouth with the back of his hand. "Show no mercy. Show them what it means to face an elementalist."

"Why are you so worried about this anyway?" She sat on the edge of her bed.

"I—" he cleared his throat, "When the spies reported the information to us about the opponent for this battle, I thought I recognized the name of the leader."

"Who was it?"

"It was my dad's name they listed as the leading commander."

"Your dad?"

"But he's a coward. I can't picture him getting caught up in any of this. I don't even know what happened to him after my sister died."

"That's why you're strung up over what's coming." Eilene patted the bed next to her.

He reluctantly sat. "Yeah, I suppose."

"I'm sure that whatever happens, everything is going to turn out alright.

This isn't the first battle we've faced or the first Rogue any of us has killed. It'll just be a normal day."

"Normal?" Scott scoffed.

"Yeah, you don't think this is normal?" She bumped her shoulder into his playfully.

"Maybe I convinced myself that our lives hidden away was 'normal', but if I think about it—have we ever had a normal moment?"

"I never had a job other than the Council." She laid on the bed. "I certainly wouldn't call that the normal experience."

"Eilene," he placed a hand hesitantly on her thigh. She hummed, and he continued. "Promise me you'll be safe in this battle. If you don't think you can win, step away."

Her brows crinkled together, and she sat up again. "What?"

"If anyone makes it out of this battle, I want it to be you."

"Scott, they aren't going to annihilate us. We're more powerful than them." She wrapped her fingers around his. "Why are you so worried about me? You've seen me fight. I haven't even been injured yet—you have. If we should be worried about anyone, it's you."

"Just promise me."

"This is war. I can't promise that. Why are you so insistent on it?"

He licked his lips. The breath rattled in his chest. His mouth worked for a few moments without making any sound. Her fingers tightened around his. Finally, he said, "I'm in love with you."

Her lips parted in surprise, and he caught the audible hitch in her breathing.

Scared and panicked at his own admission, he turned his gaze away from her, latching onto the first item where she wasn't in his peripheral. Words flooded out of him. "I couldn't really say anything before because I knew you had feelings for Dwayne. I mean, we also can't really have relationships or family being on the Council, so that was another roadblock—but the biggest for me was him. I can't even hold a candle to him and the support he's given you over the years. I'm practically a nobody. I don't have the same close relationship with others like the rest of the Council does. But I was thinking since the Council is no longer really bound by the old rules that maybe it would be allowed. To have a relationship. Not insinuating we would—that's up to you, really. I mean, any of the Council members could have a family now. There's no sense of remaining hidden like before. Really, I was just thinking I might have a chance at that 'normal' thing with you. I totally understand if you don't feel the same. I'm not exactly—"

An explosion outside cut him off. He looked at her briefly to see a swirl of mixed emotions battering through her mind. A second explosion, closer, sent them running for the door. The clouded expression in Eilene's eyes vanished as they stepped outside. It was as if he hadn't just laid his heart bare in front of the one person who could destroy his entire world.

Screams rent the air on the third explosion, and they both double-checked their belts for their weapons. Scott flew a moment later and let the wind whip his mind into shape for their current situation.

He spotted Eilene's water whip tearing through the crowd below. Somehow, HISS' army pierced far behind their camp line to reach the Council tents. He flew high to keep away from easy shots and fumbled for his own weapon. Scott got his hands on the Sclopētum. He chose the ranged version and whispered, "cōnferō" to trigger the sight. He leveled the crosshairs on one of the enemies and fired. The sagitta impacted their skull, and their body fell. One of their companions spotted him in the air and made a cry to the others. A ranged fighter on the other side stepped back and fired at him. He moved out of the way without hesitation. He trained his own sight on the shooter and fired.

Before he could tell if his shot hit, he felt the change in wind currents as a bullet tore through the air behind him. With only a moment to choose what to do, Scott released his control of the wind and dropped like a stone. He angled himself on the fall, so he would impact with the back of a Rogue. His feet hit the shoulders of the Rogue, and Scott rode him to the ground. The Rogue slid through the soft mud and landed face first, dead from the impact. Scott stepped away, rolling out his shoulders. The rush and impact from free falling always messed up his spinal alignment.

From his belt, he selected the Lūcis Harpē, a scimitar style blade with curved light which only cut on one side. Getting the feel of returning to Armōrum, he did better with tēlōrum, he flipped the handle around the back of his hand before catching it in his palm again. He slid his thumb across the activation key, and the blade extended. He slashed to his right and cut down another Rogue making great strides against an elementalist.

"Make sure you're using your ability," he called. "They won't hold back with theirs."

The elementalist at his side nodded hesitantly before turning to the next opponent and expending a lethal discharge of electricity. Scott pushed through the opening. Except the opening was wider than he anticipated. No longer an opening, but a flood of retreat. As quickly as they appeared in the camp, the Rogues disappeared into the dry forest land. He watched them retreat with the same curiosity and confusion as the other elementalists. Eilene stepped up next to him a moment later.

"I don't think that lasted more than thirty minutes."

Scott checked his watch. "Twenty-eight as of right now."

"How do you know?" She tilted her head to see his face.

"I subtracted about five minutes off from when I entered your tent." He took several steps away, but she could still see the pink color in his ears.

"Scott—"

He turned around with his hands shoved in his pockets. He continued to walk backward, barely avoiding a collision with a medical elementalist. He didn't look at her. "Now's not really the moment to talk, is it?"

Eilene shook her head; he must've seen because he turned around with hunched shoulders and assessed the battlefield.

April 12, 2319

The same style of battle happened four more times across the tenth and eleventh. A close penetration to the heart of the camp followed by an immediate retreat. Eilene leaned over the strategy table set-up in Scott's tent and moved a few pieces around uncertainly. They couldn't find the reason for the strange attacks.

"There has to be a pattern," she muttered under her breath, glaring at the board. She had the list of Rogues open on her tablet along with all the information passed along by Carmen and Ulrick as they discovered it. The notes file updated as she pulled it toward her to peruse again. Luana's handwriting scrawled across the page. Next attack wouldn't be until the thirteenth. Similar plan as previously. "Why? What is with these quick attacks?"

Scott looked up from his phone. "What's going on?"

She gestured blandly to the tablet and moved aside to another section of the three-dimensional terrain map where she crouched to get a different view. They barely talked to each other about anything other than battle plans. Despite the fact Scott confessed his feelings, he kept refusing to discuss it; he said it wasn't the right time to return to their conversation. Eilene, frankly, was pissed with him. *He should've never said it in the first place if it's the wrong time. He knew the battle was coming. We have until tomorrow to plan for an attack*, she thought. Another part of her knew better. *He's scared.*

Scott moved across the room to look at her tablet. He made sure to take the long way around the table to avoid walking next to her, and she rolled her eyes. As much as she understood his aversion, she still wanted to confront him head-on and deal with it. Although, the last time she did, a few hours after the first battle, he startled like a deer and flew out of reach. Across the table, Scott cautiously picked up the tablet and read the new notes.

Eilene touched the terrain in a few different locations, marking off the main exit points the Rogues took after their attacks. They glowed a bright yellow. She followed those points up with where they launched the attack in bright green.

Scott let out a sharp exhale of breath; it took a moment for Eilene to process it as a laugh.

"Something funny?" she asked.

"They're playing tag."

Eilene didn't say anything, but she gave him a curious look. He reached over the table, having to slightly prop himself by pulling a leg onto the edge just to avoid standing next to her. She resisted rolling her eyes again, *barely*. He drew a line between each attack point and exit in blue, then used red to mark the previous exit to the next attack. It formed a zig-zag pattern moving around the edges of the camp.

"If I took an educated guess, I'd say they started here." He used purple for the coordinating line. "And they'll attack here tomorrow." Another purple line. "I'm almost willing to bet they're sending in just small portions of their forces to grab our attention and slowly surround us."

"I'll send out a few regions to intercept." She pulled herself from her crouched position.

"No, no battles. There'd be no way to accurately time it. It may also be a ploy. We need reconnaissance to confirm that's what is happening."

"I'll send out small teams, then. Strong ones in case of patrols." She moved to the tent entrance and stepped out to speak with the Secretaries of the Army about their request. Her right-hand, Satō Akira, assured her he would handle everything they needed. "Arigatō, Satō-san."

"When is everyone scheduled to arrive?" Scott asked when she stepped into the tent again.

"Dwayne, Scarlet, and Series said they'd be here by dinner. Ethan and Kristen for breakfast. Luana and Hans are still out on when they'll arrive. They got caught up in some political issues." Eilene purposefully walked past him, brushing her elbow against the back of his jacket, as she returned to the table. He stopped breathing for a moment. She picked up her tablet and brushed past him a second time. "I'm going to eat lunch."

"There's my sister!" Dwayne held his arms wide as he climbed out of the pod to see Eilene and Scott waiting for their arrival. She ran forward and hugged him.

"I've missed you!"

Dwayne picked her up and swung her in a circle. Her legs barely missed hitting Scarlet, who told them to be careful. Series started laughing at the scandalized looks of the Field Marshals from Scott and Eilene's units.

"Sorry, Mulan."

The Field Marshals helped create a barrier between the lower ranking military members and the Council, but they still drew a large and curious crowd. Some watched with wide eyes as they celebrated their reunion. Eilene decided to fully hitch a ride on Dwayne's back, despite their four-inch height difference, and he humored her by bracing his hands under her thighs and carrying her toward the Council tents. Salama, Samuel, and Merjem followed their Council members out of the pod and gathered a small crew to help with assembly of their tents.

"Scott told me he's in love with me," Eilene said as they approached the door to her tent. Nobody was around except Satō who she knew wouldn't say anything.

Dwayne nearly dropped her. "He finally found the courage?"

Eilene sighed and slid gracefully from his back. "I suppose, except we were interrupted by HISS' attack. He won't talk to me about it. I've tried multiple times, but he just runs from the conversation."

"Oh, please try to confront him in front of me. I could do with some entertainment." Dwayne held the door open to her tent and followed her inside. "How does he run?"

Eilene bit her lip. "Runs is the wrong word. He flies."

Dwayne thought for a moment. "So, shoot him down. You can get him with a water whip. You're next to a river, you could probably propel yourself pretty high. Scare the crap out of our Mosupologo."

She laughed. "I'm not going to chase him down. Corner him, sure. Except he's very good at avoiding being cornered."

"Ah, so I get to tackle him and hold him down." Dwayne took over the chair at her desk.

"I am not going to stop you, but I have a feeling Scott is stronger than you."

Dwayne let his mouth form a scandalized O. "With these guns?" He flexed.

"Life versus Wind." She pretended to weigh them between her hands.

"Exactly! He's effortlessly strong because of his element. Sure, I can heal illnesses and reattach limbs, but for all that physical stuff, I had to work hard to get where I am! I could totally take him."

She curled on her bed, still laughing, and watched Dwayne swing himself in circles in the office chair.

"What are you going to tell him?" he asked after their giggles died.

"I've never had anyone like me before—at least, not that I'm aware of." She pulled her pillow to her chest and squeezed it. "I've gotten very used to being around Scott. There's something easy about being with him."

Dwayne crossed his arms but didn't interrupt.

"In some ways, I wonder if feelings for him have been growing for a while."

"How long?"

She pressed her face into the pillow, thinking. "I'm not sure. Maybe since I joined the Council?"

Dwayne gasped dramatically. "You were cheating on me?"

Eilene chucked the pillow at him, and Dwayne didn't defend himself. The pillow hit his face and landed in his lap. He spun it between his fingers.

"I'm glad you can at least reciprocate his feelings on some level. You both deserve each other, honestly."

Her eyes narrowed at his response. "You knew."

"Knew what?" Dwayne made his best attempt at an innocent smile, but Eilene knew better. He was never innocent.

"You knew he had feelings for me!" She looked for another projectile to throw.

"Well, when he comes to me asking me not to lead you on—it's really obvious," he said.

"He did *what*?" Eilene's mouth fell open. "Really?"

"Oh yeah. Remember the text you sent when we were fighting in Quezon City after I got shot?"

"No!" she said. "That was over a year ago."

"Yeah, and I told him a year ago to talk to you about his feelings. He's very good at sitting on them."

Eilene tugged the end of her braid.

"I'll braid your hair if you want to run your hands through it." Dwayne knew her well.

She picked up the habit from Luana. *It's not the worst one*, she supposed. Eilene pulled the tie free from her braid and shook out her hair. They weren't supposed to be attacked until the next day. Her fingers pulled at her hair, and tingles erupted along her skull as the strands released from their tight hold.

"How long has he been in love with me?" she asked.

Dwayne shrugged. "No idea. That wasn't part of the conversation."

"I'll come up with a plan to corner him."

"Do you want dinner first or for me to braid your hair?" Dwayne asked.

She ran her fingers through the wavy strands. "Dinner. It's nice having my hair down."

> **Change of plans. Just received word. Attack in five.**
> Luana

Eilene grabbed her hair tie as soon as the notification crossed the screen of her phone. She quickly pulled her hair into a messy ponytail.

"What's the deal with these spot battles?" Dwayne asked as they verified their weapons.

"Scott came up with the idea this morning that they're playing tag and slowly surrounding us. Scouts went out earlier and already confirmed the intent. They're small battles of not much note with a quick retreat on purpose."

"Drawing our attention," he hummed. "Shall we go give them a little hell?"

She grinned. "Just a little."

April 13, 2319

Hans and Luana arrived in the middle of the night with little fanfare.

They only had one tent set-up to save on time, and none of the other Council members wanted to enter the tent to let them know about breakfast. The five engaged in their version of a quiet argument over the issue just outside the tent door and provided entertainment for the Field Marshals. Hans opened the door to the tent, fully dressed in his military fatigues.

"Morning," he said.

"Have a good night's sleep?" Scarlet grinned like a bobcat.

"No, there's inconsiderate people arguing outside."

"Breakfast?" Dwayne offered. "Namune and Naledi got delayed."

"They're the ones you should be teasing." Series flicked her braid over her shoulder.

Identical grins spread across Dwayne's and Scarlet's faces.

"Oh no," Eilene said. She crossed her arms with a frown. "The two of you spending more time together created a monster."

"This is why Scarlet's parents think you're dating," Series said.

Eilene, who had just taken a drink from the bottle on her hip, spat out her water, laughing. "Do they really?"

"Apparently, denying the accusation is not enough to dissuade them." Scarlet adjusted her military hat.

"Congrats on the wedding," Eilene gave Dwayne a firm slap on the back.

"What'd you get us for a gift?" He followed her across the camp to the mess hall.

"Apologies, the order's been delayed indefinitely."

"That's disappointing. I could do with a new set of towels."

Scarlet pushed Scott's and Series' shoulders after the duo. To Hans, she said, "Wake Luana and get her to breakfast. We don't know when HISS' tag attack will arrive today."

"What about this area here?" Luana pointed to a point across the lagoon of the Paraguay River on the interactive map. "Could we use the trees and foliage to help camouflage us?"

"I'm concerned about how many people you think we can fit in a single tree." Hans stared at her. "Have you seen those trees?"

"That is not what I was suggesting." Luana rolled her eyes.

"Mom! They're flirting again," Dwayne whined reaching over to poke Scarlet.

"Why am I the mother in this situation?"

"We're not flirting." Hans flipped Dwayne off.

"Sorry we're late," Ethan opened the flap of the tent. He ushered Kristen inside with his hand on her back.

A quelling look from Luana halted any of the prepared teasing from Dwayne, Scarlet, and Series.

"You're in time to help us break the game of tag the Rogues started." Eilene climbed onto the edge of the table. She leaned over to point at the area Luana asked about earlier. "The problem with the Laguna Capitán is that it looks accessible and great, but a good portion of the land around it is a bog. Would be absolutely horrid to navigate for just about everyone."

"How'd you know it's a bog?" Series looked at the line of trees and shrubbery picked up by the three-dimensional scan.

"I can sense it." She drew a line along the beach to the northeast of the town along the edge of the lagoon. "The water, I mean. I know it's there lurking under the surface of what we see."

"What's the line for?" Series asked.

"Oh, it's showing the line between the plain and the wetland. The side we're on is great for farming. That's why I told them to set-up the camp on this side." Eilene returned to her perch on the edge and lost her balance. She let out a startled scream.

Scott appeared behind her to right her position. When his hands lingered on her waist a moment too long, neither said a word. Dwayne gave her a discreet thumbs up.

"So, that means we can't use it." Luana frowned.

"I didn't technically say that. It's a great asset to Water elementalists, but it would be a downside for literally everyone else—I mean Air could get away pretty quickly and not deal with it. Earth would also probably have an advantage with the mud," Eilene said.

"What if we were to bait them?" Ethan asked.

"How?" Kristen crossed her arms.

"We send in a crash party against their camps surrounding us. It's made up of the elements who can't navigate the bog. We take as many alive as possible to get information. Lead the others toward the bog, break off, and those who can navigate take over from there. If we play it right, we can get off with a near full capture of the entire force here with minimal deaths."

"A slight on your character," Dwayne said.

"I know! Who thought I, of all people, would suggest less deaths? I'm going to have to really hold back my power." Ethan grinned.

Kristen rolled her eyes at her boyfriend. "It's not a bad plan."

"Agreed, we should do it." Scott checked the weapons on his belt. "I think we should let them hit one more time in their little game of tag before we fumigate."

"Fumigate?" Eilene gave him a scathing look. "You're back with the synonyms."

He glared at her and crossed his arms, but he didn't say anything.

"That is two steps backward," Dwayne mumbled into Eilene's ear.

"Alright, vote for if we want to follow the plan set forth by Ethan. Everyone in favor say, 'Aye'," Luana said. Not one Council member denied the action. "Great, we can plan our *fumigation* after their next attack."

April 15, 2319

Dwayne volunteered to stay with Eilene, Hans, Scott, and the rest of the coordinating elementalists as a healer in case of a bloody battle when the Rogues realized the ambush. The group, except the Water elementalists, waded through the deep muddy water, and it seeped into their clothes. The Water elementalists walked across the water without slipping under. Dwayne lifted one of his legs from the bog and frowned at the mud.

"How hot is it here?" He fanned himself uselessly.

"Don't ask the American that question," Hans groaned.

"Thirty," Eilene said. When Scott quirked an eyebrow at her, she continued, "in Celsius. Eighty-six for the American."

"We should've worn waders over our gear." Dwayne pretended to vomit.

The area smelled like hydrogen sulfide gas from the decomposing plants. Eilene didn't mention the dead body of an undefined animal; she sensed it floating near Scott who already had a permanent scowl.

"Hindsight is always twenty-twenty." Hans spotted the same body as Eilene, and they exchanged a quiet and meaningful look. He swallowed thickly and followed her lead.

"What is this?" Scott asked as it brushed past his leg. He reached down.

"Don't!" Eilene and Hans yelled at the same time.

Scott froze. He straightened his spine and cautiously moved three steps to his right. Eilene nodded.

"Dickens, you'll warn me if I'm getting close to something similar to Mosupologo, right?"

"Absolutely not."

"I should've expected that."

"I could warn you, Tautona Tebogo." An excited Earth elementalist volunteered from behind the Council members. The woman wasn't one of their many Field Marshals.

"Ah, thank you, but it's okay. I was just messing with Dickens." Dwayne tried not to feel guilty over her disappointed expression.

Eilene hid her laugh behind a vicious coughing fit; Scott's lips twitched. Hans hid his grin behind his hand.

"There's a stretch of land just ahead of us. It's pretty solid. I'd say we spread out there and wait for the Rogues to try to cross the lagoon." Hans pointed to the sand. "The bushes would provide some cover, and this mud is going to do wonders for our camouflage."

"I may never smell again," Eilene said.

The line in their ear crackled as Ethan's voice washed over them. "Ya'll in position? We're ready to rush."

Hans lifted his hand to his ear to trigger his voice. "Not yet, almost across the bog. It's hard to cross in waste deep mud."

"Dwayne!" Eilene shouted, interrupting their flow. "Don't step there."

Dwayne stopped; his leg suspended in mud. "Please tell me I am not about to be eaten by something large and hideous."

She shook her head and lifted him out of the bog with a burst of water.

"What happened?" Kristen asked after she heard the shout over Hans' line.

"The bog suddenly dropped and went incredibly deep." Hans closed his eyes to focus on searching for the solid land under the water. "This is going to cause a crossing problem for us."

"How long do you need?" Series asked.

"Maybe about ten minutes." Eilene joined in the search. "It'll be great once the Rogues come for us. I think we could use the bog to our advantage. Fully bait them right to us. They'll think they have a straight shot."

"Love the idea. Think you could put me down, Dickens?" Dwayne called.

"I'm looking for a safe location. If you're up for drowning, I'll drop you now."

Dwayne kept silent until Eilene found the next part of solid land and set him down twenty-five feet ahead, well into the shoreline.

"Water elementalists!" Eilene called. "Take the Earth elementalists. We don't want to disturb the bog too much. It'll only hurt our chances in dragging out the enemy."

"Air, to the sky!" Scott lifted himself from the bog, followed by the others. Eilene carefully lifted herself from the bog with as little disturbance as possible. They landed on the sandy shore while Dwayne waded his way toward them.

"Alright, Namune," Dwayne said into the earpiece. "Smoke 'em."

The screaming terror was almost immediate. Smoke rose into the sky as the elementalists tore into the first camp, driving them toward Laguna Capitán. They waited about fifteen minutes before the first line of soldiers cleared the ridgeline and ran for the bog.

"Showtime," Eilene said.

The Rogues ran into the bog, struggling to make progress through the water. The first few reached the drop point and screamed as they sank.

"Pull them out! Take them alive." Hans ordered; they broke free of the bushes and charged into the bog.

This time, the elementalists used their abilities to their full capacity to manipulate the treacherous land. They had no need to keep the bog land undisturbed. They pulled the Rogues free of the thick mud and several from drowning on the drop point. However, a new line of Rogues ran into the street above the river armed to the teeth. There were a lot more Rogues than reconnaissance originally reported.

"I think it was a bad idea for me to get stranded on this side of the lagoon," Dwayne said.

"Want a lift?" Scott floated into the air holding out his arms.

Dwayne shrugged and let Scott lift him into the air and across the water.

"This was such a bad plan." Eilene ran across the bog just ahead of Hans who lifted the earth under the water to match each step.

The pair returned to shore just in time to intercept the armed Rogues before they shot into the crowd. Eilene retrieved the Lūcis Fuscina from her belt with her right hand. She thrust forward at the same time her thumb triggered the activation key. The trident extended in front of her and through the torso of one of the Rogues. She pulled back avoiding the blood spray. With her left hand, she opened the water canister on her other side and shot boiling water into the faces of the Rogues attempting to flank her.

For a moment, Eilene caught sight of Hans twisting his foot and trapping several Rogues underground with just their heads above the soil. Eilene spun the handle of the Fuscina in her hand and jabbed the blunt end into the chest of a Rogue running pell-mell toward her with no melee weapon. The Rogue flew several feet before falling on their back. They cried out as pain danced through their spine. Eilene lifted the Fuscina above her head and threw it full force where it impaled a Rogue against a tree before the light portion of the blade petered away. The handle fell to the ground a moment before the Rogue.

Eilene grabbed the Jaculum from her belt before spinning on her heel and raising her other leg to kick another Rogue to her back. He grabbed her ankle and pulled. Without proper balance, she fell face first into the dirt. The Jaculum handle spun away and disappeared among the crowd of feet. The Rogue smirked at her for only a moment before her ability sizzled through the air. She froze him where he stood. She yanked her foot from his grasp and pushed herself to her feet.

"Eilene!" Dwayne yelled over the crowd. He fought his own group of five Rogues with his Jaculum. "Scott went down! He got shot. I don't know where he is. I saw him fall."

Everything slowed down around her. She forgot to breathe.

Dwayne's hand wrapped around her arm. *When did he get there?* He dragged her toward the river. Eilene watched his mouth move, but she couldn't hear what he said. He shook her, and she made a distressed noise. All at once, she heard everything. Pained screams. Shouting. Her own cries of distress.

"Dickens! Go!"

Eilene stumbled into the bog, and mud soaked the material and climbed to her knees.

In delayed response, she ran across the water searching for bodies. Just past the drop point, she found Scott sinking and tangled in bog plants. She stopped just above him in the bog, except she couldn't pull him out of the water. He only sunk further.

This is going to be so gross, Eilene thought just before she took an unneeded deep breath and dived. She pushed through the mud. The earth messed with her control. She couldn't let it stop her from reaching Scott.

She felt the earth pressing in on her chest. Mud filled her mouth, dry and gritty. Her body was actively trying to remove the danger of the water and making every bit of earth that much more dangerous. It was a slow sink to the bottom like being stuck in quicksand.

Her hand wrapped around a familiar wrist, and she tightened her grip. Eilene pulled until she had her arms under Scott's. Grip tight around his chest, she kicked back, fighting against the mud to pull them free and up to clearer water.

They broke through the surface with Eilene gasping for air. She used a blast of the river water to lift and carry them to the shore where the fighting raged. She pushed Scott onto the ground in front of her and kneeled over him. Mud covered him from head to foot.

"Scott?" Eilene patted his cheeks. He didn't respond. "Scott?" She used her power to search his lungs for water. She found a significant amount and carefully removed it hoping it would revive him. Scott choked then went deathly still. Eilene repeated his name again, but he didn't respond. She checked his pulse, and it felt too slow. "Dwayne! Help! Dwayne! What do I do?"

"I'm here," Dwayne skidded to a stop next to her.

"He's not breathing!"

He tapped Eilene to the side and quickly ran a scan of Scott's body. Green light emanated from Dwayne's hands, and a moment later, Scott coughed violently. He pushed himself up blinking through the mud clogging his vision. He vomited to the side, expelling the same mud.

Eilene pulled him into a tight hug. "You're okay."

"Why are you covered in mud?" he croaked.

"I pulled you out from the bog where you were drowning." She pushed the mud away from his eyes with her thumbs.

"I got shot," Scott said.

Eilene nodded and continued trying to clean the mud from his skin.

"No offense, Dickens, but the both of you smell terrible." Dwayne choked on his own bile.

She cringed under the weight of the mud tangled in her hair. "It might never come out."

"Do you still have weapons?" Dwayne spun the Jaculum over their heads as a Rogue tried to take advantage of their distraction in an attack.

They immediately checked their wrists and belts. Scott still had his gear, but Eilene only had the Scūta on her wrist and a short range Sclopētum with a singular case of ammo already loaded.

"It's time for me to use the river." Eilene scratched at the drying mud on her elbow. "Tell everyone on our side to get clear. Evacuate the houses just in case."

"Try not to kill anyone." Dwayne switched channels on the radio in his ear.

"Oh, they're much worse off being captives." Eilene stood and took several steps to the edge of the river.

She watched the rush of retreat from the elementalists, and the Rogues cheered thinking they won. Except, as her own military ran for the hills, she threw out her arms and the river into the lagoon exploded into a wall of water rising high above the Rogues. Eilene shifted the water, and it crashed over the shore. The roar of the wave drowned out the screaming.

She rode the wave, churning the Rogues to the top where Air elementalists lifted them clear and to the Earth elementalists who put the power suppression handcuffs on each one. Eilene directed the water back into the river where it sloshed before settling into a serene muddy mess.

"That water did little to help you clean up," Dwayne said when she rejoined him, Scott, and Hans.

She frowned.

He put his hands up in surrender. "Alright, I'll hold off on the jokes for now."

CHAPTER THIRTEEN

Evening

Vander watched the wall of water rise out of the river, and his mouth fell open. Abdiel's hand wrapped around his arm and pulled him in their retreat from the elementalists. Vander pointed his weapon at the ground and ran, except someone slid into view just ahead of them and they were on fire.

"¡El diablo!" Abdiel shouted.

The ball of fire tore toward them, and Vander threw himself against Abdiel; they tumbled to the ground and rolled across the dirt field. The elementalist continued their crusade and sent several Rogues to their knees; the other elementalists arrived in support and captured the Rogues.

One such elementalist descended on Vander and Abdiel, and without thinking, Vander threw out his hand at the sight of the weapon. It *popped* out of her grip. She stared at the empty space in surprise. Vander's ability never came in handy before.

In the next second, Abdiel grabbed Vander by his shirt and rolled them out of the way as the woman sent a whip of fire slamming on the ground right where they were. Debris rained over them.

"We're taking them alive!"

Vander didn't understand what the fireball said, but the woman swinging the whip hesitated just long enough for them to jump to their feet and attempt a retreat. They dodged between the sparse trees. Vander grabbed Abdiel's arm and pulled him toward the town instead of joining the others. However, a person cloaked in darkness holding a double-ended scythe halted their path. He swung the weapon through the air one-handed, and both men froze.

"If the person on fire is el diablo, who the hell is that?" Vander pointed to the newcomer.

"Tu peor pesadilla," the man said.

The devil, who gave chase to their retreat, and the nightmare conversed in English for a moment, and it sounded playful—joking. Completely not appropriate for the situation. Abdiel tried to pull him away, but Vander's feet were stuck to the ground. The man pointed the scythe at them, and it waited just under Vander's chin.

"Kneel," he said in Spanish.

Their knees collapsed under them, and they submitted to capture.

More whispered mutterings between the two followed; Vander and Abdiel remained on the ground waiting for their inevitable doom.

"At least it will end by your side," Vander whispered in Sranan Tongo.

The fireball extinguished, and a woman stood in her place evaluating the battlefield. Small strands of brunette hair pulled free of her ponytail and drifted around her face. She lifted a hand to her earpiece and spoke for a moment before listening. The nightmare also rid himself of his cloak, and Vander assessed his broad shouldered frame and red hair.

"¿Habla español?" The red head turned to Abdiel and Vander suddenly.

"Sí," Abdiel said, "pero mi pareja no habla español. Un poquito."

The man nodded and relayed something to his companion. She nodded before communicating something to the others. A familiar blur blew past Vander and Abdiel kneeling on the ground in front of the Council. Abdiel's eyes widened in shock. A moment later, it stopped and a blonde woman with tanned skin spoke furiously to the others in a low voice they couldn't understand. The man jerked his thumb toward the two on the ground.

The newcomer whirled to face them with a look of determination. "¿Qué sabes sobre un hombre llamado Ryan Everton?"

"Everton?" The first woman spoke sharply.

The blonde waved her away and waited for Abdiel's reply.

Abdiel chewed his tongue before responding. "Él nos llevó a la batalla."

Vander really wished he understood Spanish better. He at least recognized the name of the person in charge of the attack—although Ryan acted rather reluctantly from Vander's point of view—and Vander figured the elementalists asked about him for information on HISS. Something about Ryan's name threw them off.

Two more women hurried down the path toward the group. Their captors quickly filled the pair in as they nodded and joined the congregation.

The blonde bent down in front of Abdiel. "Te llevaremos para interrogarte." She gestured to Vander. "¿Puedes decirle a tu pareja?"

Abdiel nodded before relaying they would be taken for further interrogation. Vander supposed it was the best-case scenario. He recognized Ryan's name a second time before the blonde pointed in the direction of the elementalists camp they attacked several times. *He must be captured, too.*

"I think they captured everyone," Abdiel whispered under his breath. "I don't really understand the English, but it sounds like the people who died were unavoidable. They tried to save all of us."

"Why? To keep us alive for the Council to do away with later?" Vander spat. "We're Rogues. The elementalists aren't going to keep us alive for long."

Abdiel frowned but didn't say anything further.

One of the newcomers finally looked at the captives, and she did a double take. She recognized them—but Vander never met her before. She pointed to them and whispered something furiously. The man waved for another person to join them, and he gave an order. The person nodded and came to their side before helping them stand and leading them toward the elementalist encampment.

"You know," Abdiel whispered, "earlier when that blonde appeared—"

he stopped speaking.

"I know," Vander said. "It looked like the thing you can do."

"You don't think I'm—" again, he couldn't say it aloud.

Vander decided not to say anything. Abdiel took the hint and stayed quiet while the elementalist at their back led them into a purple tent at the heart of the encampment where none other than Ryan Everton kneeled under the watch of two guards.

"You used our real names earlier," Eilene accused as they met up with the other Council members. They already relayed what happened at their side of the battle.

"Yeah, don't expect me to make a habit of it, Dickens." Dwayne crossed his arms. "I had to get your attention."

Eilene laughed.

"You know, that's a relief," Scarlet said. "I was worried he didn't actually know our names."

"So, we have a few captives who gave us information. We put them in my tent," Kristen cut in. "One of them is named Ryan Everton."

Scott's posture straightened immediately.

"I think the both of you should try and clean up before we confront them." Luana pointed at Scott and Eilene caked in dried mud. They nodded stiffly and headed toward their tents where they had private showers.

"Something's going on between them," Series said.

Dwayne shook his head and led the way toward Kristen's tent. "You have no idea."

"Do you think Ryan is Scott's father?" Luana's fingers threaded through Hans'.

"Based on his reaction, most likely," Series said.

Eilene returned to the group first squeaky clean and wearing civvies. She adjusted the strap of her bright pink tank top and stuck her hand in the back pocket of her cutoffs.

Dwayne picked up a loose strand of her hair and rubbed it between his fingers. "I'm getting you a box of blue hair dye, and we are fixing this mess. A blonde one for you, too, Mulan!"

They both rolled their eyes before everyone broke into a bought of laughter.

Scott showed up a moment later, in a clean military uniform, with just a bit of mud stuck under his nails. He didn't say anything but pointed to the tent.

"Do—" Luana cleared her throat. "Do you want to go in first?"

Scott shook his head.

"I understand." Luana opened the tent flap.

Eilene reached out to touch Scott's arm, but he pulled away and gestured for her to follow the others in. She clenched her jaw to keep from saying anything.

"Please! Don't kill me!" Ryan cried when he caught sight of the newcomers. "Please! I'm one of Tyr's right-hand men. I will give you any information you want. Please don't kill me."

The Council looked to Scott, waiting for him. He stared at the older and broken version of his father. He no longer resembled the young and virile researcher who married a member of a biker gang. However, he could still see Melissa in every part of his father. He couldn't quite remember how many years had passed since he last saw his father.

"We're not going to kill you, Dad."

Ryan's head shot up to stare at the Council for the first time. "Scott."

"If you're one of Slattery's, you must be familiar with my father?" Luana asked. It took a while for Ryan to look away from his son, but when he did— his eyes recognized her despite never meeting.

"Mason's daughter," Ryan said. "Luana, right? He told me all about you."

Her eyebrow quirked, but she didn't ask anything more.

Kristen walked across her tent and collected the chair from the desk. She wheeled it back and offered it to Scott. He tried to refuse, but she insisted, and he sat.

Dwayne pointed to the other two in the tent. "Do you know them?"

Ryan shook his head. "Not personally. I think we picked them up in

Suriname during Rogue recruitment for HISS."

"Suriname?" Eilene perked up. At Ryan's nod, she whirled around and said, "Waarom heb je besloten om je bij HISS aan te sluiten?"

The sudden Dutch startled one while the other looked confused.

"Meestal voor Abdiel." The first nodded at his companion. "HISS beloofde ook dat ze ons zouden vrijlaten."

Eilene repeated the first question to Abdiel, but he shook his head.

"Abdiel spreekt geen Nederlands. Hij kent Spaans en Sranan Tongo. Mijn naam is Vander."

Eilene nodded. She turned back to the Council. "That one is Vander, the other one is Abdiel. Abdiel doesn't speak Dutch. He speaks Spanish and a language I haven't heard of. Vander joined HISS because of Abdiel, and they promised the Rogues freedom."

Luana pinched the bridge of her nose and sighed. "Their freedom? What is HISS thinking? How can they promise something like that when they're planning on killing us? The Rogues are literally us with no ability to control one of the nine. This is ridiculous."

"Tyr was willing to promise them anything to get them on our side even if we took it back later." Ryan said.

"¿Sabías que HISS podría matarte al final de todo esto?" Kristen repeated their main question to Abdiel.

Abdiel nodded hesitantly. "Vander cuestionaba constantemente su promesa."

"¿Y tú?"

"No."

"Vander questions it more than Abdiel," Kristen reported. "Whatever promise they made, Abdiel agreed without question."

"Disculpe," Abdiel said.

"¿Sí?"

"Antes, tu habilidad se parecía a la mía."

Kristen froze. The others stared at her. "¿Qué?"

Abdiel repeated his statement.

"What is it?" Series asked.

"Abdiel says he has the same ability as me."

"It's not out of the realm of possibility." Luana shrugged. "We don't know how many we killed or mislabeled."

Eilene asked Vander if he observed something similar between Kristen and Abdiel's abilities, and he agreed. "So, Abdiel might be a Supernatural elementalist."

"And Vander is a Rogue," Ethan said. "What are we going to do with all these Rogues, anyway?"

"I think we should take them back to Elementōrum Patriam and try to integrate them into our society," Eilene said.

Scott shook his head and decided not to look at her. The others stared.

"Eilene, Rogues kill those around them." Luana unfolded her arms and fought off making fists at her side.

"When they're scared! That's when their power acts up. Our powers do the same thing when we get emotional."

"When did you formulate this idea?" Dwayne asked.

"Last month when HISS started killing our people using alcohol as a biological weapon." She crossed her arms. "Scott supported it."

"I did not!" he snapped. The Council jumped. He wasn't prone to sudden outbursts. "I didn't say anything about it. I agreed it was similar to what Hans is trying to do with the Uns, that's all."

"Alright, this is not the time to debate this." Luana waved them off from a further argument. "Right now, we need to focus on HISS. We have one of Tyr's right-hands who can hopefully give us information on what he's doing. We'll keep the Rogues alive until we make a decision as the nine. They'll be POWs on Elementōrum."

"What about Abdiel?" Kristen pointed to him.

"Ask him if he'd like training to use his power or to be a POW," Hans said.

Abdiel chose to be a POW. He didn't want to be separated from Vander.

"Right," Luana clapped her hands together, "now that's sorted. Ryan, what can you tell us about Slattery and HISS. Don't leave out any details."

Ryan started his story. He told them how Tyr found him in Key West where Ryan moved after losing Scott and Melissa. Tyr originally approached Ryan because he wanted to discuss what happened to his daughter. Ryan, thinking he was a man who needed a pick-me-up, agreed to meet with him. When Tyr admitted his true goal, Ryan tried to walk away, so Tyr bribed him. Made the medical debt he was in disappear overnight. Ryan figured he would help Tyr find a little information and have a way out—it was all he wanted.

Except, when he found the information, Tyr twisted it. He offered Ryan the chance to "fix" future generations. Undo the mutation and save other parents from the heartache he experienced. Ryan jumped in headfirst to HISS and helped Tyr. Then, they needed someone with military experience to really make their attacks helpful. They traveled to Tennessee and cornered Mason Ford. Tyr bribed him with information about his daughter—made the guess from some data she was still alive. Mason joined only to find Luana.

They started chasing down elementalists for human experimentation. They tried going after Kristen, but she escaped. Ryan helped kidnap two children, including the one at the mall. He never saw his son there because Ryan fought Eilene. He recognized her, and she him. Scott looked like his mother, so she never would've made the connection between them.

Tyr declared war. Countries started pulling away from long-standing agreements and backed HISS. The Council revealed themselves. Ryan and Mason saw their children for the first time in many years—the catalyst for their fading loyalty. They weren't as disillusioned by the promises Tyr made.

They were stuck. Slattery had blackmail information on them. Ryan and Mason followed his whims. The reason why Mason ended up in the battle in Georgia; why Ryan had a hand in building the testing facility where HISS experimented on elementalists; why Mason was there now overseeing the experiments; and why Ryan oversaw collecting and leading the Rogues into battle.

Mason and Ryan tried to work from the inside when they could. They made sure the elementalists overheard their plans to attack the Philippines. They delayed testing and altered its requirements, so it would never quite work.

Ryan and Mason had no freedom from Tyr.

"So, my dad is being held hostage?" Luana asked.

Ryan nodded solemnly. "He's in charge of the facility, and he must run semi-legitimate experiments on the elementalists we captured. Although, I heard from Tyr recently, and he mentioned whatever data he got from Mason's half-baked experiments might be useful to him. He already has a prototype of the weapon. I've seen it in action, and it works. If Tyr finds out I gave you information, I'm dead."

"I think he'll know soon enough that we took you captive." Dwayne crossed his arms.

Scott swallowed past the lump in his throat. "Dad, we can protect you."

"You don't have to. I understand if you want to kill me." Ryan sat on his feet. "I deserve it."

"You don't," Scott said. "We'll take you as a POW. You'll be safe where Tyr can't reach you. Eventually, after the war, we can reevaluate our relationship."

Ryan shook his head. "I don't think there's anywhere Tyr can't get to."

"Mr. Everton," Ethan kneeled in front of Ryan, "what can you tell me about the weapon Slattery made?"

"It's designed for use specifically against you."

"You know who I am," Ethan said.

"Ethan Silverspoon, a Death elementalist." Ryan's knees ached, and he tried to shift and stretch them out. Dwayne noticed and grabbed him a chair to sit in. "There's more like you."

"We saw, last year in Tyr's video declaring war," Hans said.

"Yes, that was one. Tyr is bragging he found more."

"It's not confirmed?" Luana sat on Kristen's bed.

Ryan shook his head. "There's not much I can confirm about Tyr anymore. He only tells us what we need to know. I think he stopped trusting us at some point—or he never did."

"Well, from what we saw, the weapon is incomplete." Ethan shrugged. "For all we know, he could be bragging about it just to play up an advantage and scare us off. There's no point in backing away from our plans now."

"Ethan, you don't have to be the one to face Slattery," Scarlet said.

"Yes, I do," he laughed. "Series saw it. The future is unchangeable. I can beat him, I know it. This weapon he boasts isn't going to work."

"It might," Ryan said.

"I'm not going to stop trying to bring down Tyr and HISS for a '*maybe*'."

"Ethan, I've seen the weapon in person. I saw how close it is to perfection. In fact, it worked near the end before Mason and I managed to get the child out of the house. If he does have a Death elementalist, Tyr will kill you in a one-on-one battle. It will give him the power HISS needs."

"All the more reason for me to go against him. It could be a flaw. The original elementalist you saw the weapon work on could've been too weakened. Anything would work against them in that scenario. I know that just as well as everyone here. I'm the only one of us who has a chance." Ethan jabbed his thumb into his chest.

"You can't throw yourself at the enemy. He wants you. Tyr wants to make an example of you." Kristen's voice broke around unshed tears.

"I'm not throwing myself anywhere. When I meet Tyr on the battlefield, I will be prepared. I'll train harder in our down time. I'll strengthen my powers. I'm not going to die by his hand."

"Ethan, please, don't do this. You can step back, no one will blame you," Series said.

"When I went through Council initiation, I swore to protect the people of my country. I won't have it be the other way around. I'm not going to run from this. I'm not a coward," Ethan said.

"No one would call you a coward for stepping away from a well-known and proven danger. One of us can take Tyr on," Dwayne spoke calmly.

"I know I can do it." Ethan puffed his chest a little. "I may be one of the newest Council members, but I know the extent of my abilities. I'll take Slattery down and clear the way for us to pave a new life at the end of the war."

"I can't talk you out of this either, can I?" Kristen bit her lip to hold back tears.

Ethan reached out and took her hands. "I'm going to be okay."

Scott looked away from the affectionate display. His eyes met Eilene's.

When she noticed him looking, she gave him a soft smile.

Ryan cleared his throat. "There's something else I should tell you. I'm afraid it would injure even you, Ethan."

The Council gave him their full attention.

"Mason sent word in a coded message of something in development. We don't know when they're going to be tested." Ryan took a shaky breath before admitting, "Bullets laced with alcohol."

"Would that work?" Luana looked at Dwayne.

He nodded stiffly. "If the alcohol gets in our bloodstream, we're done for."

"Tautona Tebogo," Salama, Dwayne's right-hand, called from outside the tent, "we need you immediately in the medical tent."

"Can someone else not step in?" Dwayne glared through Ryan without really seeing him.

"No, sir," Salama said. "Nobody has the skill required." They heard her steps fading as she walked away before they returned. "The rest of the Council may want to come as well."

They exchanged uneasy glances.

"I'll catch up in just a moment," Kristen said. "I'll have Gloria organize where Vander and Abdiel should go—the problem is Mr. Everton."

"Put him with the other POWs for now. We can reevaluate later." Scott stood from his chair. "Let's hurry to the infirmary."

Dwayne stared at the bodies laid out in the temporary morgue. From a quick glance, their deaths didn't make sense. The bullets the Rogues fired didn't hit any fatal locations. Each elementalist should've made it to the medical tent and been healed.

"No cause of death?" He gestured to the doctor standing in the corner with a tablet.

She shook her head. "Not that we could ascertain, Tautona."

Dwayne stepped forward without further questions and put on a pair of gloves to examine one of the bodies. Green light filled the room and made the corpses look worse. Despite his permanent frown, Eilene saw the way he shifted his weight to his opposite foot when he found something concerning. He pressed forward and requested a pair of tweezers from one of the nurses. When he had them in hand, he pressed into one of the open wounds fishing for something only he could sense.

A moment later, he pulled a bullet from the wound.

"Don't touch it," he said. "I need to run a test." A nurse gently collected the object with a sterile towel. He gestured for another to approach. "Take a blood sample from each body. I have some tests I want to run."

While the machine in the corner tested the blood samples, Dwayne carefully placed the intact bullet on a tray before prying the casing open with his tools. From the inside of the bullet, a small vial slipped onto the tray. It was leaking, cracked from the pressure of firing but not quite following its intended use. Carefully, he cracked the vial further and sniffed. Dwayne frowned and reached for a secure container to place the pieces in. He cleaned the tray and put all the items in the box before throwing it in the trash.

The machine beeped in the corner, and the nurse collected the results. A startled look passed across the nurse's face before he handed the results to Dwayne. The Council member threw the results onto the counter.

"Exactly what I thought." Dwayne pulled off the latex gloves and threw them in the trash.

"What is it?" Hans asked.

"Those bullets Ryan mentioned are already in action."

April 16, 2319

5.41, -143.16, Devil's Gate

Mason's phone buzzed on the desk next to him. Tyr just left his office with the next set of paperwork and information. He would be in the lab working with the new weapons. One of the engineers had an idea to make the bullets more effective.

We know. Next location? -

Lubear

Mason fumbled the phone as he hurriedly tried to text a response.

Kpalime, Togo. June. No specific date.

They must've captured Ryan, Mason thought. The only explanation for his daughter having a direct line of communication with him. She responded a moment later.

You in for the movies this weekend?

Mason's brows pinched in the middle as he stared at the message. He wasn't familiar with the code, but he figured it must be a message. He saw the small dots indicating typing on the other end.

You there, man?

It clicked. He needed to delete his previous messages and pretend it was a wrong number. It would hide the truth from Tyr.

Sorry, man. Wrong number.

He quickly thumbed over the previous messages and sent them to the trash before searching the memory files on the phone and purging them completely. No other messages came through, but he could pass along information to the elementalists. His chance arrived.

April 19, 2319

Fuerte Olimpio, Alto Paraguay Department, Paraguay

Scott sang along with the songs in his playlist as he spent the afternoon cleaning his tent. They would ship out the next morning to Elementōrum Patriam, and he needed to have everything packed and ready to go. They would wait for further information before moving in on Togo to face HISS again. He regretted how he didn't have a moment to discuss what happened with Eilene. Everything moved too quickly, and he had a lot of experience avoiding people he didn't want to talk to, but he was glad the Council wouldn't be splitting into their own groups anymore. He missed being with family.

The song changed to a deep bass beat before a familiar gravely and crooning voice filtered from the speakers. Scott didn't typically listen to archaic music, but Eilene's and Dwayne's tastes rubbed off on him over time. He found the artist on his own through a few algorithm recommendations. Scott tapped his foot to the steady beat. He closed his eyes as he danced around the tent to the second chorus. He reached the small bridge before the third chorus and stared up at the ceiling thinking irrevocably of Eilene. Scott felt like he would be her downfall if she did feel the same as him. He wasn't anywhere near good enough for her—she deserved the universe.

The emotion bled into his voice as he sang. The song faded to an end.

Before the next song could start, a voice from the doorway of the tent said, "I didn't realize you did so many things."

He whipped around to see Eilene leaning against the wall with a small smile on her face.

"I've never seen you act so loose before."

A faint blush spread over his nose, and he stuttered, unable to formulate a response.

"What was the song? I really liked it."

"'I'm Not A Saint' by Billy Raffoul," he said.

She hummed. "It's amazing how much we can relate to a song which talks about doing things we physically can't." She noticed his pinched brows and continued, "the smoking and drinking."

"Yeah, I suppose it is a bit odd."

"Good." She hadn't moved from the doorway. An unexplored expanse separated them. "So, how long have you been sitting on the fact you're romantically interested in me?"

The blush darkened his cheekbones. Scott's attraction to her didn't stop at romantic. "I'm not sure. I never noticed until it was too late."

"Too late?" She tilted her head to the side. "You make it sound like it's a bad thing."

"Well—" he gestured without point.

"Do you need help packing?" she asked. "I already finished my tent."

"Why are you here?"

Eilene flushed a faint pink. "I can't stop thinking about what you told me before the humans and Rogues attacked."

Scott chose not to respond. He watched her shuffle from foot to foot. She uncomfortably crossed her arms and stared at the floor.

"I'm not sure I can reciprocate the depth of feelings you have for me, but I want to try dating you."

He took several hesitant steps forward until he stood in front of her. "You're sure?"

Eilene bit her lip and nodded.

"Can—" he breathed deeply, "Can I kiss you?"

"Yes," she said.

He grabbed her elbows and pulled her closer. She released her crossed arms, and her hands grabbed the edges of his jacket. When he leaned in, he closed his eyes the moment before his lips pressed against hers. It was softer than he expected.

Scott watched the movies, saw the scenes where the couple gets together. He knew he was missing something, but he wasn't sure what. Eilene pulled away, and he panicked until her lips parted, and she pulled his bottom lip between her teeth. His hands slid around her waist and pulled her to him.

"Sorry, I'm not good at this," Scott whispered.

Eilene laughed; her breath rushed over his lips. "That's okay."

"Blow to the ego."

Eilene moved her arms to around his neck and pulled him back for a quick peck. "Seriously, do you want help with packing?"

CHAPTER FOURTEEN

Sunset

April 24, 2319

The Academy, Elementōrum Patriam

Returning home to the Council chambers felt like a breath of fresh air. When they flicked on the lights, everything was as they left it.

In the middle of the night, a notification on Eilene's phone woke her from a restful sleep next to Scott. She rolled away from him to collect the device from the nightstand.

"What is it?" Scott asked groggily.

She read the message quickly. "They finished translating the image from the book. Scarlet wants me to look at the translation. Apparently, there are some questions."

"What image?" Scott swung his legs out of the covers to climb out of the bed.

"The image from the book with the nine elements. We sent it in for code breaking and translation forever ago, but that kind of stuff takes time.

Especially since the image was so small and compressed. I remember it had Binary code and Italian," Eilene said as she pulled on a jacket and jeans. "Scarlet and I got this." She tucked the phone into the pocket of her pants. "You can go back to sleep."

He shook his head. "I'll come with. I'm interested." He reached for his slippers. "Are we meeting with anyone?"

"No."

"Good, I'm wearing my pajamas."

"What is the stone from the earth?" Eilene magnified the page on her tablet.

"No idea, but whoever has it becomes the drug trafficker of the nine." Scarlet examined the translation notes more closely. "Granted, the translator did note 'courier' may be a better suited word based on the context."

Eilene and Scott burst into laughter. Eilene said, "Drug trafficker?"

"Oh, we are so taking performance-enhancing drugs to get the powers of the nine. How do we do that?" Scott pressed a finger to his lip to hide his smirk. "These instructions seem to leave out the ingredient list."

"What are you three laughing about?" Ethan pushed open the door to their meeting room, rubbing sleep from his eyes.

"Drug trafficking," Eilene said with a straight face.

Ethan dropped his fist to his side, and his lips parted slightly. A moment later, he turned around. "Alright. Have fun."

"I scared him," Eilene lamented. "Ah, well." She flipped a few pages on her tablet. "So, there's some sort of stone from the earth which may or may not give us the power of the nine elements?"

"I think so," Scarlet said. She checked the translation notes. "Although, the border says something along the lines of only those who swear can gain the ability—so maybe there's a duality to it?"

"Is it referring to the swearing in of new Council members?" Scott suggested.

Scarlet gasped. "That makes sense. So, how do we find this power?"

"It's wherever the heart of the nine is." Eilene reached a hand behind her to scratch her back. "I really hope it doesn't mean we have to become gravediggers. I'd rather not violate the tombs of the nine."

"Maybe it's something we get just from being a Council member?" Scarlet held her hands out in front of her. "How do you control Water?"

Eilene blinked. "It's so natural at this point, I have to think about how the teachers trained us." She flexed her fingers. "It's kind of like, just knowing there's water in the air? If I really think about it, everything around me always has this sensation of feeling *wet*."

"That sounds disgusting," Scott said.

"Well, how about you with Air?"

"I'm not sure. It feels normal." He frowned. "When I want to fly, I just kind of picture the air currents in my mind."

"I like to imagine the molecules creating friction," Scarlet said. "That's how I get lightning." Her hands sparked. "However, every bit of my power is so drastically different. I mean, creating a tsunami isn't just molecules and friction."

"And throwing boiling water or freezing someone in ice is a lot different than just," Eilene held out her hand, and a small ball of water hovered above her palm, "getting water."

Scarlet held out her hand, but only a small storm cloud formed in the corner. "Either we'll need a lot of practice, or it's not as simple as being a Council member."

"How would you pass your powers down?" Scott pointed to the Italian line which read, *the nine send forth their accumulated knowledge to establish world order.*

"I don't know," Scarlet traced the edges of her tablet. "Elements aren't inherited."

"I feel like we're running in circles." Eilene ran her fingers through her hair. "I say we leave this information as is. It's clear we don't have the resources to understand it." She stretched. "I'm also exhausted."

"I'll share what we found with the others and see if anyone else has any other ideas." Scarlet waved the other two off. "Have a good night."

Scott threaded his fingers through hers as they returned to his bedroom.

May 3, 2319

Ethan took command of the training facility in the Council chambers early in the morning. He used the panel on the side wall of the sparring room to tell the computer how many enemies to generate, what they should respond to, and what weapons they should carry. Ethan selected the maximum variations he could before overloading the system—something he learned the hard way a few days after their return to the chambers when he momentarily flipped the power grid. He gripped the Lūcis Falcēs handle in his hand and watched the screen count down the time.

Ten. Nine. Eight.

He momentarily wished real battles had a timer.

Seven. Six. Five.

Ethan spun the handle between his fingers.

Four. Three. Two.

They needed to get the system updated to recognize his *Death Fog* as he named it.

One. Zero.

The projected military rushed him from the panels in every direction. Ethan slid his thumb across the activation pad for the Falcēs, and the familiar double-sided scythe extended in front of him. He spun the handle and hooked the weapon behind the projections before pulling and watching them collapse.

Ethan didn't think as he reached for another weapon with his right hand, the Lūcis Ēnsis, from his belt. He lost a lot of his sense of self since joining the Council. *That's never mentioned during initiation,* he thought bitterly. Ethan's Ēnsis cleanly hit the last projection running at him with a melee weapon raised, and the environment faded. He bit his tongue. Since he increased training to deal with the inevitable, his non-dominant hand weapon handling almost matched the control of his dominant. He didn't like dual wielding, especially when his left hand held a typically two-handed weapon; however, he didn't like feeling overwhelmed, more.

Not that I'll ever be overwhelmed, he thought. Ethan shifted his jaw to release the tension. He heaved a worn-out breath and stretched out the sore muscles of his shoulders. He came close to overworking himself, but he also didn't think other options were viable. Ethan needed to grow as fast as possible to have the best chance of tearing down HISS when the text came from Mason.

He tugged at the bun on the back of his head until it loosened into a ponytail. Ethan stretched his arms over his head then held his arms out in front of him, palms up. The Death Fog rolled off him in waves until it filled the entire training space. He could faintly see through the fog, and two people stood outside the training room watching. He pushed them out of his mind and focused on what control he had.

Ethan curled the fingers on his left hand. He felt the solid weight of a false handle. The fog around him transformed into a whip, and he hit against the wall farthest from him, hard. *That's new.* Ethan pulled the fog back, wearing it like a cloak. He didn't know what the whip would do, and he had no one to test it on without risking killing them.

He grit his teeth. The more Ethan got to know his power, the more he disliked it. He needed a frame of reference.

Kristen knocked against the windowed wall. Instead of her usual smile, she had a frown on her face and nodded toward Hans. The latter stood with his arms crossed watching Ethan with something unreadable on his face, but Ethan thought he knew the man well enough to recognize it as grim. Ethan reined in the fog and cracked his neck before walking to the door.

"Your power is terrifying," Hans said. "It's grown a lot from destroying a few lawns."

Ethan shrugged, but he couldn't suppress the pleased quirk of his lips. "I just have no idea how much control and power I have. I don't know what it can do."

A short breath burst from Hans' nose. "I'm not sure any of us really know the true capacity of our powers." He pressed his tongue visibly against his lower lip. "Theoretically, couldn't I have the same amount of power as Vasha? Couldn't we tear the world apart again?"

"Could've sworn we were already doing that." Kristen scratched the space between her eyebrows.

"Luana wants you to do a demonstration of your powers—instill hope for the future." Hans didn't share the same sentiment based on the growing frown.

Ethan crossed his arms. "I'm assuming this isn't up for discussion."

Hans shook his head. "Sorry. We argued over it for two hours this morning"

"We eventually gave in." Kristen reached out to touch him, but Ethan didn't relinquish his defensive posture.

"Am I going to have to kill anyone?" Ethan asked.

"I don't know." Hans shrugged.

"Did you tell Luana I'm not interested in being a show pony?"

"What part of arguing for two hours makes you think we didn't point out every stupid flaw in another one of her stupid plans? She's on edge like the rest of us, and I'm not in the mood to have my eyebrows singed off." Hans dropped his hands to his side, fists clenched. "I swear she was ready to burn the academy to the ground. I'm sorry we have to put up with her still."

Ethan took a deep breath and stepped toward the locker room to change out of his exercise clothes. "For a brief moment, I thought she acknowledged she wasn't god."

Hans cleared his throat to hide his laugh. "Yeah, I thought so, too."

Ethan pulled his shirt off as he stepped into the locker room. The small hitch in Kristen's breath reminded him of the scratches. His ears turned a faint pink, and he was glad Hans didn't say anything. Ethan walked toward the showers. "Well, I'm about to give her my own personal brand of Hell."

"With powers like that, I'm sure Hell is real," Hans chuckled darkly. "What are you thinking?"

"Nothing you want to know about."

Hans bit the tip of this tongue. "Just promise you won't kill her."

"Who do you think I am?" Ethan paused. "Don't answer that."

Ethan took a long shower and used the hot water to ease the tension in his muscles. He had a fight with Slattery to worry about—Luana did him no favors by pulling him away for some special militant intimidation tactic. Ethan didn't come to a solution under the hot water, but he firmly decided he wouldn't participate in her game of scare tactics.

Hans and Kristen waited patiently for him filling the empty space by ignoring each other and playing games on their phones, catching up on Council work, or texting other members to update, and annoy, them.

"You ready?" Hans put his phone in his pocket as Ethan tied his shoes.

"As I'll ever be." Ethan left the room in a flurry of building anger.

Hans jumped to his feet and chased after him. Kristen followed hot on Hans' heels.

They caught up just as Ethan forcefully threw the door open to the meeting room. Series jumped so badly she nearly fell out of her chair.

"I'm not going to be your propaganda pet," he said.

Hans and Kristen froze in the hall behind him.

Luana narrowed her eyes. "I don't think you get to make demands."

"Oh, but that rule doesn't apply to you."

Hans shouldered his way into the room to stand between Ethan and Luana. The other Council members stood from their seats preparing for a fight.

Luana opened her mouth to say something scathing, but Ethan cut her off.

"If you want to scare HISS, find another way. Propaganda for my powers is off the table. I'm not going to kill someone for the sake of killing. You can if you want to, but it'll do nothing but further their claims about us." Ethan turned on his heels and was halfway out the door when he said, "This is a Council of nine people not one. Stop pretending like you're all-powerful. The intimidation tactics are old."

May 14, 2319

5.41, -143.16, Devil's Gate

Mason hated having his closest confidant missing. *Well,* he thought, *not missing. He's with his son.* The exact place he wanted to be. Instead, Mason leaned against the glass window and watched the ongoing experimentations. On one side, he had a direct line of view into the facility where they put the elementalists under anesthesia; the other hosted the weapon testing for developmental feedback.

The days spent with little daylight and no change sent him spiraling into depression. He watched as the weapons testers lined up a row of test subjects with their backs to the firing range. Mason flinched as a new round of bullets fired and hit the children. Several cried out in pain, and the bullet exploded on impact with the wall. The others vanished as they exploded on a rotation timer inside those elementalists. The latter collapsed to the floor as the drug inside the bullets, liquid ecstasy, overtook their system. Medical professionals rushed forward to collect them and ensure they didn't die. They significantly lowered the dosage after the first few tests when the subjects couldn't be revived. Just like with alcohol, diacetyl in vapes, and carbon monoxide in cigarettes, not to mention all the other dangerous chemicals, the elementalists proved weak to any strong drug. Due to limitations, coming directly from Tyr when Mason complained about the deaths, they could only use small doses of liquid ecstasy and not try less harmful drugs for reactions. Tyr still wanted to see if the exploding bullet would get into the elementalists blood streams where it would do the most damage—and potentially affect Death elementalists.

Granted, the tests were woefully incomplete. Of all the elementalists they added to the facility, only one controlled Death. Qíng Yí. Mason wasn't willing to put her up to the tests in case they legitimately lost her. Tyr didn't need to know. The more information Mason could keep from him, the better.

His phone rang, but he didn't recognize the number at the top of the screen. He hesitated briefly before answering.

"Dad, pretend it isn't me. We're on a secure line." Luana's voice invaded his ear, and Mason had to fight back tears.

"What do you need?" he cleared his throat.

"Is there any way you could pull rank with HISS and Tyr to add a new recruit with high security clearance?"

"Can't say I'm particularly trusted since our *friend* went missing." Mason heard Luana shift the phone away from her ear on the other side. Someone whispered something he didn't understand.

"Got it," Luana said. She sighed. "Any word on HISS' next attack?"

"None of what I told you has changed."

"Dad," she paused. A *thud* came from her side of the line. "Ryan told us you were both working together in some capacity when you could."

"That's correct."

"I'm choosing to trust you." Luana sniffled.

"I'll contact you with updated data as soon as I have it. The timed bullets are not yet perfected."

Luana audibly swallowed. "Thanks."

The line went dead.

June 13, 2319

The Academy, Elementōrum Patriam

Luana's phone buzzed on the desk next to her. The Council looked up from their various duties in the conference room. Not many of them spoke directly to her after Ethan's outburst; they talked around her where she could hear but never asked for her opinion. They led votes and signed or vetoed proposals. She reached for the device, and her father's name read above the notification message.

> **Kpalime. June 15th. T with weapon. Plans to face all C.**

She didn't respond, but she knew Mason would see the read receipt before erasing the traces of the message. Her hands shook as she spoke, "It's time."

Luana set her phone on the projection screen where everyone could see the message.

Hans pressed a button on the side panel. "Mobilize all units. Shipment to Kpalime, Togo in seven hours. Battle commences within forty-eight hours upon arrival."

Sirens blared through the academy and followed in a flood through the streets to announce the call for all military personnel. The Council left their tasks unfinished and joined the harried fray, packing for what they hoped would be the last fight against HISS.

June 14, 2319

Kpalime, Plateaux Region, Togo

"Look at this gemstone I found last week in Ricci." A soldier pulled something out of his pocket to show his friend.

"Wow, that kind of looks like Water," the friend said.

"Doesn't it? I bought it for that reason. Reminded me of my element. Thought it might be a bit of a good luck charm."

Eilene froze in the doorway of the transportation pod. *Gemstones.* The military flurried around them amid war preparations. Scott took a step away from the pod. Eilene grabbed his arm. "Wait, we have to go back!"

"What? Why?"

"I figured it out. The translation from the book." Eilene's fingernails dug into his skin. "I know how we can control the nine elements—how you do it."

"How?" Series appeared behind them.

"In your vision, do you remember seeing yourself or Scott wearing some sort of stone?" Eilene asked.

Series' nose crinkled as he focused. "Yes, I think I faintly remember seeing something like a stone on a necklace."

"The stones of the earth!" Eilene hopped in place. "The swearing in of new Council members! The heart of the nine! It was there the entire time— in our chambers."

"The initiation room," Scott said.

"Inside the crystals." Series' face split into a wide smile.

Scott glanced over his shoulder at the rush job of assembling tents and arming the military. "You both should go back and get the stones. I'll cover for your absence."

Eilene kissed him quickly before climbing into the transportation pod with Series. "Be ready to control the nine when we get back."

The Academy, Elementōrum Patriam

Eilene and Series ran through the Academy without fear of who they might startle. Many people did jump out of their way, reminiscent of the day they ran to save Ethan—and they were doing it again while everyone else waited in another country for their return. Eilene felt every hard slam against the marble flooring ricochet through her ligaments. They turned sharp corners and clumsily kept their feet running under them. On one corner, the top of her shoe impacted with the back of her ankle.

She let out a hiss of pain but kept her feet under her despite a near stumble into a faceplant. She wouldn't worry about the bruise. They had to get to the stones.

Series reached the door head of Eilene and fumbled with the lock. It didn't want to read her genetic signature to unlock the door. They hadn't used the mechanism in so long; it felt weird to have the door locked. If they ever left before, their people were too scared to get close without summons.

Series broke her nail impacting the sides of the reader in her haste. She pushed the door open and ran. Eilene didn't bother closing the door. She followed Series' frantic run through the winding corridors until they reached the initiation chamber.

Series flipped the switch to turn on the control panel to open the doors to the lower space where the doorways lay out below them in a circle. While it only took a few seconds for the electricity to meet the control panel and boot up, it felt like forever. Eilene smashed her hand on the green button; it lit up, and the doors slid open. They shuffled down the steep stairs awkwardly until they walked through the first open door.

"How are we going to get up there?" Series stopped.

Eilene didn't hesitate and hovered in the air, using a blast of water from her hip flask. She grabbed the handle of her Lūcis Secūrēs from her belt and smashed it hard against the outer casing.

"Careful!"

She didn't need the warning. The gemstone inside the crystal shards rested in a secondary metal casing ready to be strung onto a piece of jewelry—although the metal had aged and rusted. They wouldn't be able to use it safely. She brushed away the green shards carefully before removing the Tibetan Turquoise.

Eilene tossed it to Series who caught it deftly. "Dwayne's."

Series pocketed it carefully with a nod. They would remember every stone and who they belonged to. They had to. Eilene jetted her way to the next crystal on her right.

"This is yours." Eilene tossed the Rutilated Quartz next, and Series tucked it into a different pocket to help differentiate the stones. They followed the counterclockwise pattern around the room collecting each stone. Star Garnet for Kristen, Fire Agate for Luana, Boulder Opal for Hans, Ethiopian Opal for Scott, Moss Agate for Ethan, and Spectrolite for Scarlet. Eilene tucked the Labradorite for herself safely in her own pocket.

Back on the ground, she nodded to Series, and they started the same hurried trek out of the Council chambers. They took their time to lock the door properly behind them for security purposes.

When they returned to the parking garage, they were greeted by a small parade of workers who showed them the supplies they managed to collect for jewelry making. They inspected the collection of items and chose what they thought they could use before thanking them and climbing into the pod.

Eilene and Series pulled out their stones first and set to work with the tools removing the metal casings. Since they didn't have a mold or a proper new casing to fit each unique shape, they forewent something fancy. Eilene wrapped the stainless-steel wire around Labradorite until it fit the form and provided no opportunity for the stone to slip through the wire. A good portion of the surface was obscured, and Series' didn't look much better than hers. She attached a small eyelet to the wire before threading it onto a chain.

"Think it'll work?" Series asked. She held hers in front of her, leery and anxious about putting it on.

"Everything else matched up to this point—we found the stones."

"But the book could be wrong. Maybe the original nine were just special." Series dropped her hands a little and the chain slackened.

Eilene held her breath and quickly slung the necklace around her neck. She breathed out slowly. "I don't feel any different."

Series slid her own around her neck. "Maybe it was a legend?"

Eilene picked up the small pocketknife with the jewelry supplies in her left hand and pressed one of the blades into her finger until it bled. She dropped the knife and wrapped her hand around the cut. A dim green light emitted from her palm, and they both gasped. When she pulled her hand away, the finger looked as it usually did.

Series snapped her fingers, and a small flame leaped from them.

"Amazing!" Eilene stood up and tried to fly. She managed to smash her head painfully into the roof of the pod, and she dropped back to the floor clutching her throbbing skull. "Bad idea in a small space."

"Your eyes were glowing! We have to make the others." Series grabbed the other gemstones from her pocket and scattered them among the supplies. "This will change everything."

"We could end the war, here and now." Eilene dropped to her knees and grabbed the Ethiopian Opal. She wrapped it in wire a bit more carefully than her own stone. "This is the end."

June 15, 2319

Kpalime, Plateaux Region, Togo

Scott nearly lost his concentration as he spotted Eilene flying across the battlefield making a beeline straight for him. Rain rushed past his parted lips as she pulled to a clumsy stop and hit the ground hard. She staggered under the impact, and pain settled deep in her bones.

"I need way more practice," she gasped.

Scott wrapped one arm around her waist and pulled her to the side as he lifted his Sclopētum and parried an attack from the enemy.

"You got the stones," he shouted in her ear, barely audible above the din of battle.

Eilene nodded furiously. "I have yours." She pulled the necklace free from her pocket and slid it over his head. The opal settled against his chest. In his uniform, it didn't sit evenly, and would swing during battle. She imagined it resting between his pectorals in any other outfit, and her cheeks warmed. She leaned up to speak in his ear. "It doesn't feel any different, but just try wielding another element, and it'll work. We'll all need proper training later."

He gave her a soft affirmative whipped away by the wind. He pulled away and shook water from his hair. "I should go."

"Scott!" Eilene called him back.

Her lips smashed hard against his. He didn't have time to think. Her arms wrapped tightly around him trying to convey all her hope they could bring the war to an end. She felt the twitching and strained muscles of his arms and shoulders. The sinews pulled under her touch as he grasped her ever closer.

This kiss was nothing like their first. It was confident, rushed, and terrified. Their teeth collided, but they hardly paid any mind. His hands wrapped possessively around her waist. For just that moment in time, it felt like they weren't two separate people. Finally, she pulled away. More necklaces clutched between her wet fingers.

"I have to go," she said.

He nodded, unable to form words.

"Be safe." She slipped away from Scott and vanished into the crowd.

Scott launched himself in the air and reached for the new power thrumming through his veins. He felt it, just on the edge. His nerve endings tingled—like static shock. Lightning sizzled through the air around him and struck several of the opposing army. He never felt power like it before. The flames came next in swirling patterns. The earth heaved and threw off their footing. The Death Fog rolled off him and swept toward the crowd, but it didn't extend as far as Ethan's.

He had the power of the nine.

Ethan loved the feel of the Lūcis Falcēs in his hands. He could spin it with one hand or use both for a stronger hit—either way, he resembled the nightmare depictions of Death. With his own cloak of death, he could wrap around himself and strike out at the enemy. A rush of power washed over him, and he smiled at every fallen body. His eyes slid to the next attacker as a curl of black smoke dropped his last victim to the ground wide, eyed and dead.

The attacker backed away in terror but was pushed forward by the crowd of bodies. They lifted their gun and fired three bullets in rapid succession at him, but every one passed through Ethan's head without a trace. He licked his lips and grinned. They dropped to their knees in front of him.

"Spare me!" the human yelled. "Please!"

Ethan considered them for a moment. He could show mercy, but he had little desire to in face of the encroaching armies. He knew the future Series saw would pass on that battleground. Ethan flipped the double-sided weapon around in his left hand. He hooked one side around the back of their neck.

"Give me a reason." Ethan sensed the movement behind him and let his ability grab the new attacker from behind. The body fell into the mud with a sickening *slurk*.

The human in front of him stuttered. Their eyes slipped to the new body and choked.

Bored of the attempt to beg, Ethan rolled his eyes and pulled his arm back. The weapon slid through their neck with nary a sound above the *rabble*. He watched the head land open mouthed in the mud before he stepped over it and pushed through the crowd.

He saw Tyr at the top of the hill fighting with his specialized weapon— the thing rumored to kill Ethan. He didn't believe it would work. The last time they saw it used on a Death elementalist, it was speculative at most— and the child was clearly under duress which would affect their abilities.

Ethan was not in the same position. He was stronger. He knew what he could do. Tyr would leave the battlefield in a body bag, and the elementalists would finally have the upper hand on the humans. It felt right.

He swung the weapon at his next victim, fighting another elementalist and watched it remove the human's arm. *Not quite what I wanted.*

He looked to the ridge and saw Tyr making a retreat down the other side of the hill. Ethan shook his head to clear the rain from his hair and took off after him. He had little traction climbing the muddy slope and had to use his Falcēs as a hiking stick.

By the time he reached the top of the hill, mud covered his clothes up to his knees, and several strands of hair fell out of his bun from the rain. He pushed the loose strands back and spat some of the water from his mouth. Before he had a handle on where Tyr fought, someone fired their weapon at him. It passed through him, but it felt different. Ethan felt "grazed" if he put a word to it. He turned in surprise to the attacker who looked all too pleased to have him at the top of the hill. The human holstered their weapon and raised their right leg.

Confused, Ethan lifted the Falcēs and spun it in his hand to attack, but the boot of the human met his chest with a painful blow. He unwillingly let go of the weapon and hit the ground hard. The mud paired with the slope sent Ethan spinning and sliding to the base. Mud filled his mouth and eyes; he did his best to spit it out and use the rain to wash away the mud clouding his vision. He pushed his hair back again and turned his face into the rain. The rivulets washed across his skin. Ethan scrambled into a crouch when he spotted Tyr just a few yards in front of him. Without his preferred Armōrum weapon, he grabbed the handles of the Lūcis Ēnsēs. He didn't particularly like the single-bladed sword style weapon, but he preferred it to the Tēlōrum. Based on the weapon Tyr held, he planned to make it a sword fight as well.

Ethan snorted. He knew the weapon wouldn't work against him, no matter its style. Tyr practically invited him to kill him. He tightened his grip over the handles and felt the leather slide in his grip. The rain would only hinder his melee fighting style, but he had his cloak.

Except, the cloak of Death receded quickly. Ethan stared at the black tendrils, and his brows pinched together. Something happened to him and his abilities. Something he wasn't familiar with. He raised his left hand to his ear to trigger the communication device.

"Can anyone hear me?"

"I'm here," Kristen's voice sent a rush of calm through his nerves. Series and Eilene chimed in moments later.

"I have Tyr here in front of me. I'm going to fight—but something is wrong with my abilities. I need backup."

Static from the other side as they engaged with their own enemies.

"Ethan, if something's wrong, you can't fight. Back off. We can come at Tyr another time." The panic bled into Kristen's tone and sent a shard of cold ice through his heart.

"I can't do that," he said. "We may never get another opportunity like this. I'm the best chance we have at taking out Tyr."

"Ethan, we have your gemstone. Just wait like five minutes, then you can have the power of the nine," Series said. "Please, just wait."

Tyr took a step forward and raised the weapon.

"I can't. He's engaging me." Ethan licked his lips. "Hurry."

Ethan pulled the dual Ēnsēs in front of him and stood slowly. He could hear the panic of the three in his ear, but he tuned them out to focus on Tyr prowling forward. Tyr twirled the sword around the back of his hand before catching it by the hilt again. The silver color of the metal glinted against the blue light emitting from Ethan's own. Flames erupted from the center of the sword and shot out through the top and the holes along the blade. After a moment, they turned a bright blue color with white near the hilt as they persisted against the rain.

Ethan watched the water sizzle and turn to steam as it pounded against the blade. A feeling of unease settled over him, but he couldn't explain why. The Council tried everything against Ethan. He couldn't be killed.

"Have fun trying to survive this, monster," Tyr said.

He lifted the blade, and Ethan watched the arc of its swing with just enough time to parry the blow against his own weapons. He shifted forward to toss Tyr free with his right arm before swinging in with his stronger left. Tyr jumped back in time to avoid the blow to his abdomen, and Ethan's frown deepened.

Ethan took a breath and reached for the Death cloak, but he had no energy to summon it. *What happened to me?* He swallowed hard. Everything had been as normal until the human at the top of the hill kicked him in the chest. *Did they do something?*

"You can't kill me," Ethan said. "You don't know how many times I've tried to do it myself."

Numerous occasions confirmed what he said—except he did know of one time when he almost died. The Council kept him in a cell in extreme conditions. He still had limits to his ability.

A spray of bullets, which missed another elementalist, blew through his stomach as if to prove he couldn't be killed. He felt the same strange "grazing" sensation from before. *Something is wrong.* Ethan swallowed against the pain and did his best to not let it flicker across his face. Tyr's mud-stained smile gave him the feeling he failed.

"I've been forging this for months. It will destroy you." Tyr lifted and pointed the claymore weapon at Ethan again.

"I'm looking forward to your failure." Ethan moved as quickly as he could; the mud clung to his heels and made loud sucking noises.

They met in the middle and matched blade for blade, hit for hit. Two weapons against one gave no advantage as Tyr's strange expertise on the battlefield emerged with each meeting. Ethan parried his weapon close to the hilt of Tyr's and pushed up. Before he could bring his left arm in for a lower hit, he watched as the heat from the sword broke through the blade of the Ēnsis. The sharp sizzle as the metal burned under the heat and seared under the rain made Ethan jump back. He stared at the broken weapon sparking in the rain.

"You took her from me," Tyr said. "You took her and turned her into one of you."

A muscle jumped in Ethan's forehead, but he didn't reply.

"She was all I had left," he said. "And you made her a threat to humanity! You made her a killer!"

Ethan held the Ēnsis horizontally in front of him as a blockade in case of an incoming attack. Then, he said, "She was born an elementalist."

Tyr's shoulders shook. "I'm going to remove the mutation. There is no happiness for humankind when you are still alive and mutated. You'll only continue to tear apart our lives."

"You and HISS are the ones killing us."

"You're the killers!" Tyr yelled.

He ran forward with wild swings. Ethan parried. One pushed past his sword and clipped him in the shoulder. Ethan hissed in pain and dropped the useless hilt from his right hand. He touched the open wound. His cocky, adrenaline-fueled ease at never being wounded by any weapon fled his body. Blood ran over his fingers.

"It worked," Ethan said numbly.

His breathing turned heavy. He stood frozen at the feeling of his own blood on his hand. Mud ran from his hair into his mouth. He lifted the bloody hand to his face and wiped. Blood and mud smeared across his skin; Ethan yelled as he ran toward Tyr with his own unplanned attack.

"I thought you wanted to die," Tyr spat.

Ethan humored him with another blow. "I thought I was unkillable."

Tyr landed a melee blow to Ethan's stomach with his knee. "You should be terrified right now."

He lost his solid grip on the Ēnsis in his left hand under the strength of Tyr's blow. He fell into a kneeling position against the ground. Ethan reached for his belt and tried to find another weapon to help him. Anything would work. Except none of them matched his needs. He couldn't release a Lūminis Pyrobolus without hurting himself and other elementalists. He reached instead to trigger the Lūcis Scūta on his wrist, but it was gone. *It must've fallen off when I rolled down the hill*, Ethan realized. He had no other tricks up his sleeve.

Ethan felt the heat of the claymore against his throat. He grabbed the deactivated hilt from the mud. His eyes trailed the figure of Tyr standing above him with a manic grin. Ethan said, "You're not going to win even if you do kill me."

Tyr laughed. "I'm just getting started. Once I kill you, I'll start on the rest of the Council. From there, your kind will fall at my feet. None of them have any knowledge of the real world."

Ethan lifted his Ēnsis, and light erupted between him and Tyr as he pushed the weapon away. He felt the rain kiss against the burn on his neck. Ethan pushed himself to a standing position. He would not die kneeling before his enemy.

A couple of hard hits from Tyr sent his weapon flying across the crowd. Ethan didn't know where it landed.

The rain pounded against his back. "You'll never touch them."

"I wouldn't count on that." A snarl curled the corner of Tyr's lip as he jabbed his blade straight in front of him. The tip met Ethan's chest.

Pain seared through him as it pierced past his fatigues and armor. "I've put all my trust in them," he choked. Ethan coughed blood onto Tyr's hand. He felt the heat cauterizing the wound, but a pierced heart wouldn't be healed. Tyr pulled the weapon back, and Ethan coughed again. His blood hit the flames and released a coppery smell. The flames vanished.

Someone shouted his name from a distance, but he didn't know who. Ethan fell to his knees when the sword left his chest. Blood dripped along the metal and into the mud. Ethan watched it swirl with the rain before he fell onto his back.

Tyr stood over him, grinning. "Stupid decision."

ELEMENTALISTS WEAPON GUIDE

Lūminis: Used to indicate a ranged (**Tēlōrum**) weapon.

Lūcis: Used to indicate a melee (**Armōrum**) weapon.

Arcus: A bow; recurve, compound, longbow, and barebow. Plural is **Arcūs**.

Manuballista: A crossbow; recurve, compound, reverse draw, rifle, pistol, bullet, and repeating. Plural is **Manuballistae**.

Sclopētum: A gun; handgun and long gun. Plural is **Sclopēta**.

Pyrobolus: A bomb; incendiaries, blast, time-delayed, command-initiated, postal, projected explosive, and commercial. Plural is **Pyroboli**.

Sagitta: Ammunition; all types. Plural is **Sagittae**.

Ēnsis: Single-edged sword; various styles in one-hand and two-hand wielding. Plural is **Ēnsēs**.

Rumpia: Double-edged sword; various styles in two-hand wielding. Plural is **Rumpiae**.

Jaculum: Spear; unlike a historical spear, the shaft of this spear can also be used as a slicing weapon. Plural is **Jacula**.

Fuscina: Trident; similar to the Jaculum, the shaft is a viable weapon as well as the base. Plural is **Fuscinae**.

Bipenne: Double-headed axe; offers one- and two-handed options. Plural is **Bipennia**.

Falx: Scythe; offers single-sided and double-sided head options. Plural is **Falcēs**.

Secūris: Handaxe. Plural is **Secūrēs**.

Scūta: Shield. Plural is **Scūtum**.

ACKNOWLEDGEMENTS

This book wouldn't have been possible without the outpouring of support I received for book one, *Incomplete*. I was pleasantly surprised by the number of people invested in my series. People who wanted to read my writing and who couldn't wait for book two to arrive.

I hope that everyone who has supported my journey will continue to enjoy the series that I'm putting forth. Compared to the first book, which is setting up the series, this book has less background information and more war. It was interesting to write this story based on historical elements that I then saw coming true around me with little power to stop it. I will continue to speak out for others who experience similar events as seen in my writing.

Of course, like with the last book, I had many people working on my "team" who helped with the production of this book. They were mentioned in the dedication, so I hope you will return there, look them up, and give them a lot of love.

Thank you to all the new friends I've made through publishing, and on the Threads app. What a great community of writers to be a part of.

And now...

An unedited excerpt from *Incinerate*.
Book three in the Elementalists trilogy.

The guard stomped against the ground to catch her attention. Qíng Yí looked up from her tablet and the doodle of a dragon. The guard waved for her to follow, and she did without complaint. She assumed they would return to the medical room where she laid unconscious for a couple hours before returning to her cell completely unchanged. However, the guard walked her in the opposite direction of the testing room, and she followed him, uncertain. They never deviated from what she came to know as "normal". It wasn't the nature of the facility. They never told her what they did in the medical room when she futilely tried to ask every time the "experiment" ended.

A door at the end of the hall stood open, and a line of children filtered inside, and Qíng Yí joined the queue expecting a medical room for group experimentation. She wouldn't be witness to the passive screaming and pleading of a passing child who found terror in the medical room where Qíng Yí only found frustration; she would see whatever the facility did in real-time. Inside the room, the children came to a surprised halt. Qíng Yí looked over their heads, one of the tallest since she was seventeen, and a colorful array of furniture bombarded her instead of the medical equipment she knew well.

Qíng Yí shuffled her way around the smaller children until she could move into the room. She claimed a violently bright colored bean bag for herself. A small play area and toys that Qíng Yí had little interest in sat in one corner. Overall, the room wasn't made of a different material than their cells, steel, and it was painted the familiar white color, but the room had spots of brightness in colored rugs and beanbags. She held onto the tablet the doctors gave her after one of her experimentation sessions. The tablet had a few games, but she mostly used it for drawing. She didn't consider herself an artist, but she liked doodling across the blank canvases and letting her mind wander.

Occasionally, Qíng Yí wrote notes. Thoughts she had while in her cell. Some notes detailed experiments she thought the facility might be actualizing—however, she never came away with any wounds. She saw the other children and teenagers, never any adults. The guards had no hesitancy in leading her past the other subjects in the halls. She saw the patterns with the others. They would wait until they returned the first to the cell before collecting another, but Qíng Yí was always there to see them leaving and entering. Wounds open and bleeding as they stumbled down the hall. The bloody prints on one of her gowns when another subject grabbed her and screamed something unintelligible in her face. The person carried down the hall by a guard with their foot missing haunted her nightmares. Qíng Yí was different. She never came away with any wounds, no pain, no missing limbs. She had nothing to show she lay in that room, the same as every other subject.

Another child bumped into her. Their mouth moved around a word she thought resembled an apology. She couldn't hear it. Qíng Yí was born Deaf with a capital D. No hearing. No cochlear implant. She grew up communicating on paper and using SgSL, or Singaporean Sign Language. Qíng Yí also couldn't read lips.

She knew the studies. Even experienced lip readers could catch maybe sixty percent of a conversation. The general Deaf population, maybe forty. She went to a Deaf school where they communicated in sign language. Her parents learned sign to communicate with her. No one in the facility had the ability to communicate with her outside of writing messages, and the doctors only ever dismissed her via a message on the wall panels.

Qíng Yí still didn't know why they chose her for the facility. The doctors refused to give her information. She assumed the others knew more than her, and she desperately wished for some information from any source.

She didn't know why the guards suddenly allowed them to be in a room together. Almost three months they spent locked away in a cell. No contact. Qíng Yí set the tablet in her lap and watched the others engage in a game of tag. One ran around her bean bag to avoid the outstretched hand of the other. Another teenager, alone, sat in the corner with eyes clearly fixed on her instead of the game. The young man expertly dodged the others as he made his way across the room.

He said something. Qíng Yí shook her head. He pointed to the tablet. She held it a little closer to her chest. He made a motion through the air as if writing something, and Qíng Yí hesitantly held the tablet toward him. She hoped the guards would give it back to her if he tried to steal it. It was the only way she could communicate with the doctors. Although, they never gave her any information or responded to her questions.

He returned the tablet a moment later. On the screen, written in messy Mandarin, she read: "*Did the experiments make you Deaf?*"

Qíng Yí erased the message and wrote her own. "*I was born this way.*"

He didn't make a move for the tablet again, but he did sit in the bean bag chair next to her. She opened a game on the tablet, a merge style game, and played for a few minutes. He tapped her on the shoulder. She handed him the tablet.

"*What do they do to you?*"

Qíng Yí stared at the question. "*I don't know.*"

His brows furrowed. "*You don't know?*"

"*They don't tell me.*"

"*They're experimenting on us,*" he wrote. "*It hurts a lot.*"

Qíng Yí took a long minute to write her return message. "*It's never hurt me.*"

His eyes matched the size of a gǎiwǎn.

Qíng Yí licked her lips and wrote. "*Why are they experimenting on us?*"

Hesitantly, the boy scrawled the words, "*We're elementalists,*" across the tablet.

Qíng Yí dropped the tablet. A guard walked toward them. She quickly picked up the tablet and erased the message. She pursed her lips, stood, and moved away. He didn't try to follow her. The guard returned to his post. She finally had a reason for why they chose her. Why they brought her to the facility. Why they put her in that room. Except, she didn't feel like an elementalist.

She couldn't be. Qíng Yí sunk into a small chair at a children's kitchen playset. She set the tablet on the wood stove. She picked up a wooden skillet and twirled it in her hand. Qíng Yí hated that the facility didn't tell her anything about the experiments, but she never understood why.

She set the skillet down, picked up the tablet, and returned to the beanbag chairs. One of the guards shifted to watch them. She repeated her question, "*Why are they experimenting on us?*"

He paused, quickly erased the message, and wrote, "*The war.*"

Qíng Yí pressed her lips into a thin line and doodled a small flower into the corner. She knew of the war. It took the world by surprise and sent communities spiraling. She saw the fall-out and the actions taken against known elementalists in her hometown. Her family worried about the growing tension. She'd seen the rise of ghettos on social media before her capture. She didn't know how the guards determined she was an elementalist when Elementōrum Patriam had no record of her existence.

She moved from her doodle and wrote, "*My name is Tan Qíng Yí Joy.*" The last three letters were written in Hànyǔ Pīnyīn.

"*I'm Sūn Tiān Kuò.*"

Qíng Yí smiled. "*We should be friends.*"

Tiān Kuò nodded excitedly. "*Teach me signs,*" he wrote.

She bit her lip. She never taught anyone her language before. Tiān Kuò pointed to the beanbag. She showed him the sign. Delighted, they repeated that pattern over and over throughout the time the guards allowed them to play in the room.

City of the Uns. Elementōrum Patriam

Esebelle Berlusconi crept through the back halls of the capitol building in central. She wasn't technically allowed there, but she coerced a janitor into allowing her to borrow their all-access key and a janitorial cap. Despite the elementalists supposed "resolution" two years previously, she didn't feel satisfied with the changes.

Sure, Marcis was a corrupt politician. Everyone saw it clearly afterward, but she wanted more than a change in their government positions. She wanted to bring down the institution of the elementalists. Equipped with her phone, she looked around corners with the camera to avoid any personnel who knew she wouldn't belong. She hurried down the hall and hoped the security camera operators wouldn't pick her up as an unwanted.

She pressed the janitor's key to the lock mechanism on another door and slipped into the archives room. Several boxes sat on shelves with necessary physical records, but she only had interest in the information on the computer in the corner where a worker sat reviewing data. They didn't turn to face her which caught Esebelle by surprise. She shifted and closed the door softly behind her, and she caught a glimpse of the employee's wireless headphones.

Esebelle crept behind one of the shelves and considered her options. She would need to access the computer unlocked. Since she led the original "uprising", the other Uns didn't trust her with government power. The Uns on her side turned up in overwhelming numbers to vote her and Maxim Aliyev into high positions.

Except, Esebelle reminded herself, *Maxim left us behind to go play buddies with his brother and the Council.*

The desk's occupant spun in their chair. They reached for another file on the sideboard. Esebelle shrank further behind the shelf. If the worker used their peripheral vision, she'd be caught. She didn't have a weapon to take them out in a worst-case scenario. However, she needed the information on that computer.

If only I planned more before I left, she bit her tongue hard to keep in the annoyed sigh she almost let escape. She didn't want to take risks in case the song or track ended.

The typing on the computer paused, and the chair creaked. The worker stood and moved their phone to their pocket from the desk. Esebelle retreated to the far side of the shelf in line of their view from the computer, but also deeper in shadows. The worker didn't notice the movement and left the room.

Esebelle hurried around the shelf to the desk. They left it unlocked. She grinned and started searching the files for trigger words. She found a few that looked interesting, opened the files, and snapped photos with her phone. Esebelle didn't know where the worker went, and she needed to be out of the room before they returned, or she wouldn't escape without being caught. She closed the files again to hide her trail and left.

She pulled the janitorial staff cap further over her eyes. She made it to the end of the hall where an unassuming door, which only opened from the one side, waited. Esebelle could escape through there and no one would be the wiser. She returned the cap and badge to the janitor she borrowed them from in a non-descript closet.

She exited the capitol building and took the long dirt trail to the rebellion's old warehouse. No one used it anymore, considering all the new construction, and she generally had the place to herself. Esebelle liked having a quiet place to work. It was also private. They worked hard to take all their computer systems offline from the Uns and elementalist grid. She had a secure line to almost anywhere in the world.

When she entered the room, dust tickled her nose, and Esebelle fought off a sneeze. She would clean after sending her message. She sat at the computer desk and booted up the systems allowing her to circumnavigate the security system. Within a few minutes, she pulled up her email and drafted a message.

Here are the files you wanted. I hope they help. Stay in contact. -UEB

Join the Discord for Elementalists and get

engaged in conversation with others and directly

with the author.

AUTHOR BIO

SI Foote loves English and well-written literature. Her favorite subject to study is linguistics. She is a supporter of the FanFiction community as it helps build writers' abilities. She is a member of the LGBTQIA+ community as an Asexual (like several of her characters). She currently lives in Utah with her Teacup Yorkie, Cinnamon.

For More Behind the World of the Elementalists
Visit https://www.sifoote.com